PRAISE FOR DANCING WITH ETERNITY

"In the far flung future, the human experience is a much different one indeed. *Dancing with Eternity* is a science fiction novel set in the fortieth century and following the misadventures and failures of Mohandas in an otherwise more perfect universe. Humorous and thoughtful, *Dancing with Eternity* may prove a fun read for science fiction fans with a strong interest in deep space travel and other elements of the far flung future."

—Midwest Book Review/Small Press Bookwatch

"Two thousand years from now, people don't die; they just reboot, choosing what to remember, what to forget. The results are not always what they—or we—expect. In *Dancing with Eternity*, John Lowrie has imagined a richly detailed world of space travel among colonized planets by characters whose minds and bodies alike are malleable, the specs stored on the 'net' and retrievable when necessary. The storytelling in this novel is lush and highly imaginative, and backed by the author's encyclopedic knowledge of our world and his deep understanding of what makes us human."

—Jerry Stubblefield, author of *Homunculus* (Black Heron Press)

"*Dancing with Eternity* is not only a terrific E-ticket ride of speculative fiction, it is also a very thought-provoking novel of ideas. I got swept away by the scope of the story, and spent many hours contemplating the moral, ethical and social challenges of 'rebooting.' Anyone who enjoys reading either Kim Stanley Robinson or Neal Stephenson will get a big kick out of this book!"

—Hugh Hastings, Actor

"In *Dancing with Eternity*, John has constructed the idyllic science fiction novel with all the elements that real fans crave: adventure, mystery, space travel, alien worlds, hard science projections, and a wonderful cast of characters from a future society. But, more important, the book dances with timeless philosophical questions that may require hard-thinking, real-life answers much sooner than we realize."

—Frank Simcoe, author, *Ridiculous Destiny*

"An utterly believable depiction of other worlds and races, imagination drips from every page. John Patrick Lowrie has more talent than any human being has a right to possess. A triumph of science fiction. I only wish I'd written it!"

—M J Elliott, Editor of *The Whisperer in Darkness, The Horror in the Museum, The Right Hand of Doom,* and *The Haunter of the Ring*

"As an ex-NASA tether specialist and consultant on the Shuttle tether missions, I found this a refreshingly accurate narrative of what it might be like to experience such life and related activities that (are) outside our normal realms."

—Dave Lang (NASA, ret.)

"As I was enjoying this book, stepping through a delightful minefield of lifeless sacred cows, I found the advanced computer concepts presented within assembling themselves in actual experiments in the real world without!"

—Chuck Pliske (NASA, ret.)

"At a time in which we are increasingly uncertain about our future, Lowrie creates a plausible scenario in which there is no death as we now experience it, and explores how such a world would play out. In the process, he challenges our traditional beliefs about love, sex and spirituality."

—Janet Pliske, D.D.

"*Dancing with Eternity* is a fascinating sci-fi thriller that depicts the world as it might be in the future .... It is a fairly quick read because the flow of the storyline keeps you fascinated and intrigued. This is one book that sci-fi enthusiasts should put on their 'must-read' list."

—Tracey Rock for Reader Views

DANCING
WITH
ETERNITY

A NOVEL

Dancing
with
Eternity

A Novel
John Patrick Lowrie

**CAMEL
PRESS**

Seattle, WA

CAMEL PRESS

Camel Press
PO Box 70515
Seattle, WA 98127

For more information contact: www.camelpress.com.

Cover design by Jeanie James, Shorebird Media
Cover illustration of the spacecraft by Phil Howe

DANCING WITH ETERNITY
Copyright © 2011 by John Patrick Lowrie
www.johnpatricklowrie.com
www.lowrie.camelpress.com

ISBN: 978-1-60381-810-0 (Trade Paper)
ISBN: 978-1-60381-812-4 (eBook)
Library of Congress Control Number: 2011929572
10 9 8 7 6 5 4 3 2 1

Printed in the United States of America

This book is dedicated to everyone who has lost a child or a parent suddenly and senselessly.

And always, always to Shawnessy.

Acknowledgments

Thank you to all my tireless, infinitely patient friends: Jadd Davis, John & Celeste Deveney, Hugh Hastings, Eric Jensen, Jason Kappus, Ian Lindsay, Phil Howe, Teresa Metzger-Howe, Terry Moore, Frank Simcoe and of course my beautiful and insightful wife, Ellen McLain, for all your feedback on the manuscript. And to my editor, Catherine Treadgold, whose hard work and belief in me made this book possible.

And a very, very special thanks to Chuck Pliske (NASA, ret.) and Dave Lang (NASA, ret.) for their help on the physics of the skyhook and wonderful conversations about things technical and futuristic.

This book would not be what it is without all of you.

CONTENTS

Part V: Eden

Part VI: In Transit

Part VII: Brainard's Planet

PART I
VESPER

CHAPTER 1

Ignorance covers humanity like a thick wool blanket, with tiny pinpricks of knowledge peeking through here and there. Whenever we manage to connect a few of the dots to form a picture we think we're pretty hot stuff, and I guess we are. I mean we've never met anyone who can do it better, but I can't decide if that really means we're good at it—or if it's just a very slow track.

I've been around a long time; you'd think I would have learned something. I don't know. A man starts acting funny when he's run out of options. Thinking becomes a strangely bloated yet pointless exercise. I hadn't worked in ten months. I hadn't paid my rent in two. The woman I'd been shacked up with had gotten tired of my scales before I did and by the time I got tired of them I was too broke to have my genome reworked.

Actually, the scales were probably the start of this current decline. I'd tried to deduct them as a professional expense. I'm an actor, among other things, and I figured if full body scales didn't constitute a costume, what does? The SRS disagreed and popped me for four thousand DCU, blocked my net access when I didn't pay, and told Shaughnessy that if she tried to lift with me aboard they'd impound her ship and arrest her for cultural pollution.

I guess they didn't like the show.

So Shaughnessy explained to me how much she liked my work and what a great asset to the production I was and how much she hated to lose me but these things happen and if I could get this straightened out and hop the next ship to Heaven (which was where the tour was going next) and by the way did I know any actors on Heaven? You know, just someone to fill in until I hooked back up with them. I told her I'd never been to Heaven. At that point it looked like I had as much chance of seeing Heaven as a 14th century heretic.

I went down to the port to see them off. I don't know why. They punched a hole in the sky and kept on going and I stayed behind.

There is something about watching a starship lift off when you were supposed to be in it that is almost indescribable.

So there I was in New Spanaway, a city that is a textbook victim of imperial planetary economics: a pre-fab metal and plastic blister plopped down in the middle of the jungle on the wrong side of Vesper, which is actually a pretty nice globe. Vesper as a whole has a good balance of trade, big tourist business; you've probably heard of it if you've done any traveling in the home worlds. It's the third moon of Golgotha, a huge super-Jovian gas giant that was one of the first extra-solar planets to be discovered, back around the end of the second millennium. Of course, everyone around here claims it was *the* first to be discovered, but who believes a bunch of hundred-and-fifty-kilo, bio-engineered SyndicEnts? I mean, you don't disagree with them, but you don't necessarily hang on their every word, either.

But we happy denizens of New Spanaway were far removed from the pleasure palaces and tourist traps; they're all in the other hemisphere, where Golgotha's cream and rust banded immensity fills half the sky. No, there's only one place to go in your off-hours in Spam-town and I was in it, looking for a way out.

I saw her in the mirror over the bar when she came in from the verandah. She would have been hard to miss. She was over two meters tall, long limbed and slender, and covered from head to toe in sleek silver fur that lengthened into a thick mane on the top and back of her head. Her eyes were large, almond-shaped and the color of emeralds—no cornea visible, just these two liquid pools of green fire split by black cat-pupils. If she wasn't rich, she must have been at one time. The fur job alone must have set her back a bundle, and I didn't even want to think what the eyes cost her. She wasn't wearing much more than I was, not a surprise in the tropics when a person's spent that much on her skin, and I should know. But what the hell was she doing here?

The contrast between her relaxed, fluid grace and the utilitarian rust of 'Burbs place was one of those images that can throw into focus the ironies of an entire socio-economic power structure. She walked past the playpens on her way to the bar, passing through humid shafts of mid-afternoon sunlight that read her body contours like a laser scanner. I tried to look at the bottom of my glass and think about something else.

'Burbs didn't stare at her; I'll give him that. But then, I don't think 'Burbs had hormonal or pheromonal reactions anymore. He hadn't had them removed or anything; they'd just eroded away naturally. Her polychrome nails clicked on the teak counter top as she sat down like—like she owned the guy who paid the guy who paid the guy who made the stool.

"What'll it be?" 'Burbs' voice was like the town he inhabited, a victim of economics. Hers wasn't.

"Give me what your scaly friend is having." I looked at her reflection in the mirror. Not just because she'd referred to me. Her voice made me think of warm honey flowing over brass. It reminded me of a singer I'd been in love with. A long time ago.

"He's no friend of mine." Nice guy, 'Burbs. He turned away to fill a glass with the home brew I'd been living on for too long, turned back to set it down in front of her.

"He have a name?" More honey. It made the scales on my arms stand up slightly; I could feel air under them. 'Burbs looked at her like he was convincing himself that he was too old and too mated to care that she wanted me instead of him.

"I'll ask him." He glanced down the bar at me. "Hey, Lizard, you gotta name?" I actually look more like a pangolin than a reptile, but when one of the regulars started calling me Lizard a couple of months ago I let it stick. The number of phonemes it shared with "loser" resonated with my current bout of sardonic fatalism.

"You couldn't pronounce it," I said into the glass. I was playing for time. In my present state I couldn't believe that a beautiful, rich, or even ex-rich, woman would care if I was breathing, let alone want to know my name. I figured she was from the System Revenue Service, or worse yet, from Planetary Tectonics, here to kick me off the dole and into a job in the 'works, where 'Burbs lost his voice and his right arm and probably his pheromonal reactions.

"Not very friendly, is he?" She didn't look at me as she said it, didn't even look at my reflection, and I tried not to look at her. That voice was really getting to me. Take away the fur, the eyes, the body contours, even the possible wealth, and the voice alone would have been enough to make me curl up in her lap. I started to wonder if she had backup outside, if I could squeeze through the window in the can and sprint down the alley before she called her goons. And where the hell would I go then? "Better get him another one of these," she said as she tapped her nails on the glass.

She was buying me a drink? Who was this femme? 'Burbs looked at her like she might be dangerous, then he looked at me like I was a slightly embarrassing skin condition, then back at her. We were the only ones in the place besides a couple of SyndicEnts wired into la-la land in the playpens. She was obviously ready to get down to business. She placed her palm on the softly glowing square inlaid in the teak in front of her. Whatever the readout was on 'Burbs monitor, it must have impressed him; he shrugged, filled another glass and sent it down the bar to me.

I stopped it with one hand, turned my head and looked squarely at her, checking out the verandah in my peripheral vision as I did so. There was the beef, all right, the size of a small mountain. Looked like a Primate 3, or maybe even a 4, I couldn't really tell; it was backlit by the sun outside. Jesus, Allah and Vishnu, what had I wandered into?

It started to rain, one of those wonderful tropical afternoon cloudbursts where the sun shines right through the fat drops, turning them into millions of fire opals. It didn't seem to bother her pal outside. He didn't move. I hoped the drumming on the roof masked the pounding of my heart.

I looked back at her reflection and met her eyes. Her pupils had dilated in the semi-darkness of the bar and were almost round now. They were enormous. Looking into them gave me the strangest sensation—a kind of dynamic equilibrium, like I'd just stepped off a cliff and there was nothing left to do but enjoy the ride and hope for the best.

"Go ahead and drink it. It's paid for."

Which is more than could be said for the three I'd already had. I stared into those bottomless eyes for a moment, then dropped my gaze to the brew in front of me so I could think. You see, I was still entertaining the fantasy that I was a free agent, and I was already discovering that thinking was not something I did well while I was looking at her. I opened my mouth to say something like, "What's your game …" or "How did I get so lucky …" but opening my mouth was as far as I got. She wasn't from the SRS or any of the syndicates; those organizations for the advancement of human degradation might do a lot of things to you, but buying you a drink in the local dive wasn't one of them. The theory that despite her dazzling appearance and apparent wealth she just couldn't find a boyfriend and was irresistibly drawn to me was just as easy to discard. I knew that somewhere there was a devastatingly incisive verbal riposte that would unmask her and leave her utterly at my mercy, but I couldn't come up with it.

"I understand you've been off the net," she said, "for almost a year. How do you keep so healthy?"

I met her eyes in the mirror again. Bad choice. "Exercise," I croaked without thinking, "and I watch what I eat."

She smiled easily and slipped off her stool, leaving her brew untouched. Three steps brought her next to me. My nostrils filled with her and my pulse rate went up. "Innovative," she said, then looked over her shoulder at 'Burbs. "Do you hide the good stuff in the back?"

'Burbs said, "Whadya need?" And she replied:

"How about a bottle of eighty year-old brandy?"

"Brandy? I don't think I—"

"Why don't you go check?" All without taking her eyes off me. 'Burbs stared dumbly at her back for a minute, then got the idea and disappeared. She put her arms around my neck, brought her lips to my ear and breathed, "Where can we talk?" I thought furiously as the chills went down my spine. She wanted privacy? This was a factory town. The Trades like to know what's going on with their "employees." I thought some more.

"You been to the beach?" I asked.

She smiled and my pulse went up again. "Sounds nice."

"Meet me at the monorail in half an hour."

"I can hardly wait." She kissed my jaw line, smiled again, turned and swayed outside into the rain and sunshine. The mountain followed her up the Alley. I turned back to the bar and looked at myself in the mirror.

'Burbs came in after a minute carrying a bottle of something. He looked at me, looked around the place, and said, "Whadja do to her?"

I continued to look at my reflection as I drained the glass in my hand. Then I turned to him. "Why do they call you 'Burbs?" I asked.

"What?"

"Why do they call you 'Burbs?"

He looked at me for a moment. "I dunno, 'cause I grew up in the 'burbs, I guess."

"What 'burbs?"

"Whaddya mean?"

"Which 'burbs did you grow up in?"

He put the bottle down. "You know, the 'burbs."

I looked at my empty glass. "You don't even remember what planet you started on, do you?"

He began to wipe down the bar. "What are you tryin' to be cute?" he said.

And a spear of empathy touched my heart as I realized that he didn't.

I walked out into the Alley, turned my face to the sky and let the rain beat on me for a while. I guess I was hoping it would clear my head. Paradise Alley was actually outside of New Spanaway proper, welded and glued and lashed together out of anything the "retired" could salvage from the 'works or the jungle. Gold light burnished the wet metal surfaces of the shops around me, the harsh, industrial lines softened by an occasional clump of bamboo or dumbcane or shefflera pushing through the cracks in the black plastic paving blocks.

I turned my head and looked down to the edge of town and beyond. Out from under the brooding, black base of the thunderstorm the sky was blue and the rainforest brilliant green, patched here and there by the lighter green of nutriCrop fields, sloping down and down to the thousand meter cliffs of Nohili Point. And beyond that to the sapphire sea and the twin, verdant fangs of Lehua and Nihoa, patiently defying the waves. Prime was low in the sky now; there were probably no more than six or eight hours until nightfall. Its nearly horizontal rays shone right under the thunderhead, illuminating the rusted, chaotic tangle of piping, catwalks and cooling towers downtown that reached clear up into the base of the storm. Paradise Alley opened onto the southwest thoroughfare right across from the seemingly endless reduction yards, row upon row of towering condensers and evaporators stretching all the way to the perimeter. I started walking toward them. Even with a rainbow forming in the distance, this place was a bad idea.

Right at the corner a traveler's palm had managed to make a home for itself and somebody had carved something in the basket weave of fronds just above the trunk. It said, "Free the Spam-town 70,000."

I was thinking I might be able to make it 69,999.

The first tube I came to dropped me out of the weather and into the corrosion-streaked labyrinth of the underground. I descended past the employee residential levels to the Mall: a fairly wide thoroughfare lined with various company stores. Spam-town was really just a huge tectonic management plant surrounded by a Gordian knot of auxiliary and support facilities. You were never very far from the 'works, but here on the Mall you were literally walking under a cannonade of colossal conduits, slanting up from the magma sink under the center of town heading for the huge heat exchangers that could be seen from anywhere on the surface.

I passed the dark entrance to the auditorium where I'd given my last performance with Shaughnessy's touring company. Ten months or an eon ago. I cursed her name one more time and slipped down the narrow alley between a Reality outlet and the nutrition dispensary that I was living behind. The woman who ran it had seen the show and taken pity on me when she heard about my tax trouble. It turned out that pity hadn't been her only motivation. She'd offered me this place, at a very reasonable rate, or so it seemed at the time. I was hoping to slide in and out without seeing her.

My palm opened the lock on the steel door to the storage area. I'd jimmied it a few months back to allow myself an escape route without having to go in and out through the store. It was old and cheap, it hadn't been hard to reprogram. When the bolts threw I stood there for a minute, listening. She was a nice old bird and I really didn't want to see her right then.

Nothing. I slid the door back far enough to slip inside and padded between the racks of nutrients, supplements and pre-packaged meals to my digs in the back. Pulling back the sheet that served as a door, I stepped down into a couple of inches of water. Great. Living in the tropics, right next to something that dealt in thousands of degrees Kelvin in temperature differentials, you came to expect a little condensation, no matter how much insulation they used, but this was worse than usual. Something must have blocked the drain again. I didn't have the time or inclination to deal with it right then; I just hoped the moaning and banging of the magma sink would mask any noise I made.

I knew what I was looking for and it wasn't where I'd left it—a serious breach of etiquette on Sheila's part. She'd evidently been digging around in here again. It was her place, after all, but you really don't mess with another person's medicine bag.

I just had the feeling that I was going to say yes to anything Miss cat-eyes had in mind. I knew she wasn't from around here, and there wasn't a chance in hell that she was thinking of moving here, and that meant that whatever she had planned was going to happen somewhere else, which was fine by me. But I didn't want to leave without my past.

The accusation had been unjust. It was where I'd left it, after all. Sheila'd just hung some lingerie over it; the silk was full of her scent. Her perfume wasn't expensive, but it was full of memories. It's funny how a woman's smell brings back just the good ones. The soft, fluid material was cool on my palm as I lifted her things off the hook on the wall. The scales on the backs of my hands were smooth and supple—I wasn't worried about snagging the material. I got my pouch and hung her garments back where they were, which seemed deceptive, somehow, like I was trying to conceal that I was leaving, but it didn't seem right to throw her stuff on the bed, either. I thought about leaving her a note, but I wasn't absolutely positive that I wouldn't be back.

I'd bullet her when I got back on the net. If I got back on the net.

Everything was in the pouch; I checked. Eighteen little fragments and talismans, one from each time I'd re-booted. Eighteen. Shiva, was I really that old? My fingers moved, almost involuntarily, to my shoulder to feel for the one not in the bag, the first one. I'd had it mounted in my left shoulder plate when I got my scales. The shiny, pitted texture was reassuring, a connection across the years and light years. It was just a little piece of chondritic meteorite that I'd found on Arcadia Planitia when I was a kid. Growing up on Mars. Back when the system was The System and Draco was just a constellation.

I always get a little melancholy when I think about leaving someplace that I've lived in for a while, even a place as wasted as Spam-town. The known galaxy is just so vast these days. Even if you never get out of Draco, even if you never leave the home worlds. Hell, most of the people living on Vesper had never come to this hemisphere, let alone this town, and never would. The chances of my ever returning were microscopic.

I decided to clean out the drain for Sheila. It wasn't very romantic, but it was something.

As I slipped back into the alley I heard her voice from the store, "Mo, is that you?" I closed the door as quietly as I could and headed toward the street. Just as I turned the corner into the Mall I heard it open again.

"Mo?"

I was on the main escalator to the surface taking the steps two at a time. God, I'm a heel sometimes.

CHAPTER 2

The storm had moved off to the east and the deep blue of the sky fought with the ocher, umber and brick of the 'works. Angel hair wisps of fog still clung to the cooling towers and the air was electric. Cat-eyes was waiting for me when I got to the monorail platform, her image dancing on wet metal. Her fur was slicked down and sleek from the rain; some of the things that had been more hidden when I'd seen her in the bar were less hidden now. It didn't make it any easier for me to keep my guard up. Her muscle stood silently beside her: loyal, patient and ominous.

My melancholia vanished when I saw her.

She smiled. "I wasn't sure you'd come," she said, and I wondered if it was true. She looked like she believed that she meant it.

"I had some things to take care of."

"Mm." She looked me up and down. I couldn't tell if it was an appreciative glance or merely archival. "Shall we?" She gestured to one of the white, lozenge-shaped cars waiting on the rail. She wasn't wasting any time.

"Yeah, let's," I said, trying to sound calmer than I was.

The cars were spacious for four people—two seats facing forward, two facing back. She preceded me into the rear seat and I sat down beside her. The mountain sat in the two rear-facing seats and generally took up the rest of the cab. The thing was definitely a Primate 4—it must have weighed three hundred kilos. I'd never seen so much hairy meat propelled by two legs.

Our weight triggered traffic control and the door slid closed. An unnecessary light and a very necessary air conditioner came on and we started down the rail; there was only one other destination.

She started to speak and I cut her off, "This is a really nice system," I said, "All the cars are mic'ed, so if you run into trouble halfway down the line all you have to do is yell for help and they come get you."

She smiled again and looked out the window. "That is nice," she said.

We picked up speed and the 'works started to flash past us. Rust and plastic, towers, grids and arrays, the leviathan heat exchangers dwarfing everything else.

"This is an interesting place." That voice again, only now she was sitting right next to me, her thigh practically touching mine. "Do you like it here?"

I looked out the window, too. It was easier than looking at her. "Yeah. Yeah, I like it fine."

"What do they do here?"

Small talk. Good idea, we had a ways to go and nothing important to say until we got there. "Um, mostly magnetic field and earthquake management."

"Oh?"

I tried to think of something that would be both impressive and unrevealing, but all I could come up with was "I never actually worked here—"

"Yes." Wrong subject. Don't talk about me. Or her.

"Uh, you see, Vesper's tidally locked on Golgotha. That's why all the resorts are on the other side of the planet."

"Hmm-m." Honey flowed in my ears and soaked my brain. "I thought Vesper was a moon."

"Well, yeah, it revolves around a planet, so I suppose it is a moon. But it's big enough to be a planet," I was even boring myself. I wasn't used to this. When I was on tour with Shaughnessy, I was the glamorous one. Ask Sheila. Sheila. "It seems like a planet. I suppose you could call it a manet, or a planoon." I was babbling like an idiot, or a tour guide. But she laughed. Various intriguing things happened within and about her torso when she did. I figured the easiest way to remain polite was to look out the window again. Looking in her eyes was still a risky option if I wanted to pursue my own agenda.

We had reached the edge of the city. I could see Paradise Alley poking drunkenly out into the bush. There was 'Burbs' place, where I'd first seen her. Cat-eyes. I didn't even know her name yet but I was hoping I'd never see 'Burbs place again.

Her laugh had given me confidence; I forged ahead. "Anyway, being tidally locked means that its rotation period is about ninety-two hours, the same as the time it takes to revolve around Golgotha."

"Must make for long sunsets." She was playing right along. I would've liked to act with her. She could improvise. I wondered what else she could do.

"It makes for long everything," I said. We gazed out the windows in silence for a moment.

We were moving over the jungle now, an endless, variegated carpet of rosewood, banyan, fig, and who knows how many other kinds of deciduous trees, interrupted by sprays of royal palm, traveler's palm and banana. All genetically engineered to thrive on a ninety-two hour day. The mid-afternoon thunderheads had cleared and you could see all the way to the mountains, a range of twelve-thousand meter peaks that were icy white even here in the tropics.

She took a deep breath, almost a sigh, that came from somewhere lonely and painful. It made me look at her. Without looking at me she said, "So, what do they do with magnetic fields?"

What *was* her game? "Ninety-two hours is too long," I said. "I mean Vesper doesn't spin fast enough to make one of its own. Magnetic fields. They had to plop these magma sinks down around the equator to spin up the core."

"Mm." She still stared at the jungle gliding by. Our large, hairy companion just stared.

"You need a—" I wasn't sure she was even listening to me, "you need a magnetic field to have any kind of stable, thick atmosphere. And an ionosphere. To keep out radiation. Golgotha's got a wicked radiation belt and we're just on the outer edge of it. When the developers came in they needed the field or the biosphere wouldn't take."

"You seem to know quite a bit about it."

She was good. I backpedaled, "Oh, just what you pick up hanging around the joint."

Her fur was drier now. She fluffed it with her hands, passing them over her arms and thighs, digging her fingers into her mane, rubbing her stomach. She seemed to rouse. She turned to me and the smile and charm turned back on again. "And how do you keep earthquakes from happening?"

And I was caught by her eyes. "We don't—I mean, I don't do anything. I just happen to be here. *They* don't keep them from happening; they make them happen." She just kept looking at me. And I kept looking at her. "Lots of them." She was slowly moving her hands up and down her arms, shoulder to wrist and back. "Little ones. All the time." Little silver waves preceded them going up, didn't coming down. "So the big ones never have a chance to—" She had musicians' fingers, long and tapered.

"Build up?" she finished for me. Did she intend that as a double entendre? I thought about smiling at her. I almost did, maybe one corner of my mouth curled up a fraction.

The rail suddenly curved and we were gliding along the edge of the cliffs, heading out to the point. We would be pulling into Nohili soon. Out her side of the car the ocean was a thousand dizzying meters below us. Out my side the jungle sloped gently up and up to Spam-town, which looked like the Emerald

City left out in the rain for a couple of centuries.

The view was spectacular. Even if you'd been to the Valles or the Ginger Islands on Shangri-La or Hawaii on Earth, it expanded you and diminished you at the same time. Her body reacted visibly in a manner that I was beginning to wish wasn't so visible.

"My, that's quite something," she said, leaning toward the sea. Lehua and Nihoa were ahead of us, thrusting out of the azure metallic water off the point like needle-sharp stepping-stones. For people with really long legs.

"Yeah," I said, looking, too, "The scenery on Vesper can be pretty overwhelming. The gravity's low and the tidal strains from Golgotha have produced some amazing tectonic fracturing. It's why they have to manage crustal movement. Everybody wants to look at the cliffs and mountains, but nobody wants to put up with the processes that form them."

She turned back to me with a wry smile, "You seem to know about a lot of things." One eyebrow arched, "Or is that just something else you picked up hanging around the joint?"

"Yeah, I— well, you know—" I kept trying to talk, but stuff like that came out instead. "Anyway, it makes sense," I went on gamely, or lamely, "I mean, large-scale disasters put a pretty heavy strain on the net. You can only re-boot so many people at one time. It ends up being more economical this way."

"Yes, I'm sure it does." She looked out at the sea again and then gasped as we were suddenly over nothing. The rail crosses a gap in the cliff. We could see the waterfall that cut it making the dive to the beach in three mind-altering plunges. I thought she'd be impressed. She was.

Just as suddenly we were gliding just above the treetops again. She laughed. "Well, you certainly know how to show a girl a good time, don't you?" I smiled as the car decelerated and glided into the slot in the plain metal platform that was Nohili station.

The door slid open and we let the mountain lumber out first. It seemed the only reasonable solution. Then we stepped out onto the silver boilerplate and felt the sea breeze rising off the cliffs caress our faces. It filled me with salt air and made little dancing ripples in her fur. Every muscle in the universe seemed to relax.

"This way," I said, pointing to the stairs down into the jungle. We clanged off the final step (I was proud of them for not collapsing under King Kong) and onto a dirt path that had been worn through the greenery. We brushed by hibiscus, elephant ear and tree ferns as I led us out to the fork. I took the left trail that went out to the point.

"Aren't we going to the beach?" she asked.

"No, I thought—" and I stopped. How did she know we weren't? I started again, "I thought, just in case some Trades jafo was listening in on 'Burbs place this afternoon, we'd stay up here. Just to be safe." Now I was really confused. She seemed genuinely surprised when we went over the falls. Could she fake that? And why would she?

"Yes, of course. Good idea."

She wasn't giving anything away. If she'd just slipped, she didn't seem to be worried about it. I guessed I'd find out soon enough.

We wove our way out to the very tip of Nohili Point. As we neared the end of the trail, the trees got shorter and finally gave way to billows of flowering bushes and scrub sheared off and shaped by the wind. The summit of Lehua was just a little lower than we were, sharp as a spike and dripping vegetation. It looked so close that you could jump over to it. It was actually almost half a klick away, with Nihoa peeking out behind it. And the ocean a long, long way down in between.

"Well, if they can hear us out here, I guess we're re-cyc anyway," I said. "What's the story?"

And she told me, her hairy chum filling up a couple of meters of trail behind her.

"I need a man who's off the net. No ties here. Nobody that would miss him for a couple of years, maybe longer. I need someone who's crewed before. I think you're him." The flirt was gone. She was all business now.

"Crewed what, a starship?"

"Yes."

This was getting intense. "What size?"

"It's a seven-seater."

"Hmm. Lucky seven."

"Yes."

"You're the Captain?"

"Yes."

"Got a Pilot?"

"Yes."

"Astrogator?"

"I just need a crewman."

Meat for the engine. "Where are we going?"

"We'll make several stops before we head for our final destination."

Well, she didn't answer that one. "Wait a minute. Why does it matter that I'm off the net? I'll be back on as soon as you plug me into the engine."

"I'm on an eye-ess."

Eye-ess? What the hell was an eye-ess? Eye-ess? I. S. An Independent—"You're on an Independent System?"

"That's right."

Okay. Not rich. Not mega-rich. Mega-giga-filthy-howling rich. "What's your name?"

"Let's call me Steel."

Let's, I thought. You didn't answer that one either. I wondered if she got the historical allusion. I doubted it. A twentieth-century dictator who wiped out large parts of his own people through weird farming practices was most likely outside her ken. Probably a company name. Or maybe she was just poetic.

"You want to know mine?" I said.

"Mohandas. People call you Mo." Oh. Like that.

"How about that?" I gestured at her friend. "Does it have a name?"

Her face broke into a smile again and life seemed worth living. "Ham? Don't worry about Ham; he's not for you. He just takes care of me."

"I'll bet he does a good job." She scratched Ham behind the ears and got nuzzled in return. Okay, he was a big cupcake. He still made me nervous. One thing still bothered me. "So, you came to Spam-town to look for a starship crewman? Why? I mean, I'm a fluke. Everybody else around here is indentured to the Trades."

"I was lucky to find you. As to how we came to be here, that really doesn't affect this transaction."

Well, that cleared *that* up. "What do you pay?"

"I'll double standard crew scale, pay off your back taxes, and at the end of the trip I'll re-boot you."

Wow. "Nice benefit package."

"What do you say?"

Good question. Run off with some femme I'd just met; fall through infinity to someplace she won't name, for a whole lot of money and a great health plan. Or I could go back to my hole in the back of Sheila's store, until she kicked me out, and run up a tab at 'Burbs' place.

Like I said before, a man starts to act funny when he's run out of options. "Let's go take a look at your ship."

"I know crewmen like to look over a ship before they sign on. I'm sorry, but I can't offer you that option."

"Why not?"

"The ship is not available."

"What do you mean? Why can't we—I mean I just want to—"

"The ship is in orbit."

"In orbit? Around Vesper?"

"Yes."

Curiouser and curiouser. A woman rich enough to have an independent system leaves her ship floating around in space. Why? All the re-fit facilities were on the surface. Spam-town had a nice port complex; it needed one for all the trade it did. "Well, won't it have to land to pick us up?"

"No."

No? How the hell were we going to get up to it? Walk? Take a cab? Jump real hard? Surface to orbit shuttles had been obsolete for centuries.

"I'm sorry I can't tell you anymore. I'll have to have your answer now. I know it's a bit of a squeeze play, but I'm afraid it can't be helped."

'A bit of a squeeze play.' Holy mother of Lao-Tse.

She suddenly looked a bit unsure of herself. Then she said, "If it makes any difference, it would mean we would be together."

Nice gambit. I didn't feel like biting right then. I said, "Together? How together?"

And she looked away from me. Out at the sea and Lehua and Prime and the sky and the endless, bottomless universe. "You know, on the ship."

I felt like a heel for the second time in an hour, a fairly heavy dose of self-loathing even for me. She didn't need this from me. She was offering me a job. I needed a job. Granted, it sounded like a job that would probably get me imprisoned, enslaved, or permanently eradicated from the space-time continuum, but what the hell.

"You don't need to promise me anything like that," I said. She looked back at me. "I usually don't have too much trouble finding company when I want it." I don't know why I said that, and I regretted it right away, but there it was.

"I didn't mean—"

"Forget it." I looked at her one last time as a free man. "Okay. I'm your boy. What do we do now?"

CHAPTER 3

I could see her relax, like she'd just found out she wasn't going to have to shoot her dog after all. It made me tense up. I wasn't sure I liked being that important to her, or anyone.

I was already second-guessing myself. What kind of job was it that made a person act like that when they found someone to do it? I couldn't read anything in those liquid eyes but relief—a lonely, exhausted relief propped up and propelled forward by an almost frightening determination. For a moment we just stood there with the wind massaging us and roaring in our ears, the moss green cliffs arcing away to the north and south, cut here and there by lacy cataracts and free-falling horse-tail flumes. I could barely hear the pulsing white noise of the surf—far, far below us. I wanted to say, "Listen, Cat-Eyes, why don't we forget about your little project and set up shop right here? We could have a nice little surf 'n' turf place at the end of the rail and sell shells to the tourists that say 'I saw the other Vesper—Nohili Point!' when you hold them to your ear." I wanted to say it. But I didn't.

It was interesting to watch her compose herself. She was very efficient at it. One or two short breaths and poise slid back over her like a curtain. "I'd like to leave right away," she said. "You don't need to go back for anything, do you?"

I looked at my new boss, trying to bury any romantic fantasies. "No," I said, "I imagine I can get along without anything I've left behind."

"Good. We have about five hours of daylight left and I'd like to use it." She gave me one look of generalized approval, turned and walked briskly back into the forest. Ham lumbered after her.

"I'll just follow along, shall I?" I said to where they'd disappeared, and started walking.

I caught up with them at the entrance to the tube. It was just a few meters down the trail to the beach, right under the monorail platform. It descended inside the cliff to the desalinization plant at the foot of the point. You wouldn't think they'd have to distill salt water right in the middle of a rain forest, but the magma sink heat exchangers had a thirst that matched the temperatures they dealt with. Cat-Eyes (I didn't know if I could ever think of her as "Steel") looked at me as I walked up.

"We're under a fairly acute time constraint," she said, and she looked at the tube entrance. Then that wry smile came back. "But I need to see what kind of shape you're in. Come on." She started off down the trail.

In a few meters we came to the edge of the gorge cut by the waterfall we'd ridden over. The trail switchbacked down the south wall. "Trail" may be an exaggeration. It dropped the thousand meters to the beach in just over a kilometer, a meter down for every meter forward. But some stretches were fairly level, which meant other parts were watch your feet and hope the root you're clinging to doesn't pull out of the cliff. It had never been built, just worn into the rock and jungle by the employees. This was before the syndicate, in its infinite mercy, decided to let them use the tube to go swimming. I guess they finally figured out that it was cheaper than re-booting them when they fell off the trail.

I'd been down and up it before—one of the things I did to keep healthy after I got kicked off the net. I didn't know how she knew about it, I didn't know why she wanted to use it, and I didn't know why we were going down to the beach in the first place. All in all I felt the master of my own destiny.

The work started right away. To get over the lip of the gorge and onto the south wall you had to scramble fifteen or twenty meters, maybe the height of a six-story building, down a web of strangler fig roots to the first ledge. Twenty meters of root ladder can be kind of airy in any circumstances, but this one was at the top of a thousand meter drop, with a jet of water off to our right that we could watch falling and falling and falling, down and down until it shattered in a small pool that was still only a third of the way down. Then another long fall into another tiny pool and the final, timeless plunge to the minuscule strip of sand at the base of the cliff. The hammered steel ocean was softened at the shore by tiny white fingernails of surf.

Steel hesitated at the edge. "Wow," she said.

"What's the matter?" I asked.

She just stood there for a moment. I think she was hesitant to show any weakness to me. "When we came up this it was foggy. You couldn't see anything but the route in front of you."

"Why didn't you take the tube?"

"I didn't know about it." Determination hardened her. "Let's go." She grabbed a handhold and swung down onto the web, picking her footing, but moving with speed and grace.

And why were you down there in the first place? And how did you get there? And where were *we* going, and why? And several other questions of that general ilk. I waited for her to get a safe distance below me and started to descend, Ham bringing up the rear.

Everything was still wet from the rain; it made the bark as slippery as a politician's promise. There's nothing quite like the rush you get when your feet start to slide with nothing under you but air. Your arches cramp, it shoots up your calves, through your inner thighs to your groin, your stomach does something very strange and then—POW! Your pulse rate triples, it zings down your arms, and your palms and inner wrists ache from how hard your fingers are gripping. I made it down to the ledge with my dignity fairly intact. Ham climbed like his arboreal progenitors. Of course, he had two more thumbs than I did.

The ledge at the bottom was comfortably wide and descended steadily but moderately for a while. Cat-eyes, or "Steel," or "Captain Steel" led us downward, sometimes with staggering views of the falls and the ocean, sometimes burrowing through leafy tangles of shrubs and vines. As often as not we would be scrambling down root ladders or bare rock. The roar of the falls would crescendo as we approached, then recede when the trail switched back the other way, in a regular, soothing rhythm. Steel kept up an impressive pace.

The gorge enfolded us like a green womb. Each measured negotiation of a fractured rock face, each heart-pumping glissade down the grease-slick, ropy chaos of a root system pushed the lip of the falls farther above us. Each quiet, leafy tunnel, each thundering, misty turn behind the diamond column of water brought us closer to wherever we were going. As the silver ribbon of the monorail bridge receded above me so did the last ten months of my life. 'Burbs place and vacant idleness, Sheila's room and the sad, mechanical physicality that never would have blossomed into intimacy, the oppressive, corrosive sterility of the 'works. Time had stopped for me in Spam-town, and Cat-eyes had started it again.

And what would I do with that time? Before Spam-town had been Shaughnessy and the show. We'd played forty cities on fourteen worlds in the last five years. And before that, other companies and other shows, other tours, other cities, other planets. I'd been an actor for most of the twenty years since I'd last re-booted in Palermo on Mondoverdi. Before that … Before that was the last time I'd been old, truly old.

I'd put off re-booting because I didn't want to decide what I'd have to forget. There was too much I'd wanted to remember, and you can never keep it all. Though a lot of things fade over time, holos or Realities or even smelling a certain spice or perfume will bring them flooding back. But once you log off and restructure, after you come back, the parts you didn't keep are *gone*. Gone. Mary wasn't gone, but parts of her were. I hadn't saved the day she left. The house on Scarpus wasn't gone—I could see the bedroom, her dressing table, her silk scarves draped over the mirror—but my things were missing. I could see out the back window, over autumnal hardwood hills rolling to the horizon, but the glass wind chimes hanging by the door were silent. I hadn't saved their sound. I couldn't remember how we got into town. And even if I bought a Reality, even if I went back to Scarpus and traveled the same route, it wouldn't connect to anything. There was nothing to connect to. It would simply be a new experience for me, connected to my life now. To 'Burbs and Shaughnessy and acting and Cat-eyes. Not to Mary. Nor to my life before Mary, nor the life before that, nor the one before that. But to the pieces of all of them that I still had in me.

And now Captain Cat-eyes Steel. I watched her easy, loose-jointed dance over the rocks and drops in the trail in front of me. Once again I'd connected myself to someone else going someplace else. Heading out. On the road again.

We stopped at the first pool for a drink. It was loud and misty and invigorating. A riot of ferns sprouted from the rock, and moss dripped like green velvet. Looking up at that much water, falling so far, was just as impressive as looking down at it. It danced and weaved when the breeze changed, individual drops exploding into spray in mid-air, thundering and thundering endlessly into the rock-lipped pool. Then Steel was off again, leading us to the next stretch of broken stone to clamber down, another ledge, another leafy arcade, and down and down and down. The tourmaline ocean slowly turned to brass as Prime imperceptibly slipped toward the horizon.

When we were almost down to the beach, we stopped on an outcrop overlooking the water, close enough to hear the surf over the roar of the falls. She tossed a question at me over her shoulder that took me by surprise.

"How did you get involved in the uprising on Valhala?"

I didn't answer for a moment; I didn't know what to say. That she knew about my role in it raised one question; that she wanted to talk about it raised another, and I already didn't like the answer to either one. I looked at the white sand below us, a blank page rhythmically cleansed of memories by the caress of the waves. I remembered Valhala. I could have easily chosen to forget it, an option offered to me every time I'd re-booted since then.

"That's something I don't really talk about," was what I said, but what I was thinking was much less laconic. I already figured she'd looked over my C.V. on the net from what she knew about me, but that only covered my last three 'boots. I kept it that way deliberately. The Valhala Uprising was way before that. Ancient history, clear back in the twenty-eighth century, when armed conflict still made a weird kind of sense to some rare groups of people under some highly unusual circumstances.

"I'd like you to talk about it with me." She turned and looked into my eyes. And what was in hers? Compassion? Or merely patience?

"Does this have to do with the job?" I said, stalling.

"I like to know the people I command. What's formed them, where their hearts lie. It helps me to know how they'll respond in a crisis." Innocent enough. Could be true.

"Well, I was there," I stalled some more, "you pretty much had to choose one side or the other."

"Not everyone fought." She wasn't going to leave this alone.

"No. Not everyone." How do you talk about something like that? The universe was a different place back then. Had Steel ever witnessed what I had? I didn't know how old she was; I didn't know anything about her.

"Do you keep in touch with anyone from that time?" That voice was so rich and compelling, it would have been easy to fool myself into thinking she simply wanted to get to know me better. Standing there looking at the ocean, Lehua, Nihoa, and the point towering above us to our left, the sand and the cliffs stretching away to our right, I wanted it to be true. But I just didn't buy it.

"No." I looked back at her. "Not for a long time."

"Your wife—"

"It seems you know a lot more about me than I do about you." There was a little more anger in that statement than I would have liked, but she seemed to accept it. She smiled—deferentially? Maybe.

"Fair enough. We'll talk more later. We may not be so different from one another as you imagine." And then she was on the net, or her independent system. "Marcus, is the boat ready?" She listened for a moment. "Things take time. I moved as quickly as possible." Her voice was quite different. "How is he?" Steel. Definitely Steel. Captain Steel. "We'll be there in fifteen minutes. I'll want to move out immediately."

Ten months was a long time to be off the net, but I wasn't sure that I missed it. She looked at me again, "You're a complex man. I think you'll make a good crewman." The honey was back, but now it was mixed with my experience of her. She turned and started down toward the sand. I followed. Ham followed me.

CHAPTER 4

There was always a feeling of 'I came down that'? whenever I hit the beach and looked back up at Nohili, stoic, silent, transcendent. It was no different this time, except that this time I wouldn't be going back up. Steel felt it too, I could tell. Even in her haste she kept looking up at it, as I did. It made me feel more connected to her, or perhaps it was just the comfort of false superiority, born of watching her experience for the first time what I had already known.

The desalinization plant was as stainless as Spam-town was corroded. It punctured soft green tapestry, dwarfed to insignificance at the foot of the unmoved colossus, thrusting its clean geometry into aleatoric waves. We clattered around the catwalk that encircled it, up from the sand, out over the intakes, and down again, to get south of it. I could see a tiny aquamarine sliver far down the shore, almost to the very tip of the point. Two specks moved around it. In another five minutes they had resolved into a fair-sized open fiberglass catamaran and two people. Five minutes later Steel was introducing me to them as we shoved the boat into the surf and climbed aboard.

It was disconcerting being with her among people she already knew. Fantasies I thought I had put away were stuffed into deeper places, although I could feel my reluctance to give them up completely. I could tell Marcus was her pilot and exec even before she told me which one he was. Chocolate-skinned and taller than Steel, almost as tall as I was, his eyes held the hardened fatigue of command. He appraised me, an unknown quantity, as he took my hand. I think my scales dismayed him, but I couldn't be sure. If he allowed himself emotions on the job they would be channeled to the task of the moment. He had no obvious cosmetic alterations; a man of his temperament wouldn't be interested in them. I thought he might be from Earth. He looked African. He said simply, "Mohandas. Welcome aboard."

"Thanks." I felt the need to reassure him, or maybe to increase my status, "I've crewed several times before. My pilot and astrogation licenses are up to date." Shaughnessy and I had often joked that we should have been in the teamsters' union instead of Actors' Equity. It often seemed like we spent more time freewheeling than we did on stage.

"Yes, I've seen your C.V." Of course. And what else had he seen?

Steel turned to the other man. Shorter, thicker, less chiseled in his facial features. "This is Jemal. He's in the number five spot." Another crewman, also unadorned, and I wondered why. He wore the same buff one-piece garment that Marcus had on. Perhaps he had his talismans mounted under it. I couldn't see a medicine bag.

"Hi." He took my hand as well; then he made his way back to the turbine and fired it up.

Prime had been refracted into a fat, wavering peach, almost connected to the shimmering, orange path that it flung across the cobalt water. We passed through the shadow of Lehua as we drove south through the gap between it and the point. Nohili's verdant cliffs flamed sanguinary in the horizontal light.

Steel started to confer with Marcus in tones of controlled tension. "Any word from Alice?"

"Yes." Marcus' voice was just as controlled. "She's found a dirigible in Kindu."

"A dirigible? Nothing faster?"

"Nothing we could use. The economy in the outback is solar-powered, hydrogen-based. Anything powerful enough to get us to the altitude we need is just too fuel-hungry. They can't afford them. I don't think we could land anything like that at Manlung La anyway."

"No. You're probably right. But a dirigible. Will we have the control we need when the time comes?"

"We'll just have to make it work."

"Yes. Can Yuri fabricate something for us?"

"Alice says he's working on that now. The dirigible frames are carbon-carbon epoxy, which should be strong enough, and there's a repair facility in Kindu that he's working with to put it together."

Steel sighed. "I don't like him working with the locals."

Marcus seemed to get slightly defensive, "He's only telling them what they need to know to put it together. He's not stupid."

"It's simply imperative—"

"Captain, I believe I am conversant with what is imperative on this voyage."

They were silent for a moment. The whine of the turbine and the hiss of the water on the hulls filled the cooling tropical air. Salmon streaks of cirrus feathered the sky to the west. We continued to parallel the cliffs south of the point.

Steel spoke again, "Does Alice think the … the … What do they call those things? The gondola. Does she think the gondola will hold pressure?"

"They use them to get over the mountains, so it should be okay for the amount of time we'll need. The main concern seems to be the size of the handle. If he makes it too big we'll never get off the ground. But the smaller it is, the tighter the altitude tolerance becomes."

"What are we talking?"

"Less than ten meters."

We were getting into some chop. The hiss of the water turned to a rhythmic slap as we started to bounce over the waves. I grabbed the railing and sat on a bag of something.

"No word from Archie and Drake?"

"We were able to see the mountains until we pulled in under the point. Except for those thunderheads the weather has looked clear and calm. They should be okay. The fact that they haven't found it necessary to call is probably a good sign."

I had no quantum of a clue what was going on, but the bag was pretty comfortable. I tried to relax. The cliffs continued to slide by; we must have been making forty knots. I saw a dolphin break the surface off the port bow.

Steel asked him one more question. "We'll make the mouth of the river by dark?"

"With time to spare. We should be a ways up it when Prime finally disappears."

"Good. And Tamika will be over Manlung La in the morning."

"Twenty-six-thirty hours sidereal. About three hours after sun-up."

"Which gives us—"

"About fifty-two hours."

"Fifty-two hours. I hope Yuri can pull it off."

"He either does or we wait another rotation."

"No. I don't want to wait. I'll have Tamika shift orbit."

"How will we explain that to traffic control? The story is thin enough as it is."

Steel thought for a moment. "It won't come to that. Yuri will be ready." She turned, came back to where I was sitting and stood over me. "How are you doing?" she asked me, her mane whipping in the breeze.

"I'm all right. A little tired, a little hungry, about as confused as I've ever been in my life. Other than that I'm fine."

She smiled as she sat down next to me. Even in the open air with the wind over us she smelled really good. Like—like bread and almonds. "Sorry about all the secrecy." She looked at me like *I* was the secret, then sighed, "Corporate stuff. You know."

Marcus turned and glanced at her, saw me looking at him, turned away again.

"Is everything all right?" I wasn't getting any less confused. The Captain was gone again, replaced by the woman who had picked me up in a bar. Or maybe someone else.

"Yes. Yes, I think it is." She sank down farther into the hull and lay back against the bag. "I'm tired, too. We've been through a rough few weeks, but I think it's going to be okay now. I was very, very lucky to find you."

Heady stuff. "Well, I guess I was lucky to be found."

She smiled and looked at her feet. "I *mean*, you were the only qualified crewman off the net on this whole planet."

Oh. "I thought you said it was a moon."

"Right," she laughed.

"Why is it so important that I'm off the net?"

She looked at me. "Not yet." Oops, the Captain was back. "I'll give you a full briefing when we get on the ship. If you still want to know."

If I still want to know. Oh, boy. "Why wouldn't I still want to know?"

"Let's wait until we get to the ship, and you can decide."

Hmm. "All right." There were so many things I wanted to know, and right then most of them were about her. But there are so many things you can't ask, so many things I wouldn't ask, and so many things I was willing to bet she wouldn't answer.

She wrapped her arms around herself. "You did very well coming down the cliff."

"I've been on that trail many times. It's hardwired into me."

"Mm. Still—" She was looking at the sunset. I followed her gaze and saw Prime just kiss the water. "They do last a long time here."

"Yes." We watched it for a while. If you watched long enough you could see that it was sinking, but ever so slowly. I tried to think of something to say. Finally, "Where did you get your fur? It's beautiful."

"Mm." She stroked her arms. "This wonderful little place in Lausanne. It's on a little street up the hill and you just lie there looking out the window at Lac Leman and the French Alps while they make you spectacular."

I thought for a moment. "On Earth."

"I'm sorry, yes. I forgot. You haven't been back to the system for a long time, have you?"

"Not for a long time."

She yawned and snuggled in beside me on the bag. I wasn't sure whether I was supposed to put my arm around her or not. I didn't.

Marcus called out to Jemal in the stern, "We're coming to the end of the cliffs. Keep an eye out."

"Yes, sir."

I looked over my shoulder at the shore. The cliffs were much lower already and I could see to the south where they disappeared altogether. I'd never been down here. I hadn't gotten farther from Spam-town than the end of the monorail since Shaughnessy had left me there. The mountains were visible in the distance, a ragged horizon of ice and rock set afire with alpenglow. Sperry and Alta were rising, a melon and a grape in the deepening blue. I looked farther up in the sky and found the crimson glint of Ruby. I was going to point it out to Steel but when I looked down at her she was asleep. She must have been tired. I wondered how long she'd been awake. Many times when people first get to Vesper they try to stay awake all day, and that can be an awfully long forty-six hours.

"There it is!" Marcus yelled, "Bring her around." The boat slued to port and headed obliquely shoreward.

We were south of the cliffs now. The shore was a dark line of tangled jungle, bloodied by the sunset. I could see the break in it where a fairly wide river emptied into the sea. That's where we were headed. The water around us turned slowly from translucent jade to a creamy brown as we entered the outflow. In a few more minutes we passed between mangrove and palm-clogged points flanking the mouth of the river. Prime was a glowering dome in a pool of fire as it disappeared around the first bend.

CHAPTER 5

I wondered about Marcus and Jemal. It could be embarrassing, if not downright inconvenient, if one or both of them nodded off while we were driving up this river at forty knots. I got up without disturbing Steel and walked up to Marcus.

"How long have you been on Vesper?" I asked him. He looked back at where Steel lay curled up. "She's asleep," I said. "I was wondering if you two needed to get some sleep, too. It takes a while for people to adjust."

He kept looking upstream like a man with a purpose, a purpose I totally agreed with; you could see logs, branches, and sometimes entire uprooted trees half-submerged in the thick, brown current. "Yes. We've been on the surface since early—what would you call it—yesterday? Seems a strange thing to call an event that happened over a hundred and thirty hours ago."

"They call them 'quads.' Most people take four sleeps per quad. A five or six hour siesta before noon, another in the late afternoon, then a longer sleep before mid-night and another before dawn. It's strange at first, but it seems to work."

"I see." A flock of birds exploded from the trees on the south bank, disturbed by our turbine. "So, you've only been up a couple of hours?"

"No, my schedule's all screwed up. I've been out of a job, and my digs in Spam—that is, New Spanaway, were down in the bowels of the 'works. I could sleep pretty much whenever. I guess I've been up quite a while. Being off the net, you know, time kind of gets away from you."

"I suppose it would. Jemal! Watch that snag to port!"

"Got it," Jemal called back.

"Well, I'm on the payroll," I said. "Is there anything I can do to help?"

He looked at me, looked at my scales, then back at me again. "Do you know this river?"

"Never been anywhere near it."

He gazed at me for a moment longer, then looked back at the water rushing past us. "I think Jemal and I will be able to muddle through," he said. "Thank you."

This guy was beginning to annoy me. "Look, Marcus—"

"I think ..." he glanced back at Steel curled up on the bag then back at me, "I think it would be better if you addressed me as 'sir.' I find a ship runs more smoothly if the formalities are observed. I don't know what your arrangement is with the Captain—"

"She offered me a job. I took it. Sir." He was really beginning to burn my ass.

"I didn't mean to imply anything else."

"I'm glad to hear it, sir."

He looked at me a moment longer, then turned back to watching for snags. "In any case," he said, "I appreciate your offer to help, but Jemal and I had a little nap while we were waiting for the Captain to return. You probably need sleep more than we do. We'll be in Kindu in about four hours."

What the heck, I thought, I'd give it one more try. "It'll be dark in an hour. It's going to be a lot more difficult to spot stuff in the water. I could take one side and you could take the other. What do you think?"

He sighed heavily, a sigh born of—what? His face was stony, unreadable. His posture was stoic, like he was refusing to be crushed under something he couldn't solve. "I apologize if I seem—" he stared hard at the river, "Yes, that's a good idea. Why don't you get some rest and I'll call you when it gets dark."

Why did I feel like I'd just joined the crew of the Flying Dutchman? "All right. I mean, yes, sir." He kept staring at the water, back straight, hands folded behind him, keeping the fabric of reality from unraveling through sheer force of will. There was nothing else to do, so I made my way aft to look for someplace to take a nap. I looked down at Steel as I passed. If anything, she was more beautiful than when she was awake. Her body was even more fluid, her features clearer, more connected. If we'd been alone I would have lain down beside her, but—but what the hell was I doing?

I thought about crossing over to the other hull, to put as much distance as possible between us, but I'd have to cross right in front of Ham to do it. He was sitting amidships, a huge, hairy pile of patience. I supposed if I wasn't doing anything threatening to Steel I'd be okay, but it seemed like one of those experiments that you might get to try only once. Ultimately, my distaste for Marcus' insinuations, even if they might be true, overcame my fear of being eaten alive. Funny how dignity can override self-preservation sometimes.

I figured it would be safer to cross in front of him than behind. I didn't want to make *him* nervous. I stepped up on deck. As I neared he looked me right in the eye. He pursed his lips and raised his chin a couple of times. I guess he was saying "hi." I stopped, thinking, what the heck, maybe I could make friends with him. He seemed to like getting his ears scratched, at least when Steel did it. I reached out a hand and his gaze shifted to it, but he let me place my hand on the back of his head and give him a rub. I scratched his ears for a minute; then he shook his head. Scratching time was over. As I was pulling my hand back he reached up and wrapped his huge paw around it, not with any force; he just took my hand in his and held it while he looked out at the water.

How long was this going to last? I stood there for a time while he meditated on the ironies of being a genetically altered gorilla-chimpanzee-whatever, riding up a river on a moon, circling a planet that was three hundred fifty light years from the globe he'd evolved on. Well, maybe he wasn't but it seemed like he might have been. After a minute or two he let go of my hand but continued to stare at the water, or maybe the jungle. Maybe he was homesick. Had he ever been in a jungle? Or had he grown up in a lab somewhere? Suddenly I felt closer to Ham than anyone else on the boat. Both of us were a long way from home, and neither one of us had the faintest idea what was going on.

"Take it easy, Hamster." I know, a pretty silly nickname for a three hundred kilo guard dog, but it just popped out of my mouth. "I'm going to go log off for a while."

He didn't look at me when I spoke, just kept staring off at the passing scenery. I slipped past him and stepped down into the starboard hull, found more sacks of stuff (it smelled like some sort of grain), laid down on them and passed out for a while.

I'd had a big day.

"Hey, Mo! Mohandas, wake up, man." I looked blearily up into Jemal's face hanging over me. "Marcus wants you to go forward and help watch for snags."

"Yeah, right. Right. Okay, I'm up," I started to get to my feet. I must have gone straight into REM. I felt hung over.

Oh, right. 'Burbs' place.

Oh, right. Cat-eyes. Steel. Captain Steel. I wasn't in Spam-town anymore, I was—

I stood up and looked over the bulwark.

It shouldn't have taken me by surprise. I knew about them. I'd read about them on the net centuries ago, when Vesper's biosphere was being designed, but I'd never been outside a city at night since I'd landed here. When I was working there just never seemed to be any reason to, and after Shaughnessy left me I was too depressed. You couldn't really see them even from the edge of Spam-town, even from Paradise Alley. The lights were too bright. Of course, people had them potted, and in Capri on the other side there was a botanical garden that had a nice display. But nothing like this.

It was night. The sky was peppered with stars. Sperry and Alta were still too low in the east to be seen in the middle of the jungle. The trees hid them. And Ruby, although much brighter than the stars, didn't give off an appreciable amount of light. It was really dark.

The flowers had come out.

Come out, maybe they'd already been out, but you didn't notice them in daylight, not in the tangle of manic fecundity that was the rain forest. But at night—

In order to make the whole ecosystem work, back when they were putting it together, the biggest problem they'd had to overcome was the forty-six hours of darkness every day. I mean once they had a reducing atmosphere established. Circadian rhythms could be altered, but sleeping that long on a regular basis just wasn't healthy for a lot of things. Birds and insects started to act very strangely. That meant the things they liked to eat weren't getting pollinated because the pollinators couldn't find them in the dark, and everything started to fall apart.

So they gave the flowers bioluminescence. Not just the cool green of fireflies; they ran the entire spectrum. Icy blues fading to rich lavenders. Luscious reds swelling to cool pinks and gaudy oranges. Chrome yellows flecked with crimson. Some brilliant, others the most delicate pastels, they filled the jungle on both sides of the river.

It took your breath away.

Not that they were all that bright. You could still barely see around you. But the turgid river was glassy smooth; it reflected the flowers and the stars. We were floating up a polychromatic kaleidoscope.

I made my way up to the bow and Marcus hailed me from the other hull. "We tried it with the running lights on, but we found this works better. The lights just make you think you can go faster than is really prudent. You can actually see farther without them, once your eyes adjust."

"Right," I called back. My eyes had been closed, so I could already see pretty well. Even so, the longer I looked, the more I could tell that the luminescence was in everything. The veins in the leaves gave off faint traces of dim emerald. The moss on the trunks showed as patches of dull jade. The way you saw logs floating in the water was by the black gap in the reflected stars. Even so, Jemal had the turbine throttled way down.

We snaked our way up the meandering river like that, with me or Marcus calling out to Jemal when he needed to avoid some obstacle. Steel must have been dead to the world; our calls never disturbed her. Ham was Ham, still and silent.

The river was already quite a bit narrower here than it had been at its mouth. Sometimes we'd come around a bend and the jungle would arch completely over the water, replacing the actinic stars with a soft gingham canopy of blooms. Once in a great while we'd pass the flickering torches of a homestead or a small settlement and our eyes would have to readjust, but that didn't happen more than five or six times in the course of the entire voyage.

The overall effect was one of an almost timeless calm balanced against the intense need to wring every possible scrap of visual data out of any stray photon that happened to hit your retina. The hardest thing was to keep your eyes on the water and not just drift off and admire the light-show. The occasional calls, shrieks, bellows and roars of whatever was out in the bush looking for groceries, or a way to keep from becoming groceries, didn't help. All in all, as eerily beautiful as it was, I was still glad to see the torches of Kindu come around the final bend.

I heard Marcus in the other bow. "Alice, how are things progressing?" The flowers dimmed out of visibility as we approached the torches lining the rough, wooden dock. "Yes, we're just pulling in now."

There were lots of other boats tied up along the waterfront, but none were as sterile as our fiberglass cat. Each was a unique work of painstaking craftsmanship— ornately carved and skillfully fitted mahogany hulls, rosewood and ebony rails, teak decks, sturdy masts reaching up out of the torchlight. The village of Kindu could be glimpsed through the trees. A main street twisted away from the dock lined with carved and thatched buildings, lit mostly by the yellow-orange of burning wood, occasionally with the cool blue of hydrogen. I couldn't see a single straight line anywhere; all was soft, organic asymmetry, as comfortably functional as an old pair of shoes. After months in the brutal efficiency of Spam-town, my soul felt bathed in warm humanity.

And there were people everywhere, their dark bronze Draconian features emblazoned with tattoos, jewelry and cosmetic genome work. I saw iridescent blue feather crests, green and gold epaulet and spine plates, some designs new to me, others centuries old. It was mid-evening and the place was jumping. Bales of grain or tubers, baskets of fish, crates, bags and barrels were being lifted onto the dock or lowered onto waiting decks.

A tall, handsome woman seemed in nominal charge of the port facilities. She took time out of shouting orders to throw us a line. Her body art took me back to the last time I was in the Pleiades—a carnelian ridge lock reigned over symmetrical peacock tattoos, with the heads at the corners of her jaw, the necks stretching down the sides of her throat to bodies that spanned her shoulders and blended into real plume tails that flowed gracefully over her arms like a robe of royalty. The tails erected and fanned out as she waved to Marcus like an old friend.

"You bullet Alice?" she smiled.

Even Marcus' obsidian composure couldn't withstand the onslaught of vivacity; he was forced to smile back. "Yes, I've just been talking to her."

"Your friend Yuri works like he's got a hobby. Don't you people ever stop to have sex?"

This forced Marcus to laugh. I was afraid he'd hurt himself; it was good to see. "Well—" I think he was looking for a witty riposte, but witty ripostes were so far out of his conversational arsenal that he would have had to rent one. He gave up and switched to what he did best.

"We're really pressed for time right now. Is Yuri at the—?"

"Pressed for time? You come back when my shift's over and I'll press you into a totally new frame of mind."

Marcus was back in alien territory, but he tried to dig his way out, "You seem even more ebullient than usual, Matessa. What's the occasion?"

Her metabolic state jumped up another couple of notches and she let out a whoop, "I just signed with Planetary Tectonics! Come Graveyard they start to re-boot me, and three months after that I'm headed for sixty years of hell! I plan to do nothing but drink and screw between now and then, so if you miss out it's your own damn fault."

It kind of took me aback. I'd re-booted eighteen times, but I'd never had to go into the trades; it was disturbing to meet someone facing that prospect. I could see it shook Marcus, too.

"Well, I ... um, I'm, uh, glad to hear—when did you say this was going to happen?"

She laughed, "Graveyard, man, Graveyard! Appropriate, yes? Come the witching hour they're gonna whisk me off to la-la-land and I'm not coming back for two-thirds of a century."

I could tell Marcus still didn't understand. He must have been younger than me by a few centuries, and younger than the person who thought up the shift names on Vesper. With four waking periods per day, they'd had to come up with something to call them, and they weren't really all that creative, just morning, afternoon, evening and Graveyard. But I doubt that one out of a thousand people, even among long-term residents, knew what a graveyard shift was, or had ever seen a graveyard, for that matter. I don't think there *were* any graveyards outside the system. Were there even any left on Earth? I didn't know.

"Hey, Matessa!" one of the dock hands yelled, "I'll treat you right, man!"

"Oh, Bartos, I don't want you," she yelled back, "you're no good."

"Oh, man, I been practicing!" All his mates laughed.

"You don't need practice, you need lessons." They laughed again.

"You could give me lessons!"

"School's out." These guys were really cracking each other up.

"Oh, you don't know what you're missing. I could take you to heaven, man."

"I've been to Heaven. It's not all that great a planet. Get back to work."

Bartos clutched his heart and fell backwards into the water, to the cheers of his fellows. A woman and a man dove in after him, ostensibly to save him, but it was obvious they were just goofing around.

"All right, all right." Matessa was laughing, too. She turned back to us. "What a bunch of yahoos." But I could see tears in her eyes. "I'm gonna miss this dump." She looked at Marcus; "You look me up, later. We'll all be at Teng's. It's gonna be a hell of a party."

Marcus climbed out onto the dock. He seemed really touched. It made him awkward. "I'll—I'll try to be there. I really will. But we really are pretty busy."

She punched him in the chest, hard. Then she grabbed him and hugged him even harder. "First things first," she said, "First things first."

Marcus was really embarrassed, now. "But I— I mean, we hardly know each other—"

"I want life around me. I'm going to be leaving it for a while." She looked him in the eye. "You do this for me."

Marcus stared back at her for a minute. He looked naked, then veiled, then naked again. "Yes. Yes, I'll be there. Teng's place."

She grabbed his ears and kissed him. Then she was laughing again, "You won't regret it! Bring your friends!" she said as she turned back to her crew. Bartos and his lifeguards were just climbing out of the water. "All right, you worthless clowns, let's get this stuff loaded!"

Steel climbed up behind Marcus. She looked rumpled and sleepy. "Looks like you found a friend," she said.

Marcus jumped. "Yes, Captain—I mean, I just—she was the one who got the boat for us. I don't really—"

"I trust you didn't divulge anything in the heat of passion?" She cocked that eyebrow at him.

Marcus' mouth worked fruitlessly for a moment, "Captain, I—I didn't—"

Steel laughed and clapped him on the shoulder, "Allah and Rama be praised that I have you, Marcus. You keep me sane." She laughed again.

Marcus wasn't sure how to take it. He looked for language, found none, then said with a smile, "I'm glad, Captain."

Steel looked around. "I feel like I've been online for a million years. I need to get some real sleep. Where's Alice? Didn't she meet us?"

Marcus replied, "She needed to try out the dirigible, and she wanted to get the solar panels, electrolysis plant and extra bag up to Manlung La, so she's on her way up there now."

Steel tensed up, inappropriately, I thought. It was strange; I couldn't figure it out. "In the dark?" she asked, and went on her I.S.:

"Alice, where are you? Alice?" She listened for a moment. "Why? You didn't need to—Yes, I know." She paused. "How are they?" Her face darkened. "I see—yes. Yes, of course." She listened for a time. "When will you be back down here?" She looked into the village. "All right. I'm going to have Marcus and Jemal go help Yuri—" she looked at me, "And Mohandas. I'm going to the inn and log off. I don't even know how long I was awake, but it was too long." She looked at me again. "Yes—yes, I'll see you then."

She turned back to Marcus. "Yuri's at the hangar?"

"I guess. He hasn't been picking up. He must be inspired."

Steel sighed. "Well, I suppose that's good. Alice says there's plenty of moonlight to fly by. She's almost at the pass." Then she looked hard at Marcus. "Drake is much worse."

Marcus said simply, "Yes."

Steel looked at the river, the boats, the dockhands, the jungle, up the main drag of Kindu, but there were no answers anywhere. I wondered what the questions were.

"I'm glad we brought him down." Her voice was as steely as I'd ever heard it. "He shouldn't be in weightlessness now."

Marcus looked for something to say to her. I think he wanted to comfort her, but there were other things, too. Anger? Frustration? Fatigue, certainly. He finally chose, "Yes, Captain."

"Alice is taking some things up to them, things they make here out of plants in the forest. She thinks they might help." I could tell Steel didn't think so, but she wanted to.

"Let's get to the inn." She started up the street.

CHAPTER 6

The walk to the inn was a very strange one for me. My future was clouded with tension and mystery, but my present was as pleasant and relaxed a time as I could remember. I'd never been to anyplace like Kindu. It looked entirely handmade. Hewn and carved and woven and pegged, it was a purely organic expression of the people who built it and lived in it. All the construction materials had obviously come from the forest, except for the hydrogen and electrical systems, but even those were utterly integrated into the flow and thatch of the place. Buildings were placed capriciously, but not randomly. The sweeping curves of the thatched roofs, the carvings on the poles and door frames, the style of the verandahs and balconies, while not uniform in any way, seemed to spring from an artistic consensus, incorporating aesthetics from many planets and centuries into a vibrant improvisation on a single theme. We walked through an open-air market that evidently served not only Kindu but the people in the surrounding bush as well. Business seemed to be good.

The inn was on the far side of the market. Steel booked two rooms adjacent to the one Alice and Yuri had been sharing and had us follow her up the stairs to hers. It seemed like Ham should have been carrying the luggage, only we didn't have any.

We passed through the sleeping room out onto a lanai that overlooked thatched roofs and jungle lit by torch light, flickering and shadowed. All except for Ham; I don't think the lanai would have held him. It was on the back side of the inn, away from the market and fairly quiet. The weather was still clear; I could see swaths of stars through clearings in the forest. We sat down around a small teak table; Steel lit an oil lamp.

"All right," she said to Marcus, "since Yuri is in the midst of a creative fervor, why don't you tell me what he's got planned."

Marcus drew himself up and tented his fingers on the polished wood. "Well, he's having to make it up as he goes along. The dirigible was the best we could do out here, given the security parameters—"

"Which have to be maintained," Steel interjected.

"Of course. But the system was designed to work with aircraft that were much smaller, quicker, and very much more maneuverable. When we lost the ultra-lights—"

"I know we'd be much better off with our original equipment, but we don't have it. Does he think he can make this work?"

"Alice seems to think so. If we can be at the right place, altitude and latitude, at the right time, the hook should be able to grapple us. If we miss, it just means laying over for another rotation."

"I really want to avoid any delay."

"I understand. But that's not the biggest worry."

"Which is?"

Marcus traced a circle on the tabletop. "As I said, if we're just in the wrong place, the hook simply misses us. If we're too low, the hook misses us. But," he looked at Steel, "if we're at the right place but too high, we could get tangled in the tether. And ..."

"And?" Steel prompted.

"If we're just a little too high, the hook could puncture the gas bag."

"Well, if that happens, I assume we'll be grappled, right?"

"The way Yuri's got it figured, the momentum of the hook would tear right through the bag and catch on the handle."

"So we wouldn't need the bag any longer, anyway."

"If the hook catches, that is correct. However, the locals haven't the capability to manufacture helium. They use hydrogen."

"Yes?"

"Which is highly flammable."

Steel thought for a moment. "I see." Then, "We'd be under the fire, which would tend to rise."

"That's the way Yuri figures."

"I don't see a problem."

"Well, the hook will pull us right up through it."

Steel looked out at the night sky. "We should be out of the atmosphere quickly enough that it won't be a problem." She looked back at Marcus. "Why does he want the extra bag?"

"Just in case the primary bag is destroyed and the hook doesn't catch. Aside from the possibility of grave injury to all of us in a remote area, which would require complete abrogation of security to attend to, there is—" Marcus glanced at me and then back at Steel.

"Mohandas has not been briefed as yet," she said, without looking at me.

Marcus nodded, then continued, "There is Drake's condition to be considered."

"How so? I can't see that this would affect it."

Marcus chose his words, "The impact incurred in a fall from altitude could cause his—" He paused. "His environmental containment could be compromised."

Steel looked somber. "Yes. How did Yuri explain the extra bag to the locals?"

"We're sticking to the accident story. As Alice and Yuri became acquainted with local conditions, they filled in the details to fit. At this point I believe the story is that our dirigible failed in the mountains and its bag is beyond repair."

"So we're replacing it."

"Correct."

"And Yuri has a way to assemble this contraption at Manlung La?"

Marcus smiled, "You know Yuri."

I was thinking I wanted to get to know Yuri as well. The conversation had fascinated me up to this point. My only concern, besides the question of Drake's 'condition'—whatever that was—was that I might know something about what they were discussing. I said, "Excuse me, but are you talking about using a skyhook?"

Steel and Marcus looked at me, then each other. Steel asked, "What do you know about skyhooks?"

I tried to look innocent. "Besides the fact that the technology is almost two millennia old? Nothing much."

The tension rose appreciably. Steel asked me, "Are you an aficionado of the history of space flight?"

So she didn't know how old I was. Maybe. "Just a hobby," I said. "You're going to use one to hook a blimp into orbit?"

Marcus answered, "That's the plan."

"Hmm," I said in a sort of neutral, nonchalant, 'sure, why not? Beats watching holos,' sort of a way. Skyhooks had been used for launching cargo starting back in the mid-twenty-first century, when interplanetary commerce was in its incipient stages between Earth, Luna, and Mars. They had never been man-rated, and had faded out of use after graviton impellers made surface launches cheap and clean. A skyhook was basically just a hub with two spokes several hundred kilometers long. It was placed in a low orbit and spun up until it was rotating as fast as it was revolving around the planet, so it behaved like a wheel on a road. As the spoke descended into the atmosphere, the end of the spoke was traveling backwards in relation to the hub at the same speed the hub was moving forward, so its velocity relative to the planetary surface was zero, and it could pick up things. *If* they had been lifted above the more turbulent parts of the atmosphere. Then, as the spoke continued to revolve around the hub, it would pick up speed until, at the top of the wheel, it was moving twice as fast as the hub, or twice orbital velocity, and you could launch your cargo into an interplanetary trajectory simply by letting go of it. It was an ingenious technology. For cargo.

Riding one in a burning blimp seemed to be an unusual way to spend one's leisure time, but then I wasn't ready to hop the next boat back to Spam-town, so it looked like I was signed up for the duration. The question 'Why?' seemed to keep popping into my head. Why, when you have a perfectly good starship, would you use an ancient, obsolete, dangerous, and in this case, half-improvised technology to get up to it? Security considerations. I could always ask what these security considerations were, but, given the nature of security considerations in general, I didn't figure I'd get an answer. *I* certainly wasn't feeling very secure, but it wasn't my show.

"The encyclopedic nature of your knowledge continues to surprise me," Steel said to me, somewhat guardedly.

"I guess I get around." I tried to look bland.

Steel examined me for a moment. "Well, I'm glad you're on our side," she said with a wry smile.

"Me, too," I replied, wondering who was on the other side.

"All right," Steel yawned suddenly, "I'm going to get some sleep." She looked from Marcus to Jemal. "How are you two doing?"

"No problem, Captain," Jemal answered. "We had a nice nap on the beach."

Marcus nodded, "We're fine for a while."

"Good." Steel looked at me. "How about you, Mo?"

I thought, 'Bed sounds awfully good; why don't we share one?' But I didn't want to test the dream, so I said, "I'm all right."

Steel nodded. "I want the three of you to head up to the hangar and see if Yuri needs any help. Marcus, how long did I sleep on the boat?"

"About five hours, Captain."

"I feel like I could use another twelve, but call me in three. All right?"

We all stood up.

"Yes, Captain, three hours." Steel walked us to the door. Marcus stopped in the hall and turned back, "Captain?"

"Yes?"

"I feel obligated about Matessa's re-boot party."

"Matessa?"

"The woman on the dock."

"Oh, yes."

"It won't be starting for a few hours, but I'd like to put in an appearance. I told her I would."

Steel thought for a moment. "Go see how Yuri is doing. If everything is proceeding apace, we'll all go. We could use a little shore leave, eh?" She smiled wearily.

Marcus smiled back. "Thank you, Captain."

"Three hours," Steel said, and closed the door.

Ham stayed with Steel. Marcus, Jemal and I exited the inn and turned away from the market to weave our way farther into the streets of Kindu, a maze-like web that could be defined, basically, as wherever someone had refrained from putting a dwelling, business or hut. Many of the dwellings had been added to and connected over the years; some were two or three stories tall. A broad thoroughfare would open into an irregular square with a moss-covered stone fountain in the middle of it, then suddenly squeeze between two ornately carved structures and become barely wide enough for two people to walk abreast. Often buildings would be connected from the second floor up and we'd find ourselves in a narrow tunnel lit with the soft blue glow of hydrogen lamps. Then, just as suddenly, it would open out into a wide, earth-packed boulevard again.

The whole aesthetic stimulated parts of my mind long dormant. It made me long for my earliest lives, when I'd been an architect in the System, fervent, driven, teamed with and married to the most beautiful woman in the world.

We reached the edge of town and started up a wide trail through the jungle. It climbed to the top of a plateau that had been cleared and turned into an airship field. But I didn't even notice the two aging blimps and corrugated metal hangar.

As we emerged from the forest I was overpowered by the sight of the mountains. We'd come a long way up the river; the stratospheric escarpment was right in front of us. Bathed in pearly double moonlight from Sperry and Alta (triple, if you count Ruby), the range climbed in dark, jungle-clad shoulders, steepened to crystalline granite cliffs surmounted by soaring, icy parapets, pinnacles and crags that seemed to reach up and touch the stars. Forested canyons in the piedmont became deep, glacial valleys at higher elevations, snaking back between hulking goliaths, inviting the imagination to question what was around the next bend. The broken, crevassed faces of hanging glaciers glinted blue in the frosty light, dissonant and removed from the balmy, tropical night air that surrounded us.

We crossed the field and entered the hangar on the far side. The cavernous interior was lit by electric lights focused on something that looked like the fossilized rib of some impossibly huge creature. A man was suspended beside it in a bosun's chair hung from a crane. His face was obscured by an elaborate headset. Several different pairs of lenses protruded from it, one of them lowered over his eyes. He was being moved along the surface of the thing, peering closely at it. Occasionally he would switch lenses and go back over an area he had just examined.

"Yuri!" Marcus yelled. The man looked up, then flipped up the monocular he had been using. He seemed to recognize Marcus; then he flipped another set of lenses down over his eyes and turned back to his work.

"What do you want?" he said.

"Why haven't you been picking up?" Marcus asked, reasonably, I thought.

"Do you want me to finish this or gossip with you?" Yuri replied testily.

"Steel just wanted to know how things were going."

Yuri didn't look up from what he was doing. "Humanity could have spread throughout the entire galaxy by now, and been well into the Megellanic Clouds, if it hadn't had to stop and furnish progress reports."

I liked Yuri already. Marcus seemed to be used to this sort of exchange. He said, "Is there anything we can do to help?"

Yuri stopped the chair and brought his face down so the lenses he was wearing actually touched the surface of the thing. "You can get me a cup of coffee. There's an urn on that bench over there." He pointed vaguely over his shoulder.

Marcus shook his head and looked at me. "You mind getting that for him?" he said.

"Not at all," I replied and started to look around the place for the particular bench he was referring to.

"This thing is amazing," Marcus said. "What do you call it?" If he was trying to butter Yuri up, it didn't work. Yuri replied:

"I call it a desperately slapped together realization of a hastily conceived solution to an absurd and utterly self-imposed situation. What do you want to call it?"

Marcus tried again. "I call it a triumph of will over adversity."

"It's not a triumph of anything over anything, yet. It's just a great big lump of carbon and glue that may or may not withstand the forces it will be subjected to." He ripped off the headset and rubbed his eyes. "Shiva, there's no freaking way I'll be able to do even the sketchiest statistical structural analysis. The thing's just too freaking big."

"Don't they have a—"

Yuri cut him off, "I'd love to give you a long list of the things they don't have, but I just haven't got the time."

"How can we help you?" Marcus asked again.

"What do you know about materials science?" Yuri fired back.

"I'm just a pilot, Yuri."

I'd finally found the coffee. "I used to be an architect," I said as I poured a cup.

Yuri looked at me with a perfect balance of hope and cynicism. "Oh, yeah? What'd you build?"

"Oh, this and that," I replied as I handed him the mug.

"This and that what?" he said.

"You want my portfolio? I don't think I have it on me," I responded.

"It might help," he took a sip. "Ever use any double-carbon?"

Okay, so I'm an egotist. I said, "My wife and I designed and built Marineris." It was a slip, I admit it.

"Marineris?" His expression changed to incredulity. "On Mars?"

In for a DCU, in for a kilo. "Yep. North rim of the Valles."

"Jesus, how freaking old are you?" Like I said, it was a slip. "Sorry, rude question. Don't answer. Let's pretend I never said it." He dismounted from the bosun's chair. "Hell, if you were working in this stuff that long ago you might even get along with this equipment. I think it was designed sometime before the first Crusade. I'm surprised it's not nuclear powered."

"I'll do my best." I looked at the headset as he handed it to me. "Looking for structural flaws?"

"Anything. Hairline cracks, bubbles, misaligned fibers, structural resonance. Their fabricators here are well maintained; they're just outmoded. On the ship I could have whipped this up in eight hours. Here it's like swimming through paste." He pointed to the various eyepieces. "These are polarizer filters, this is U.V., here's your magnetic resonance imager, over here is graviton echo, X-ray is up here—"

"They use different lenses for each?" I said, trying to keep the dismay out of my voice.

"Quaint, huh?" He started walking across the room to a console array in one corner. "You just keep those images coming, and I'll collate them over here. We'll at least eliminate one step. I don't know why I didn't just carve it with a stone axe."

I climbed into the bosun's chair and put on the headgear. No wonder Yuri was so irritable; it must have weighed three kilos.

Marcus said, "Well, I'm glad Mohandas can give you a hand, anyway."

Yuri's mood must have slightly improved; I know mine would have just taking that stupid helmet off. He replied, "Yeah, whaddya know? Steel actually managed to hire someone useful."

I couldn't see what anyone was doing. I was trying to figure out the antique optics, but I heard Marcus say, "There's got to be something Jemal and I can do to help speed up the process."

I must have pushed the right button. The vids came to life. They *were* old. It was like watching TV at the Museum of Science and Industry in Chicago.

"You know, there is something you can do," Yuri's voice again, "Go back in the office and get Yanis to show you where the winches and cable and all the rest of that stuff is. There should be some heavy-duty spikes and carabiners and a bunch of stuff. It should all be in one pile. You can take them outside so we can load them when Archie gets down from the pass."

Marcus: "Archie's coming down?"

Yuri: "Yeah, haven't you talked to Alice?"

Marcus: "Not in the last half-hour."

Yuri: "Oh. Well, she's relieving Archie so Archie can get some rest. I guess it's pretty intense up there with Drake."

Marcus: "I see. I don't think the Captain is going to like that, but that's not my problem. How do I recognize this Yanis?"

Yuri: "Oh, I guess you didn't meet him. He's the guy in the office."

The surface came into focus. I could magnify up to ten thousand times, good enough for what we were looking for.

Marcus: "Of course."

I could focus down into the interior using M.R.I. or grav echo. X-rays didn't show too much in a carbon-carbon matrix.

Yuri called after Marcus, "And don't let him sell them to you! I already paid for them!"

Marcus called back, "I understand." Then an afterthought, "Wait a minute. You pick up for Alice but not for me?"

"Alice is a lot prettier than you."

I could almost see Marcus shaking his head as he walked off.

CHAPTER 7

For the next endless time Yuri and I checked out the "handle" as well as we could. All the values were critical because it had to be light enough for the dirigible to lift and strong enough to take the acceleration of the skyhook, which was about sixty meters per second squared, over six standard gees. With no Musadhi Discontinuity to keep us comfy and cozy at whatever gravity we wanted, it was going to be quite a ride.

At one point Archie came in. I didn't get to meet her because I was under the helmet, but she, Marcus and Jemal loaded the stuff into the gondola and left for Matessa's party. Marcus must have bulleted Steel to wake her up, but I didn't hear him. I was lost in a world of microscopic carbon fibers.

After several hours of this Yuri came to the conclusion that we weren't going to get it any better than we had. In the final analysis it was either going to work or it wasn't. Steel wanted to be ready to go just after dawn, we didn't have time to fabricate another one, and we couldn't have checked it any better than this one if we had. There was nothing else to do, so Yuri shut down the work station and we headed back to the village.

Yuri knew how to get to Teng's place, which was good; I still had afterimages of log-like carbon fibers superimposed on everything I looked at. There was never any thought of going back to the inn and, perhaps, getting some sleep, or something equally pedestrian and pragmatic. I'd had about an hour in the last who-knows-how long, but by that point I was going on pure adrenaline, and Yuri told me he only slept when there wasn't something more interesting to do.

The party was in full flower when we got there. It looked like everyone in Kindu was there; we couldn't even see Steel and the rest of the crew. Teng's place was right on the river, a blaze of torchlight danced in the reflecting water.

Upstream of the docks and around the next bend, it occupied a rocky point of land that thrust out into the current. The river surrounded it on three sides, then ceased to be navigable, climbing an orchestra of cascades that sparkled in firelight and blurred into moonlight. But the real orchestra was inside, 'inside' being a relative term in tropical architecture.

Teng's place was laid out like a lotus blossom. Small, irregularly shaped platforms at various levels were cantilevered out over the water, some thatched gazebos, others open to the sky. They radiated from a larger area that was being used as an improvised stage and bandstand. An enormous array of musical instruments was being played by anyone who felt like it: gamelans, marimbas, harps, tablas, gongs, wood flutes, sitars, lutes, sarangis, oboes, an endless variety of percussion, guitars, stone chimes, natural horns ... half of them I didn't even recognize. The main group of musicians was in the central area, but people everywhere were pulsing along with the music on anything they could hit, slap, or stomp on. In front of the orchestra a woman was half-singing, half-chanting a long story. I couldn't quite make out what she was saying, but at the end of each riff the audience would cheer her on. As soon as we entered, a man slapped me on the back, shoved a maraca in my hand and pointed us to the bar.

"The natives seem to be friendly," Yuri yelled at me as we wormed our way through the pulsing mass. By the time we got to the bar we were dancing, too; you couldn't help it. People would bump up against you in time to the music and after awhile it was a lot easier to move with the beat than against it. The rhythms were infectious. Sevens and fives floated above a raga that sounded like it was in a complex triple meter. Long, sad triads wailed under triumphant, ecstatic bursts of melody that the soloists redefined each time they conversed with it.

And the food! I'd been living on nutrient packets and 'Burbs' brew for way too long. A huge luau was spread out beside the bar, luscious sprays of pineapples, mangos, bananas and limes alternated with trays of wonderful things that had been dipped in this and marinated in that and sautéed with some of these and spiced and grilled and were just incredible. They never seemed to run out of anything. My only frustration was having to put down my glass of incredibly rich, frothy, caramel-hued ale to eat something, while I added the voice of my maraca to the chorus with my other hand.

I saw Matessa, or rather, I saw two fans of iridescent blue and green eyes radiating from sturdy shoulders, down toward the center of the main floor. She was literally bathed in people. There must have been eight or ten holding her hands, clasping her waist, her shoulders, rubbing her back, her neck, her head, her feet. She was looking up at the night sky and cheering on the singer louder than anyone.

I leaned over to Yuri. "This is incredible," I yelled. "They must really love her."

"They're saying good-bye to her for a long time," Yuri yelled back. "Yanis was telling me about it. They do this for everyone. You can't make enough out here in the bush to pay for your medical, so they all have to indenture to get re-booted. This is Matessa's third time."

"What do you mean?" I asked.

A man dancing in front of me turned around to face me, without breaking rhythm. A butterfly's body was tattooed on the bridge of his nose. Wings with real iridescent scales glistened on cheeks and forehead. "She keeps coming back, man!" he yelled. "Who wouldn't? This is the most beautiful place in the universe!"

I couldn't disagree with him. The setting was spectacular, and the town itself seemed to be an ongoing expression of artistic joy and balance. But to go into the trades ... I thought about the two SyndicEnts in 'Burbs' place, hard-wired off their nut in their off-hours just to escape that which could not be escaped. Then I looked at Matessa. What would she look like in three months? Whatever Planetary Tectonics needed her to look like. Her peacocks would be gone, that was certain. Her personality algorithms would be stored, but disabled. She would still be her, but she wouldn't be able to ask for raises or go on strikes or disobey a direct order from a superior or anything else that was inconvenient to the suits.

On the other hand, Planetary Tectonics wasn't going to re-boot her just once, but twice. Once at the beginning of her sixty-year stint and once at the end. And on the second 'boot she could get her peacocks back and her personality and her looks, and her physical condition would be that of a healthy twenty-year old, free of whatever disease must be killing her now. Free to go where she wanted and do what she wanted, her whole life ahead of her.

And if she didn't want to remember what it was like to be trapped in her own body, working endlessly for people who thought of her as a machine, she didn't have to. She could have the entire sixty years wiped, like she'd never left Kindu. But she would have to live that sixty years, one day at a time, one hour at a time, enduring, hunkering down, waiting for release. She must really love this place, I thought, to come back here again and again, knowing what she was going to have to do to pay for it.

I looked around at the party. These people seemed to be almost one living entity, they were so entwined. Someone had given Yuri an a-go-go, which was cruel, I thought. He had to hold it in one hand and beat it with a stick held in the other, which left no hands for ale and food. Ah, but he'd found a friend. A woman beside him was feeding him while he danced.

"There's Steel," Yuri yelled between mouthfuls of something that looked vaguely like hummus, and may have been. I looked where he was pointing and saw her, too. In the midst of the gaudy bouquet of undulating body art her silver fur was an elegant understatement. I tried to ignore the hand that squeezed my chest when I looked at her, but I didn't succeed. She was swaying with the music, talking to some townie that I had never seen before and was suddenly intensely jealous of. I'd been off the net too long, alone too long, unemployed too long. I drained my glass in one long, surly draught and set it on the bar to be refilled.

I yelled at Yuri, "You want to go over there?" hoping he'd have some better idea.

"Sure, why not?" he yelled back. "It's a nice night. Let's dance over!" He put his arm around the waist of the woman that had been feeding him and put the a-go-go in her hand, continuing to play it with the beater in his. He picked up his glass, took a nice long draw, put the rim to the woman's lips and let her drink as much as she wanted. Then they both pulsed off in Steel's general direction, instrument and player—which was which yet to be determined. I picked up my refueled tumbler off the bar and followed them, shaking my maraca like I meant it.

Making our way through the crowd was no mean feat. As we got closer to the band the organism grew denser and more rhythmic. Just as I was about to break through the thickest grove, I got caught in a vortex and started to resonate with the hips of a woman dancing next to me. She was from somewhere in the Pleiades, too. The tattooed beak of a tropical bird made a widow's peak that just touched the chakhra between her flashing eyes. A crest of scarlet feathers blended to dark blue-green, almost black, as the long neck traveled down her back, swelling to a body and wings that embraced her pelvis above a fountain of multi-colored plumes that sprouted from the base of her spine and almost brushed the floor.

She smiled at me, took the glass from my hand, drank from it and passed it to the next dancer. Then she gave me the cabasa she was shaking, took my maraca and began to dance with me in earnest. I looked around for Yuri, but he'd been swept away in the current. All right, I thought, take a break. No more Steel, no more burning blimps, no more Drake's 'condition,' no more mystery or tension for a while. Time to let the spirit replenish. I inhaled the party and joined it.

The woman who had been singing, or chanting, evidently was finished; she walked over to where Matessa was being held, hugged and kissed her, and rejoined the throb of the dancers as they applauded her. Then, through some arcane process or perhaps no process at all, they chose another singer from their midst and encouraged him to take the stage. He'd had his body art for a long time, or else was emulating an archaic style. The thirty-fifth century, if I remembered correctly. His features were the usual Draconian blend, a sort of Afro-Eurasio-Austral-Amerind mix that ended up looking vaguely Polynesian; but his skin was midnight black, with pinpoints of white in the configuration of the constellations as seen from the planet where he'd had the work done. I couldn't tell which planet it was, he was too far away and dancing around too much, and there were too many planets anyway.

"How many verses?" someone in the crowd asked him.

"Seven!" he responded, and the crowd cheered and urged him on. The music diminished to an expectant murmur and he began to sing:

> I started in the project around Epsilon Indi;
> The desert was empty and the weather was windy!

The crowd cheered; I think you got extra points for actually rhyming.

> We made the planet and they named it 'Nirvana';
> They made us work hard, but I sure didn't wanna!

Everyone cheered again, and I laughed. He went on like that, sometimes rhyming, but usually not. He sang his lives, one extended verse for each 'boot.

Evidently Interstellar Biosphere had hatched him to help seed Nirvana, but he didn't have anything nice to say about the company. I wasn't surprised; the labor involved in starting an ecosystem on a dead globe was grueling, and IB didn't make its money by taking any longer than absolutely necessary. They worked their newbies as hard as ... well, as hard as they wanted to. I knew the woman who had been the chief ecologist on the project; she'd gotten a nice bonus for bringing it in ahead of schedule.

Of course, they re-booted him at the end of his term. That was the only thing that kept the system distinguishable from out and out slavery. The corp that hatched you basically owned your first life, but they had to give you a second one to do with as you chose. If you worked hard, scrimped and saved, invested wisely and basically got lucky, you could eke your way into a position where you could pay for your medical and not have to go back into the trades. It rarely happened that way.

This guy had managed to do it once. He freewheeled out to the outer arm on his second 'boot, got involved in some mining concern, lost all his money, and indentured with Relativity/SimulComm for his third. That must have been a bad one; he didn't remember anything about it. But they'd given him his fourth 'boot and sent him on his way. After he'd worked his way back down the arm, doing this and that, he met up with a woman on Himmel around Procyon, a woman he'd known in the mines. She had a friend in the Teamsters who owed her a favor and the friend had gotten them both into crewman's school. Things were looking up. They studied hard, graduated together and signed on with InterPlanet, hauling between the home worlds and the outlands on various ships.

He was finally paying his medical, but she wanted to buy a house. They'd argued about it. She was adamant; she'd always wanted a place of her own. She saved the money and bought a nice place on Celeste. I've been to Celeste; it's a beautiful world. But on the next trip they'd gotten caught in a solar storm close in around Epsilon Eridani, just half an AU out from the star's angry surface, closer than Venus is to the sun. They were in an older ship, the Witchwand, and evidently the storm bunker needed to be repaired; everyone on board had picked up a lethal dose of radiation. He was okay, he had medical, but even selling her house wouldn't have gotten her enough to pay for re-booting. She had to go back into the trades.

He waited for her. He re-booted and went right back to work for InterPlanet, trying to save enough money to pay for both their medicals when she came back. Sixty years he waited. He met other people, had a relationship with two or three other women, but they'd all known he was waiting for someone to return.

He bulleted her as soon as she got out. She was fresh out of the can and he had sixty years on his last 'boot, but the net kept you healthy. He looked great, he felt great, he was good for another twenty or thirty years. And, anyway, he had medical; they'd get back into sync.

But she didn't remember him. She hadn't been able to face missing him and the house and her friends for sixty years, so she'd zeroed out. Ignorance is bliss. You can't miss what you don't remember.

He'd gone into a tailspin. He lost his job with InterPlanet, lost his crewman's license, lost his medical, the house, everything. He ended up indenturing to Planetary Tectonics for his sixth 'boot and working right over the hill in Spam-town. One day when he was swimming at Nohili a fishing boat from Kindu had pulled onto the beach. He talked to the fisher folk on board and they'd told him about this place. He fell in love with it without ever having seen it. All that was left to do was work and wait, work and dream about the future, work and grieve about the past, endure, hunker down, put in his time.

When Planetary gave him his seventh 'boot, he climbed down to the beach, made his way down the coast and up the river. He'd lived here the last thirty years, fishing and carving, dancing and thatching, saying goodbye to people as they went into the trades, saying hello to others as they came out.

People cried and cheered when he finished; Matessa held her arms out to him and he went over to her. With all of Matessa's orgiastic predictions earlier in the evening I expected her to disappear somewhere with him, but she didn't. He just became the main hugger for a while.

In fact, during the whole evening I only saw her go off twice, once with a woman I hadn't seen before, and the other time with Bartos. Can you beat that? It made me wonder; was all that stuff down at the dock just white noise and Bartos actually the intergalactic stud-muffin of the universe? Or, in this time of leaving, had Matessa decided that something as fleeting and temporal as sexual technique just wasn't that important to her?

But I began to understand why she wasn't more active in that area. Nobody wanted her to leave the party, even for a brief tropical tryst. I mean, you could tell they wanted her to do exactly what she wanted, but they wanted to be close to her, too. Each exit was a fairly elaborate ceremony in itself, cheering on the participants, wishing them good fortunes and happy hunting, but it was always combined with a kind of 'hurry back' energy. Nothing explicit, but you could feel it, nonetheless.

The party went on and on. I don't think everybody sang, that would have taken weeks, but lots of people did. Their stories were all different, but all similar in many ways. One woman had started on Vesper eight centuries ago, when they were first starting the terraforming. Ten 'boots later, here she still was. She'd always indentured to Planetary Tec, and no matter where they sent her (they had projects all over Draco), she'd always come back to Kindu.

Everybody started somewhere. Most of them were between six and ten 'boots old, products of the Great Expansion of the early thirties. They'd all been hatched by the corps or syndicates to be used as labor to hew habitable worlds out of the raw material of creation. And for most of them that's what they'd done every other life. It's what they would do.

As they sang their stories I was carried into the ritual nature of it. They were tying Matessa to them by singing their pasts, collective and individual.

Pasts are not something I deal with very well, maybe because I have so much of my own. I may have been drinking more heavily than usual, I don't know. Miss Bird-tail was awfully attractive (who isn't, these days?); I was probably just trying to impress her, for the oldest and most mindless of hormonal reasons. Anyway, at one point in the evening, as someone was just being applauded for their poetic efforts, I leaned over to her and said something along the lines of, "I have more verses than anybody here." I probably put it even more lamely than that, I don't remember.

She eyed me coyly and said, "Oh, really? How many do you have?"

Crashing the gates where angels fear to have their tickets punched, I said, "Do you count the first one?"

"What?" she replied.

"Never mind," I said, "Eighteen. Nineteen. A lot."

She must have been impressed, because her eyes lit up and she said, "Oh, you have to sing! You have to sing!" And suddenly everyone around me was chanting, "Sing! Sing! Sing!" and pushing me toward the band.

How do I get myself into these things? I found myself in front of the orchestra, the musicians vamping coolly, waiting to see where my song took them, Matessa looking at me with a smile full of love and expectation and amusement at my plight, and everyone else pulsing, dancing, encouraging, marking time.

Somebody said, "How many verses?" and I replied, "Nineteen." A kind of ripple went through the crowd and I looked around to see if I could find Steel or Yuri or Marcus. I spotted them; they were all in one of the gazebos. They'd evidently been following the action, or they'd heard the crowd hush. They were all looking at me.

The music dropped down lower, both in volume and activity. The musicians were looking for me, looking for the groove, trying to match my energy. I realized that, even though I hadn't said anything yet, I'd already started. My silence was the beginning of my first verse. I saw Matessa smiling at me and I didn't want her to be lonely before she left simply because I wasn't in the habit of letting people know who I was. Even so, it was hard to start. What do I tell them, I thought, who are so much younger, who had not experienced the world before the net, before re-booting, before freewheeling, before …

I wasn't started. I was born—

It burst out of me without volition:

> I grew inside another's womb
> And fought my way into a larger room
> On the sands of Mars where my father's tomb
> Lies unattended, weathered and worn.

I didn't know how much of this they were getting. Some of the words I hadn't heard in centuries. I didn't know if the concepts had any meaning anymore, even in an historical context.

> The woman who bore me raised me up,
> And from her body did I sup,
> And from my father's mind I learned
> Why bodies bled and fire burned.

Of course, it didn't come out smoothly like that. I'd say a line, and then someone would fill in with a lick while I figured out how to make the next one rhyme. I sang about a lot of things, but as I listened to myself I couldn't help noticing the things I didn't sing. I sang about my father, a word probably meaningless to them, but I couldn't use the other word, the one for the woman, my … my other parent. Too many changes had occurred since she had been alive. For one thing, for a couple of centuries after bearing children had faded out of fashion it was considered very rude to mention that you had had a ... you know, that you had actually been born instead of hatched.

And I didn't sing about my ... the other one, the—how do you talk about these things? The words are gone. There was another person, born of the same woman, a girl. That's why I didn't mention her. After a few times of telling someone that you'd had a ... that you'd had one, and they looked at you with one of those 'Not only did *you* start by emerging from someone's body, but there was someone else who came from the same body, traveled down the same canal, the same area where a person has sex and evacuates waste and I'm trying not to look disgusted but I really am' expressions on their face, well, you just don't bring it up anymore.

So, of course, I didn't sing about how she ... how I lost her. But I sang about the first time the net saved someone, kept him from ... kept him alive until they could reach him. How wonderful and amazing it had been for all of us, storing his mind in our minds, his genome, remembering the structure of his brain so that it could be repaired when they finally got to him. And when they did, *all* of us knew it, as it was happening. Well, not every one of us, but everyone who could afford to take a nap at the time. How many of us were there then? I remembered the year it happened, 2457. There must have been fourteen or fifteen billion still on Earth, with maybe another billion spread through the solar system. Every one of us saved him.

I sang that *that* was the moment we truly realized the power of the net. Sixteen billion human minds connected directly to a single system. Even more than the first time I had a live conversation with someone on Earth while I was on Mars, and that had been pretty impressive—no speed of light delay, no loss of signal power or clarity over the millions of kilometers—the time we all saved that man, together, as one instrument, one conscious repository of memory, one processor of data, one giant thinking, believing, willing, acting organism, was the time that I, personally, knew that the world had changed forever.

And yet, what did it mean now? I looked at their faces and tried to ascertain what they thought about all this, but I couldn't really tell. I mean, how many were on the net now? Seventy billion? Eighty? Keeping people alive who had gotten into trouble somewhere beyond the reach of immediate help was an everyday occurrence. People had conversations across light years.

They gazed back at me as I had been looked at before, but not for many centuries, not since I'd become more careful about who I told what. They looked at me like I was a fossil. Matessa looked ... what? Honored? Like I was a special phenomenon that reflected well on her by raising the status of her party. I wanted to give her a good send-off. I felt guilty and appalled by what she was facing. And yet, what she was facing wasn't permanent. It was only sixty years. She would come back.

I felt tears in my eyes as I turned from Matessa to Steel and started to sing again:

> In Chryse a man met the love of his life,
> A woman so soft, and hard, and bright,
> With eyes like water and hair like night,
> Her spirit was fire, her soul was light.
> And she would consent to become his wife.

I didn't know why I was singing about her. I hadn't intended to. Maybe it was because Steel had mentioned her, coming down Nohili. I know Steel didn't really know anything about her. She probably just read an article about what I had done on Valhala when she was checking me out on the net, and my wife had been mentioned. She couldn't know anything specific about her. There was no way she could know the important things.

Maybe it was simply because I was jealous of that townie Steel had been talking to. Stars and feathers and tattoos danced as I sang.

My wife and I had met while involved in a residence project in Chryse on Mars. I was the architect, she was the ecologist. We had gotten into such intense debates over conflicts between structural aesthetics and environmental impact that we'd had to get married to give the conversation room to breathe. We'd traveled all over the System, designing, building—Mars, Earth, Luna, Ceres, Ganymede, Callisto, Titan, Triton—anywhere people needed integrated living systems.

> She was my heart and my blood and my mind.
> She was so gentle and loving and kind,
> And bitchy and fiery and stubborn and strong.
> If I am the lyric, then she was the song.

We came up with some ingenious solutions to our original problems, but the debates never stopped. The conversation just kept getting better and better.

> Ahead of us waited the time it would end,
> When everything ceases and eyes ever close.
> Our loved ones had left us, departed in myths,
> And we took our courage in stories of life
> That transcended being and breathing and strife.

But before our health failed us a striking breakthrough was made by a group of people working in the habitat at one of Earth's LaGrange points. Through the incredible computational ability of the net, they had perfected a method of restoring the human body. The fountain of youth. It consisted of literally trillions of micro-operations. Going into each individual cell and repairing DNA strands, cleaning out accumulated waste products, recalcifying bones, repairing organs, eyes, teeth, everything. Turning back the genetic clock.

It essentially gave you another sixty to a hundred years of life. It gave you a second life, a second adulthood. It was incredibly expensive, and, at that time, took over a year to complete. But my wife and I had been very successful. We had the money and the time.

It changed our lives profoundly. We were getting older, and we had been worried about which one of us would lose the other. Neither of us wanted the other to be alone. We had this romantic hope that we would somehow go together, be involved in an accident or something, but we knew that that was unlikely. We tried not to think about it.

And then we didn't have to go at all. It was astounding. We emerged from the process looking like snapshots from decades gone by. She looked younger than she had when I first met her, as I must have. But it was not only appearance, we *felt* young. We thought like young people. We were filled with drive and energy and restlessness.

That had been the most difficult part of the process to engineer, the actual re-booting. The restructuring of a human mind. You see, you could go in with the information contained in the human genome and restore muscles and organs and skin to pristine condition, but even when a brain is in perfect health it still fills up with an incredible amount of data. Memories of decades: sights, textures, smells, emotions, grocery lists, math problems, where the bathroom is, why your next-door neighbor doesn't like cats. Short-term memory wasn't a problem, but long-term memory would get to the point where things would start to blur, become confused. They had to come up with a technique that preserved the structure and continuity of your memory, while paring down the actual volume of data, so there would be room to remember your next life.

We weren't the first to go through it, but we were among the first. We became famous, in a way. Those people who could afford the process became the center of an intense debate on the net. This was during the twenty-sixth century. Things were still pretty bad on Earth, nothing like the horrors of the twenty-first and twenty-second centuries, but still pretty bad. People weren't starving anymore, but lots of people were poor, *really* poor. It seemed utterly unfair. It still seems unfair to me now, that some could go on living while others had to ... you know. If the process had been perfected twenty years earlier my parents would still be alive. Maybe.

It put a tremendous pressure on those of us who had re-booted to show those that couldn't that we were worthy of this ultimate gift. My wife and I had gone back to Earth, had redesigned Calcutta, Kinshasa, I forget how many cities, preserving their unique cultural aesthetic while making them hundreds of times more efficient. We had built Marineris on Mars with our own money, and opened it to immigration. We had worked and worked and re-booted again.

It was getting cheaper, but not much. On the other hand, the net continued to mature, so people were getting richer. You could make a very comfortable living while you slept just by allowing your brain to be used while you dreamed. A significant percentage of the population was beginning to be able to afford to stave off cessation of being.

Population pressure, which had been painfully, sometimes horrifically, brought under control during the previous five centuries, began to prowl the future like a dark demon again. Average lifespan, which had been creeping up for hundreds of years, now exploded. No one knew how many times you could re-boot, but it seemed like there was no limit.

Three things saved us from what probably would have been the worst ethical, moral, cultural disaster in history. One of them was astronomy. Since the end of the second millennium we had been finding planets around other stars. By the mid-twenty-first century we could get meaningful images of terrestrial-sized planets within sixty light years. We knew they were out there; we just had to figure out a way to get to them.

That was the second thing. Musadhi developed his graviton filter. This gave us graviton impellers, which made it almost free to climb out of a gravity well, and the Musadhi Discontinuity, which let us ride in ships at any acceleration. Whereas before, even with antimatter torches, boosting at one gee it would take most of a year to reach the vicinity of the speed of light, now we could boost at over a hundred gees and reach it in a matter of days.

The third thing was feminism. All of the starships we could have afforded to build wouldn't have been able to carry enough people out of the System to make up for the fact that we weren't ... that we were bringing people into the world but fewer and fewer were leaving it. But women had been concluding from the late twentieth century on that almost anything was more fun than having a human being swell up inside of them and then squeeze out through their most sensitive place. When large numbers of people started re-booting, the last impetus to reproduce—to carry on the line—was removed. And besides, rearing a human from zygote to adult was trying, wearing, and fiendishly expensive. Why spend all that money on offspring when you needed it to pay your medical?

Still, much more wealth needed to be generated if humanity was to overcome this unprecedented disparity between rich and poor, namely that the rich got to keep living and the poor didn't. The only way we knew how was to keep expanding the sphere of human activity, enlarge the marketplace. We went to the stars.

After our third 'boot my wife and I headed out to the project around Barnard's Star. This was before freewheeling; the trip took over six years, although it was only a couple of months to us. There was a planet they'd found in much the same condition as Vesper before people came. It had a climate that oscillated around the freezing point of water and it had plenty of water, but it was young. The atmosphere was still largely nitrogen and carbon dioxide; life had not had a chance to establish itself yet. We went there to build a new world for humanity to use. The project was run by a syndicate based in western Eurasia on Earth. They called the project, and the planet, Valhala.

It was only one of a dozen projects around the closest stars to the sun. Tau Ceti had two, as did Epsilon Eridani. Epsilon Indi, Procyon, 61 Cygni, and Alpha Centauri had one each, but would have others in the coming centuries. Wolf 359 and Lacaille 9352 produced viable worlds; the projects around Ross 128 and 154 would eventually fail.

But Valhala was very promising. There was a crushing amount of work to do to get the biosphere established; our techniques were not nearly as sophisticated as they are now. We carried a crew of two hundred, plus enough viable ova and sperm to hatch fifty thousand new people, or newbies. Calling them babies made people uncomfortable, so they didn't.

That was one of the ironies of the projects. We needed new worlds to create wealth and living space because there were too many people. People on earth needed work. But we couldn't yet afford to ship thousands of workers across interstellar distances, and most people wouldn't have gone anyway. So we made our own. We'd already learned that once you had designed, built, and programmed a robotic machine that was as autonomous, intelligent, and flexible as a person, it basically *was* a person; only people were cheaper to make. And where women were no longer willing to serve as incubators, incubators *could* be built cheaply. So you get a sperm and an ovum together in a nurturing environment and, bam! You've got a zygote. Program it for a couple of decades and you've got the end product of four and a half billion years of research and development.

Was it ethical to create people so you could send them out to do hard, grueling, dangerous work? The corps responded by saying that that was the way things had always been, only now they would re-boot their workers at the end of their shifts and give them a life to do with as they pleased. Where individual people no longer had the money or desire to make more people, the corps had both.

A lot of this history I didn't sing. I'm just recording it for my own benefit, just in case. I was sure they either knew it or weren't interested. But I sang about the work on Valhala. I thought they would identify with it and they did. They cheered as I sang about seeding the atmosphere and creating the soil, building coral reefs, starting the forests and the veldts, helping the plants adapt to the light of a new star.

The work went on and on. We re-booted a fourth time and never stopped working, it seemed. It was an odd balance: without the technique of re-booting no one would have lived long enough to be interested in projects as extended as terraforming, but without people living so long the projects probably wouldn't have been necessary.

I then came to the events leading up to the uprising. I stumbled for a moment. I looked at all of them dancing and swaying. I looked at Steel; this was what she had wanted me to talk about coming down the cliff. She and the crew looked back at me; I looked at Matessa. And I bailed. I couldn't sing about how they—how my wife—why we ... The bastard syndicates. I couldn't sing about any of it. My fifth 'boot, why I'd had it before ...

We'd been married for over three centuries, and then—then she was just gone. Just ... not around anymore. I was lost. Since I had been thirty-four years old she had been with me. We'd always traveled together, worked together. Even when we were on separate parts of Valhala there had been the net. We were never really apart. But now we were and I would never, ever have her again. Never.

I skipped the trial and the years after the trial. Things were pretty messy during that period, anyway. I could tell my audience knew something was missing, but everyone went along with it. You didn't really have to sing about anything you didn't want to. Everybody just kept dancing. The more I stumbled the more they cheered me on.

I wanted them to know that it hadn't all been free, that it had cost people a lot, everything, to make the world what it was. But in order to do that I would have had to sing things that I couldn't even think about.

Hell, it was a party, not a lecture. I tried to liven things up again, although I think I was the only one having trouble in that area. My next few 'boots were pretty wild, anyway. I didn't get married again, nobody was getting married anymore. No one knew what ' 'til death do us part' meant anymore. Not if you were rich.

And after the settlement I was rich. Rich enough that I would never be poor again if I played it smart, and I was determined to play it smart. I invested on both sides of every issue; no matter who lost I always won a little. I didn't worry about causes anymore, I didn't worry about poor people, I didn't worry about anything. I learned to improvise on the voix humaine. I got good enough to join a band, tour around and see some of the new worlds that were opening up. Music sort of took my mind off of things.

That era of my life lasted a long time. A long, long time. I jammed, I traveled.

I kept her name alive in my heart.

I wasn't lonely, or at least I wasn't alone any time I didn't want to be. Being in a band was a great way to meet women. Sexual relationships had changed so much that I'm sure my father wouldn't have recognized them. Reproduction was no longer an issue. Life-long fidelity was becoming impossible to visualize, what with everybody's lives getting longer and longer. Sex had become nothing more or less than an expression of intimacy. Like conversation, or sports, or religion.

The millennium changed and nobody looked back. They'd learned how to freewheel and the great expansion was on. There were so many planetary projects going that unemployment vanished and poverty had to be redefined. No matter who you were or what you were, you could always go into the trades. Of course mentioning the trades brought a chorus of boos from the revelers, but they were good-natured boos. They didn't blame me personally.

I did lots of different things, keeping myself busy and looking around the galaxy. Things happened. The System expanded along one galactic arm and eventually started to call itself Draco. The worlds of the Pleiades broke away and formed their own political unit, although they were still tied into the net, so they were never really separate. Brainard discovered a planet with an evolved indigenous biosphere on it. The Plague. Most of it affected me in one way or another.

I started to notice that my life was becoming cyclical. I would go through periods of doing something like playing in the band, traveling a lot, having a series of short relationships—from a couple of days to a few years long. Then I would settle down to something and someone for a few decades. But sooner or later it would come time to re-boot, and I never made it through that process with anyone again. I would leave, or I would cause my partner to leave. Something would happen, but by the time I went into the hospital to undergo the process, I was alone. I guess it was the only form of fidelity I had left.

The last time I'd had a normal life was on Scarpus. 'Boots number fifteen, sixteen and seventeen. I really thought I'd adjusted. I came to a kind of peace with it all and had become an ecological engineer, I guess in memory of her. I threw myself into it. By my sixteenth 'boot I'd worked my way up to chief ecologist of the Scarpus project. I'd personally overseen the hardwood invasion of the north temperate zone. I even named one of the forests after her. If you've been to Scarpus you can probably figure out which one.

I built a house right after my seventeenth 'boot. I met a woman, Mary. I guess we fell in love; she moved in with me and we lived in that house for over fifty years. I really thought things were going to be all right. The house was on the crest of a ridge just outside a little village that nestled up against a crystal clear river. Oaks, maples, sycamores, and ash rolled away in all directions. It was really very nice.

The atmosphere was stable; the biosphere was self-sustaining, although it would take centuries to reach full maturity. I began to think about taking a sabbatical, a sort of semi-retirement. Just sit on the front porch and watch the seasons change for a few centuries. Become the weird old guy in the woods.

It was funny, I guess. Mary was over a millennium younger than I was, and yet she'd lived several lives. She'd been around the block, as it were. We shared a lot of history, but not all of it, not even most of it. She still had things to do and places to see.

Maybe if I'd met someone my age, but that isn't easy to do.

As the time to re-boot again came closer Mary grew restless and I grew moody. She eventually left me, probably for good reason. I closed up the house and freewheeled out to Mondoverdi. There was an acting school in Palermo that was teaching the new poetic psycho-realism. I thought I might be able to figure myself out. I don't know if I did, but I liked acting. I re-booted the last time and eventually joined Shaughnessy's troupe, bought some scales, got pissed off at the SRS when they didn't like it, and here I was singing in the middle of the jungle. Cut off from the net, cut off from my money, foot-loose, fancy-free and on the road again.

I like to think they cheered longer for my song than anyone else's, but I doubt they actually did. Mine was over twice as long as most, but that's not really that much in an evening full of singing and playing, dancing and drinking, laughing and crying. I'd seen more history than any of them, but I don't think they were all that impressed by history. They'd all lived long enough, seen enough, lost enough to achieve an almost Zen appreciation of the now. Direction wasn't as important as balance; status was nothing, intimacy was everything.

Well, maybe status still carried a little weight. As I went over to pay my respects to Matessa I could see in her eyes that I had added something special and unexpected to her going-away party. When I hugged her she grabbed me around the neck and kissed me on the mouth. She was fairly glowing, but not from drink or heat. She had an intensity of spirit, of life, that could scarcely be contained within her corporal body. She swayed to her feet. "You're my talisman," she said, smiling joyfully. She placed her hands on either side of my face and gazed fiercely into my eyes. "You connect me to the past, to the future, to everything!" She grabbed my hand, "Let's go!"

It took me a minute to understand what she meant. I looked around for Steel and said, "I— uh … I came here with some people—"

"Hey, hey, hey!" She put a finger to my lips. "You had your chance to talk. Now you shut up and get the job done!"

She laughed and pulled me along. Sometimes it's better not to be the master of your own destiny.

The party went on until midnight when we all moved down to the dock to see her off. The festivities chilled appreciably when the boat with the big Planetary Tectonics logo on the bow appeared around the bend in the river and tied up at the dock. There were only two uniformed reps; I guess they didn't expect any trouble.

Matessa turned to the crowd just before she got in and blew us all a kiss. Her eyes were brimming with tears, but there was a big smile on her face.

"I love you all!" she said. "Remember me!"

One guy nearest to her raised a fist over his head and shouted, "Frag the freaking trades!" He must have been fairly drunk; he almost fell into the water. Matessa went over to him and gave him a hug. She whispered something in his ear, squeezed him one last time, then turned quickly and got into the boat. The reps cast off and the boat pulled away. She waved to us all until she disappeared around the bend.

The man shouted again, after she had gone, "Frag the freaking, freaking, FREAKING TRADES!" Others moved in to comfort him.

An older man with polychrome geometric designs on his arms and legs saw me taking in the whole scene. He must have remembered me singing, or maybe he could just tell it upset me, because he said, "He's a politician. He always says things like that."

"It sounds like he's going to miss her," I replied.

"We'll all miss her," he smiled, "but Matessa will be all right."

I thought about the SyndicEnts in 'Burbs place again. "Yeah?"

He clapped me on the shoulder. "Sure, Matessa will be fine. She's no politician. She knows the truth."

I looked at him, a little incredulously, I suppose. "Oh, yeah? What truth is that?"

He paused for a moment. He regarded me with a kind of 'You're not going to get this, but it might be fun to watch you try' look on his face. He said, "She knows you got to suffer if you wanna sing the blues."

I think I understood him. I looked down the river where she had disappeared, looked back at the old guy, then went off to find Steel and the crew.

CHAPTER 8

Yuri found me first. "Hey, party man! Steel told me to come get you. I think she's jealous."

I laughed. "What, of me and Matessa?"

"No, no." Then he paused and seemed to reconsider. "I don't think so—that is, maybe. I don't know. I think she's jealous of you because *she's* usually the center of attention."

"Well, I guess she could have sung if she'd wanted to."

"Right. Look, if you're half as tired as I am you're already asleep."

"I don't know. I'm so buzzed I don't know what I am."

"Everybody else is back at the inn. What do you say we go log off for ten or twelve hours? We've still got a lot of work to do before we leave this crazy orb."

"Yeah." Lots of things went through my head. Matessa: life force in the face of adversity. Steel: power and mystery. Mary: comfort and misunderstanding. My wife—my wife who was still irreplaceable, because of her own uniqueness, because of social changes, or because of my own need to keep her alive the only way I could, I didn't know. I thought about stability. I thought about change. "Yeah," I put my hand on Yuri's shoulder, "let's get some sleep."

We moved off up the main street of Kindu, two motes in a stream of spent celebrants quietly fading into the night.

We must have slept quite awhile. Normally the inhabitants of Kindu would have gone to bed around eighty-two and slept until midnight, then gotten up for Graveyard, but they'd shifted their schedule around for Matessa's party. I guess a lot of them just stayed up through the next shift. Graveyard was nearly over when we got up and you could tell the village was getting ready to call it a night.

I figured we had twelve or thirteen hours until dawn.

We met in the lobby of the inn. The proprietors gave us a nice breakfast, even though it was dinnertime for them. Steel, Marcus, Yuri, Jemal, Archie and I sat around one large table. They gave Ham an even bigger table and a nice tub of fruit and leaves.

Steel spoke to us as we ate. "I've been talking to Tamika. The Lightdancer is ready to go. Our cover is holding—no trouble with traffic control—and the omnicorders have actually gotten some nice footage."

Yuri said, "That's good."

"Yes," Steel replied, "we've got to finance this adventure somehow."

Oh, well. I was confused again. What were they doing? Making a Reality of Vesper from orbit? Then again, something like that might sell. Vesper is awfully pretty.

Marcus said, "The equipment is already loaded in the dirigible. All we need to do is mount the handle and take off."

Steel turned her emerald eyes on Yuri. "And you think the handle is ready to go?"

Yuri looked at me and then back at Steel. "We checked it out as well as we could. To do a really meaningful check would take a couple of weeks."

Steel thought hard for a moment. "No. We'll have to take our chances. We've been away too long as it is. And there's the question of Drake. I had to bring him down to the surface, but I don't want to keep him here any longer than absolutely necessary." She looked at Yuri again. "The design is sound?"

Yuri shrugged, "I did as well as I could with the available tools."

"And you trust those tools?" she pressed.

"They were what I had to work with."

She looked at him long and hard. Then she pressed her hands to the table and said, "All right. Let's get moving."

Steel paid our bill and we headed for the airfield.

Sperry and Alta had set already, and Ruby was quite a ways farther west, but there was even more light than before because Jumbo had just cleared the mountains in the east. It sat on the jagged horizon like a silver, cratered beach ball, pierced in a couple of places by the tallest peaks.

Attaching the handle wasn't difficult. The hangar had cranes capable of assembling entire lighter-than-air craft, but it sure looked strange. Of course the blimp itself looked very little like the first zeppelins built a couple of thousand years ago. The gasbag was spherical and spun to create lift as well as to maneuver. The handle was fixed to the ends of the frame that secured the gondola to the gasbag. But there was an extra pair of mounts part way up the handle for the extra bag that Yuri wanted to add up at Manlung La. When the whole thing was put together the handle would arch over the entire width of the blimp, held vertical by the two bags, one on top of the other. But right then it just lay on the ground hanging from the set of mounts on the ends. When we took off, it would swing underneath us till we landed at the pass. Steel pulled Yuri aside and asked him, "What the hell did you tell them we were going to do with *that*?"

Yuri laughed, "They think we're all nuts anyway," he said, "I just smiled mysteriously and said it was experimental. Our credit is good. That's all they really care about."

We mounted up. Marcus sat up front, but he had Archie fly it, as she had one trip more experience than Marcus did, having flown it down from Manlung La. We rose silently into the night air until the handle was swaying gently beneath us; then Archie fired up the propellers and headed us toward the mountains.

Manlung La was one of the lowest passes through the great spine, but even so it was over eight thousand meters up. We could see the valley leading up to it winding back into the range, flanked by colossal cliffs of granite and schist that glowed in the moonlight. As we gained altitude, the valley floor became filled with a sweeping, crevassed glacier, silently but inexorably grinding its way west.

As we rose to the height of the first ice-carved spires, the true giants beyond them seemed to just get bigger. We wound our way up the valley between them, crystalline walls scalloping back and back, up and up. Hanging glaciers sat like thick frosting on every tier, soft white blankets that were cleaved sharp and blue at the edge of the cliffs. Snow on the knife-edged arêtes fluted into countless avalanche chutes that gathered into larger snow-filled couloirs plunging dizzily to the valley floor far below. Alluvial fans of broken ice and rock encroached on the sides of the glacier there, attesting to the active nature of those chutes.

My ears kept popping as we gained altitude and I said to Yuri, "I thought Marcus said this thing was pressurized."

"It can be, but if we want to get the door open up at the pass we have to let the air pressure drop inside as it falls outside." He turned and yelled forward, "Hey, Marcus, how high are we?"

Marcus looked at the altimeter and said, "Just passing four thousand meters."

Yuri looked back at me, "We might as well put on our pressure suits now." He headed for the cargo hold in the back of the gondola.

"You have one for me?" I asked.

"Oh, yes," Steel answered me. "You're why we came down in the first place. It would have been silly to not be able to get you back up to the ship."

She was smiling at me. I smiled back. She and the crew and the population of Kindu knew more about me than anyone I had met since Mary left me. I wondered how they felt about me.

Yuri passed out the suits and we all put them on, and I have to say that Ham looked pretty silly in his. They weren't true space suits. They were lighter and not as bulky, but they would keep you alive for a little while even in a hard vacuum. Although sturdy enough for working at eight thousand meters, they reminded me of the risky nature of our upcoming voyage.

I asked Steel, "None of you are on the net right now?"

"That's right," she said. "My system interfaces with the net, but we're not directly linked."

"So you can call for help if you need to."

"Yes, but I don't think we'll need to."

"How good is your medical program?"

"It's excellent. We can even re-boot people in most cases. If we need extra capability we can borrow it from the net, but we're pretty self-sufficient. Why?"

"Well, I was wondering if you were going to put me on it."

"Of course," she said, "just as soon as we get up to the Lightdancer."

That's what I thought. "As soon as we get up to the Lightdancer."

"Yes. Everything is up there. Why?"

"Oh, nothing important." So I was going to ride a blimp to orbit without a net, so to speak. My genome wasn't preserved anywhere. If people did that the entire capacity of the net would be used up memorizing the structure of its components. It wasn't necessary in most circumstances. If you got in trouble you just went online and your genome was encoded temporarily until you were put back together. No need to fill up valuable memory with information that was always available.

Except that mine wasn't available. I wasn't on the net, and I wasn't on Steel's I.S. I was flying solo. If anything went wrong with our surefire patented planetary launch system and I got spread out over a mountainside, there I would stay. I wondered how I felt about that.

My thoughts must have shown on my face, because Steel said, "Oh. I see your point."

"Yeah," I replied, "I see my point, too."

Lots of things crossed her face. Concern, fatigue, determination. She smiled at me and said, "Yuri's very good. His stuff will get us to orbit."

She didn't realize that all she needed to do was smile at me.

We continued to wind our way higher into the mountains. The pass itself was broad and flat, a stone field swept clean of snow by almost perpetual westerly winds. To our right the sheer north face of Manlung shot up another four thousand meters; to our left the gradient wasn't nearly as steep but rose almost as far. I could see the camp nestled between two desolate mounds of talus. Some of the boulders were bigger than our gondola; some of them were bigger than the whole blimp. A pressure-suited figure left the shelter as Archie brought us in, dropping three anchors, one in the front and two in the rear. We could hear and feel the handle dragging over the rocks until they caught and brought us to a stop. The pressure-suited figure started piling rocks on top of the anchors as Archie said, "Everybody out." Jemal opened the hatch and we filed out onto the jumbled stones.

Yuri led me over to the figure that had set the anchors. "Let me introduce you to my best friend," he said.

The figure punched him in the shoulder. "Best friend," she replied, "Everybody's your best friend." I couldn't see much of her face through her helmet, but she had very pretty blue, almond shaped eyes. A shock of blond hair hung over her forehead.

"Hey, people like me. I can't help it," Yuri responded and then said, "Alice, meet the new guy."

"Hi, new guy," she said. "I'm the problem."

Yuri laughed. I didn't understand. He went on, "His name's Mo. He's actually relatively useful."

"Hello, Alice." I offered my hand. She shook it.

"Welcome aboard, I guess," she said.

"Thanks, I guess," seemed the appropriate response.

Yuri asked her, "How's our patient? Did those herbs and stuff help any?"

Alice collapsed into herself a little before she responded. "I don't think so. He's about the same."

Marcus yelled over to us, "Social time later. Let's get moving."

"Well," I said, "nice to meet you."

"Yeah."

We spent the next several hours preparing the blimp for the trip. We not only had to mount the extra gasbag, we had to bleed quite a bit of gas into it from the first bag. We'd top it off with more hydrogen made from snow as soon as the sun came up to power the solar cells that Alice had brought up, but we wouldn't fill either bag completely; we needed them to be partially deflated so the gas inside would have room to expand as we headed for the edge of the stratosphere. We also removed the two dozen lightweight seats from the gondola and replaced them with seven heavy-duty acceleration couches, plus a big one for Ham.

I asked Steel, "Aren't there eight of us?" She replied: "Drake is in a special container. We'll put him on board right before we take off. I don't want to disturb him now."

"Oh." Then I asked, "Did you bring these couches down from the ship?"

She smiled at me—that sophisticated, knowing smile that turned my volitional capabilities to mush—and said, "We rode them down. We parasail from orbit. It's fun. You'll like it."

"Yeah, I bet," is what I said, but I was thinking, 'Why?' Why would they go to such lengths to not land on the surface? Why would they design a system for commuting from orbit to the ground and back in such a low-tech fashion? It made no sense at all.

By dawn the big jobs were done. We started melting snow and separating out the hydrogen by electrolysis, pumping it into the spare bag. Our chariot to the stars looked like a big Easter basket with two huge, half-inflated eggs in it, one on top of the other. At one point Yuri looked up at it and said to me, "With any luck at all we'll crash on something soft."

The Lightdancer was in a polar orbit with a period of about eighty minutes. She made exactly sixty-nine orbits in one rotation of Vesper so each orbit brought her a little over five degrees closer to passing directly overhead. Things got tenser and more hurried as the time approached. We finally loaded Drake's pod into the gondola, but I couldn't see into it. It was covered with an insulating sheath that only left a small window right over his face. Everyone seemed very concerned for him. We moved him very carefully and gently.

That was another thing that didn't make sense. What could be wrong with Drake that the net couldn't handle? Or if security was so important that it overrode the health of a crewman, why didn't they fix him with the medical program on Steel's system? If she could re-boot people she ought to be able to handle almost anything, injury or disease. I didn't get it.

It was time to get aboard. I felt very strange—light and detached. I looked around at the harsh, spectacular landscape, the last I might ever see of Vesper. The last I *might* see of anything. Prime was low in the east, sending bronze fire across the dry interior plains to burnish the cliffs and peaks. The valley we had come up was still in shadow, Prime wouldn't rise high enough to touch Kindu or Spam-town for another hour or two.

Spam-town. What a hellhole, but I'd managed to get out of it. I wondered how Sheila was doing. Was she missing me, or just relieved that I was gone? She'd be opening the store soon. If I hadn't left with Steel I'd be sneaking out the back door and heading for 'Burbs' place. I guessed this was better.

I wondered what the hell I was doing with my life. This whole situation had been brought on by my refusing to bow to the government. But it could have been any power structure. The corps, the syndicates, it didn't matter.

Sometimes it mattered. It had mattered on Scarpus; that was the last time it had mattered. But then it was time to re-boot and Mary had left me and then it didn't matter anymore. Another cycle. Another bout of fatalism. I wondered if maybe I'd simply lived long enough, or maybe far, far too long. I wondered if my wife was still on the wheel of Karma, as my father's great-great-grandfather would have believed, or if she was an angel now, as my—as my—

If we didn't make it, would I be seeing her soon? Was that what I wanted?

"The undiscover'd country, from whose bourn no traveler returns ..." No one went to that country anymore.

I looked around at the golden mountains, the glaciers glinting fire. Out across the dusty plains, where the biosphere project hadn't yet reached. I hadn't been involved in seeding Vesper, but I had helped make more than one world. I had done many things. And now Steel needed me to help her do something, something that seemed very important to her. Perhaps it would become important to me as well.

I felt a hand on my shoulder. Steel's voice said softly, "Hey, sky pilot, are you going to start shouting at the sun like Zarathustra?"

I turned and smiled at her. "Now *there's* an obscure reference. You *must* be from earth."

She smiled back. "It's time to go. I promise you we'll get you to the Lightdancer in one piece."

People had promised me things before, but I said, "It should be a hell of a ride." We climbed in and closed the hatch.

For a while we just sat there as compressors raised the pressure inside the gondola to almost two atmospheres. Yuri wasn't sure how quickly air would bleed out once we were in space, and we were going to need all the cushion we could get. Even so, we stayed in our pressure suits. Can't have too many backups.

All of the extra guys we had rigged to keep the blimp from blowing away in the night had been taken down; the anchors had been cleared. As we settled into our couches, Marcus ordered the anchors weighed and we released from the surface of Vesper. The brooding north wall of Manlung started to slip down as we lifted, slowly at first, then with gathering speed as we accelerated upward. I could feel the alertness of the crew; there was no fear, really, but a definite state of enhanced readiness.

Marcus was in constant communication with Tamika on the Lightdancer. The tether had been unreeled for the crew's descent two quads ago so it was already at speed, ready to pick us up. Tamika was passing over the south pole as we took off and would be on the other side of the planet for most of our ascent, coming over the north pole as we approached the altitude where she would grapple us, rolling toward us like a juggernaut with a two-thousand klick diameter.

As we cleared the summit of Manlung the rest of the range came into view, stretching roughly north and south from us, a seemingly endless rampart of chiseled, icy teeth. I could see the shadow of the range stretching out across the jungled lowlands we had so recently left, the coastline, the ocean. In the other direction the inland plains stretched out to the horizon, waiting to be developed.

Marcus was flying now, with Alice in the co-pilot's seat. Alice was the newest mystery. What had she said when I met her? She was the 'problem.' Wasn't Drake the problem? Another puzzle. Maybe she was just being funny, self-deprecating or something.

Marcus said to Steel, "We're approaching 16,000 meters."

Steel said, "How's she handling?"

"Nothing even remotely resembling an ultralight."

"Are we going to be able to maintain position?"

Yuri looked at me like, 'Are these people crazy, or what?'

Marcus said, "It's going to be tough, but I think we have a chance. Every air current shoves us around. Whoa! Hold on—"

The engines roared as Marcus gunned them. We swung around to port and then steadied again. He said, "Yes, I know." Then to Steel, "Tamika's complaining that we keep drifting around."

Steel asked, "Where's the ship?"

Alice said, "It's just come over the pole." Her voice reminded me of Steel's.

Of course, Steel could have gotten on her system and asked Tamika directly, but she wanted to let Marcus have a free line.

The engines roared again as Marcus maneuvered. "Twenty thousand meters. We've arrived," Marcus turned to Alice. "You watch the altitude. I'll cover our lateral drift."

"I've got altitude, aye." Alice's eyes were glued to the instruments.

"Damn, we keep drifting east." The engines gunned again. He called out to all of us, "Everybody strap down! Ten minutes to rendezvous."

My stomach decided to visit various parts of my anatomy. Considering the way we were rolling around and the knowledge of how critically that rolling was affecting our chances of success, and, not incidentally, my chances of survival, I thought my metabolism was holding up rather well. Under the circumstances.

"Archie! Strap down!" Marcus ordered.

I looked back at where she was bending over Drake's pod. She said, "I'll strap down in plenty of time. I just want to keep an eye on Drake—"

"You can't do anything for him right now, and this elephant is hard enough to handle without people moving around. Now sit down and strap yourself in."

Archie moved to her couch, "Aye-aye, sir."

My feet started to tingle. Being in a lighter-than-air craft is unlike anything else; you're floating, but you're not weightless. You can feel gravity trying to pull you through the bottom of the gondola. And you're not really flying; you're just hanging there. With a whole bunch of planet below you and nothing but a skin of carbon and epoxy between you and it.

"How's the altitude holding?" Marcus asked.

"Twenty-thousand and three. It's really pretty stable," Alice replied, "I'm a little surprised."

"How's the navicom?" Steel asked.

"We're getting a good position, reception is clear. I've let us drift a little bit south so I can head back north into the hook. It will give us a better grapple."

Looking down out of the port I could see Manlung and the pass directly below us. Eight-thousand meters below us. Suddenly a white cloud blossomed on the east face that expanded and expanded.

"Hmm," I said to Yuri, pointing down, "Avalanche. A big one."

Yuri looked down as well. "Yeah," he said, "Prime's starting to heat up the mountains."

"Five minutes," Marcus said.

I looked at Yuri, at Jemal, at Archie, at Steel. All of them were calm, the sort of iron calm that is imposed by will and discipline. I hoped I looked the same. Just in case I didn't, I looked out the window again.

"Wow," I said, "Look at all the clouds starting to form over the mountains." It was startling how fast a row of cumulus had puffed up over the peaks. Fluffy white clouds, but you could practically see them growing.

"Mountains that big make their own weather," Yuri said.

"One minute," Marcus announced, "Get ready."

I put my head back on the headrest and snuggled down into the couch. Everyone else did the same.

"Thirty seconds," Marcus said. "Altitude?"

"In the groove," came Alice's reply. "Twenty-thousand and two."

"Close enough," said Marcus. Steel echoed him. Yuri nodded at me and smiled.

There was a bang like we hit something. I could see the gasbag above me, now fully expanded, shudder and ripple. And I felt a little heavier.

"Oh, skag!" Alice said, "We've hit a thermal. We're rising. Twenty-thousand twenty. Twenty-thousand thirty."

"Lose some hydrogen," Marcus said tersely.

"I am, I am!" said Alice, "We're going to be high. Twenty-thousand fifty. Damn."

"Here it comes!" Marcus said, "Everybody hang on!"

A superfluous statement if I'd ever heard one. I never saw the hook. The gasbag above me simply collapsed like a falling soufflé and turned into a bright orange fireball. But I couldn't really worry about it because I weighed over five hundred kilos and was fighting for breath. Burning fabric slapped down onto the top of the gondola like it had been thrown by a really angry giant, then was just as violently torn away. I could see the hook then, digging into the upper gas bag so deeply it looked like two bags; then it, too, collapsed and exploded. There was an instant when we were falling and then a huge CRACK! as the hook finally lodged on the handle. The two opposing expansion bells of its maneuvering rockets made it look like it was wearing a bow-tie.

"We're on!" Marcus' voice was strained with gee forces.

The remaining tatters of the upper bag rained past us at amazing velocity. Through the shower of flaming remnants and the red haze induced by my eyeballs flattening into my skull I could see the sky turn from deep blue to purple to black as the stars came out. I started to notice a noise, too, a high sibilance. It seemed to be coming from directly behind me.

I didn't have to wonder about it long. Marcus' strained voice announced in the headphones of my helmet, "We're losing cabin pressure."

"How fast?" Steel gritted out.

"We're down to—uh—one and a half atmospheres."

"How long until we release?" she gasped.

"Four minutes."

Four minutes lasts forever when you weigh half a ton, but we could clock our progress by watching my erstwhile home recede—not below us, but above; the sensation of down was the direction opposite the tether. We were swinging up in a semi-circle around the Lightdancer as she in turn orbited Vesper. We would reach the top of our rotation just before the ship passed under the south pole, at which point Tamika would release the hook, sending us hurtling toward Golgotha at twice orbital velocity. But the Lightdancer was much too far away to see. As we approached the top of our arc it seemed like we were dangling directly from Vesper like a chest-crushingly heavy chandelier.

Then we saw it: the rusty, banded immensity of Golgotha rising over the southern ice cap, attended by her two inner moons. Prime was off to the right with Jumbo several degrees higher. The rest of the sky was strewn with stars. The hook released and we were weightless.

Just like that. From five hundred kilos to nothing—like we'd stepped off the side of a building. We were falling through space at ten klicks a second. Falling! I grabbed unnecessarily for the arms of my acceleration couch. How long had it been since I'd been weightless? I had no idea, but it had to have been over a millennium. Space travel is so smooth these days, but not with Steel and company.

"We're down to half an atmosphere," Marcus said, "Switch to your suit air."

Great. I found the panel on my left wrist and clicked the 'internal' button. Everyone else did the same. I saw Archie reach over and do Ham's for him. Drake had always been on his own air supply. The hissing was dying away, but that was probably because we were running out of air.

I felt a sharp pang of homesickness for something I'd never seen. I was leaving Vesper behind, but that wasn't all. The Lightdancer would have to make another full orbit around Vesper to give Tamika time to reel in the tether before she could kick in her graviton impellers to follow us and (hopefully) pick us up before we ran out of air. It occurred to me that being on the wrong end of two thousand kilometers of high-tech rope might be as close as I would ever get to Steel's starship.

What do you do while you're hoping you have enough air to last until you get inside an actual, bona fide space craft? I checked my air supply. Then I checked it again. Then I looked over at Yuri who said something along the lines of "We'll be fine." Then I checked it again.

There was no way for us to maneuver now that we were in space; the blimp's propellers were now just decoration. We'd picked up a slow tumble when the hook released us and we would continue to tumble until the Lightdancer grappled us, turning over every quarter of an hour or so. It was a little disorienting, a little nauseating, but it meant the view changed out the window. I caught a glimpse of the auroras around the south pole of Vesper. Very pretty. Made me think of magnetic fields and radiation belts and radiation shielding and how much a blimp gondola would have. Not much, I figured. Oh, well, I'd suffocate long before radiation sickness could get me.

It was a long ride.

"Rendezvous in five minutes." Marcus' voice was calm. The Lightdancer was still over a kilometer away, but we could see her easily. She was a pretty ship. A conventional freewheeler, she was over a kilometer long—a sleek, tapered, conical needle covered with a flat black coating of ablative material. I could see that the habitation module was extended. A brief cylinder of lighted windows interrupted the lines of the cone just forward of the stern. Her torch was retracted; it would extend another five hundred meters out the stern when it was lit. The only thing that differentiated her from other ships like her was the gap right at her center of gravity that held the skyhook spool.

As we got closer to her I began to see some scoring on the hull. I asked Yuri about it. He started to speak, then he glanced at Steel and she answered me:

"When Drake got sick he had to drop out of the engine. We were still thirty light years out."

Wow. The middle of nowhere. Then it struck me, they couldn't freewheel with an unbalanced engine; you had to have all the components in place. "You traveled thirty light years in rational space?" I asked.

"Yes."

"At relativistic speeds?"

"That's right."

No wonder there was scoring. At close to the speed of light even hydrogen atoms pack a pretty good wallop when they hit you, and though the average density of interstellar space is only around one atom per cubic centimeter, you go through an awful lot of cubic centimeters in thirty light years, and not all cubic centimeters conform to the average. It was why all starships were long and narrow and covered with an ablative coating. Back in the late twenties, when my wife and I had headed out to Barnard's Star, they'd stopped in the Kuiper Belt along the way to pick up a fair-sized comet nucleus, just to have something in front of us to get worn away, and that trip was under six light years.

Then I thought, these people have been out of touch for thirty years. You couldn't communicate at relativistic speeds. Time dilation made it impossible to carry on a meaningful temporal relationship. It's what made freewheeling possible. But you couldn't *talk* to anyone when one of your seconds took a couple of days or even weeks for everyone else poking along at planetary speeds. And it's not like there were any other ships moving close to light-speed that you could synch up with. Why would there be? It was dangerous to travel through rational space at that kind of velocity; we lost enough ships in the early days to prove that. No, you accelerated up to just under the speed of light and immediately started to freewheel, and when you stopped freewheeling you decelerated just as quickly.

Only the Lightdancer hadn't. I mean, she hadn't been outrageously lucky. Interstellar space really is pretty empty, but if she'd hit anything of any size—like, say, the size of a grain of sand—there wouldn't have been much of anything left but gamma rays.

But what else could you do if part of your engine got sick? No one got sick anymore, not like that, if they did they just got on the net and got better again. If someone was close to re-booting and having real health problems you sure didn't hire them as a crewman. But suppose you did lose a crewman somehow, as the Lightdancer evidently had. You're forced to drop immediately back into rational space, traveling so close to the speed of light that you could shake hands with passing photons. Do you decelerate to a safe speed? No one carried enough supplies to spend years and years in transit; it just wasn't a situation that arose anymore. And suppose you did slow down enough to significantly increase your chances of surviving a major impact? At ten per cent of c it would take three hundred years to make that same thirty light-year journey, with no noticeable time dilation to make it seem shorter. Even with re-booting and Realities on the net and any other creative way you could come up with to pass the time, could you make it three centuries cooped up with seven other people on a starship? No, you'd do what Steel and her crew had done—take your chances and not decelerate until you were close to a populated star system.

What the hell could be wrong with Drake? There was only one thing I could think of, and I didn't want to think of it.

Archie said, "He's convulsing again. We've got to get him under acceleration."

I turned around to look at her. She was floating over Drake's pod, peering in the window. I looked forward at Steel.

"He never did well in weightlessness," she said to me. "That's why I had to bring him down to the surface. I wanted him to be as comfortable as possible." She looked unutterably sad. Then she got on her system. "Tamika, get underway as soon as we've docked." She looked back at Drake's pod again.

We passed between the fore and aft sections of the hull that slid closed behind us. We were aboard the Lightdancer.

PART II
F.S. LIGHTDANCER

CHAPTER 9

As soon as the hull closed, large davits swung out from the bulkhead just aft of the tether spool to grab and secure us. Weight hit us as Tamika kicked in the impellers. It seemed like she accelerated at about a standard gee; I felt about a third again as heavy as on Vesper.

The bulkhead became the floor. The huge tether spool that had stretched out beside us as we entered the ship now loomed over us, filling the diameter of the Lightdancer for a hundred meters. We unstrapped and carried Drake's pod out of the gondola and across the metal deck to a large airlock that led to the interior of the pressure hull. Even though Drake stopped convulsing as soon as we had weight, Steel was in a hurry to get him to the medical bay. We didn't even stop to take off our pressure suits after the lock cycled. Carrying him down a short corridor brought us to a lift that descended the third of a kilometer to the habitation module.

Once again Steel's money was in evidence. The ship was appointed well. Not lavishly, but all of the fittings and components were top of the line.

We carried Drake's pod into the medical bay and set it on the examination table. Archie shooed us out and sealed the bay behind her. Marcus caught Steel's eye and said, "I'll go to Control." Steel nodded and he walked off down the curving passageway, removing his helmet as he went. Ham evidently knew where he belonged, because he headed off somewhere, too. The rest of us followed Archie into the medical interface booth.

Archie turned and faced Steel. "Is there really any point in this?"

Steel took off her helmet as she replied, "I want to see if anything we did was effective. Who knows?" She turned to Alice. "Maybe those herbs you got in Kindu helped." Her tone of voice changed when she spoke to Alice. It puzzled me. There was something sing-songy about it, a mannerism I hadn't heard in a long time, like the way people talk to a pet.

Alice looked stoic and said nothing. I was struck by her freshness. Maybe that's the wrong word. Even in her grim concern for Drake she seemed, I don't know, new. Unworn. Something.

Steel turned back to Archie. "We'd better have a look."

Archie stood there for a moment, started to respond, then nodded and turned to the control panel. She waited for a moment, then unlatched her helmet, doffed her pressure suit and kicked it into a corner. I was beginning to feel like I wanted to keep mine on, but everyone else was losing theirs, so I took mine off too. We stood there holding them as we watched Archie begin to work.

The first thing she did was to evacuate the medical bay. The compressors were high quality. We could barely hear them as they pumped the air out of the chamber. She then activated filters in the observation window, making it opaque to anything but visible light, and bathed the bay in intense infrared, UV, X-rays and gamma radiation. "That ought to take care of any residual organic matter," she mumbled.

She inhaled once, let it out, and took up the controls to the remote manipulators. Slowly and carefully, she opened the thermal covering on Drake's pod. It fell away, exposing a transparent capsule. The bottom half was filled with life support equipment; the top half held Drake.

My heart rate jumped, but I think I managed to keep any expression off of my face. I'd seen people in Drake's condition before, but never in person, and not for over five hundred years. He was in the final stages. His eyes were already gone, and his teeth were exposed. Pieces of his skin clung to the sides of the capsule where he had rolled against it. The skin that he had left was running with sweat. A black, pancake-sized melanoma covered the hollow above his left collarbone and extended up the side of his neck. His forearms were raised and his fingers occasionally clenched half-heartedly. Other than that he didn't move.

"Is he in pain?" Steel asked.

"I don't think so," Archie replied. "I've got him heavily sedated. I hope he's not aware at all."

"There's been no improvement."

"What did you expect?"

Steel was silent for a moment. Then, "We can't—We'll have to—" Another silence. I think we were all afraid to meet each other's eyes. What Drake had couldn't be cured. If we tried to re-boot him the very cellular restructuring that would have saved him in any other circumstance would cause the degeneration to accelerate. He was already lost.

I still wasn't prepared for what Steel said next.

"We'll drop him into Prime after we refuel. Before we boost for Earth." She looked at Drake again. "We can't leave ... we can't leave anything. For anyone to ..."

We all stood there for a moment, looking at him, not looking at him, I'm not sure which.

Steel turned to me. "I'll have Jemal show you your quarters. Then I'd like to meet with you in my cabin in, say, fifteen minutes."

I was going to say, 'Aye-aye, Captain' but she was already out the hatch and down the passageway.

Fifteen minutes later I was standing outside her cabin wondering what I would say to her, what she would say to me. The hatch opened and her voice flowed over me. "Come in. Please."

I walked into her suite. The lighting was subdued. I faced a row of windows that reached from floor to ceiling. The habitation module must have still been extended, for I could see out. We were diving in toward Golgotha, tacking around her to head down into the inner system to the anti-matter station close in around Prime. I could see the banded globe swelling visibly as I watched.

"Please sit down," she said. She was wearing a long, lavender, satin robe. It clung and flowed as she moved. In the soft lighting her voice was so rich and compelling that it almost wiped out the vision of Drake's pathetic, ravaged body. Almost.

I took a seat, as did she. She asked me, "Would you like anything to drink?"

"How did Drake get the plague?" I answered.

She picked up an exquisite blue-crystal decanter off the small table that stood between us (it looked like twenty-ninth century Murano) and poured some of its contents into a matching glass. She lifted it to her lips, tasted it, put the glass down. Her eyes met mine and she said, "He picked it up on Brainard's Planet."

That was not the right answer. I don't know what answer I wanted—I don't know what answer there could have been—but that wasn't it.

"*On* Brainard's Planet," I said.

"Yes."

I just stared at her, trying to think of something to say that would make this all go away.

"*On* Brainard's Planet?" I repeated, "What do you mean, *on* Brainard's Planet? You can't land *on* Brainard's—"

I stopped. It was so illegal to land on Brainard's Planet that I didn't even know what they did to you if you were insane enough to try it. They didn't even really need to enforce it. No one wanted to go there. If traffic control sensed you so much as dropping a probe into the atmosphere ... I didn't know. Maybe you could get research waivers, or something.

But I knew what Steel was going to say next.

"We didn't have to land."

The skyhook. "Traffic control doesn't know about your little shuttle system."

She didn't smile at me. "No."

"They can't pick it up on their scanners?"

"I suppose they could if they were looking for anything that even resembled a skyhook, but they aren't. No one has used them for over fifteen hundred years. You really shook me when you knew what they were. They might as well scan for internal combustion engines, or covered wagons."

"They can't see a tether a thousand klicks long?" I asked.

"It's less than a tenth of a meter wide. The farther it is from the ship the faster it moves. It's basically made of diamond. It's transparent for all intents and purposes. Transparent to visible light, transparent to radar. If it occasionally happens to occult a star, what will they look for? Where will they look? It doesn't move like anything they're looking for."

"And they can't sense what you're doing through the net?"

"We're not on the net."

Of course.

I didn't know why I was asking all this stuff anyway, the answers were rendered moot by Drake's condition. He *had* the plague. Steel had every reason to tell me she hadn't been to Brainard's Planet if she had; she had no possible reason to tell me she had been if she hadn't.

"But why?" I asked.

"Why what?"

"Why the hell was he on Brainard's Planet to begin with?" I was filling with the surge of anger you get when you see someone hurt by stupidity or negligence. It's too late to prevent it, so you try to undo it by proving it was too stupid to have happened in the first place.

Steel didn't rise to my implied condemnation. She sat quietly for a moment, then picked up her glass again and looked at it. The muscles in her throat worked. I got ready for the lie. Then I decided to preempt it by asking something she might answer.

"Are we going back there?"

She looked me in the eye. Sadness, weariness and determination. "Yes."

"Why?"

Another pause. It lengthened until she got up and walked to the window.

I was oscillating between rage, incredulity and panic. I don't think I yelled at her, but I might have: "You know what happened to the Brainard expedition. You have to."

"Yes."

"You know what happened to Elysium after they limped back to it."

"Yes, I know."

"They had to sterilize the whole planet. Five hundred million people. Gone. Just like that. Plants. Animals. Everything."

"It was horrible."

She wasn't looking at me. She had her back to me, staring out the window. Golgotha's mass bulged hugely toward us, getting nearer and nearer.

"It didn't stop there," I drove on, desperate to prove to her and myself that this wasn't happening. "Paraiso: gone before they figured out what was happening. Cielo: gone. Who knows how many more would have been obliterated if they hadn't let those planets die in quarantine."

"I was alive then. I remember."

I didn't recall standing up, but I was on my feet. "Almost two billion people." I didn't know what else to say.

She turned back to me. She looked at me as though she didn't want to be separate from me. "You've met my crew," she said.

"What?" I didn't know where she was taking me next, and I wasn't sure I wanted to go.

"My crew," she repeated. "You've met them, worked with them."

"I've worked with everyone but Drake." The anger was still there. "He didn't seem to be up to doing much."

"They're a good crew," she continued. "They're not insane. Or stupid. Or easily duped."

I thought about them. Marcus, Yuri, Alice, Archie. None of them were brainwashed or spineless or even particularly easy to get along with. Maybe Jemal. I hadn't met Tamika yet. "Yeah, okay. I think I see what you're getting at."

"Do you think they would go along with something like this if they didn't think there was a very good reason for it?"

"Okay, okay," I sat down again, "I see your point. But I haven't heard any 'very good reason' yet." I was still breathing hard.

She sat down across from me. "You've been through a pretty big shock," she said. She gazed into my eyes for a moment, then covered my hand with hers. Chills ran up my arm. "Do you think you're ready to listen?" she asked.

The question was: was *I* insane or stupid or easily duped? I withdrew my hand from under hers, which caused her hand to drop down on my knee where my hand had been. It didn't help.

She sensed my discomfort and pulled away, sitting back in her chair. "Okay," I croaked, "let's hear it."

She looked at me for a long time. Then, "I am a good person."

I looked back at her. "Sometimes that isn't enough," I replied.

She sighed. Then she started again. "The potential pharmaceutical resources contained in an entirely alien biosphere are immense. Almost beyond imagining. Brainard realized this when he first discovered it."

"A fat freaking lot of good it did him. Or anyone else."

"It's been over five centuries. We've learned a great deal since then."

" 'A great deal.' " I still couldn't believe I was having this conversation. "Your education doesn't appear to have helped Drake any."

"We tried to plan for every contingency." She looked at her perfect fingernails. "We'll do better next time."

"What the hell happened?"

The muscles in her throat worked again. Okay, I thought, here it comes. "His environmental suit failed."

"Failed," I echoed. I was watching her like a man whose life depended on it.

"Yuri analyzed it in quarantine. The upper gasket in the left knee joint had a microscopic pin hole in it." There were no joints in the suits we had worn up to the ship, so I assumed she was talking about different ones. I said as much.

"No, no," she responded. "Our E-suits are much heavier. Fully armored."

"And you're saying you missed this flaw in Drake's?"

"No. His suit integrity was intact when he left the ship."

I waited. So did she.

"What happened?" I was determined to get the whole story out of her, even though I knew, even then, that she'd get me to believe I had it whenever she thought I knew enough.

"He was involved in an incident with one of the natives."

Oh, this was getting better and better. "You mean he was attacked?"

She ran her finger around the rim of her glass. "I always think it's a mistake to impart human emotions and motives to the actions of a species we don't fully understand."

" 'Don't fully understand.' " Was she nuts? Brainard had been totally unable to establish any kind of contact with them, even though the dominant species seemed to have a complex social structure, something that might have been kind of like an economy, the ability to work with metals, even things that Brainard was convinced were religious artifacts. I remembered something my father had said when I was about fifteen. The last time I'd thought about it was when Brainard had been sending back his first frustrated reports. Eleven hundred years earlier my father had been reading about the SETI program being run at the radio installation on Iapetus, and I'd just wrecked the family rover after he'd told me not to drive it. He said: "How can we expect to be able to communicate with alien civilizations when we can't even talk to our own children?" I wondered again what he would have thought of Brainard's expedition.

"Well, we understand them a lot better than Brainard did," Steel said. "You know that both Draco and the Pleiades have had remote sensors in orbit around the planet for the last five hundred years?"

Every once in a while something would be published on the net when they thought they'd come up with some significant part of the puzzle, but it always turned out to be not very significant. "Yeah, I know," I said, "Did they actually get something useful?"

"Some things that turned out to be useful," she looked me in the eye, "and some that might potentially be revolutionary."

I could smell it then. Money. Whatever Steel was after was going to translate into wealth, one way or another. It didn't make me happy. "You think it's going to be worth it?" I asked.

"What do you mean?"

I wanted to be careful how I phrased what I was going to say next. She had me at a tremendous disadvantage. I was on her ship and I wasn't on the net. I spoke quietly and slowly. "There is a human being in sick bay right now who at one time had a good shot at living—if not forever, then a very, very long time. No one knows how long." Swirling bands of Golgotha's stormy atmosphere slid urgently past the windows behind her. "It doesn't look like he's going to do that now."

Unexpected tears filled her eyes, but her gaze didn't waver. "I know," she said, "We thought we had a safe system. We—we knew how Brainard's party got infected—"

"How?" That had been the problem. No one could figure out how the plague had started, how it had spread. Brainard had taken all the usual quarantine precautions; it hadn't seemed to make any difference. No one even knew what the plague was, except that it was horribly, horribly lethal.

"It's not really an infection, the way we think of infections."

"How do you know this?"

"I—let me tell you what we know." Her countenance wasn't pleading. I don't know what it was. Imploring, I guess. "What we think we know," she amended.

The south temperate band of Golgotha's atmosphere filled the windows with creamy whorls and eddies. We were close enough now that individual cloud formations could be seen climbing above darker layers below. Lightning flashed in thunderheads that were torn asunder by titanic winds.

I listened.

She stood up again and paced slowly around the room as she spoke, only occasionally making eye contact with me: "We don't think there's an actual virus or bacillus involved. There seems to be a substance excreted by certain life forms—I won't call them animals; we're not sure how to classify them yet—that they use to communicate with each other, if that's the right term. It seems to affect communal activity in the colonies, anyway."

"How do you mean?"

"Well, we're not sure, but their albedo changes right before they move the colonies. They get shinier, like they're covered with sweat, or slime. It's difficult to get good data when you have to observe them from orbit."

"How do you know they're communicating?" Storms flashed past till we crossed the terminator into darkness. The lighting on her face changed when we did. Blue electricity flickered and raced across the black face of the gas giant.

"We're not certain, but there are definite patterns of interaction that seem to correspond closely to the level of reflectivity on their skin. We assume they're communicating. But that's not what's important." She paused. "This substance seems to be able to migrate through metals, ceramics, silicates, even many plastics without altering its chemical structure, or if it does alter, it changes back once it's through. That's why we think they're using it as some sort of signaling mechanism. We've seen individuals separated by an iron dike appear to 'talk' to each other this way. We're pretty sure it's this substance that caused the plague."

"Why? I mean, how do you know?"

She turned and looked at me, "Well, for one thing, I'm standing here talking to you."

"You've been on the surface, too?"

"All of us have. All except Marcus. He stayed on the ship to operate the skyhook."

I felt like I'd just dived into a toxic waste dump. Nowhere to run, nowhere to hide. "I suppose," I said, my mouth suddenly dry, "if you were contagious it would already be too late."

"If what we think is right, it doesn't really spread by contagion. It's not really a disease."

"I'm sure that will comfort me as I'm decomposing."

She smiled at me. "You're safe. If we had been wrong, we'd all look like Drake by now. Our E-suits work; we know they do. It's just that Drake's suit was compromised."

"How was it compromised?" I wasn't really feeling any better. I could feel my eyes rotting, my skin falling off my tortured flesh.

Her eyes focused on the past—a sad, unchangeable past. "It was so strange, and it happened so quickly. They're really magnificent creatures, they move with a ponderous grace that is almost like dancing ... They don't seem to notice us at all, or they didn't. It's so hard; we don't know what motivates them. Why they do what they do." A fuzzy, orange arc was spreading out behind her as we approached the dawn. "Drake wasn't behaving in any way that we thought was threatening. He was just walking along a trail, not on point, not in the rear, just walking along. One of the creatures was grazing to our right, about five meters off. We really didn't think anything about it. We'd been much closer to them before and they hadn't reacted at all." She watched Prime rise over thick, endless tempests. "A—a pseudopod caught Drake's leg. We didn't even see it, we just saw him trip and fall down. We didn't know they could extend them so fast. We didn't think they did anything fast." Prime's light played over her body as it rose. "It wouldn't let go. We beat on it, tried to pry it loose, anything we could think of. Then, for no apparent reason, it did. It retracted without bothering any of the rest of us. The creature just went on grazing as though nothing had happened." Boiling turbulence receded: clouds became weather systems became counter-rotating bands of rust and cream.

"That doesn't—How did—?" I faltered.

"We think it was a combination of the torque applied to the knee and a dilute hydrochloric acid that the pseudopod seems to have excreted." She stared out the window. "We tried to plan for every contingency. We'd just never seen that sort of activity before."

"The rest of your suits—" I didn't want to finish the question.

"There was some minor erosion on our gloves and forearm plates, nothing too deep. It was the duration of the contact and the tortional stress to the gasket that caused it to fail. Drake's alarm went off as soon as his suit was holed. We got back up to the ship ... as soon as possible. We hoped we might be able to save him, but he got sick soon after we started to freewheel."

"How did you keep it from spreading?" I still felt like it was too late to be asking anything. I couldn't believe they'd been successful at containing it. No one had before.

"Once we knew how to make the E-suits, developing quarantine procedures and facilities was relatively easy." She turned to me and allowed herself a smile, "Relatively."

I was at an experiential impasse. I didn't know what to believe. I was almost certain that she wasn't telling me everything, and yet Drake *was* sick and everyone else wasn't. It wasn't impossible that Steel had come up with a way to deal with the plague, but on the other hand, why ask me to meet her in her private quarters? Wearing a slinky dressing gown? I just had a feeling that her technique in dealing with the plague wasn't nearly as sophisticated as her technique in dealing with me.

"All right," I said, "We've been talking for a while now. Have you come up with a good story to tell me about why you were there in the first place?"

She smiled at me again. Like she'd been caught. And she liked it. It made me feel very powerful, and *that* made me feel utterly defenseless. She didn't press her advantage. She didn't sit down next to me or casually brush up against me or run her fingers through her mane or stretch or any number of things that she could have done. She was very, very good.

She pinned me in her emerald gaze. "Brainard's Planet has been under observation for over five centuries," she said. "We think their life-spans may be longer than that." She paused to let it sink in.

I stared into her eyes and tried to put it together. Something 'revolutionary,' she had said. Having to do with pharmaceuticals. And long life spans. That would make a whole lot of money.

What was she driving at? We already had long life spans, unlimited life spans, maybe. We had to re-boot every eighty years or so, but so what? It got the job done. People had tried various ways to lengthen the time between re-boots, and we had, to a certain extent. They'd tried splicing genetic material from long-lived species into the human genome. It hadn't worked. I said, "So what? Joshua trees have long life-spans, so do Sequoias—"

"Trees don't have central nervous systems."

I chewed that over for a while. I thought of the possible ramifications. And the ramifications of those ramifications. And the ramifications of those.

I was beginning to get the picture.

CHAPTER 10

I made my way back to the common room. It was down one deck, in crew quarters. Our meeting had ended with several things unresolved, the main one being whether or not I wanted to continue to be part of this venture. I now understood the need for airtight security. Besides the flagrant illegality of visiting the surface of Brainard's Planet, there was the matter of patents. How many substances could be mined from the biosphere if Steel really had come up with a workable system for dealing with the plague? Pharmaceuticals and genetic engineering had completely changed the shape of the economy in the first half of the third millennium, had changed the nature of human life from a closed curve to an open-ended arc. What were the possibilities in harvesting a completely independent line of evolution?

Would any of it be useful at all? There was no way to know without going in and getting samples. All of the things Brainard had collected had been lost in the plague.

But what if something useful was found? I thought about what Steel had implied: sentient beings on Brainard's Planet had central nervous systems that lasted centuries, not decades. Could their genetic material be spliced with ours? Did they have genetic material? Did they have cells? I wanted to find out.

But if we *could* use what we found there, if we could extend the useful life of a human brain to more than five centuries, what would that mean? I thought of Matessa and the rest of the residents of Kindu, and all the people everywhere that had to go in and out of the trades to be able to afford re-booting. What if they only had to 'boot every half-millennium instead of every six to ten decades? They'd have five centuries to save up for the operation instead of less than one.

They wouldn't have to go into the trades anymore.

How would the people at Planetary Tectonics feel about that? And Interstellar Biosphere and Relativity/SimulComm and all the rest of the corps? Their labor pool would evaporate.

VENGEANCE! rang in my head with a surge of adrenaline that made me pause at the hatch into the common room. I needed to be careful. I'd stumbled into something that might change the future of humanity as profoundly as rebooting had. It could shift the balance of power from the suits to the workers in a way that no one *I* knew had anticipated, even in their wildest extrapolations.

This could get really ugly.

I needed to remember that it had nothing to do with the loss of my wife. She'd been gone for over a millennium. Steel didn't know how that had gone down. It wasn't why she was on this mission. She had her own motivations—maybe humanitarian, maybe profit oriented, I didn't know—but it had nothing to do with me.

In my heart, though, it had everything to do with the dull ache of loss and self-doubt and recrimination that I had lived with for all these centuries. I needed to be very careful. I needed to check things out very thoroughly. I needed more information.

In order to get it I needed to get back on the net. Or at least onto Steel's system. I had to do that anyway. Steel had sent me down to find Archie and get connected so I could plug into the engine after we re-fueled. Archie was sitting at a table in the common room.

"Say, Archie." She looked up at me. Her features were clean and sculpted. Her eyes were large, dark, and incredibly tired. I thought: She's losing a patient. How long had it been since anyone had lost a patient? Her loss gave her a profound beauty. I almost didn't speak, but then I did. "Steel wants you to connect me. Do you have time to do that now?" I asked.

"Sure," she said. She looked into a mug of something, tea, maybe, that was in her hand, put it down on the table, then pushed back her chair. "We'll have to go back up to medical."

"Uh, you can finish your drink," I said.

"What makes you think so?" She got up and walked toward the hatch. I followed her, looking for something to say.

What I found was, "I'm sorry about Drake—"

"We all are." The tube hatch opened in front of her and she stepped in. I stepped in after her. "Medical," she said, and the lift began to rise. Two decks up we stepped out and started down the corridor, the same corridor I'd helped carry Drake down earlier.

We turned into the medical interface booth and I started to get nervous. I didn't want to see Drake again. Even though I believed Steel's quarantine methods worked, believed that the rest of the crew were confident they worked, in my gut I could feel the ferocity of the disease. No one who was alive then, who hadn't zeroed out since then, felt anything but horror about the plague. To be this close to it was like being naked in a swarm of angry bees. I tried to get smaller, to give the disease less of a target.

To my relief Archie had turned off the main lights in the medical bay. The dim red glow of the night watch lamps was all that drifted through the observation window. They reminded me how tired I was. Even though we'd left Vesper a few hours after dawn we'd been up more than an entire shift.

Archie stopped and checked on her patient, noting the readouts on her board and then looking through the glass. Almost against my will I followed her gaze into the medical bay. Drake's pod was backlit, soft red refracted through plastic, forming a stygian halo around his silent form. His silhouette was blurry, as though the inner surface of his pod were coated with something translucent. I asked Archie about it.

"That's it," she said. "As far as we've been able to tell, that's what causes the plague."

A pointless fight-or-flight adrenaline rush raced up my thighs. "All that got in through one tiny pinhole?"

She made a small adjustment to something, perhaps his pain medication. "No," she said. She walked over to the net socket—I thought of it as the net socket although it only plugged in to Steel's system. It was the standard recliner; all of the important parts were in the headrest.

"No?" I asked.

"Have a seat," she said. I did. She gently pressed my head back into the headrest and turned to another control panel and readout. She called up a scan of my brain on the screen. I couldn't see the bio-chip at the base of my medulla— it was far too small—but I was sure she could. She knew what to look for. "We don't know too much about the stuff yet. It's—" she glanced over at me, "very dangerous." She looked back at the screen and zoomed in on my brain stem. "We can contain it now, but we haven't developed a whole lot of tools to handle it."

"Steel told me it migrates right through most things."

"Mm." She'd tapped into the bio-chip, and a full readout appeared in a box on the screen. "You were last updated January 4, 3895?"

"That's right," I said, "On Scarpus."

"Mm. Just over a century ago." She touched the control panel in a couple of places. "We'll give you some new stuff. I'm sure Steel would want you to have it." She touched the board once more and the electric zing! you get when you patch back in ran through my nervous system. For a second or two different digital matrices were superimposed over my view of the room, then my eyesight went back to normal. "That's it," she said as she turned back to me. "I think I'll hit the sack." She waited for me to precede her out of the booth.

She was an absolute font of information. I wondered if she and Steel had gone to the same school, or if this was simply the way all doctors behaved. I decided to press a little further. "If all that goop didn't get in through the pin hole, where did it come from?"

"You want theories?" she asked. "All right, I'll give you theories. Just be sure to come back in a few decades and I'll give you some different theories."

I laughed. "I guess anything is better than nothing. I just, you know, if I'm going to be around this stuff, I'd like to know, um, anything …"

"Yes, I know what you mean." We stepped into the lift. "Crew quarters." We started to descend. "My best guess is that it contains at least a hundred and perhaps as many as five hundred different enzymes. One of those enzymes allows it to pass through our cell membranes. When it does, it seems to head directly for the cell's lysosomes, where the cell stores many of its own enzymes. I'm not at all sure what happens next, but the end result is that the cell's enzymes are altered to mimic the enzymes in the invading substance. Somewhere along about then the cell's membrane falls apart, like someone poured acid on a balloon, and the cell explodes. Well, not explodes, really. It just loses its integrity and dies. But before it does it becomes a factory for the new enzymes, making enough to attack many more cells."

"Wow," I said. The lift door opened and we walked out into the corridor. "You've seen all this? I mean, you've looked at it under a microscope or something?" We stopped outside the door to her quarters. She turned to me.

"No. It's a theory. If I could get the stuff to stay on a slide long enough to look at it through a microscope without it migrating through the slide and the microscope and destroying me and everybody else, I would. We'll figure out a way to do it, but the engineering is going to be tricky." She opened her door. "What I know is: whenever this stuff comes into contact with biomass from a terrestrial ecosystem—that means us—tissue starts to degrade rapidly. As more tissue is destroyed more of this stuff shows up, even if the tissue has been isolated in a container that the stuff can't migrate through." She leaned against the door jamb. "But 'stuff' is such an unscientific word, don't you think? I much prefer words like 'enzyme' and 'lysosome.' When I make up a scientific theory I hardly ever use the word 'stuff.' Polysyllables obfuscate a preponderant ignorance with so much more style and panache."

I smiled at her. Then I thought of something else. "How did you ever learn how to contain it?"

"Trial and error. We kept sending little samples of biomass down to the surface in containers made in various ways. Eventually we started to get results."

"What was it that worked?" I asked.

"You'd have to talk to Yuri about that," she said. "It has to do with super-long chain polymers and grids of half-micron thick silver wires and random, non-repeating frequencies of alternating current. But he's the genius who put it together. I wouldn't presume to try to explain it."

"Well, thanks for telling me what you know."

"Any time," she smiled back. "And now, unless you're going to offer me some really excellent conversation or some really excellent sex, I think I'll go log off for a while."

I laughed. "Yeah, sounds like a good idea." I didn't know if she was serious or not, but I still hadn't recovered from Matessa, I had designs on the Captain, and I had work to do. As she turned away, I said, "Um, one more thing ..."

She turned back. "Yes?"

I tried to look through those dark wells of gritty weariness that masked and revealed her. "Do you know what Steel is trying to do on Brainard's Planet?"

She took a moment to answer. "I know what she has done."

Hmm. What did I want to ask her? Do you think she's utterly insane? No. Do you think we have a chance of living through this? I didn't really want to ask that either. How about: Do you think I'm a fool for being as attracted to her as I am? If she knew the answer to that one I probably didn't want to hear it. Then, out of nowhere:

"Was Drake a friend of yours?" Even though he was technically still with us, he'd certainly lost his perspective.

She seemed to consider the language I had used, parsing the sentence for clues to my real meaning. "A friend," she said, and I couldn't tell if she was confirming or merely echoing, tasting the words to see if they were true.

"It must be ..." I started. There were no words. Maybe there never had been, even centuries ago when people had talked about these things. "Do you think ..." Was this what I wanted to ask? "Do you think ..." Protocol closed my throat.

"What?" She examined me. "Do I think it was a good idea to go to Brainard's Planet?"

Something like that. "Yes," I said.

It took her a little while to weigh her duty to Steel, to her profession, to a person she'd just met. "At this particular point in time—" She examined her hands, hands that were very capable but ultimately limited. "I wish it hadn't cost so much."

The Lightdancer drove in toward Prime as I made my way to my quarters. I walked down the curving corridor reproving myself for not screwing up my testosterone level and responding to Archie's implied request. I still wasn't sure if she'd been serious, but she certainly could have used the distraction. Realities are fine, but there's nothing like the awkward spontaneity of sticking your elbow in someone's ribs while looking for an erogenous zone to take your mind off your troubles.

I stopped by the common room to pick up a sandwich and something to drink, then retired to my new digs. Nowhere near as posh as Steel's suite, nor as large, but clean and functional. It gave me pause to think that it had probably been Drake's before mine, but if I was going to worry about the risk of infection, or whatever it was that the plague did to you, I might as well have jumped off the ship right then. If it *had* been Drake's cabin someone had done me the courtesy of removing his personal effects.

My bunk was equipped with a system interface and I was anxious to get started. I wasn't sure how long I was going to be able to work because, though the net couldn't use *you* unless you were asleep, you had to be awake to use *it*.

I raised the bunk to semi-sitting position, took a crisp chomp of sprouts and rye, and logged on. The universe opened before me. My cabin faded to a peripheral glimmer and my mind filled with the multi-dimensional matrix of the main library. Steel's system was very nice; I wondered how many drones she had on it. I saw the net gate and it made me think about bulleting Sheila, just to let her know what had happened to me, but I was stymied immediately. Security. I could request information off the net but I couldn't send data in any other format. It made perfect sense—I just hadn't thought about it—but it reminded me of my status or lack thereof.

So, down to work. I called up Brainard's Planet, chose my favorite voice for the interface, and laid back while it talked to me. There was quite a bit for a globe that had only been visited once (officially). Astronomic and geophysical data: It orbited a G-type star, a little brighter than the sun, some twelve hundred light years farther out from the galactic center than the earth was. Seen from Earth, it resided in Cancer. It orbited a little farther out from its star than Earth did, about a hundred eighty thousand klicks, fourth of eleven major planets in its system. It was a double planet, even more so than the earth-moon system. Its companion was almost half its size. It was larger than earth, had a diameter of over fifteen thousand klicks, gravity almost two standard gees, atmospheric pressure at the surface over four times what it was on earth. Flying would be easy there. Reducing atmosphere very similar to earth's: nitrogen, oxygen, various trace gasses. You could breathe it if you didn't mind getting the plague. Inclination to its orbit was negligible, less than a degree, and its orbit was almost circular. It didn't have seasons.

If it had been a dry world it would have resembled Mars in one way: the northern and southern hemispheres were divided roughly at the equator by a large drop in elevation. Whereas on Mars the highlands were in the south, here they were in the north, and the southern hemisphere was mostly ocean. There were a few minor island chains, but basically Brainard's Planet was one big continent on top and one big puddle on the bottom.

This was interesting. There was a Reality taken from orbit, filed thirty-two years ago by "40. Jahrhunderts Stahl Wirklichkeit, AG." Arty name. They must have made it a couple of years before they left, before Drake's infirmity caused them to be out of touch for three decades. I called it up. Like most Realities, you could travel around in it through any of the original viewpoints of the omnicorder, plus an enhanced matrix of extrapolated viewpoints. In effect, I could wander around in orbit looking straight down for a map-like view or pan in any direction to see things more obliquely. I could zoom in and achieve an effect like walking around on the planet, but there would be holes in the data, particularly if I got into a complex texture like a forest or something. Anything not visible to the omnicorder from its orbital path was, of course, not available to the data bank. You had the option of asking the program to fill in any missing pieces with fractal-generated images, but I didn't use it. I wanted to see what was there, not some figment of an equation's imagination.

I disabled the tactile inputs. The omnicorder had been in weightlessness, but I was in a nice, comfy bunk under acceleration, so why get nauseated? I wasn't going to be able to touch anything on the surface, anyway.

It was funny. I wasn't actually going to be there, I was just entering a Reality of the place, and yet I still felt my skin crawl. Brainard's Planet was simply terrifying.

I held my breath and engaged the program.

There it was, floating benignly in space. A half-and-half, blue-and-brown marble swathed in dazzling white swirls and streaks of clouds. It didn't particularly look like the doom planet; it was just a planet. Because of the density of the atmosphere, the temperature gradient toward the poles was very mild, almost non-existent. There were no ice caps. Still, most of the land-based biota were confined to a broad band in the lower latitudes. The farther you got from the southern ocean the more arid the land became until, about halfway to the pole, it was lifeless desert.

I watched it rotate for a while, then I zoomed in on the northern tropics. The band of life resolved from a dark greenish brown smudge to a multi-hued carpet. It was easy to see the colonies. Intricate structures of multi-storied chambers and passages, knotted and intertwined like a plate of pasta. As I moved in closer I could see the creatures moving ponderously along the thoroughfares, looking more than anything like giant beige walruses or slugs with sort of crab-shaped carapaces on their backs. It was impossible to tell which end was the front, unless you assumed it was the one pointed in the direction they were moving. They wandered slowly until they suddenly jumped back to their original positions as the omnicorder passed out of range and the program looped back to the beginning of the data.

I moved out into the countryside. Rolling fields or forests of lazily waving lavender and pink tubules. Sea anemones writ large, I thought. It was hard to tell scale. There was nothing familiar to compare anything to. I wandered around. Rivers, hills, some impressive mountain ranges—how do you study a whole planet? I could have spent centuries, but I wanted a different kind of information.

I backed out and called up Brainard's expedition. There were the five Realities Brainard took on the trip, his personal log, and then it branched out into different subjects: the plague, xenobiology, Elysium, et cetera. I called up the fifth Reality, the one he made on his final trip to the surface, his last attempt to communicate with them:

I am in an environmental containment suit of a vintage half a millennium old. I don't feel well. My skin is clammy. I realize with a start in the Mohandas part of my brain that it isn't sweat on my skin; I am producing the seeds of my own destruction. I can see Brainard and the rest of the party ahead of me, brushing through fat lavender sausages that wave in the thick breeze. Above the sea of undulating tubes the top stories of a colony can be seen. We break out of the field onto a broad sort of path that winds toward the structure. There are creatures moving on the path; they don't notice us. I am not surprised.

The sides of the creatures are not beige at all. They are no particular color, but change color all the time like the skin of an octopus. Sometimes sudden changes of overall hue, other times complex patterns scrolling and swirling. We think this is how they communicate with each other. Our recordings of them have revealed structures and repetitions, but of course the code is unbreakable because it's not a code, it's a language. It must be a language. If we can only get them to pay attention to us, perhaps we can begin to understand what they are saying.

We enter the colony through a long circular passage that twists and climbs before opening onto a large area surrounded by flowing structures. Their sense of shape and proportion is exquisite; the lines are clean and elegant. As colorful as their bodies are, their buildings are drab and uniform in shade, the brown of fired pottery, of old iron, of earth.

We set up our light screen. We don't know where their eyes are—if they have eyes—but we can't believe they would display such patterns on their skin without being able to detect them somehow. We set up the screen beside a major traffic artery and hope they will respond.

Brainard is excited, though his voice is hoarse. He has not been feeling well either. We suspect we have picked up something from the biosphere, although we can't see how; our E-suits are in good working order. He directs the assembly with his usual enthusiasm and good humor. We are optimistic we will obtain results from our experiment.

The power packs are ready. We connect the screen and begin to play back the patterns we have recorded on our previous sorties to the surface. No response. We turn the screen to see if it makes any difference; it doesn't. We try different patterns, patterns we recorded in the colony, the very courtyard where we now stand. Still nothing. Brainard, through his unflagging optimism, is showing the effects of the repeated disappointments. We know there is some key we are missing, some overlooked behavior, some ancillary stimulus that tells them to pay attention, but we can't think what it is. We go on and on. We turn the omnicorder on one of the creatures and feed it directly into the screen. The echo is immediate and accurate but still gets no response. It gets dark and we still keep at it, trying different patterns, different lengths, different intensities of light, anything we can think of. We know this will be our last trip to the surface. We are running out of supplies, so we drive ourselves past exhaustion.

In the end, nothing works. Nothing. So far as we know they aren't even aware that they have been visited by beings from another world. The contact that we have looked forward to for so many centuries remains an unfulfilled dream, a frustrated, unrequited overture. We are defeated.

We are out of time, out of supplies, out of energy. We pack our equipment, trudge dispiritedly back to the lander and lift off. It has been an exhilarating time, an amazing success, but ultimately baffling. Home calls to us across the light years, and we know we have a long wait in quarantine when we get there.

I pulled out of the Reality and back into my cabin, logging off for a moment. It was emotionally difficult to even spend time with this information again. It had been so terrifying for everyone when things kept getting worse on Elysium, and when we started to lose people on Paraiso and then Cielo we really didn't know if this might not be the end of humanity, of every terrestrial life form.

We essentially wiped out primitive biospheres on several worlds during the great expansion. Brainard was still the only person to have discovered a truly evolved, integrated ecosystem, but there had been ten or twenty planets where primitive life had existed. Scientists and many other people had howled when those worlds were terraformed, but the corps had grown powerful and the need for wealth and living space was universally accepted. How could you advocate saving a few smears of self-replicating slime if it meant that some people couldn't afford to re-boot? Terraforming was so colossally expensive even when you started with an earth-like planet—and finding earth-like planets was no picnic—that asking them to leave a world alone once they had located it was deemed unreasonable and economically unsound. The corps were given free rein. It was an open question whether anyone could have stopped them anyway.

When the plague had started the collective guilt of our rapaciousness had resounded like the knell of the Grand Inquisitor. Ancient religions that had withered away when re-booting had replaced funerals were revived with the fervor of the condemned. The twilight of the gods had arrived.

And then it didn't spread beyond Cielo. Draco lived up to its name and quarantined the three planets by force, at one point shooting down starships that were attempting to flee the inescapable horror. Nothing that had touched the three doomed planets was allowed to enter any inhabited star system. Almost two billion people were destroyed. Three entire biospheres. Draconian measures, indeed.

There was a hew and cry to raze Brainard's Planet too, but cooler heads prevailed. We still had no idea what the plague was, how it had interacted with us, anything. We needed Brainard's Planet to study, even if we could only look at it from orbit. And ultimately, to my own personal pride in my species, we couldn't bring ourselves to annihilate an entire complex of living beings, even if it meant leaving a horrible danger extant in the universe.

The aftermath of the experience resounded for centuries. I suppose it's still going on. We had seemed invincible. We had conquered space, we had conquered time, we had learned to live forever. We had even learned to conquer ourselves. War and murder and rape had become incomprehensible aberrations fading into the misty past of alchemy and superstition. Why try to terminate a person's perspective when all that happens is they get re-booted and you have to go into the trades to pay for it? How do you rape someone when all the victim has to do is log on? Suddenly you're not raping one person but sixty to eighty billion people and all of them are pretty upset about it. Our very language had changed to fit our new perception of the cosmos and our place in it. We seemed destined to be the perfect reflection of the divine thought, conversant with the face of God.

Then Brainard had discovered his race of city-building walrus-crab-slugs who seemed to talk to each other but didn't even notice us, and something from their planet mowed us down like we would inconvenient bacteria. All we had been able to do was cut and run, leaving our fallen to their horrifying fate.

And I was going to that planet.

CHAPTER 11

W e didn't have much to do until we refueled. Travel within an inhabited system is largely automated. Marcus and Tamika divided the piloting chores, which weren't much. They didn't even have to stand their watches in control if they didn't want to, but usually they did.

I spent the work shifts helping to re-fit the Lightdancer and the evenings doing research on the net. The more I learned about the two expeditions to Brainard's Planet, Brainard's and Steel's, the less sense the whole enterprise made. There was an urgency about it that I didn't understand. Why rush into the most dangerous place in the galaxy? As far as I could tell, there weren't any other corps sniffing around. If Yuri's E-suits were still a secret—and it certainly looked like they were—then no one else would want to go anywhere near Brainard's Planet.

The various housekeeping chores required to prepare the ship for an interstellar hop gave me a chance to get to know the crew better. As I had presumed it would, my singing at Matessa's party had created more questions than it had answered; they were as curious about me as I was about them. They wanted to know what it was like in the old days; I wanted to know—well, I guess I wanted to know what the hell I was doing on this crazy ship and whether or not I was going to live through the voyage.

They were an interesting group, very individualistic, yet highly integrated and, apparently, committed to the project. Marcus was the iron man, quiet, determined, "The Slave of Duty." Archie—more philosophical and dry, did her work bearing a weight that seemed greater than just her failure to save Drake. Yuri was the clown genius, wry and mercurial, manic and creative. Tamika, whom we didn't see as much because she was busy piloting the ship, had a quick, agile mind and an eclectic curiosity. Jemal was an open book, and Alice, more of a closed one.

Then there was the enigma leading us all—tall and beautiful, warm yet unavailable. Or maybe just unattainable.

I could feel the tension of Drake's impending fate weighing on everyone—it weighed on me—but Yuri's fatalistic optimism seemed to keep us moving forward, and when that lagged, Marcus' iron professionalism picked us up by the scruff of the neck. Still, Drake was in his pod, already apart from us, a silent pilgrim awaiting a journey untaken in five centuries.

It was very odd. All we could do was talk about it. We, as a species, had forgotten what it was like to be faced with inescapable fate. Aside from a brutal reminder five centuries ago, we had successfully deleted inescapable fate from the vocabulary of our experience. But the eight of us—cocooned in our tiny technological womb, a microscopic needle driving through the ungraspable distances of Prime's planetary system, distances that were dwarfed to nothing by our coming interstellar voyage—were staring into the eyes of the greatest distance of all. One of our number would be diving into a star soon, to be reduced to plasma, sub-atomic particles, energy. Memories. I don't suppose it had ever been easy, even back when it was accepted as inevitable. Back then it happened to everyone sooner or later. You were always hearing about it happening to someone, sometimes large groups of people. Sometimes someone close to you, sometimes someone hundreds or thousands or, after we settled Mars, even millions of miles away. It was always happening. But these days it didn't happen to *any*one. Only now it was happening to Drake.

It was hardest at mealtimes. When we were working, cleaning, re-fitting, when we had concrete tasks in front of us, we could push Drake into the same corner to which humanity had consigned the entire experience of Brainard's expedition: off, away, not present. When we ate, though, there I was where Drake had been, consuming what he would have consumed, breathing what he would have breathed, and by his absence he returned to us, asking the unaskable. We'd try to answer, but it was difficult. It was a struggle between our need to talk about it and an equally urgent need to avoid talking about it.

"Didn't they used to think," Jemal asked me one evening, "that a person's perspective didn't stop when their body did? That it, you know, went somewhere else? It was still out there, it just wasn't on the net anymore?"

I twirled my pasta around my fork for a while and thought of many things. "Well," I said looking around the room, "they didn't actually 'think' it, not the way we think things now." Steel's eyes were on me, and Archie's. Alice's weren't. "They ... believed it."

"Heaven." Alice didn't look up from her food as she spoke.

"Alice ..." There was a reproving tone in Steel's voice and manner that I didn't understand. Alice looked at her, then back at her meal again.

"What about it?" Jemal asked. When Alice didn't answer he turned back to me. "They don't still think that on Heaven, do they? I've been there. I don't remember any—"

"Not the planet," I said. "Heaven used to be a—kind of mythological place, where people went when, you know, when they weren't alive anymore. Some people believed that, anyway."

"Right, right," Yuri chuckled. "It was kind of like warp drive, or hyper-space, or the fifth dimension."

Marcus shook his head. "You need another hobby, Yuri. Those old movies are rotting your brain."

"Hey," Yuri shot back, "Annette Funicello is my dream woman."

"Who," Marcus looked reluctant to ask, "is Annette Funicello?"

"Don't get him started," Archie said.

He was already started. "Who's Annette Funicello? *Beach Party*, man! *Beach Blanket Bingo! Back To The Beach!* She was Frankie Avalon's chick! Oh, man. Kowabunga!"

"What language is he speaking?" Marcus asked.

Archie shook her head and took another bite. I, for one, was glad we'd wandered onto another subject.

"Frankie was the Big Kahuna," Yuri was informing me now. "They'd break up because he'd go gaga over some other chick, but they'd always get back together again. But, you know?" he leaned in conspiratorially, "They never had sex. Not once. No matter how glad they were to be back together. That's how I know she's secretly in love with me."

"Congratulations," I said.

"And if her perspective is still floating around out there somewhere, all I have to do is rig up a net gate that can bullet her, and there I am!" And there was the subject again, waiting patiently. But we were deft at avoiding it.

"I saw a movie once," Alice said. "I don't see how you can watch them. Everything is reduced down to this little, flat rectangle. When things are outside the movie they just cease to exist. You can't turn your head to look for them or anything. They're just gone until they pop back in again. No wonder people were crazy back then. It's solipsistic."

"That's what made them great!" Yuri would not be swayed. "Where are the artistic limits in a Reality? It's the infinite cage. When you can do anything, what's worth doing?"

"I like Realities," Jemal said. I got the impression that Jemal didn't feel like he had that much to contribute to most of the conversations on board. He tended to be careful and offer only what he felt sure of.

"I called one up last night," Alice said. "It was really good. *Contact Binary*, have you done that one?"

She was looking at me, so I shook my head.

"Bellalinda is in it. She's fantastic. Say, you're an actor. Do you know her?"

"No." I laughed. "I didn't get many chances to make Realities. I was mostly a theater actor."

Her interest slumped. "Oh." She shouldered her disappointment and moved on. "Anyway, I think she's beautiful."

"I suppose everyone does," I said.

"I'd like to look like her someday."

"Why?" was drawn from me without thinking. Alice had her own face, clear blue eyes, an inquisitive nose, a pugnacious set to her jaw, and a full mouth that could be soft enough to sleep on or hard enough to wrest answers from the sphinx.

"Because she's beautiful," she replied, as though I had questioned the most remedially self-evident tautological premise ever uttered.

But you're beautiful, too, I started to say; and then, What is beauty? and a few other worthless homilies before I settled on, "Well, I wouldn't try it if I were you."

"What do you mean?" she asked around a mouthful of salad.

I could see Steel in my peripheral vision, checking me out, watching me like—what? I didn't get it. Like she was waiting to see how I performed. I said, "She'll sue you. All the big Reality stars have their genomes copyrighted now. Don't you remember—" and then I thought, maybe they didn't, "a few centuries back they did this big biographical Reality about, who was it? Estella, or Excella, or something like that."

"The Extasya Story," Yuri filled in.

"Right," I said, "Extasya. It was a really big deal at the time. Extasya was a huge star who'd been making Realities for—I don't know—a couple of centuries, anyway."

"She'd also had sex with all the richest people in Draco," Archie inserted with the mildly judgmental envy of a person who hadn't.

"Who was that actress who played her?" I asked.

"Arcadia," Yuri replied.

"Right," I continued, "There was a huge row between Extasya and the studios about who was going to get to play her. Extasya, the Greatest Star Who Ever Lived."

Marcus said, "I think she wanted to play herself."

"Right," I said, "a lot of people did. Other people thought it was all a big publicity campaign."

"Which it no doubt was," Steel added.

"So what happened?" Alice asked me.

"Well, either Extasya or her publicity people, or both, considered her to be the most beautiful woman in the known universe. They said that anyone else would be a disappointment to her fans. But the studio wanted someone who could bring some objectivity to the part. I think they convinced her that it would be more titillating to the public, more 'real,' if someone else played her. But the studio had to agree that Arcadia would have her genome altered so she would look exactly like Extasya in all the phases of her life."

"And then Arcadia turned out to be twice the actor Extasya had ever dreamed of being," Yuri interjected.

"Right," I answered, "it was all over the net for years, it seemed like. Arcadia won all kinds of awards for her portrayal and she basically went on to eclipse Extasya completely."

"What did Extasya do?" Alice asked.

"Didn't she try to make Arcadia get her genome re-altered?" Archie replied.

"The courts ruled against her," Steel said from the end of the table. "They said that no one could force another person to undergo surgery."

"But, I mean, what did she *do*?" Alice asked again. "Did she keep being a star?"

"Oh," I said.

Yuri looked quizzical. "What *did* she do?" he asked.

Archie said, "I think she made a few more Realities. The scandal gave her quite a bit of pull at the outlets."

"Yeah, that's right," I said. "She played a whole succession of these egomaniacal predatory vamps that everyone loved seeing humiliated in the end."

"Yeah, I think I did some of those." Jemal found another subject he could contribute to. "She sure was sexy."

"But what did she do after that?" Alice asked.

We were stumped. What do you do after you've been the Greatest Star Who Ever Lived only now you're not anymore? Go into retirement? For how many years? How many centuries?

"I haven't heard about her in a long time," Yuri said. "I wonder what she *is* doing."

"Yeah," Jemal agreed.

"That's one thing Drake won't have to worry about." Archie looked at her coffee and we looked at her. There it was again.

"What's that?" Steel asked, gently.

Archie didn't return her gaze. "What to do," she said, "He won't have to worry about what to do anymore."

We were quiet for just a moment. Then Archie obviously regretted bringing us back to the subject and said to Yuri, maybe a little too loud, "Anyway, I thought Dotie Foster was your 'dream woman.' What happened to her?"

"Jodie Foster," Yuri corrected as he got up from the table. "That was before I discovered the 'chick' concept."

The meal was breaking up. We all rose and started rinsing dishes, placing them in the sterilizer. The mundane domesticity was comforting.

"Okay, I'll bite," Archie said, evidently feeling it was her job to lift our spirits again, "what's the 'chick' concept?"

I guess Yuri wanted to lift our spirits, too, because he jumped right back in: "You wouldn't understand it. It's too weird."

"Sure I would," Archie said, making a good effort to sound interested.

"No, no," Yuri responded, "it's cosmically weird. Multi-dimensionally weird. Weird like the mist-being from the Crab Nebula."

"What the hell are you talking about?"

"Sorry. Another movie. Star Trek 12: The Lost Generation."

"What the hell is the 'chick concept,' you freaking skag-head?" Archie turned to me in exasperation. "I don't know why I let him drag me into this stuff."

Yuri laughed. "I'm actually still working on it. I need to do more research."

"You're making this up, aren't you?"

"No, no! It was a real thing. Chicks only existed for maybe fifteen or twenty years around the middle of the twentieth century."

"What was it, some kind of early genetics experiment?"

"Not genetics. Social Dynamics. Most chicks were named Connie. Connie Francis, Connie Stevens. I think there were some Darlenes, too, and, of course, my dream woman, Annette."

Alice looked at me, "He's gonna drag this out forever."

"That's the thing with Yuri," Marcus put in, "If you let him go on long enough, he'll tell you something so utterly esoteric that it will be completely unintelligible."

"Hey," Yuri leapt to his own defense, "I told you it was going to be weird."

"Could you just boil it down to the basics?" Archie asked. "I'd like to get to bed before the universe degenerates into uniform entropy."

"Okay, okay." Yuri grinned like a coyote. "It's really kind of interesting."

"But weird," Archie added.

"Very," Yuri agreed. "Like I said, I'm still doing research, but it seems to be based on—" he looked around to see if we were hooked; we were, "it seems to be based on not having sex, but wanting to really, really badly."

There was a pause while everyone looked at him like he was the mist-being from the Crab Nebula. Well, almost everyone. Alice didn't seem all that interested, which I thought was strange, and of course *I* saw what he was driving at, but then, I'm older than most manufactured biospheres. Archie shook her head and said,

"I'm going to bed. Anyone want to come with me?"

"Sure," Jemal said.

Archie put her arm around Jemal's waist and gave him a squeeze. "That's what I like about you, Jemal. You don't talk. You're just a pretty face."

Jemal laughed and squeezed her back. They went off down the passageway together.

We made the re-fueling station on the fourth day, my 'days' being earth-standard again. It had been a long time since I'd worked with a twenty-four hour day, but Steel's med software had a very nice circadian adjustment program in it; I didn't have any trouble.

Galactic Positron had built the station only fifty-million klicks out from Prime so they'd have lots of solar energy to run the colliders. It extended in an arc three-hundred-thousand klicks long. A baby. I hear the one around the Sun now goes literally *around* the Sun, but that's down in the heart of civilization. They need a lot more fuel. Fifty-million klicks is nice and cozy when you're talking about stars: closer than Mercury is to the Sun; we had to retract the habitation module. Anti-matter is relatively dangerous stuff, so core exchanges are fully automated. It went without a hitch. It did mean being weightless for about twelve hours, though, which gave Archie a chance to worry about Drake for a while.

My stress level started rising in earnest after we'd re-fueled. I knew that I only had seven days or so, ship's time, to make up my mind about the operation. Three and a half days to accelerate, three and a half more to slow back down. Freewheeling time didn't count; for one thing, it wasn't 'time' at all. For another, I'd be busy.

So seven days. Then we'd be on Earth and either Steel would have a new member of an expedition to the most terrifying place humanity had ever known, or she'd have a great big security problem. And I wasn't sure how she'd handle the second option.

After we got our new anti-matter core we swung north of the ecliptic to tack around Prime itself, using her gravity to get us pointed toward Altair, with the Sun between us and it and the center of the galaxy beyond. In the opposite direction, almost nine hundred light years away, Brainard's Planet awaited my decision.

But before we could boost for earth we had to discharge our sad cargo. It wasn't a problem with traffic control. Starships usually drop their waste before they boost. Traffic control didn't know that our waste had once been part of the net—that we had to leave Drake to the fierce mercy of Prime in order to get through Earth Customs. They didn't know that we were going to experience the permanent loss of an irreplaceable human perspective, a perspective that, under other circumstances, might have traveled the breadth of the galaxy, visited other galaxies, experienced the end of time. They didn't know we were about to commit the first murder in over a millennium.

We weren't equipped for it. I mean, we had the hardware to do the job; it was a simple mag-rail launch of Drake's pod. What we didn't have was a common experience to call on, a ritual, a mode of being. I was the only one there who had ever lost anyone close, and that had been centuries and centuries ago. We all gathered in the launch bay, almost by instinct, or maybe curiosity, or perhaps a primal need for physical proximity to a willed act of diminution of the tribe. We couldn't see Drake. His pod was once again swathed in the thermal covering that had protected it on Vesper, the idea being that once the temperature rose high enough to burn through the blanket, Drake and the pod would flash into plasma almost instantly. It seemed the best way.

The launch bay wasn't small, but we all seemed to crowd together anyway. Steel was at the launch panel and would be the one to actually execute the maneuver. Archie was checking read-outs on a hand-held display. The rest of us stood mutely, wondering what we were observing.

"He's asleep?" Steel asked Archie.

"Unconscious," Archie replied. "He won't feel anything."

Steel took a deep breath. We were all watching her, but she was staring at Drake's pod, perhaps taking one last chance to will him back to health. She touched a green light on the panel and it turned red as the inner hatch opened to the mag-rail. Drake lowered gently into the rail tube and rested there for a moment before the hatch closed and the light on the panel turned back to green. We looked for something to say. Steel touched an amber light and we could hear the compressor evacuating the tube; the light turned to green when the compressor stopped. Another green light turned red as Steel opened the outer hatch. Although we couldn't see it, we knew the end of Drake's pod was now bathed in the blinding glare of Prime's unfiltered light. It made him seem farther from us. Did it make him seem closer to the cosmos? I don't know.

Steel's finger hovered over the launch initiator. She spoke, and her voice was as clear and beautiful as I had ever heard it: "Let the ship's log show that on July thirty-first, in the year thirty-nine hundred ninety-seven, at twenty-two-oh-one Greenwich Mean Time, corrected, ship's exobiologist Drake was placed in the launch tube of the starship Lightdancer—" her voice faltered for just a moment, "—and launched into space." She touched the initiator and we felt a muted thump. The mag-rail kicked Drake into free orbit, an orbit that would end at Prime's surface, only he would never make it that far. "He was eight-hundred seventy-one years old."

What else was there to say? We stared at the tube hatch, or maybe the bulkhead or the bottom of our souls. We searched but found nothing. Steel turned to me and said, "Mohandas, I'd like to see you in my quarters," and she strode out of the bay. I looked around at everyone else, but they offered no answers, so I followed Steel down the passageway.

"Tell me about your wife," she said to me, her features shadowed. Light from another room, her galley, maybe, spilled through an archway behind her, filtering through colored glass sculptures that floated on shelves. Pools of color caressed her fur. She sat with her knees and ankles together, her elbows on her thighs, her chin pressed into her fists. Her eyes weren't on me. They were still looking at Drake.

"What do you want to know?" I asked, thinking: 'How is this going to cleanse your hands?'

"Everything," she replied, sitting very still. Then she returned to herself, made herself relax a little, not much. "How you met, how you—Where did you get married?" Her eyes sought mine and I knew what she really wanted to ask, but I answered what she had asked.

"Syrtis. On Mars."

"Was it in a church?" The word sounded strange coming from her lips. Another ancient word.

"A Hindu temple. My father ..."

"Yes. You had a father." She looked back at Drake.

"Yes." I wanted to help her. As angry as I was with her, I wanted to love her, to heal her. To own her.

"Were there a lot of people there?" She had started to rock gently. She was hugging her knees now.

"A lot of people. Both our—our families," another ancient word, "our friends. Their families. Their friends." I watched the loneliest woman I had ever seen. "No one could believe we were actually going through with it. I guess our fights were pretty legendary."

"What did you fight about?"

"Our work. How my work interfered with hers, actually. She was usually right."

She rocked.

"Did you like to fight?" she asked, her voice getting smaller.

"Yes, I suppose we did." I wanted to sit next to her, but I didn't know if I was supposed to. "I guess we liked to do everything, as long as it was us doing it."

"Where did you go after—you know, for your—what did they call it?"

"Our honeymoon?"

"Yes." She had hugged her legs into her chest. Her chin was on her knees.

I sat across from her so I could look into her eyes. I perched on the edge of the seat so I could be closer to her. I rested my elbows on my knees, with my hands out in case she wanted to hold them. "We went to one of the shepherd moons. I forget which one."

"Around Saturn?" Pools of tears trembled in her eyes.

"Yes. The one they made the resort out of. Have you been there?"

"No."

"They kicked its orbit about five degrees out of the plane of the rings. You swing above the rings for half an orbit, then down through them and you're underneath for the other half. It's very beautiful."

She kept looking at Drake. And rocking. Rocking. "Was *she* beautiful?"

I took a chance and put my hand under her chin. I brought her head up so she was looking at me. "As beautiful as you are," I said.

"Captain?" Marcus' voice came over the intercom.

"Yes?" Steel replied.

"The pod is gone. We tracked it until it vaporized. It was a good burn. You told me to let you know."

"Yes," she said. "Thank you." She looked at me again. Her chin started to tremble and the tears spilled over her eyelashes and ran down her cheeks. I put my hand on her shoulder and she fell apart into wracking, convulsing sobs. Standing, I swept her into my arms and crushed her to my chest. She hugged my neck and buried her face in the pit of my shoulder while she cried and cried and cried until the universe refused to end and she was still there, holding me, being held by me, living in the present.

After some time her breathing steadied but she kept her face buried in my shoulder. A little later she got braver and looked up at me. She said, "I must look awful."

"No, no," I replied, "you look great with snot running down your face. Most people couldn't pull it off, but you really do."

She giggled, which, owing to the viscous condition of her nasal passages at the time, turned into kind of a snort, which made her laugh, which made her start to cry again. I stood there rocking her gently back and forth for a time—a long time, maybe.

A while later she said, "I must be getting heavy."

"No, not really. Well, maybe. Yeah, I guess you are."

She laughed again. "You can put me down if you want." She continued to hug my neck.

"Where?" I asked, and kept rocking her for a while.

Then she said, "My bed's in there."

I looked where she nodded. She still couldn't let go of me long enough to point. I walked through the archway, and the lights came up softly as we entered the room. I started to put her down on the bed.

"Don't let go of me," she said.

"All right." I lay down beside her, my arms still enclosing her, her knees curled up and her head on my chest.

"I need to blow my nose."

I looked around.

"There are tissues over there." She nodded again.

I saw them beside the bed and handed her one. She blew and said, "More." I handed her a few. She blew again, wiped her eyes and her face, and curled up against me, maybe tighter than before.

We lay a long time like that. She would occasionally shudder, and sometimes she would cry some more, then she would be still. A long time later she asked me, "How long were you married?"

I knew what she was leading up to, and I wasn't sure I wanted to go there, but I said, softly, "A long time." I breathed. "Over three hundred years."

We both breathed for a while.

"Were you happy together?"

"Yes," I said, hoping I was telling the truth, and, upon reflection, knowing that I was.

Then: "You have a strong heart."

"What?" I lifted my head.

"I can hear it beating." And then she started to cry again, but not for as long this time.

Then, a little later, she said, "How did she—How did—" We had reached where she needed to be, and, I guess, where I needed to be, too. But I checked anyway:

"On Valhala?" And she nodded. So I looked in my heart for where I kept that story and wondered if I could take it out. I started, because I needed to, but I didn't know how far I would get.

"We'd always re-booted together. Just ... to make sure that, that nothing happened, you know, to separate us."

"What if one of you got sick?"

"We were pretty lucky. Both of us had been born and raised on Mars"—and I thought, what an odd phrase, 'born and raised'—"so we missed out on a lot of the stuff that was going around Earth at the time. Even back then the net kept you pretty healthy. We never were involved in any life-threatening accidents. I suppose we should have been—the line of work we were in."

I was quiet for a while, and Steel was content to wait. Then: "It was a big deal, getting to go out to Barnard's Star back then. Any of the early projects. We were going to save the world, and I guess we did. Nobody knew if the projects were going to pay off. They were so incredibly expensive. I guess they completely re-defined the term, 'risk capital.' " I could feel my heart tightening as I got closer. "Of course, all the corps were risking *was* capital. We were the ones taking the real risks."

"What happened ... to your wife?" I could tell she didn't want to make me go there if I didn't want to, but she needed me to. And I think she could tell that I needed to as well.

I breathed deeply and tried to balance myself. "She just ... got old and faded away. Congestive heart failure complicated by pneumonia. But it could have been anything. She just got old."

"Why?"

I breathed again, but the anger was dagger sharp and bright as the taste of blood. I had refreshed it each time I had re-booted since then. "It was kind of a test case," I said. "The corps got cold feet when the project fell behind schedule so they ... pulled out."

"Out of what?"

"Out of Valhala. Out of the entire Barnard's Star system. They just cut us off. They got scared that the Valhala project wasn't going to show a profit so they cut and run."

"So you lost your jobs?"

I allowed myself a sardonic smile. "We lost much more than that. We'd all put our fortunes into the Valhala Corporation. There wasn't any use for money on Valhala. There wasn't anything to spend it on, just us, so the corp set up a fund for us back in the System. When they declared bankruptcy, the fund was frozen."

When I didn't continue she prompted me: "Well, you said there was nothing to spend money on—"

She felt me tense up. Maybe I hugged her a little harder, I don't know. I tried not to squeeze the life out of her; it was not her I wanted to hurt. "It takes money to re-boot," I said, in as calm a voice as I could muster.

"Oh," she said, very small. Then, "Yes."

We lay there for a while.

"But you had already 'booted?" she asked.

"Yes," and for some reason my heart calmed again, as though the admission brought me back into balance with the cosmos. But I hadn't really admitted anything yet. I lay there in that moment of calm, knowing her next question was coming, but, somehow thinking that it never would, that I would be permitted to rest there forever in the present, the future and the past merely ghosts held at bay by their equilibrium. But she did ask.

"Why?" And I stared at the overhead of her bedchamber. On a starship driving around a sun three hundred and fifty light years from my home world and hers, a sun she had turned into a funeral pyre. How much did I want to help her? How much was I willing to expose to her to soothe her grief, to show her she was not alone in the universe with her unbearable act? But it was my aloneness, not hers, that drove me. Perhaps I had finally found someone who had committed a crime great enough to enfold mine. Perhaps the shock of watching Drake's termination had jarred me to a place where I *could* speak. Perhaps, after so many centuries, I simply needed to speak. In any case, I found myself discarding the various excuses and half-truths I had nurtured for so long. I shed them as a ceremonial robe before bathing in my own cleansing fire. And I told her.

"She had been in Neue Bayern, on the other side of the planet, working on the montane forests, and I had been building the habitat at First Landing. We'd only been able to see each other once every two or three months for the past several years. We got together on the net, of course, but, you know, it's not really the same."

She listened.

"And there was a ... woman working for me. She was out of sync with me. She'd just re-booted before joining the building project and it had been, oh, sixty years or so for my wife and me. It's funny, I suppose."

"What?"

"She'd only had one 'boot and I was about ready for my fifth, I must have been three centuries older than she was, but the only difference that seemed to matter was our *apparent* ages. She looked young and I looked old."

"You were attracted to her?"

And having tasted honesty, I seemed to crave it, so I said, "Yes." But I couldn't push myself any further. I needed help. Steel gave it:

"You re-booted to be attractive to her?"

And I said, "Yes," again. It was either harder or easier the second time. It wasn't the same.

"And the corp pulled out before your wife could re-boot?"

And that was the most expensive "Yes." of all.

"Was that what started the uprising?"

I lunged at the anger of politics to escape the baffling labyrinth of my culpability and loss. "No," I said, "the uprising had already started. It was the uprising that had put us behind schedule. I didn't join the uprising until I had my own personal vendetta to goad me." I didn't know who I was angry at.

"What started it?" I think Steel was helping me then as I had helped her. She could see how I used the anger to cauterize the wound and she offered me access to it.

"The newbies ... The corps—" I started again: "In order to get the idea of manufacturing human laborers past all the people they had to get it past, the corps promised to re-boot all the newbies for free at the end of their first life and let them do whatever they wanted with their second."

"Yes?"

"But, of course, what could they do? Where were they? On a raw planet over five light years from civilization. They could either keep working for the corps or take their chances in the desert. And there were no chances in the desert."

"So they had to keep working—"

"Yes, only the corps had a plan."

"You knew about the plan?"

And that was an expensive "Yes," too.

"What was it?"

"They encouraged the newbies to reproduce. They figured it would be cheaper than re-booting them. Only the newbies didn't know it was an either/or situation. They figured since they'd worked for the corps their first life and gotten re-booted at the end of it that was just the way it worked: work for the corps, get re-booted." I reflected that a lot of us had thought a lot of things back then that had turned out not to be true. "Then, during a childbirth, one of the women started to hemorrhage. She didn't make it. There was nothing in the budget to cover 'booting her. So, she just ..."

I thought about that funeral. On the edge of the desert. Her mate hadn't worked on the habitat project so I hadn't had to deal with him directly, but everyone had questions. Why hadn't she been saved? It was part of my job not to answer. Just don't tell them anything, they'd said. Leave it to management. They'll deal with any unrest.

"Of course," I continued, "she wasn't the last. In any big project there are bound to be accidents." I remembered one in particular. A young man had gotten in the way of a structural member and had his leg amputated. He had bled to death while I watched. "Once the corps were assured of a new generation of labor they stopped fixing the old one. Two or three, here or there, the newbies could be placated. Each manager they went to for answers told them something different from the one before. But eventually the numbers got too great to explain away. The stories got too thin."

"And you joined it after ..."

"Yes."

We lay there for a long time, holding each other, until Marcus' voice came over the intercom again:

"Captain?"

"Yes."

"We're ready to maneuver for Earth."

"I'll be right there."

We headed for control.

CHAPTER 12

I don't think I was ever so glad to leave a beautiful woman's bedroom in my life. I think she felt a little better. I don't know if *I* did. I don't know.

It felt great to get back into the control room of a starship, though. I really needed the feeling of walking into the nerve center again—the rest of the crew in their places, the ship already moving several hundred thousand klicks per hour relative to the star we were about to leave. I felt, rather than heard, the slow throb of the impellers. They're never precisely in phase. Their resonance created a sub-sonic swell like the breathing of a sleeping god.

"You're number four," Steel said to me and headed for the Captain's interface. Back to business. If we'd bared our souls to each other for the last couple of hours no one would have known it. I climbed into the recliner she had gestured to between Yuri and Jemal. As I logged on, the navigational matrix flooded my vision, digital updates flickering and scrolling. I synched in with the rest of the crew, and the black glass instrument panels of the control room faded to a dim ghost as the graphic built to solidity.

Steel's system was nice. Little features like the fact that everyone's digital voice was nearly identical to their acoustic ones let you concentrate on the task at hand without any distractions. Marcus was bulleting traffic control:

[1\TC>F.S.LIGHTDANCERREQUESTINGTRAFFICUPDATE
<1/TC]
[TC\LD1>YOURECLEARFORPRE-
FILEDJUMPPRIMESOLDIRECT<TC/LD1]

Once they'd learned how to laze neutron streams, anti-matter torches had jumped in efficiency, but it meant exhaust plumes maintained their integrity for a couple million kilometers before things like solar wind started to dissipate them. We needed to make sure no one was behind us for a long, *long* way.

Four-dimensional gravity-well graphics undulated in cool green grids across the-star dusted space behind my eyes. Every star was preceded by a vivid blue directional vector, the speed of the stellar motion indicated by the length of the arrow. Steel logged on:

[*\1>CONFIGURESHIPFORJUMP<*/1]
[1*>CONFIGURESHIPFORJUMPAYE<1/*]

Marcus' reply was calm. There was a muted clang followed by the sound of huge machinery. It took about five minutes for the torch to fully extend and lock into place.

[*\1234567>FINALNAV<*/1234567]

Steel directed the unitary mind that we seven crew members had become to crunch the numbers on the final course corrections. We dipped into the net and resonated with 40 or 50 billion sleeping brains scattered all through Draco, the Pleiades, and the outer arm, each one a unique point of perspective on the whole of human-occupied space. The sun was three hundred fifty-two light years away and moving about ten klicks per second relative to Prime. Every ten-billionth of a nanometer we got closer to being pointed at exactly where it would be in a week would save us a significant amount of anti-matter. Prices being what they were, it was worth doing the math. Steel must have liked what she saw:

[*\1234567>ENABLE<*/1234567]

There was a short hesitation as we waited for all the zeroes to line up. Then we felt the tiniest blip in gravity as the impellers were shut down, the torch was lit and a standard gee was filtered out from its crushing thrust.

I was headed for home, moving almost a thousand meters per second faster with every passing second.

[*\1>I'LLTAKEFIRSTWATCH<*/1]

Steel's digital voice was nested in a steady stream of evolving Nav graphics.

[1*>AYECAPTAIN<1/*]
[1\34>YURIMOYOUVEGOTTHESHIP<1/34]
[1\2567> THERESTOFYOULOGOFF<1/2567]

A chorus of 'Ayes' and five concentric ripples in the data flow as the rest of crew broke contact.

I was grateful to get the first watch. I could feel the texture of the net already massaging my re-opened wounds. While navigating it's almost impossible to nurse a grudge, carry a torch, or think about what you should have said. You're experiencing a large portion of the galaxy from billions of points of view simultaneously; ego is mathematically incompatible. Prime was behind my eyes and Sol was in my heart. The outer arm extended to my finger tips and the core of the galaxy was at my feet. Every nerve-ending was a star. Nebulae drifted through my muscles. We flew and my sternum throbbed with our growing velocity.

[3\4>SOMERIDEEHMO?<3/4]

I felt Yuri flip through me. No matter how many times you crew—and I'd been on more jumps than I could remember—the metabolic acceleration of synching in with the Nav net, of becoming the cosmos through which you're traveling, is impossible to ignore. It's like going to sleep in prison and waking up on top of Olympus Mons with the ability to fly. Enthusiasm bubbles up in you and floods you like the warmth of hot soup on a cold day.

[4\3>KOWABUNGA!<4/3]

I replied as I barrel-rolled around him.

[*\3 4>HEYBOYSLETSSEQUENCE<*/3 4]

Steel's digital voice sliced through my heart effortlessly and she was Cat-eyes again: mysterious and playful, available and unattainable, honey over brass.

Sequencing is simply the process of checking your connections with each individual piece of the net. It's accomplished by actually slowing down your normal access rate. The illusion of four-dimensionality on the Nav net is produced by accessing each perspective for a single time quantum; this allowed us to seem to be looking at everything from all angles at once. When sequencing, that's slowed down to about one per nanosecond, or a billion contacts per second, which gives time to get feedback and status on each one while still running through the entire net in about a minute. But the perceived effect is pretty mind-altering. I forget how long they finally decided a time quantum was— they keep refining their figures—but I know that at normal access rates we're zipping through the net several million times a second, tagging each perspective. This provides us with a smooth, four-dimensional experience of the ship's relationship to the galaxy. Spending a nanosecond with each contact, though, is slow enough to make our relationship to the data temporal again—that is, it actually takes time—so that the experience of the data itself is simply spatial, or three-dimensional.

So we spend a little time with everybody. If there are half a billion contacts on a planet, half a billion people sleeping, we spend half a second zipping around that planet. We scream around the known galaxy in a roughly widening spiral starting from where we are out to the contacts that are farthest away—in our case out in the outer arm—in under a minute. Don't get me wrong, going four-dimensional is a rush. It's so unimaginable that I can't even really remember what it's like after I've logged off. Maybe that's why sequencing is so intense. It better resembles normal experience, in that you're moving in time through a familiar spatial environment. You're just doing it so *fast*. The ultimate roller coaster.

This is what makes crewmen so boring at parties. If you make the mistake of asking them about crewing, they just get cranked up, talking with more and more enthusiasm and making less and less sense.

[*\34>SYNCHANDMELD<*/34]

Our digital representations floated together, head to head, or rather, brain stem to brain stem, forming the corner of a cube, each of us at right angles to the other two, defining the three spatial dimensions. We then spread our arms into six more, scissored our legs into six more, twisted our hands and feet and spread our fingers and toes into sixty more for a total of seventy-five. This was a good, high level of dimensionality. The higher you're synched in the more accurate your maneuvering is. It was good to know, whatever other misgivings I had, that Steel had a well-trained crew.

However, we needed a prime number, and seventy-five isn't one, so with Yuri's and my male projections and Steel's ample, twin female projections, we snared four more for a total of seventy-nine. It's always good to get sexual tension into the calculations anyway. There's nothing more focusing than the basic creative force. As violet energy streams coalesced into writhing ropes emanating from our virtual extremities, we pulled them back to our sides and melded into one body—female and male, void and presence, yin and yang.

[3*4>TAKEMEHOME!<4*3]

It was getting hard to tell who was talking and who was listening as our brain functions meshed at deeper and deeper levels, but I thought I recognized Yuri's style. Or maybe it was mine.

[*34>SEQUENCE<43*]

And BAM! we were off—zipping around Vesper. I saw Kindu for 200 billionths of a second, Spam-town for 20,000. I think I picked up Sheila but I couldn't be sure. A nanosecond is so short even on the Nav net. And JumboNewArielFaraway HeavenCelesteCirceShangri-LaUltimaThuleMondoverdiNirvanaParadise ElysiumScarpusValhala and on and on and on, streams of individuals in millions and billions in villages and towns and cities and continents and planets and planets and planets. Down through the system and out to the Pleiades and out to the outer arm and out and out.

And back.

[*34>SEQUENCECHECKED<43*]

Honeybrasssteel.

[4*3>47,981,768,332CONTACTS!ANiceROUND
NUMBER<3*4]

That had to be Yuri.

[*34>NAVCHECK<43*]

And we crunched numbers again. We danced with the developing Nav
graphics. Cool green gravitons caressed us like silk stockings. We flew through
the cosmos and traveled within ourselves. At the end of the first watch we were
cooking along at almost 30,000 klicks per second.

"Perspective!" Yuri gesticulated. "Perspective, perspective, perspective!"

Steel and I nodded in agreement. We were back in the common room, the
ship now being flown by Marcus, Jemal and Alice. It's always like that after the
first watch. Your mind is so jazzed by the experience you've just been through
that you have to get together and debrief.

"This is why we have to keep expanding." Yuri's eyes shone with the conviction
of the true believer. "Push farther out into the galaxy. Beyond the galaxy."

"Absolutely," Steel agreed.

"The imperative is placed on us by our ability to perceive."

"If we have a purpose in the universe it is to hold it within ourselves and
cherish it."

"Embrace it," Yuri added.

I jumped in. "The cosmos was obviously lonely or we wouldn't be here." I was
just as fervent as they were. How many times had conversations like this taken
place? And yet this one was as vital as any of the others I'd had. I rubbed my eyes.
"It was so clear this time. What's our maximum parallax these days? I swear I
could see the big bang."

Yuri shook his head, "They've opened a project out beyond New Moorea in
the outer arm. We must be looking at close to ten thousand now."

"Ten thousand light years," Steel mused. "Can you imagine ...?"

"What?" I asked.

"What it was like, you know, back ... It must have been like being blind."

"Oh, you mean back ..."

"Back in the old days," Yuri finished for me. "Back when there was just the

System."

Yuri and Steel laughed at the improbability of an age so dark. Then they simultaneously remembered that I had been there. They looked at me like they'd just unearthed me at an archaeological dig.

"Well, it wasn't—" I started, then: "At the time we thought we were cutting edge. We *were* cutting edge. We were pretty proud of terra-forming Mars, of having mapped and modeled the human brain."

"You were alive when they did that?" Yuri asked.

"I'm not quite *that* old. That was back in the early twenties. I think the Farrell Group finished their work in the twenty-second century. Maybe even the twenty-first. I forget."

"Wow," Steel shook her head. "It's hard to even conceive."

"How did people talk?" Yuri asked. "How did they think?"

'How do they think now?' I wondered. But I said, "It was really Wickes' work on dream states that made the big change."

"Wickes?" Steel puzzled, "I don't think I've heard of him."

"Me neither," Said Yuri. But he knew who Annette Funicello was. Were we getting wiser or just more bizarre?

"Her," I said, "She was the person who finally analyzed and codified pan-dimensional mental activity. You know, prescience and telepathy."

"You talking about Wickes?" Archie sauntered into the room, her hips gently swaying. In our heightened, post-Nav state, the three of us locked onto their warm, galactic curves as though her uterus was the source of all matter and energy. "Whoa! Settle down, folks. I just bonked Marcus' brains out before he went on watch. I'm resting." She sat down at the table. "Now what were we talking about?"

With some effort I pulled my eyes back up to hers. "Uh, right. I was just saying that it was her work that made the net possible."

"I suppose so," she replied, "although you certainly couldn't have had it without bio-chips. And Wickes could never have understood pan-dimensional thought processes without the Farrell Group's working model."

"Yeah," said Yuri, "we were talking about them, too."

"But without Wickes' discoveries the net would have been limited to speed-of-light information transfer," I cut in. "We never would have been able to converse between Mars and Earth, never mind between star systems. Never mind freewheeling."

"I guess I never thought about it," Steel said. "I get so used to something being there that I don't question it." She laughed. "I just complain when it's not up to specs."

"What did she do?" Yuri asked.

"Well, she studied dreaming—"

I cut Archie off, "But what she really did was to figure out *why* people went pan-dimensional."

Steel: "How so?"

Archie: "Well, there'd always been lots of anecdotal evidence of prescient visions and dreams—"

Me: "But no one could ever make it happen with any consistency in a laboratory."

Archie: "Same with telepathy. They did all kinds of experiments with, I don't know, with decks of cards. With all kinds of things."

Me: "Right. To see if someone could visualize what someone else was looking at."

Yuri: "What the hell were they trying to prove with that?"

Archie: "Who knows."

Me: "The really brilliant question Wickes formulated was: what *don't* people have telepathic and prescient experiences about?"

Steel: "What do you mean?"

Archie: "Well, the early research into this stuff was kind of scattered. They didn't know what they were looking for. They were just acting on stories about how this or that person had had an experience. So they were trying to duplicate it in a laboratory."

Me: "Right. But Wickes was the first to realize that people always had visions about *people*, or things that were going to happen to people."

Archie: "And usually about people who were important to the person who had the vision."

Me: "Right. Nobody ever woke up in a cold sweat with the utter certainty that something was going to happen that wouldn't affect anyone."

Archie: "Right. And if somebody had a feeling that someone was in trouble, it was almost always someone that the person cared deeply about."

Me: "Someone they felt close to."

Yuri hopped back in, "You see? Perspective! Just what I was saying. What is close to us looks important. What's important to us looks close."

Steel smiled and rubbed Yuri's shoulder. "You're three steps ahead of me, Yuri, as usual. I still don't see how this got us to the net."

"It goes all the way back to Bertrand Russell. Leonardo da Vinci! Plato! Lao-tse!" Yuri's eyes were shining again.

"Okay," Steel said, still rubbing his shoulders. "We'll get to them in a minute. Let's finish up with this Wickes person, first." She turned back to me.

"What Yuri's talking about, I think ..." I looked at him.

"Speak on, o Big Kahuna," he said, smiling.

"... is the difference between our perception of a thing and the thing itself."

"And which is more *real*," Yuri laughed.

"Or which can be demonstrated to be real," Archie put in more sedately.

Steel said, "I'm going to take a wild guess here and say the object itself. Right?"

"Not according to Bertrand Russell." Yuri was the Cheshire cat.

Steel laughed, "Okay, okay. Back to Wickes—"

"Wickes decided that the reason telepathy research never got anywhere was that they were looking for the wrong thing," Archie stated.

"Right," I said. "That it didn't have to do with 'reading' another person's mind, or picking up their 'vibrations' or anything like that. It concerned the nature of what she called a 'perceptual node'—"

Archie: "Meaning any sentient being."

"—and its relationship to what it perceived. She postulated that, like Einstein's description of gravity, space and time curved through yet another dimension. The dimension of perception."

"But there are lots of perceptual dimensions," Steel said.

Yuri: "One for each perceptual node."

Steel: "Right."

Me and Archie: "Exactly."

Archie continued, "She said that, like Einstein's two dimensional model: you know, where all the stars and planets are like steel balls sitting on a stretched rubber membrane, causing little dimples that stretch it into a third dimension?"

Steel: "Right."

Archie: "Well, Wickes made a model where the dimples weren't made by an object's mass, but by its importance to the observer. So that even a star as large as Betelgeuse would make only the tiniest dent to someone on Earth, even if they could look up in the sky and see it directly. Whereas their best friend or a close relation would make a huge impression, even if that person was on the other side of the planet."

"Or on a different planet," I added.

"She modeled this membrane as a sphere—"

"With the observer in the middle."

"Right. And everything that was or had been perceived was out on the surface of the sphere. The more experience and value that surrounded any particular object, the heavier it became, the greater the impression it made on the surface of the sphere and the closer it dropped into the middle of the sphere where the observer was."

"So physical distance didn't matter—" Steel started.

"In the perceptual dimension it didn't even exist," Archie answered. "Time didn't exist. All that existed was the perceptual relationship between the observer and the perceived."

"Well, this sure starts to sound like what we do on the net." Steel's eyes kept flicking back and forth from Archie's to mine. Yuri was grinning like a tiger and kicking his legs under the table.

"With this model she could go back to the people who claimed to have had these experiences and try to formulate them mathematically. Then she programmed them into the Farrell Group's virtual brain and sat back to see what would happen."

"And it dreamt," Yuri said.

Archie nodded.

"Wow," said Steel, "that must have been something."

"Well," I turned to her, "it turned ego-centrism into something that could be used, instead of just a fact of human existence."

Yuri got up and poured himself a cup of coffee. "And when you hook up billions of these perceptual nodes on the net—bingo!—perspective vanishes."

Archie nodded, "The point of view ceases to be a point."

"That was the thing." I was getting cranked again. "When Wickes' discoveries were applied to the net time and distance could be bypassed. If you tapped into minds that were in the pan-dimensional dream state you could communicate instantaneously."

Steel shook her head, "And that eventually led to freewheeling. Hmm." She got up and started cooking. That's the second thing that hits you after a watch—hunger. But you have to kind of re-enter the material plane first.

"Time dilation!" Yuri had put his coffee aside and was pulling things out of the pantry. "Perceptual nodes approaching the speed of light. Other perceptual nodes moving at planetary speeds. Dissonant frames of reference! Temporal perspective vanishes. No time, no space, no relevance—Wango! Off you go into the wild atemporal yonder."

Tamika wandered in and joined the fracas. I hadn't spent much time with her to that point, but she was nice—high energy. Kind of a female Yuri. She looked at him as she walked in and said, "It sounds like *someone* is still violating causality."

Yuri's reply was concise, if somewhat inelegant. "Bite me," he said. "If you bite me, I will be bitten. If I am bitten, I will bite you back. If I bite you back, we will have sex. If we have sex, we will go to sleep. Cause and effect." He stuffed a lettuce leaf into his mouth.

"Mo?" Steel asked me, "Do you know when they first noticed the effect of time dilation on the net? You must have been around th—Oh, I'm sorry."

"That's all right," I replied, "I'm getting used to it. Again."

"You're just such a treasure trove of experience."

"Walking history book, that's me." My voice was not utterly free of ironic inflection.

"It was the first interstellar flights, wasn't it?" Tamika sat down across from me.

I nodded. "They expected it to have an effect. They didn't think it would provide anything beneficial." A bowl of Yuri's special salad appeared before me. I gave it the attention it deserved. "I mean, Yuri's right—"

"Kowabunga!" he set out glasses and started pouring the wine.

"—in that it really was just a matter of perspective, or the triumph over perspective." That sounded pompous to me even as I said it. Oh, well. More salad.

"Leonardo da Vinci!" Yuri helped himself to the piece of art Steel had produced and passed the bowl. "He knew that if you wanted to make a two-dimensional painting look like a three-dimensional perception of the world, you had to lie about size relationships. You had to deliberately and systematically distort the truth. Seeing isn't believing."

"The same turned out to be true for time," I said between mouthfuls. "It was just a lot harder for us to understand that because, whereas spatially every person had their own unique point of view—"

Yuri: "Everyone sees their own rainbow."

"—everyone was at the exact same point in the time continuum. Our view of time was just as distorted as our view of space, but every individual's perspective on time was identical."

Yuri: "Temping isn't believing, either."

Archie: "Until people started to experience time dilation."

Me: "Right."

Tamika: "That must have turned people's minds completely inside out, the first time it happened."

Me: "The thing that surprised us was that we didn't fall out of contact. The contact just got really strange."

Steel: "I'll bet."

Tamika: "How did people react to the experience?"

The others turned to me as well. It made sense, I guess. This was probably the juiciest gossip they'd heard in centuries—how the human race lost its virginity. They wanted all the details.

I thought for a moment. "We didn't know what to think, at first. We couldn't figure out what we were looking at."

"Kow - a - bunga!" Yuri was kicking his legs again.

I laughed, "Yeah. It was ..." I searched for an image and suddenly tears came to my eyes. "It was like losing your family."

They got very quiet. Intense. Focused.

"You know?" Maybe they didn't know. "Everything came unhitched. Nothing was perceivable. Our minds were so geared to being temporal ... sequential. I guess it must have been like before a baby learns to see. Lots of input— overwhelming amounts of input—but no way to make sense of it."

Tamika said, "I'm sorry, I don't know what that word means."

"What word?" I asked.

She tried to get her mouth around it, "B—bebby?"

"Oh," I said, "its like a newbie."

"Oh, okay. I'm with you."

I thought some more. "It was just—we didn't have—I mean, *now*, we have a whole rational, spiritual framework to place the experience in, you know? Then— we were just winging it."

"Yeah!" Yuri was grinning again.

Archie shook her head. "It's just unfathomable to me how people could think that space-time was *it*."

"A few centuries earlier they thought the sun went around the earth and the universe was made of nested crystalline spheres."

"Yeah," she nodded, "I guess so."

"But it wasn't just the way we thought of the universe," I started again. "It was the way we thought of ourselves."

"Mm," Yuri said, "Humanism."

"Right," I agreed. "You have to remember that it was a pre-perceptualist culture. The concepts 'important to me' and 'important' were almost universally thought of as congruent."

"God is on our side," Yuri again.

"What's that mean?" Tamika was like a shark smelling blood when there were new concepts in the air. New to her.

Archie answered, "You know, paternalism? Paternal power hierarchies headed by quasi-parental deities?"

Tamika: "Whoa, you lost me."

"Well, it was—let's see, how to put this—"

Yuri: "Static belief systems."

Yuri's obtuseness was helpful as always. "What?" Tamika said.

Yuri asked her, "Do you have a concrete, unchanging system of beliefs about your relationship to the cosmos?"

"What are you yapping about?" she replied. "Of course not."

"People used to." He was the Cheshire cat again.

"A concrete, unchanging system of beliefs." She wasn't buying it.

"Mm-hmm," Yuri grinned.

"How the hell did *that* work?" she asked. "What did they do when they learned something new?"

"You have to remember," I hopped back in, "people used to live only a few decades."

"And there were whole centuries where they didn't learn anything at all," Yuri added.

"Hmm." She was starting to buy it.

"Some really insightful person would come along and say some wonderful things that no one had thought of before. Someone else would write them down in a book and that was it. The word had been received from the fountain of absolute, unchanging truth and people would fight wars over which book was right." Yuri could be quite eloquent when he bothered.

"I guess they couldn't see how ignorant they were," Tamika mused.

"They were so alone," said Steel. "The only ways they had to get to know each other were conversation and sexuality." Then she looked at me. "What are you grinning about?"

"Oh, sorry," I answered. "I was just thinking: this sure beats the conversations I had back at 'Burbs' place."

Her smile had history in it. Our history, I thought. I hoped.

It was a great meal. It wasn't until the end of it that we sort of collectively realized that Drake was still gone.

And he wasn't coming back.

CHAPTER 13

The boost watch-list was a modified watch-in-three with either Steel, Marcus or Tamika heading the watch and the other two positions filled from the remaining five crewmen. In the three-and-a-half day boost there were fourteen six-hour watches, so we got mixed together pretty well. The only two people I didn't get a chance to work with before we started freewheeling were Archie, whom I felt I knew, at least a little, and Alice, who was one of those people that the more I got to know her, the less I got to know her.

She was very quiet most of the time, but unlike Jemal, I always felt like she had something to say. She just usually didn't say it. Her hair was a thick, tousled blond mop, strands of which she would regularly brush out of her eyes. She was quite a bit shorter than the rest of us, but she seemed tall. Her limbs were long for her body, like a dancer's. Kind of a miniature Steel without the fur. But at the same time she often seemed smaller than she was, sometimes in a way that made me want to take care of her, sometimes in a way that made me want to watch my back.

Alice didn't spend as much time in the common room as the rest of us. I ran into her a couple of times hanging out with Ham in the corridor. She'd wrestle with him or chase him around, but when she saw me coming she'd stop until I'd gone by. It wasn't that she was unfriendly, but there always seemed to be something in front of her eyes, a dark thing that never went away. She could be very funny, with a biting insight that could really take me by surprise; then, other times, she wouldn't say anything at all.

And she had this uncanny quality as if—I don't know—as if she wasn't quite used to her body. She wasn't ungraceful, but sometimes her hands would wander around like a cat's tail, rubbing her arms, brushing at her hair, not knowing quite where to rest. And there were strange gaps in her knowledge. Odd stuff, like the Extasya story. Where could she have been to have missed that? It seemed like there had been decades and decades when you couldn't log on without getting lurid details shoved into your cortex, and yet she obviously had never heard of Extasya.

One time when Yuri and I were coming off watch together I asked him about Alice. He looked at me with that 'Is this joke on you or on me?' look of his and said, "What do you want to know?"

"Well," I answered, "she's kind of different, isn't she?"

"Yeah, I suppose she is."

I didn't want to be impolite, but I wanted to know anything I could piece together about this project. It was hard to ask about what I suspected—you just don't. I didn't know if *Yuri* knew. So I asked, "Does Steel have a license to manufacture newbies?"

Yuri laughed, "Newbies? Why would she make just one? There's no profit in that—and whatever else Steel is, she's a good businessman."

"Yeah, I know it doesn't make any sense. But I didn't know what else to think. Alice is so ..."

"Yeah, I know," Yuri mused for a moment. "She isn't a newbie." He scratched his throat. "Steel probably has the connections to buy a single, but she wouldn't. I don't think she would. I'm sure she wouldn't."

"I don't mean to pry. I was just thinking about what Steel's doing on—on ..."

"Brainard's?"

"Yeah."

He raised his eyebrows. "What? You mean, like, a guinea pig or something?"

"Yeah, you're right." I shook my head. "Even *I* know her well enough to know she wouldn't do anything like that."

"Drake got exposed completely unintentionally. I was there."

"Of course. I didn't mean to say ..."

But Yuri wasn't offended. He was thinking, too. "One thing you need to understand about Steel." He looked at his foot. "She picks up strays. You know what I mean?"

"I suppose *I'm* one."

"Yeah. I don't know how long Marcus has known her. A long, long time. But he's got a story. I've never heard it, but I know he's got one. We've all got one. *I've* sure got one."

I laughed, "Oh, yeah? What's your story?"

"You'll have to get me a lot drunker than you were in Kindu to get me to tell it."

"Mm. Sorry. Didn't mean to—"

"That's okay."

We'd been walking down the corridor and were now at the hatch to Yuri's quarters. He opened it and motioned me inside.

After he closed the hatch he said, "I don't know where Steel found Alice. She was already with her when I signed on for this trip." He sat on his bunk. I rested on the back of his chair. "You might have noticed she's kind of protective of her."

"Yeah, I think I know what you mean."

"Something must have happened to her on her last 'boot. I don't know what, but something bad. Really bad. I've never met anyone so totally zeroed out. I mean, she knows *nothing* that went on before a few years ago."

"Hmm. Do you think whatever happened to her is what is motivating Steel to, um, pursue this project?"

Yuri looked at me strangely, like he wasn't sure how to answer, or how he wanted to answer. "Well, I don't know," he finally said. "Maybe. But I really, *really* doubt it. If we get what we're going after on Brainard's, the entire fabric of civilization is going to be turned inside down and upside out. Huge fortunes are going to be made and even bigger ones are going to vanish like the last cookie in the bag. Seems like a little overkill to shake the entire galaxy just to get back at somebody for doing something to one person." I thought of my wife and wondered. "I mean, sure, Steel likes her. They seem to have a special relationship. But then, she has a special relationship with Marcus. With Archie. With me, for that matter. And," he looked at me meaningfully, "with you, so it would seem."

I looked back at him. "Hmm," I said.

Yuri laughed. "Can't figure her out, huh?"

I made that little exhalation that sounds like a laugh but means 'No, I'm not having sex with her and I'm not sure that I wish I was, or maybe I'm only trying to convince myself that I'm not sure that I wish I was.' Then I said, "I can't figure out why she would—" I stopped and looked at Yuri. "Did you know where this trip was going when you signed on?"

He waited for a minute and said, "Yeah."

"And you think it's worth the risk?"

He thought longer this time. But eventually he said, "Yeah, I guess so. I'm here. Of course, we thought the risk was a lot smaller until Drake got messed up."

I looked at my palms, "How did this whole thing get—do you know what got Steel started on this project?"

"It was something she and Archie cooked up."

"Cooked up?" That sounded kind of casual for an undertaking of this sort.

Yuri shrugged, "Put together. They'd been involved in some research project somewhere. Archie doing the research and Steel providing the funding, I imagine."

"What were they researching?"

"I don't know. Something that got Archie interested in Brainard's Planet. She was the one who was collating the data coming out of the remotes there."

"And when they noticed the long lifespans ..."

"Long lifespans. I suppose you could call it that."

"What would *you* call it?"

"Well, if Archie says they have long lifespans, that's good enough for me. Certainly nothing seems to die there."

"Nothing? I thought it was only the big slug creatures."

"Hmm." Yuri thought for a moment. "You know what loam is?"

"Sure," I said. "Soil. Dirt."

"Made up of decaying plant matter."

"Right."

"There's nothing like it on Brainard's Planet. Not that anyone's found."

"Huh."

"No corpses of anything that we've ever run across. Nothing that looked like it had been something healthier at one time. Nothing that you could call a predator. We've never seen anything *eat* anything."

"I thought the slugs grazed on those pink tubules."

"Brainard called it grazing. We call it grazing. But we don't know what's actually going on. All we know is that it doesn't hurt the tubules. The slugs don't even have mouths. Not that we've been able to see. We know there's some sort of chemistry going on, because the composition of the tubules is different after the slugs pass by, but not in any profound way. We assume that either the tubules are nourishing the slugs in some way, or the slugs are nourishing the tubules. We're not sure which. Or if. Maybe both. Maybe neither."

I thought for a while. Then I shook my head.

Yuri laughed. "Kind of boggles the imagination, doesn't it?"

"You think we'll be able to apply anything we find there to humans?"

"You'd have to ask Archie. She and Drake did all of the exobiology. I just make stuff."

"You designed the environmental suits." I meant it as an appreciation.

Yuri looked at my eyes, maybe looking for recrimination. I hope he didn't find any. "Yeah," he said.

We both sat there for a moment. Then Yuri said, "You can only design to the parameters you know about."

"That's right." I patted him on the shoulder. "It's amazing you got them to work at all."

"I suppose." He lay back on his bunk and looked at the overhead.

"You going back to Brainard's Planet with Steel?"

"Yeah," he said, "I imagine I will. I imagine we all will."

"Why?"

He thought for a while. Then, "What do you mean?"

"Well …" I was stumped. If he didn't know … "It's—I mean, Drake's *gone*. You know? Mistakes on Brainard's Planet are costly. You really want to stretch your luck?"

He looked at me for a moment. I'm not sure what he was trying to find, but he said, "We'll work the bugs out. We'll do better next time."

I didn't know what to say so I sat there, nodding like I was agreeing with him. Work the bugs out. Hmm.

"How about you?" he asked.

"Me?"

"Yeah, you going?"

Well, there it was, the 'You Bet Your Life' question. "Well, that's … that's what I'm trying to figure out."

"It'd be good to have you along. You know a lot of stuff."

I laughed, "A lot of stuff. Yeah."

"I guess," Yuri started, "I guess it's impossible to conceive of your own cessation, even after you've seen it happen to someone else."

I wasn't so sure. Of course, I'd had more experience seeing it happen to someone else than he had.

"You know it's illegal to go there," I said.

"Pff! Michelangelo robbed groves to study anatomy."

"I think you mean 'graves.' "

"What did I say?"

"Groves."

"Ah, it's an archaic concept anyway."

"We seem to have done our part to bring it back."

"Hmm."

I got up to leave. "You okay?" I asked.

"Yeah."

"Thanks for talking to me."

"Any time."

I let myself out.

Steel was flying the ship with Archie and Yuri when Marcus, Jemal and I came on to relieve them for the final watch. We were moving almost 270,000 klicks per second, say from Earth to Luna in about a second and a half. Temporal communication on the net was already being affected. Later in the watch it would become impossible. At the same time, the Doppler effect was making it harder and harder to navigate by optics; the stars in front of us were crowding together and blue-shifting, the ones behind doing the same and red-shifting. This is why all of the intense Nav is done early in the boost. By the last watch all you can do is lock down and hope you're pointed in the right direction.

We relieved them not in control, where they were, but up in the engine. Freewheeling engines are always placed at a starship's center of gravity to facilitate rapport between the ship and the crew. This had made me wonder where they put the Lightdancer's engine when I first saw the skyhook spool, because that had to be at the center of gravity for very basic, mechanical reasons. But of course the skyhook was only used in orbit with the torch retracted. With the torch extended the center of gravity moved back about two hundred meters.

I felt the reverent quiet that I always do when I walk into the core. I've been to the cathedral at Chartres on Earth and the feeling it gave me was similar, but that was caused by architecture and ancient beliefs. This was a calm anticipation of otherness, expansion beyond physicality. Perhaps a realization of those very same beliefs, I don't know. The engine itself hung over us, a sphere five meters across hooked into the ship through seven umbilicals as thick as your arm. Life-support and auxiliary machinery hummed quietly along the walls. Tamika and Alice were with us—moving at the speed we were it wasn't wise to have people wandering around the ship, so they were there to mount up early, even though we wouldn't need them until we started freewheeling. Yuri and Archie would join us soon, leaving only Steel in control to interface between the engine and the 'real' world. Ham, of course, would just be a passenger.

Soft blue lights flickered on as we approached the lockers. Inside each locker was a midnight black freewheeling suit. We stripped down and started greasing each other up. It's not really grease, just an electrolytic salve that facilitates contact between the tactile nerve endings in the skin and the receptors in the suit. The suits are probably what disturb people most about freewheeling; I mean, if they've never crewed. They fit you like a second skin. Everywhere. Yeah, even there. And there. All those places. The ship is wired directly into the nervous systems of the crew because, while we don't need a ship to freewheel, it's kind of embarrassing to drop back into rational space without it. And the only reason the ship freewheels is that we're in it.

Of course, unless you can run really, *really* fast, you still need a starship to get you up to the speed of light—and you need to be going that fast to achieve pure stereotempic parallax. Time and no time. Motion and stasis. Everywhere and nowhere.

I meditate on the nature of the process every time. I can't help it.

We stood in a circle, greasing each other's backs, contacting each other, digging our fingers into pressure points, massaging muscles and tendons, synching in physically. Then our own chests, faces, necks, stomachs, genitals. Alice did my legs for me and I returned the favor. Bottoms of feet, between the toes, scalps, behind the ears, shoulders, arms, buttocks. We glistened as we opened the lockers and donned the suits.

They don't activate until you close them. As I pressed the seam up the center of my face I felt the suit turn fluid, sliding under my scales, into my ears to rest gently against my eardrums, into my nostrils and down into my lungs, mating with each bronchial tube, between my lips and teeth, around my tongue, down my esophagus and through my entire digestive track, ultimately meeting itself. The thought always hits me that we're really just tubes, like the simplest sponges.

As it slid under my eyelids my vision came back. It always seems a little enhanced by the suit; I'm not sure why. We all stood there encased in black fabric, life-support hoses flowing from our faces, silver connector strips highlighting our contours, looking like we should be in a modern dance troupe.

"Let's mount up," Marcus said, his voice removed from me by two interfaces. He depressed the lever beside him and seven hatches opened at equidistant points around the sphere, one right on top, three more making an equilateral triangle about a third of the way down, three more in another triangle toward the bottom. Elevators lifted us to the hatches where we slipped into our brackets feet first and then we were inside the sphere, the polished silver interior encompassing us finitely and infinitely. The armature adjusted to our various heights until the tops of our heads just brushed the inner surface, our feet pointing at the center.

Marcus, Jemal and I logged on. The dilation effect was already very noticeable. We see solids because our brain interprets the interference between two flat pictures supplied by our eyes. At the speed we were going it was as if someone had taken our eyeballs and moved them about five feet apart, only temporally instead of spatially. By the time we achieved the speed of light it would seem like they'd been moved to opposite ends of the universe and pointed at each other.

[1*>READYTORELIEVEYOUCAPTAIN<1/*]

Marcus was calm as always.

[*\1>YOUHAVETHESHIP<*/1]

[1*>AYECAPTAIN<1/*]

[*\1>WEVEPASSEDTHROUGHMOSTOFTHECOMETSHELL BUTKEEPALERT<*/1]

Steel was referring to Prime's Oort cloud. Most single stars have one. It's easy to avoid most of the skag floating around a star simply by boosting up out of the plane of the ecliptic, but comet shells orbit so far out from their primaries they tend to be spherical. There's no way to miss them.

They weren't a problem in the old days. Back when we boosted at a single gee we were well beyond the heliopause and into interstellar space before we got even close to the speed of light, but with higher rates of acceleration, luminal velocity started being achieved much closer in. At these speeds you're not worried about anything as prosaic as a meteor punching a hole in the hull. Anything that hits you completely annihilates equal parts of you and itself, proton by proton, creating showers of muons, gluons, who-the-heck-are-youons and lots and *lots* of energy. This can be very inconvenient.

I actually met a man once who'd been through a catastrophic collision. It had happened five years before I met him and he was in a really *bad* mood. Fortunately for him he'd been fabulously wealthy before the incident—it kept him out of the trades—but his medical bills still wiped him out. That's not what was souring his disposition, however. He knew the right people and he had all the time in the world. He'd get rich again. The proximate cause of his annoyance was much more immediate.

They don't tell you this when you're a passenger, but there's one way of re-vitalizing that's even more expensive than re-booting. *Much* more expensive. In cases where your person has inadvertently turned into an expanding cloud of sub-atomic particles and gamma rays, it makes very little sense to try to collect and re-assemble them—very labor intensive. And you have to be Johnny-on-the-spot or they're scattered all over the galaxy. This is why they actually upload your genetic code and the structure of your brain onto the net for the last half of the boost phase—the speedy part. When you're backing down the other side of the jump it's not a problem because you've flipped over and are being preceded by your torch, which does a very nice job of clearing a path for you. It's only the last few hours before you freewheel that this extraordinary precaution is taken.

Even so they only dump your structure onto the net, not your actual memories. With all the people traveling between stars these days, that would really clog things up. But if the unthinkable *does* happen, like it happened to this guy, they can speed-dump everything before you vaporize. Even matter-annihilation explosions are limited to the speed of light—it gives you a couple of pico-seconds to get the job done.

But now your problems have just started, because you're missing that mortal coil that makes food taste so good and sex put a bounce in your step. Your net storage charges are skyrocketing and you don't have any way to make money. But they have your genetic code so they whip up a zygote (at a moderately exorbitant fee), incubate it (at a moderately exorbitant fee times nine months), and start feeding you back into it as fast as the developing brain can take it. By the time your newbie is three or four years old it can handle your complete personality algorithms and quite a lot of your memories. In another year or so you're back in business—but not *quite* back to normal.

When I met this particular guy, he was about a meter tall and had only the finest, downiest hair anyplace but on his head, and what he talked about most of the time (he was fairly drunk—this was during my musician years; he'd come up to me on a break in some dive I was playing) was how his penis hadn't been good for anything but evacuating liquids for the last five years and it wasn't *going* to be good for anything else for another seven or eight. Actually, I'm not sure if he was irritable because he was randy or because all the femmes in the joint were treating him like he was 'cute.'

Anyway, the chances of running into anything sizable are vanishingly remote, but it keeps you on your toes.

Thinking about that guy brought up something else that I wanted to ask Steel about, or Archie, if either one of them would give me an answer. Maybe they would. Also something that I would have to check out on the net, but later.

Yuri and Archie joined us after a little while and Marcus sealed us in. The engine was complete. As we continued to build velocity, temporal communication with the net ceased and we concentrated on short-range micro-meteor surveillance and interdiction. 'Short-range' is a relative term, of course. We were traveling a million klicks in under four seconds and inching closer to the speed of light with each passing second. We had to survey a very tight cone of space in front of us a couple million klicks deep but only six hundred across, anything farther from our path and we would flash past it before it had a chance to get in front of us. Two million kilometers is not very far as astronomical distances go—say five times the distance from Earth to Luna—but we had to scan that volume of space continuously for every tiny piece of matter. If we hit a speck of dust it would impart enough energy to us to knock us significantly off course. It's nerve-wracking.

At the same time interaction with the net was mutating pan-dimensionally. Dividing consciousness and concentration between space-time and the view of literally *everything* that starts to come into focus is the most challenging part of crewing, but it has to be done. Freewheeling itself is more like deep Zen meditation than anything else, but those last few hours, last few minutes, last few *seconds* before you drop out of rational space can seem pretty irrational.

After an eternity of this I heard that beautiful sound, made even more beautiful because it was Steel's voice delivering the input:

[*\1 2 3 4 5 5 6 7>TENSECONDSTOJUMP<*/1 2 3 4 5 6 7]

Then Marcus:

[1\2 3 4 5 6 7>SYNCHANDMELD<1/2 3 4 5 6 7]

And the seven of us resonated at astonishingly profound levels. It's astonishing every time. Then honey over brass again:

[*\1 2 3 4 5 6 7>FIVESECONDS<*/1 2 3 4 5 6 7]

Marcus released the armature and let the seven-pointed star made of us roll freely inside the sphere, seeking our own specific resonance with the pan-dimensional universe. Thus the term 'freewheeling'. Then:

[*\1 2 3 4 5 6 7>THREE...TWO...ONE... - -

And we were backing down the other side, several light-hours and three and a half days from Earth.

PART III
EARTH

CHAPTER 14

Earth had changed.

How long had it been? A long time. A thousand years? More. The whole system had changed.

By sheer chance we were able to tack on Mars coming in. We approached the system from a little bit north of the ecliptic plane and used the planet's gravity to swing us around into line with everything else orbiting the sun. We could have come directly into Earth if we'd wanted to waste the anti-matter. Using Mars was cheaper. Still, missing Earth by a mere hundred million klicks after traveling three hundred fifty-two light years is damn fine shooting.

The anticipation of seeing Mars again clutched my chest, though. I could picture Arcadia in my mind—the struggling patches of vegetation huddling against the cold, the endless, rock-strewn dust, the domed city, the lake we had made ...

Mars isn't red anymore. There are oceans, real oceans. I don't know how deep they are, but they must cover a third of the planet. Forests, fields, grasslands—it was strange—I just couldn't make a connection to it. There it was, my home world. At closest approach we were only two hundred klicks up. We flew almost directly over Marineris, the arcopolis I had built with my wife, and I couldn't feel anything but a sad detachment. It was in my memory—I would never wipe those years—but it was so little like what I remembered. It's surrounded by jungle. There are waterfalls arcing into the Valles so tall we could see them from space.

My wife would have been pleased. She had engineered many of the biological invasions that had matured into the blue-green world beneath me. I missed her more acutely than I had in a long, long time, because I could see the product of her work, and because our home as we had known it no longer existed.

After we flew under the south polar cap (it's much larger now) and away toward Earth my home turned back into a globe receding behind us—and I knew that it *was* my home. I didn't want it to leave, but it kept getting smaller. My fingers longed to dig in its earth, my feet to walk upon it, my lungs to breathe its air and my face to feel its winds. I ached for the endless, rusty deserts that were no more.

And then it was gone. Just a bright star lost in the night, a star that wasn't even the right color anymore.

The change in Earth was even more astounding. Of course I'd seen realities on the net over the centuries, stories of its gentrification after the Great Expansion, of its depopulation, of the enrichment that was the product of being the hub of an interstellar civilization, but I still wasn't prepared.

We landed at Nairobi spaceport (it was nice to know the Lightdancer could actually land on a planet) and monorailed north to Europe. The little I experienced of east central Africa seemed like one huge garden and animal preserve—endless herds of wildebeest and impala, families of elephants, chimps and baboons, cantankerous rhinos thumping across the veldt. (If it was the veldt. Maybe that's farther south, I forget. Too many planets.) Ostriches and secretary birds and shoebills and kites. Flocks of flamingoes so pink they were almost orange. It was amazing.

The sprawling, desperate slums that had been so prevalent when I was last on Earth were nowhere to be seen. The architecture in Nairobi was all a product of the thirty-fourth century neo-traditionalist movement. As Earth had become too expensive for most people and they emigrated to the projects, the face of the planet had changed. On the projects everything was new: architecture, social structures, even biospheres. So the people rich enough to stay on Earth gradually became interested in all the things they had torn down, plowed under or forgotten in the last two thousand years. The one thing they had, the thing that people on the projects could never buy no matter how rich they became, was history. Ancient traditions, ancient artwork, ancient architecture. People that had made their fortunes depleting the planet's natural resources, habitats and gene pool were suddenly interested in being surrounded by natural beauty, and they had the money to pay for it.

There were two ways to live on Earth now: one was to be a mega-rich member of one of the syndicates, the other was to supply the syndicates with something they wanted. There weren't any farmers left on Earth; there were groundskeepers, gardeners and ecologists. There were farms, to be sure, but crops were largely ancillary to the primary function of keeping the bucolic countryside bucolic. There weren't really any architects, just architectural historians. The only things

I saw that looked like they'd been built since the industrial revolution were the spaceport and the monorail. Of course the technology was there. It was just hidden behind stone walls, frescoes and thatched roofs.

As Yuri put it, the whole planet had been 'Disneyed,' whatever the hell that means. Archie preferred to think of Earth as an open-air museum, but Yuri said that of the structures now standing on Earth less than half were historical. The rest were just a creative team's idea of what it might have been like.

We left Marcus in Nairobi. He was heading west to someplace called Senegal. As we continued north, the Sahara was just as vast as I remembered and the bridges linking Tunis to Malta, Malta to Sicily and Messina to the toe of Italy were spectacular. The rest of the crew split off in Florence, heading for the pleasure palaces of Paris and a well-earned liberty. Steel was going home. For reasons I figured out later she took me with her.

So there we were again, the three of us—Ham, Steel and me, sitting in a monorail car not unlike the one that took us to Nohili Point, maybe a little bigger. But now the scraggly pines, stately cypresses and sprawling vineyards of the Apennines floated past us, giving way to the wheat and mustard fields of the Po valley, which in turn gave way to the chalky cliffs and blue waters of the Lago di Garda and the rising foothills of the Alps. Every promontory, every commanding height up the valley of the Adige was topped by a medieval Italian castle, or something that looked like one. The Brenner Pass had been used four thousand years ago by Roman legions and the Germanic tribes they fought to civilize. Two millennia later it had been a crowded tangle of transport systems for surface vehicles and electric power. Now its slopes were once again dotted with wooden chalets connected by winding lanes. The concrete ribbons of the old superhighways had been dismantled centuries ago, the marching steel towers strung with electrical wires torn down without a trace. All the heavy traffic was underground now in hypersonic tubes. The only thing that interrupted the sweep of the mountains was the monorail. It made one graceful, curving line up the side of the valley, supported on tall stilts to keep it above the threat of avalanches. Other than that, we could have been in the eighteenth century.

We crossed over the pass, descending into the glacier carved valley of the Inn and what had once been the Holy Roman Empire, the Eastern Kingdom, Ostereich, Austria. Innsbruck straddled the crystalline river, a filigree of pastel upper stories topping sturdy stone arcades. We followed the curve of the Inn as it descended into the plush, green fields and patchwork forests of Bavaria.

Where Rome was antiquity and Florence the Renaissance, Munich was Baroque. Onion-domed cathedral spires rose above tiled roofs bound by facades that seemed to know no straight line. After pulling into the arching iron and glass of the Hauptbahnhoff, we changed to a spur line that took us southwest to the village of Oberammergau. Here squat shops with ornate wooden eaves and thick, white walls were painted with scenes of alpine life and ancient mythology. In the pre-perceptualist past, the story of the execution of Jesus had been re-enacted here every year. Pilgrims had traveled great distances to witness it and be comforted by its promise of eternal life. Now we *had* eternal life, or something close to it. Our hejiras were made in different dimensions, our stories gained through very different paths. The weight of four millennia of history made me feel foolishly and insignificantly young, an unusual sensation for me.

It was in Oberammergau that I began to get a better idea of just how wealthy Steel was. A bearded, liveried servant met us at the station wearing a felt hat and driving a horse-drawn carriage. I think they were antiques—the carriage and the hat, I mean, but probably the driver as well. Two footmen helped us in before mounting their posts on the rear and off we went, clopping down the cobbled road. The way opened onto rolling countryside bounded to the south by abrupt mountains. The Bavarian Alps are beautiful—steep, sudden, and clad with dark firs—but a bit of an anti-climax after the colossal massifs of Vesper.

Riding to Schwangau took as long as the trip from Nairobi to Munich. Steel pointed out her home to me from the carriage as we approached. Turrets and spires sprouted from the top of a rocky crag, filling it so completely as to seem an organic outgrowth of the stone. Its windows opened serenely onto verdant fields rolling away to the north and the immediate backdrop of the Alps to the south and west. Steel smiled at me with a gentle, powerful pride.

"Neuschwanstein," she said, "I think you'll like it."

I knew of it. Her home had been built in the nineteenth century by a mad Bavarian king who wished he had lived in the twelfth. A schlossfantastiche, a fairytale castle for a lonely man who had never grown up. Frustrated with the maneuverings of parliamentary government, he had longed for the absolute power of a medieval prince. Had he been granted that power he would have used it to send chivalrous knights on quests for the Grail. I wondered if my hostess had any similar bents as our matched white steeds pulled us up the final curving drive, through pine forests. We approached the arched gate flanked by crenellated, witch-capped towers.

Where the imagery in Oberammergau had been Christian, here it was Teutonic. A statue of Siegfried gazed boldly from the peaked roof of the main residence. Paintings of dragons flamed high on the walls. As we walked through the courtyard and into the wing where Steel's force of servants, accountants and lawyers were housed, I kept expecting some sort of welcome. After all, she'd been out of touch for three decades. It seemed like they'd be excited to have her back or upset with her for being unavailable, or something, but we were allowed to make our way into the residence unmolested.

She fairly ran up the sweeping marble staircase that filled the north spire. "It's so good to be home!" She smiled at me. Even Ham looked excited.

The reception I was expecting finally took place in the grand entrance hall at the top of the stairs. The room was not square but slightly trapezoidal, being at the junction of the two wings of the Schloss, wings set at a slight angle to conform to the shape of the crag on which they perched. Smart cooks in snowy aprons and tall hats stood in echelon behind their chef wearing the tallest and snowiest hat of all. Maids with soft bosoms billowing out of the tops of their dirndls and lace caps pinned in their hair curtsied eagerly behind solemnly bowing manservants in sky-blue brocade vests, satin breeches and white hose. At the fore of this impressive retinue stood a powdered wig and a rich coat of the same Bavarian blue, with deep lapels and cuffs sculpted with silver braid and bright buttons. This construction was occupied by a long-nosed, diffident scaffold of a man. His bow was the haughtiest and most deferential. His greeting, eloquent and concise, was delivered in mellifluous tones and echoed by his subordinates down the line. It was too perfect. As Steel hugged him and greeted him in turn I didn't know whether to laugh or run for cover.

I stood gaping at the hall as Steel moved from person to person, shaking a hand here, kissing a cheek there. I'd studied this place back when I was an architect. I was having trouble believing that I really knew the person who owned it now. The Romanesque vaulted ceiling was a manic phantasm of color. The ribs of the vaults were painted in helixed ribbons of blue, white, red and gold bordered by hallucinogenically repeating arcs of the same four colors. They were supported on white marble capitals carved to represent animals and knights. The vaults themselves were arched fields of gold filled with marching rows and columns of red and blue medallions in a frenetic gingham, bordered with thick strips of green and more gold. And that was just the ceiling. The carved oak panels that lined the walls waist-high were surmounted by huge, romantic murals depicting scenes from Teutonic legends, legends the mad king had commissioned to be set as vast musical dramas, Gesamtkunstwerke, the most colossal musical expressions of the age. Less than a century later music from those dramas would be played in human extermination camps, played for the gaunt victims as they were herded to their destruction.

I told myself to take it easy, take a deep breath. No matter how old Steel was (I still didn't know) she had been born centuries after that horror. She'd probably never heard of Hitler *or* Wagner. That was ancient, *ancient* history and too much new history being created to bother with it.

Still ...

"Mo!" Steel beckoned, smiling her warmest smile, "Come here and be presented!"

"Oh, right. Sorry." I walked over to the—the what? The butler? The maitre d'hotel? The capo di tutti capi? I had no idea.

Either Steel didn't feel it was necessary for me to know his position or she assumed I already knew it, for she simply introduced me: "Jean-Léon, this is my friend Mohandas." He bowed crisply. "He'll be staying with us for a few days."

"Bien entendu," Jean-Léon replied, making no judgment of me or anything else.

"How ya doin?" I asked.

"Tres bien, m'sieur," and he made no judgment about that, either.

And so on down the line: the manservants, the cooks, the pretty maids all in a row. One of these, Anna was her name, caught my eye in particular. I can only describe her, given her Rabelaisian surroundings, as 'saucy.' Jet hair whose undisciplined wisps caressed her cheeks, icy blue eyes that held veiled and overt promises of things perilous and forbidden—this in an interstellar culture where nothing had been forbidden in centuries—and, I'll admit, bosoms that were even softer and more billowy than those of her colleagues.

I think Steel noticed me noticing her. I didn't observe this at the time, but looking back on it I'm sure she did.

"I suppose Krupp is already here?" Steel queried Jean-Léon.

"Il vous attend dans sa petite chambre." Why did he keep speaking French? If he liked dead languages why not German? Or go all the way and speak Latin. Or Greek. Or Mesopotamian. Only on Earth—

"Good," Steel frowned, "let him wait." She looked at me, "He's been bulleting me ever since we re-entered the system." Kind of made me wonder who the hell he was. Back to Jean-Léon: "I'm going to go wash the road off of me." She clocked the net. "It's just after three. Tell him I'll meet him in the throne room at six."

"Mais oui, Madame," he bowed.

She gave me a grim smile. "That way the sun will be in his eyes."

Steel had a throne room. A *throne* room. The thought kept going through my head as I stood on the highest battlement of the tallest spire, looking out over lakes and wooded hills and the sun setting over the Alps. She was in it right then, meeting with Krupp, whoever he was. What did that meeting portend for me? For Steel's expedition?

What was I doing getting involved with a woman who owned a throne room?

I wished Yuri were there. Or Archie, or even Marcus. Or that I was with them, with the crew, getting stupid in Paris. I looked at the sky, waiting for it to get dark.

I thought: if I were back in 'Burbs' place getting drunk, trading insults with the regulars and generally avoiding going home to Sheila, I wouldn't have had the courage or imagination to even dream of being trapped in a castle like this with a woman as beautiful as Steel, and yet there I was—wishing I were someplace else.

Steel *was* a beautiful woman. And Yuri was right—I couldn't figure her out. Why she sought me out for emotional companionship I didn't know. I didn't know why it mattered to me that she did. I gazed down over the parapet, seeking vertigo. The foreshortened cylinder of the upper spire grew like a cone-capped asparagus out of its octagonal, crenellated stalk. Crowns of fir trees stabbed up at me from a dizzying distance below. The balcony wrapped around the spire like one of Jean-Léon's lace cuffs, suspending me between earth and sky.

Between Earth and Space.

The sky was getting darker. The first stars were already out. Sunsets were a lot faster on Earth than they were on Vesper, just a little faster than they were on Mars. I walked around to the east side of the tower. Mars had been a hundred million klicks from Earth when we came in; it was in opposition. It would be rising as the sun set. The sun was in Leo so Mars would be in Aquarius. I waited.

Why would Steel risk everything, *everything*, to go to Brainard's Planet? I'd spent almost two weeks with her crew on the Lightdancer trying to figure it out and I was no closer to an answer. Potential fortunes to be made—all right, but how much fortune did she need? She was already the princess of her own fairytale. Was she really interested in social change? What could she have gone through that would have convinced her it was important enough to possibly destroy herself, her perspective, permanently and irretrievably?

What had she lost that she needed to do *this* to regain it?

The sky in the east had turned indigo. Sagittarius' whimsical teapot poured to the south. Capricorn, less picturesque but just as recognizable, swam next to it. On the eastern horizon Aquarius reigned with an extra star, a blue star. The baleful eye of war no longer glared in the skies of Earth. It had been turned to water.

"I hope I'm not disturbing you." Steel emerged from the small wooden door and stepped up beside me.

"No," my voice tore like paper. Thoughts of home filled my throat.

"What are you looking at?" She rested her hand on my bicep, hooked through my elbow. My nostrils expanded to encompass her smell.

"Just looking. Your home is beautiful."

She smiled up at me, then followed my gaze. "So is yours," she said.

"Hmm." Rolling Bavarian fields twinkled here and there with hearth lights. Alpine shoulders bulked deepening blue, gnawing at the fading sky. "How did your meeting go?"

"Well ... meetings," she leaned her head on my shoulder. You'd think I'd learn, but that voice ...

I asked her, "Is everything all right?"

She hooked her other hand over my elbow, nesting, pulling closer. "I'll probably have to meet with him again before we leave, so things could be better. But, yes, they're moving along."

"How long do you figure to be here?"

"On Earth?"

I nodded.

"Just long enough to refit the Lightdancer. About a week."

I nodded again.

"Not long enough for you to get home to Mars, I'm afraid."

I allowed a small, comfortable chuckle to acknowledge her insight. We stared at the sky for a while. Then she asked:

"Would you like to go home?"

"I don't know." The last bruise of daylight was leaving the sky. The ragged southern horizon was a velvet silhouette.

"You've already helped me a great deal. I don't know how we would have gotten back to Earth without you."

This sort of language always embarrasses me. I didn't know what to say, so I didn't say anything. She continued:

"I paid off your back taxes this afternoon."

And I wondered how I felt about that. My chest expanded. My spine lengthened. Weight was removed. On the other hand, I hadn't really won, they'd gotten their money. Even though Steel had paid them it was money I had earned. Was earning.

And I thought about that. I guessed Steel knew that I was thinking of leaving the crew. Jumping ship. Mars was right there. I could see it. I still knew people there.

"You can get back on the net now if you want to." Her voice caressed the deepest parts of me.

"I—thanks," I said. What was she doing?

"I guess I just want to say ..." she paused and looked at the night, "thank you for all you've done. Not just crewing. Talking to me. When I ... When ..."

"It's okay. Really. I—"

"You've been very good to me. In ways you didn't need to—"

"No. No, I ..." What did I want to say to her?

"I just—You'd be, have been, a wonderful part of the crew. I hope you'll—No. What I wanted to say is—"

"They're a great crew. I love working with them."

"Yes. I know. I mean, I've seen."

On the other hand—"I think they're all a bunch of psycho mutants," I said, "I mean, I have to tell you, I still don't see why—"

"That's what I wanted to say," she turned me to her, looked up into my eyes. I could feel her gaze in the soles of my feet, and my heart turned sideways in my chest. "You can leave if you want to. It's—it will be—I'll understand. I'll pay you for the jump from Vesper. That should be a tidy sum right there. And I'll throw in the back taxes as a token of my appreciation. For a job well done. Above and beyond the call—"

"No. Wait." What was I saying? Starlight reflected in her huge green eyes. Were they ingenuous or ingenious? "I don't want to go any place." Was I nuts? I breathed and teetered and my mouth opened and this is what came out of it: "I'm in. For the whole trip. I said I was and I am." I'll just check my brain at the door, I thought. I'm obviously not using it.

Her eyes moistened. "Good," she smiled, "Good. I'm so glad you'll be with us. I know it must seem crazy, but it really is for a good cause. I—"

I think, right then, in that flushed moment of relief and happiness, she almost told me what was really going on. But then she didn't:

"I could have found a replacement, but it would have taken time and we really don't have any to spare." She hugged me. She put her arms under mine and slid her hands up either side of my spine and laid her cheek and breasts on my chest. And inhaled. "We have so much to do and so little time."

Yeah, I thought. Let's all race off helter skelter to the Planet of Doom. We only live forever. Wouldn't we feel silly if we got there late and all the good Doom had already been taken?

I took a chance: "What's the rush?" It was a good move. She was still hugging me so I could feel in her body when her mind checked out the option 'candor' and immediately filed it away for possible later use. Or not. But she was smooth, she didn't pull away from me. She kept holding onto me as she spoke:

"Well, the Lightdancer has to be refitted—"

"You mentioned that."

"And we have to get new ultra-lights. Check out the skyhook—it wasn't really designed to withstand hydrogen fireballs, you know."

"I admit that hadn't occurred to me."

"I need to get my genome reworked. And yours."

Oh?

"And we have to come up with a strategy for dealing with this new behavior."

"What new behavior?"

"The creatures. What happened to Drake. I don't want it to happen to anyone else." She hugged me a little harder, unconsciously, I think.

I hugged her back. "Any ideas how we'll do that?"

"I've got Yuri working on it."

"I thought he was in Paris."

I could feel her smile. "Yuri works best when he's got a lot to distract him." That sounded right.

Her breasts really felt nice against my ribs, rising and falling with her breathing. We stayed that way for a while. I thought about a lot of things; I'm sure she did too.

She, of course, hadn't answered my question; she hadn't told me why she was in such a hurry.

That night I tried to get back on the net and found that, even though the System Revenue Service was through with me, Steel evidently wasn't. The SRS flag was off my address, but I still couldn't access it—security considerations, no doubt. So, no mail for *me*, and no way to communicate with the outside world.

To alleviate my feelings of cybernetic isolation I did a little more research. I'd been wondering why plague victims hadn't been able to upload and wait for new bodies to be grown for them, like that guy I'd met in the bar. Even if re-booting exacerbated the effects of the plague they should have been able to give up their infected bodies and store their minds on the net.

The short answer was—they could. Over five thousand people had survived the plague by doing just that. After that the net simply became overloaded with storage demands. Too many people, too little capacity. Brainard and most of his party had elected not to, wanting to gather as much information as they could from their own destruction, and, perhaps, not wanting to live in a world where they had unleashed such misery.

But many, many people had. They'd had to do it in the very early stages, when symptoms first became apparent, because soon after that the cellular interface between the medulla and the bio-chip became too degraded to function. But they'd done it.

That left me with one question, the question I had been afraid I was going to be left with. Re-booting had simply accelerated the effects of the plague, and the plague had spread so fast the net had been unable to handle everyone wanting to upload. Almost two billion perspectives had been lost.

Almost two billion.

It was the magnitude of the disaster that had turned it into a disaster.

So.

So why hadn't Drake uploaded?

Anna visited my room that night, billowing bosoms and all. I was feeling so confused and manipulated that I took her up on her offer.

CHAPTER 15

I spent the next few days climbing up and down the trail that begins behind the Schloss and goes to the top of the Tegelberg. Steel was busy lining things up. There was really nothing I could do to help her, and she had intimated there would be some heavy climbing work involved in this job, something having to do with getting on and off Brainard's Planet, I guessed, so I figured I better keep the edge I had developed on Vesper. Climbing also helps me think, and I needed to.

It's a very pretty trail that starts out by crossing a beautiful gorge and waterfall on an airy footbridge that's supposed to be even older than the castle. It then grinds its way up the mountainside in a series of steep switchbacks through open alpine forest. It has some nice views—a couple of which are right on the edge of the cliff overlooking the Schloss. At one of these I saw an ancient wrought-iron cross and plaque that had been placed there in memory of someone who had fallen. The date on it was 1957.

Only on Earth.

The trail finally ends up at an old Jagerhut—you can see most of Bavaria from it and they serve a great lunch. Three hours up and an hour and a half down—it was a good workout. Steel's system was keeping me in shape, but, like sex, nothing beats the real thing. It felt wonderful to leave all the intrigue behind and just pull pine-scented air into my lungs as I labored up the mountain. The higher I got, the larger the world became; finding my problems in it became increasingly difficult as expanding perspective shrank them.

My first lunch at the hut was glorious. The sun shone electric out of a neon-blue sky. The air was so clear I could pick out individual stones in the facade of the Schloss, which looked like a trophy fifteen hundred meters below. I sat at a rough table on the wooden deck outside the hut, chewing on rustic cuisine delivered by a flaxen-haired Fräulein (I thought of her as a Fräulein even though she spoke Systemic like everyone else. Everyone but Jean-Léon, that is). Location is everything in dining—a simple sandwich was transformed into one of the best meals I'd ever had.

I don't know why, but when I was finished eating I pulled my medicine bag off my belt and emptied it out on the table in front of me. My lives lay scattered across the rough wood in a little constellation, sparkling in the sun. There was the lock of Mary's hair I had kept, there a music crystal my band had made on Helios, there a vivid branch of coral from a reef I had designed on—which planet? The one I did before Scarpus. It has a Chinese name—Singing Garden, something like that.

A fragment of etched double-carbon from Marineris, a tiny foam-steel model of the habitat I'd built at First Landing, an eagle talon I picked up somewhere out in the outer arm. Little things. Little pieces of pieces.

And there was the thimble computer with my wife's genome stored on it. It was one of the last computers ever made, just before the net took over all those tasks. I picked it up and rolled it between my thumb and fingers. I hadn't put it on in—a long time.

I had never even fleetingly entertained the idea of cloning her—it would have been silly. It wouldn't have been *her*. The genetic material would have been the same but her appearance and even her personality would have been the product of what she ate, what she learned, how she was treated by those around her. Her perspective would have been unique, as different from my wife's as Steel's was, or Yuri's. Or mine.

I just felt better having the information close to me, the information that had resulted in her.

At that moment, however, I was thinking the thimble might serve another purpose. I put it on my finger to check for unused memory. It still had a couple hundred million giga-bytes left. Not much, but it would be enough.

Steel was being so careful with security that it made me wonder how far she'd go. I was still cut off from the net. It didn't look like she was planning to let me back on any time soon. Reasonable, under the circumstances, but then, the circumstances were rather unique. It occurred to me that her offer to re-boot me at the end of the trip might play right into her security needs. Particularly if things didn't turn out the way she hoped. Particularly if she 'booted me herself, on the Lightdancer, independent of the net. I'd always been very careful about re-booting. If you go to just anyone you can end up like 'Burbs, adrift in the universe with big holes in your past.

I was betting that she wouldn't think to look through my medicine bag, and, even if she did, that she wouldn't know what a thimble computer was.

I started recording this memoir. Just in case.

Memoirs are always suspect. I wonder how much I am improving myself, how much credit I am conveniently taking, how much blame I am conveniently spreading around.

The third day started out much as the previous two, sunny and vibrant, but a cold front moved through while I was up on top, and weather socked in quickly, as it only does in the mountains. The temperature dropped and wind started whipping spitting gusts of rain sideways and even upwards. I watched my step coming down.

The storm had really started to kick it up when Steel bulleted me on her system: [Mo, where are you?]

I grabbed onto a tree, "About half-way down the Tegelberg trail. Why? What's up?"

[I need you down here. Please hurry.] And she signed off.

It's hard to hurry when rock is wet and everything that had been dirt has turned to mud, but I did my best. The wind had knocked some dead-fall across the trail about a quarter klick above the gorge. It wouldn't have been a problem except that the stripped trunk was slick and I was moving pretty fast. I bunged up my ankle.

I was hobbling down the last part of the trail when I heard her voice. I thought she had bulleted me again until I realized it was echoing off a bluff beside me:

"Get off me!"

I started running. As I came into the cut in the rock above the gorge I saw her on the footbridge—an insignificant ribbon spanning the chasm a hundred meters above the top of the falls. There were two men with her, one tall and fragile, the other, huge. Great, bulging muscle mass turned arms into thighs, thighs into tree trunks. Meaty pectorals rippled with frustration. His traps seemed to grow directly out of his head. I hadn't seen that sort of hyper-testosterone genome work in a thousand years. At least not on anybody who wasn't in the trades.

Ham was with her, too. He had interposed himself between Steel and the behemoth, but the wood deck of the bridge was slick. He was having trouble keeping his footing. Muscle-boy lunged at her again. Steel backed out of range but had to lean backwards over the rail to do it. The tall, wispy man was trying to calm things down, to no great effect.

The hulk managed to catch one of her wrists just as I reached the bridge. Ham stood up under his arm, tore him away and kind of tossed him back toward the center of the bridge, but Steel collapsed, holding the arm he had grabbed. There was an unnatural curve in it. I rushed into the fray not sure what I was going to do, shouting colorful phrases like "What the hell—?" and things like that.

The bridge wasn't very wide, but I managed to step over Steel and around Ham to confront the thug. He didn't even look at me. His attention was riveted on his target. I yelled at him, "HEY! Calm down! Calm down—" He stood up, grabbed my shoulder and punched me in the chest. I heard a rib crack, but I managed to catch one of his ankles as I fell. This slowed him down enough for Ham to get a bear-hug (a gorilla-hug?) on him and keep him from reaching Steel again. He was struggling to get free and I was holding onto his foot for all I was worth when he suddenly drew his leg up to his chest and kicked it into the air—with me on it. This guy was really strong. I came down on the bridge railing with my legs and lower torso on the wrong side. A scarlet spear of fire flashed through my chest. He kicked again and I was dangling from his foot, nothing under me but a lot of air and rushing water. The railing came up at me and I caught it, but my chest was killing me. I couldn't pull myself up. I managed to wrap my arms around two struts and hang there, elbows on the deck, my body swinging below it. The foot I'd let go of slammed into my face. He would have kicked me again if Ham hadn't been getting control of the situation. He wrapped his legs around the legs of our meaty friend and was squeezing the breath out of him with his arms. His ape mouth opened amazingly wide and feral jaws closed on the guy's cranium; a big canine punctured a temple. It didn't take the guy long to settle down.

Steel struggled to her feet, cradling her arm, seething with pain and rage. "You atavistic moron! What the hell do you think you're doing?" Her eyes were green fire. "Nobody touches—" She was too angry to finish. He wasn't going to answer anyway. His eyes had lost focus. He hadn't been able to breathe for about a minute. Then Steel saw me dangling from the rail struts. "Mo! Mo, what are—? Are you all right? I mean, oh, my—HAM! We've got to get him up from there!"

Ham looked up at her. The tall guy looked impotently down at me. I don't think he could have lifted his spirits, never mind two and a half meters of ex-Martian, and Steel's arm was broken.

Ham started to release Mr. Muscle, but Steel said, "No! No, don't let him go!" Which gave Ham a conundrum, and put me in a bit of a spot as well. I don't think either one of us could figure out how he was going to hang onto the guy and pull me back onto the bridge at the same time. Ham looked at Steel inquiringly, the man's skull still in his mouth.

The tall guy was no help at all. He just stood there, frozen. Finally, Steel said, "I don't know! I don't know, just get rid of him! I don't want him around me!"

Ham came to a decision. He stood up carrying his limp prey in his teeth and casually threw him over the side. I saw him flash past me to fall down and down, splash into deep water and slide over the lip of the falls. Ham then reached a long, simian arm over the railing, grabbed me under the armpit and swung me back up onto the bridge. Simple enough. I almost passed out from the pain in my chest.

I sat on the bridge deck feeling woozy as Steel got on her system: "Jean-Léon! Jean-Léon, Krupp is coming down the Poellat." (The name of the stream). "Ham threw him off the bridge. He'd been quite violent." She listened. "Yes, yes. Try to fish him out before there's brain damage. I don't want to have to pay for re-booting him. We're coming down now. We'll be there in a few minutes."

I coughed up something sticky and metallic—I really wasn't feeling too well. The sun was coming out again, I could see it reflecting on the wet wood, but it seemed to be getting darker anyway. And the bridge kept swaying around. That wasn't right. I started to say something to Steel about it, but ...

" ... "

" ... why I continue to counsel against ..."

" ... Krupp has always ..."

" ... guess that's my decision, not yours ..."

" ... "

... the sky was a deep blue, a royal blue, almost a midnight blue, spattered with gold five-pointed stars ...

I was in a golden hall ... gold on gold ... Thick shafts of mote-filled sunlight spilled in between wine-colored columns of porphyry ... gold Byzantine arches covered with interlocking polychrome filigrees sat on lustrous gold capitals ... brilliant blue pillars of lapis lined the gilded upper gallery ... color everywhere ... a huge, Byzantine crown hung above me, gold, covered with white candles ... Saints in bright robes conversed solemnly, golden glories emanating from their bearded visages ... I saw Jesus standing in a golden field, surrounded by cherubim, attended by seraphim, adored by John and Mary ... On the—floor? Was it a floor? Fantastic animals and feathery trees cavorted and danced ... Broad stairs of creamy marble ascended to the apse where a magnificent throne of gold and ivory stood ... And on that throne sat—sat—

Steel. Talking to the tall guy.

Or maybe yelling.

"You were there," she was saying, "and I had logged on."

He nodded, trying to placate her.

"Look what he did to my man!"

"Yes, yes—"

"He was simply trying to protect me!"

"Krupp has had—"

"Krupp should freaking re-structure!" Steel was really mad. I couldn't really figure out why, but then, I couldn't really figure out why I couldn't move. Somebody passed between them and me. I couldn't see who. I was only seeing what was right in front of me. Outside of that circle things were really fuzzy.

"I was going to say that Krupp has had issues with you since you maneuvered him out of this place. I've always thought it unwise to provoke him. I still think so."

"This has nothing to do with him."

"He seems to think it does."

Oh! I was in a nano-doc. There must be something wrong with me. It covered me up to my chest. I could see a large bandage on my shoulder. A cool hand was laid on my forehead. A familiar hand.

"You're right," Steel was saying, " 'he seems to think.' He doesn't actually think, he just seems to—"

"Estelle, this attitude will do no good. First your escapade on Eden. Now this adventure. You can't really blame him for feeling—"

"He BROKE MY ARM! Do you understand?"

Eden? What the hell was Steel doing on Eden? Didn't she ever go anyplace legal?

"Yes. He was out of control. He will be counseled."

"I'm not paying for his 'boot. I logged on. I have it all recorded. You were there."

"Yes, I was there. I'm sure it will all be worked out."

"He's paying for my arm, too. And my—" she looked at me. "Mo! You're awake. How are you feeling?" She descended the steps and came up beside me.

"I ... uh, I'm not sure ..."

She put a finger to my lips. "Don't try to talk now. Just rest. Archie's here."

Archie's face swam into my field of vision. "Hi, sport," she said. "If you're gonna dance, you ought to learn the steps first." She smiled at me. I don't think I'd ever seen her smile like that before.

Steel came back. Had she left? I had no idea. "I had them bring you in here so I would know when you woke up," she said, leaning over me. Her eyes filled my vision. "I have even more to thank you for, now." She kissed me on the mouth.

"Thank you." No, that wasn't right. I should have said—what?

"You take it easy." It was Archie again. "You got a pretty good concussion, there. Not to mention a punctured lung. We'll have you out of there in a few minutes."

"Good." That sounded right. No. "Thank you."

"   "
...

I was in a cave—no. I was in a bed, an intricately sculpted fantasy of a bed, under a heavy, sky-blue coverlet that was embroidered with golden vines and white swans. The impression of a cave was made by the carved wooden canopy—a fantastic puzzle of dozens of interlocking Neogothic spires and steeples, delicate and pointed, thick with ornamental buds and boles, connected by fairy arches and flying buttresses.

Outside the window I could see the Poellat gorge, the delicate footbridge arching over the falls. Across the room a thick, oaken door, carved to resemble a cathedral window, opened beneath a pastoral scene from *Tristan and Isolde*. Archie walked through it.

"Feeling any better?" she smiled.

"Yeah," I croaked in return, "Much better. What room is this?"

"You got the royal treatment. Steel gave you her room. It made it easier to keep an eye on you."

"Oh."

"How are you doing?"

I sat up and looked around. "Uh, much better, really."

"They've made some improvements in nano-docs in the last three decades. I've got some catching up to do."

"Yeah. I bet."

"Let me just check some things ..." She sat down on the bed and started doing doctor stuff, thumpings, peerings, various invasions of privacy.

I asked her, "I was in the throne room, right?"

"That's right." She shined a small light in my left eye.

"Hmm. You know ... when I woke up there, I ... I thought ..."

"What?" She shined it in my right.

"I thought maybe I'd—I mean, I thought I was in—"

"Does that hurt?" She dug her fingers into my ribs.

"No."

"How about that?" She dug in a different place.

"No."

"Good. Your rib seems to have knitted up just fine."

"It feels okay." She listened to my lung. I asked, "What's the story with this Krupp guy?"

"He kind of went crazy, didn't he?"

"Kind of."

"It's that damn genome work of his. They have to keep his system flooded with so many hormones and steroids ... Let's take this off and see how things are progressing." She turned me around to get at the bandage on my left shoulder.

"What happened to my shoulder?"

"He roughed you up pretty good. Tore a couple of scales off."

"Oh. How does he get away with acting like that?"

She peeled the dressing away. "You mean, why don't they fix him?" There was a bright pink place where the shoulder plate and the plate under it had been ripped away.

"Yeah, I guess. Why would he *want* to act that way? How can he get so disconnected?"

Archie chuckled knowingly. I hate it when people do that. She asked me, "How long have you been off the net?"

"Me? Just under a year. Why?"

"Have you noticed yourself getting a little paranoid? A little reclusive?"

I didn't answer. I didn't know what she was driving at.

"Developing a little bit of 'me against the cosmos' attitude?"

"Maybe."

She prodded my shoulder. "Tender?"

"Nope."

"You ever wonder how people in the syndicates live with the idea of sending their fellow human beings into the trades? You know, enslaving them, turning them into human machines?"

"I guess I always assumed they were callous bastards."

Archie laughed as she bundled up the bandage and threw it away. "Interesting and oddly appropriate choice of phrase. It shows your age." She turned to me, "Do you think *you* could do it?"

"What? Send people into the trades?"

She nodded.

"No."

"You've worked for the corps, haven't you? Weren't you an architect or something?"

"Yeah."

"Then you've worked with people who were in the trades. Worked over them."

"Yeah, but I tried not to work them over."

Archie smiled at my attempt at levity. "You felt connected to them. One with them."

"Yes. Very much so."

"You notice you never rose into management."

I nodded. She sat down in an ornate wooden chair whose cushion matched the coverlet on the bed. She was right. I'd always been in the creative team, whether it was to design buildings or eco-systems, never management.

"You never will," she said. "You've spent too much time on the net."

"What do you mean? Everybody's on the net."

"We're not. Steel isn't."

"That's because—"

"Neither is Krupp, or his tall friend, Daimler. Or anyone else in the syndicates."

"What are you talking about? How would they—"

"Oh, they interface with the net. They communicate with it, they check up on it. But they're not on it. They're all on independent systems. Like Steel. Think about it. Have you ever bulleted a syndicate member on the net?"

"I've never had any reason to—"

"They always came to you, right?"

"Yeah, I guess so."

"Like they do with everybody else."

"But why? Why aren't they on the net?"

Archie examined me for a while. Then she said, "Psychological necessity. Their positions require them to do things that connected people couldn't do."

"Things that ... Yes."

"You lived through that time," she continued. "You should remember what created the necessity for this economic system."

I thought about it. Going to the stars. To build ... "So everyone could afford to re-boot."

"That's right," she nodded. "We had to create wealth on an unprecedented scale. We had to invest on an unprecedented scale. The cheapest possible way we could do it *still* almost bankrupted us."

I thought of Valhalla. "Yes." It had been so very, very expensive.

"It's the paradox of our time. Everybody hates the corps because they take people into the trades, an inarguably evil thing to do. Tantamount to slavery."

"Yes."

"And yet if it weren't for the trades none of those people could afford to re-boot. They literally owe their lives to the corps."

"And the syndicates that control them."

She nodded. "To answer your initial question: there are two reasons people like Krupp get away with their behavior. One is that people like him are necessary to the system."

"How so?"

"The corps have always needed people who were aggressive, ruthless. Competitive. It's how they survive. The question is ..."

"What?"

"Do we still need them to survive?"

I thought about that for a while. Then I said, "What's the second reason?"

"Oh," Archie allowed herself a little, sardonic laugh. "The second reason is they can afford to pay the damages." She stood up and patted me on the shoulder. The uninjured one. "You see? One afternoon in a nano-doc and a good night's rest and you're back to normal."

"Right," I laughed, "Are you going to put my scales back on?"

Archie looked at me, "What do you mean?"

"You know, the ones he tore off me."

"Oh. I don't know. Steel said you were going to be getting your genome re-vamped anyway."

"Oh, right," I remembered, "but you have them, don't you?"

"N-no, I don't think we do. Why?"

I was getting alarmed. "Where are they?"

"Hey, settle down," She placed her hand on my arm. "What's the matter?"

"You have the bigger one? The shoulder plate?"

"Not so far as I know. Why?"

"It had a small meteorite mounted in it. Remember?"

"Yes," she nodded. Then, "Oh, no! Was that a talisman?"

"My first. From my first life."

"Oh, Mo! Why did you have it in such a vulnerable place?"

"I didn't think I was going to get beat up and thrown off a bridge," I snapped.

"I'm sorry. Of course not. Well, maybe they found them, have them somewhere. Maybe they just didn't give them to me, you know, in all the confusion."

But they were nowhere to be found. Washed down the Poellat. Probably in the Danube by that time. Gone.

We asked Jean-Léon if Krupp had had anything in his hands when they fished him out, but no. "Non. Non, rien. Je regrette." He seemed genuinely concerned.

I'd had that little cosmic rock since I was nine years old. Some damages can't be paid.

PART IV
CIRCE

CHAPTER 16

After I recovered we got off Earth in a hurry. The only stop before we left was the little shop Steel loves in Lausanne. We both got re-worked. Another mystery. My scales are gone, as is her fur. Her eyes are back to normal, if you call spectacularly beautiful, almond-shaped eyes normal. Her corneas are visible, her irises round. Their color is closer to blue now than green. And we're both quite a bit shorter. We could pass for Terrans from an earlier epoch. Why? Don't ask me, I only work here.

Of course everyone changes appearance from time to time, particularly if you're moving from planet to planet. The Lightdancer had bulked all of us up so we could handle Earth's gravity after the gentle pull of Vesper. Then she slimmed us down a little when we headed for Circe, our first stop in the Pleiades. That sort of thing you hardly notice, these days.

I remember one time, in the early thirties I think, they made a huge reality about ancient Earth. It was one of those sweeping historical (or semi-historical) romances, filled with privateers and sheiks and wooden ships. The hero and heroine were two Africans that were captured and sold as slaves, one to an Arabian Emir, the other to a Don somebody-or-other in South America somewhere. The story was long and improbable, but very romantic.

For decades afterward there were Africans everywhere. If you didn't have gleaming black skin you just weren't stylish.

Then they did one about an Icelandic edda and everyone had red braids and freckles for a while. And there was a huge one that aspired to enact the entire Bhagavad-Gita—I don't think one out of ten people understood it, but for a while everyone looked like me.

Now *I* look like me. And I assume Steel looks like she originally did. Only both of us have lost about half a meter.

It's funny about her eyes, though. You get used to seeing a person through their eyes. I can't tell if she's more available or less.

The crew had a great liberty in Paris. I guess Alice particularly had a good time. They saw the new band, TAUToLOGy, in concert. She and Yuri came back singing, "I PERsonally LOVE you, 'cause THAT'S the way I FEEL." Yuri also managed to convince everyone to tube out to Malibu on the west coast of North America to go surfing. They even got Marcus to come up from Senegal. Tamika got a great suntan.

Steel was a little peeved about it. If anyone had actually managed to drown in the ocean, it would have taken them three months to re-boot. This would have delayed things, either while she waited for them to come back online or while she looked for a replacement.

If anything, she's in a bigger hurry now than before we got to Earth. I think she's worried about Krupp and Daimler coming after her, but I'm not sure. Krupp has to re-boot, himself, which gives us a three-month head start, but Steel seems worried, nonetheless.

We're in the Pleiades now. Four hundred stars in an open cluster just twenty-five light years across. Compare that to the thirty or so within twenty-five light years of the sun and then toss in streams and whorls of interstellar dust and gas glowing blue in reflected starlight. The sky is an opal filled with fire.

We've come to Circe to pick up the new ultra-lights and some other new equipment Yuri has been designing. And to meet for some reason with the curator of the Antigone Institute. Circe is a ringed planet, like Saturn, except that the planet itself is terrestrial. It was the first project in the Pleiades, originally colonized in the twenty-ninth century by militant separatist neo-Feminists. Even after all this time it's still about eighty-five percent femmes. They were first going to call the planet Lesbos, but the majority thought that was too obvious, so they decided to name it after the sorceress who turned men into pigs. This ruffled a lot of feathers at the time, but I guess the war taught people how expensive ruffled feathers can be. The name is still considered an act of open contempt or defiant patriotism, depending on who you ask.

Speaking of feathers, they're everywhere: crests and tails and bird tattoos. Not everyone has the avian genome work that's characteristic of the Pleiadean style, but it's pretty prevalent. It's like walking around inside a casino floor show.

We landed at Medea spaceport and immediately tubed out to the Antigone Institute, so we didn't get to see much of Boleyn. That was a shame; I would have liked to spend some time there. From the Institute we could see the skyline across the bay. They've gone far beyond anything else I've seen in the use of structural free-form Lucite. Boleyn itself is completely transparent—soaring, whimsical shapes inspired by long-stemmed cocktail glasses and melted chandeliers. Suspended globs and spires are connected by airy bridges that look like they liquefied and were caught by the wind. With the rings behind it arcing up across the southern sky it's absolutely stunning.

We've made so many beautiful places.

The Institute itself is housed in the dome that covered the original colony before they finished engineering the atmosphere and could live outside. It's huge. The old service airlock has been transformed into a grand, arching entrance that leads into the main gallery—still the largest collection of bio-aesthetics in the known galaxy.

Steel had us stop in the tree-orchid grove beside the waterfall. Petals like tongues and arms and slippers, white dappled with royal, flame blending to sullen coals, stamens crowned with shocking chrome-yellow pollen: the blooms were the size of cartwheels. They waved lazily above us on ten-meter stalks as thick as my thigh, spangled with mist.

"Lys said she would meet us here." Steel spoke above the roar of the falls. "Mo," her new eyes were grave, "I'd like you to come with Alice and me ..." I looked at Alice. Alice looked detached. "After what happened at home—at Neuschwanstein—I think you should know ..." The rest of the crew was a study in the variety of ways one can disguise heightened interest. Marcus straightened, glanced at Steel, and was stoic. Archie studied her hands. Yuri had climbed up a few feet on the rocks around the waterfall; he adroitly extended a look at Steel into an invitation to Tamika to follow him up. Jemal was the worst at it, the most ingenuous. He had to realize that everyone else was disinterested before he found a bed of plume-flowers to give his attention to.

And then she didn't go on. "Yuri?" she said. He looked down at Steel from the rocks. "You know where to go?"

"Sure." Marcus glanced at him; Yuri adjusted. "Yes, Captain. I remember. I just hope they remember *me*."

"What do you mean?" Steel asked.

"Well, it's only been a couple of years for me—it's been over three decades for everybody else."

Steel smiled. "Yes. Lys was pleasantly surprised to hear from me. But don't worry. I'm sure she has everyone alerted to your impending arrival. Marcus?"

"Yes, Captain."

"You can get everything loaded?"

"I'm sure we'll make out all right, Captain. They've still got a dedicated freight tube direct to Medea. Security looks good."

"Good. Archie?"

Archie looked up from her digital studies. "I've already filed my reports—"

Steel tensed slightly, "Nothing about Drake."

"No, of course not. How could I?"

She eased again. "Of course."

"But I could use a little time to collate my notes."

"Certainly. Would you like to go back to the ship?"

"No. I can do it here. If that's all right."

Steel gazed at her with that same mix of empathy, patience and determination that I had seen before. "Yes." She looked around at everyone, "We shouldn't be long."

For a moment we waited for Lys to arrive and I tried to decide who to observe. My eye was drawn to Alice, her hands behind her, digging a toe into the dirt beside the tile path. When I glanced at Archie she returned my gaze, eyes filled with caution, with weariness, with the search for wisdom. Aluminum geodesics arched far above us. Macaws and Birds-of-Paradise flashed brightly through the air.

An explosion of white rounded the curve in the path and stretched her arms out toward Steel. "Well, it looks like the Flying Dutchman rounded the Horn after all!"

As they embraced I recognized her. Even so, even though it made sense that Steel would move in these circles, I still had to ask Archie, "Is that—?"

"Lysistrata-24. Yes."

"The person who—"

"Who negotiated the Treaty of Alcyone. And signed it."

I remembered. She had changed her style of plumage since then, but her face was unmistakable. Wow, I thought, we are playing in the big leagues now.

She took just a second to take in Steel's new appearance and then looked around at the rest of us. Where hair might have been, white feathers sprouted. From a pronounced widow's peak (*There's* an archaic term. I wonder what it's called now?) dazzling plumes grew into a tufted crown that erected as her facial expression brightened. The line of feathers continued down her spine, spreading into a snowy peacock's tail five feet long. Ivory eyes the size of my palm tipped each quill. Her pubic mound was covered in a soft triangle of white down.

She smiled and her tail spread slightly. "Everyone looks like they're holding up fairly well." Her eyes rested on me for a moment. Wariness? Acceptance. She turned to Steel, "It was disappointing to hear that Drake decided to leave the project. He was a very good resource." Then back to me, "But I'm glad you found someone to take over for him."

Steel came over to me. "This is Mohandas. He's already proven to be very valuable. To the project and to me."

Lysistrata-24 appraised me. "Good," she said. She took my hand, "It's good to meet you."

"Uh, thanks. Me, too. To meet you, I mean. It's an honor." How do you talk to the person who managed to end the most devastating war (psychologically as well as physically) humanity had ever fought? It was like meeting Lincoln. Or my namesake. She moved over to Alice:

"Sorry we have to put you through this again," she said, putting an arm on her shoulder, "It must be getting rather tedious." She smiled warmly at her.

Alice just shrugged and looked somewhere else. "It's okay," was all she said.

"Well." Lysistrata-24 appraised Steel. "Shall we?"

Steel nodded and beckoned me to follow with her eyes.

The Institute is much more than just the Botanical Gardens, of course. It's the largest center of learning and research outside the solar system, established right after the war. Maybe to make up for it, I don't know.

We followed the path through the engineered gardens until we came to a Musahdi lift that carried us far above them, rising past terraced galleries and displays dedicated to various subjects—natural history, technology, medicine. There was a wonderful holographic working model of the brain based on the Farrel group's work; it was about fifty stories tall. You could walk around inside it and follow the nerve impulse patterns.

About two hundred stories up we stepped off onto a balcony that led into the war archives. I could tell it was less visited than the lower floors. It was lonelier, sadder. It had been a war that had produced no heroes, only horrors. We passed under a large plaque that read "The War of Liberation."

"Hmm," I said absently, "I'd always heard it called the Pleiadean War." Or the Feminist Insurrection, but I didn't say that.

Lys smiled. "You must be from Draco," she said.

A hologram filled one entire wall to our left. It was one of the early rallies in Benazir Square, in the original Boleyn—the one that had been destroyed. Thousands of women filled the square, dressed in fashions of the last millennium. They faced the huge dais backed by the colossal banner that had become so familiar on the net: the curved white raindrop of the Yin sign centered in a field of red.

Then I saw her.

"There you are!" I said, feeling like a rube as soon as the words left my mouth.

The three of them stopped and looked at the image. There was Lysistrata-24 standing on the dais, to the left and slightly upstage of Saba and Indira-3. Everyone on the platform had iridescent black plumage—but they weren't uniform; there was a wide variation in style.

"Hmm," Lys smiled—wistfully? No, she was too dignified to be wistful. There was regret there, though, and pain, and some residual anger. I wondered who she was angry at. "It's hard to believe that was over a thousand years ago."

I nodded.

"We celebrated our millennial five decades ago. It was quite a party."

"I'll bet."

We moved on.

Another hologram: a wrecked spaceship on a cratered plain under a harsh, black sky. Beside it a mosaic of faces—a memorial to the four thousand men who had perished. I had to stop and listen to the docent—it was a warm, female voice:

"On September 17th, 2934, the transport Karachi lifted from Circe bound for Monde Bleu in Draco. It carried 4,022 forced male émigrés as part of Circe's controversial gender purification program. At the time tensions between the newly formed Pleiadean Congress and Draco were very high. In July of 2934 the Congress had passed the Independent Network Act, taking the 4.3 million women of the Pleiades off the net. The Draconian High Command responded by mounting an expeditionary force that was en route to the Pleiades to 'restore order.' Due to a malfunction in the Circe planetary defense system, the Karachi was mistaken for a Draconian military vessel and fired upon. Severely damaged, the Karachi impacted on Circe's largest moon, Ariadne, and all aboard were lost."

There followed a list of names.

"That's what started the war, wasn't it?" I asked.

Lysistrata turned and walked back to where I was standing. She looked at the image and said, "In history it's hard to tell where things start and stop, but the Karachi incident did lead to a hardening of positions on both sides."

I looked at the faces.

"It was a tragedy," she continued. "Both governments blamed the other for the wreck. Both denied responsibility."

"But it was your responsibility, wasn't it? I mean, not yours—the Pleiades'. Circe's."

"One could certainly make a case for that. We were the ones who shot them down. Of course, we wouldn't have been so trigger-happy if Draco hadn't sent the expeditionary force."

"Well, yes. But—I mean, the gender purification, the—the Independent Network Act ..." I wasn't sure I wanted to argue politics with her, but her position seemed—I don't know ... I don't know. Maybe I would have felt the same if I were her.

"Those were mistakes. Tactically and philosophically." She looked at the holo for a moment more, "A lot of us were very angry back then," then turned and walked on.

Steel wasn't just staying silent, she was staying neutral. Her bearing was balanced, non-confrontational. Quiescent. Alice was being patient—she had the patience of the powerless—and there was embarrassment, too, as if this were all somehow her fault. Not the war, but us being there. Something.

As we penetrated farther into the archives, Lysistrata continued to speak: "You're probably not aware of the conditions on Earth back in the mid-twenties. The things that led us to colonize Circe in the first place—"

"I remember," I said.

"Oh?" she turned to me as we walked past holos of the war, each more horrific than the last, "you were there?"

"Not on Earth," I answered, "but in the system." I added, "I was married."

"Oh." A different 'oh.' She searched my eyes for a moment, "That must have been difficult." Steel was paying close attention. Alice wasn't. She didn't seem to be.

"Well," I said, "I certainly learned pretty quickly where not to use phrases like 'my wife.' "

"Yes, I would imagine."

I should have just shut up—but, oh no, not me. "If you said it around any neo-feminists, you were treated like you owned slaves."

I'm sure she'd had this conversation with much better rhetoricians than I could ever hope to be. I guess I couldn't blame her for not wanting to have it with me. "Mm," she said. I plowed on anyway. I don't know why:

"If you let it slip that she was pregnant," strange how close to the surface my anger was—considering the number of centuries that had intervened, "they treated you like some kind of Nazi sadist."

She accepted my anger with grace and poise, not surprising for one of the greatest diplomats in history: "It must have seemed quite unfair to someone who hadn't been on Earth."

All I could say was, "Yeah."

"Did your wife bear children?"

"Hmm?" I guess my thoughts were elsewhere, on lost moments long ago. "Oh, uh, no. No. She was pregnant once but, uh, you know, it didn't work out. She, uh ... she, um, oh—what's the word..."

"She aborted?"

"No, no. She, ah—oh , hell, what is it?"

"She miscarried?"

"Yeah, that's it." I guess I laughed a little. It's weird what will strike you funny. And when. "It's been a long time since I heard *that* word."

She looked at me with great compassion. "I'm sorry," she said.

"What? Oh, yeah, well. Thanks. It was a long time ago."

We passed more displays. Some relics, some holos. All pretty grisly.

"Actually, we never liked the term 'neo-feminist,' " she went on, "We certainly never applied it to ourselves. The Yin were very much different from the feminists of the twentieth century."

I asked with real interest, "Oh, yeah? How so?" I found myself wanting to make friends with her. I guess I was embarrassed for getting angry.

"Well," she started, "for one thing, the technological issues were quite different. Feminism arose at a time of mechanical innovation. It dealt with the social ramifications of integrating women into the work force. The Yin dealt more than anything with the controversies caused by unlimited life extension."

"Oh, yeah, I see what you mean."

"But we also came from quite different economic backgrounds."

"Yeah?"

"Oh, yes. The feminists," she stopped for a moment to adjust a display piece, some sort of weapon, I think, "were the last in a long line of rich, privileged people complaining that their rights were being unfairly abridged." She looked back at me. "They were carrying on a long tradition; one that stretched back through Jefferson, Paine and Adams in the eighteenth century all the way back to the medieval English nobles who forced King John to sign the Magna Carta. Wealthy people, fabulously wealthy, whether you compare them to others alive on Earth at the time or any who had lived up to that time; people with nothing to complain about, really. And yet complain they did, and quite eloquently."

This was all way before my time—she obviously knew much more about it than I did. But it was interesting. "And the Yin?" I asked.

"Well," she thought for a moment. "Political movements depend on communication. Back in those days fast communication was a product of wealth. The feminists arose in the rich nations of North America and Europe where communication was cheap and easy. Where life in general was easy. They worried about things like 'glass ceilings' and whether or not advertising exploited the female form. At the same time the ancestors of the Yin—my ancestors—were languishing in the truly wretched poverty of eastern Africa and southern Asia. Some were surgically altered to make them more faithful wives—the theory being if they couldn't experience sexual pleasure they couldn't be tempted by it. Others were placed in arranged marriages as early as age four to boys they had never met, then shipped off to their new families to serve—in every sense of the word—as slave labor. They were denied the most fundamental education. They had their dress, behavior and thoughts dictated to them. They had no rights to be abridged."

I could hear the passion in her voice—and I *knew* about *this* stuff. "Yes. My— uh, my—" She seemed pretty old. Maybe she had a father, too. "My father's people originated in northern India. They moved to South Africa under the British and then to Mars a few centuries later. He told me a lot of what had gone on."

"Hmm," she nodded. "Perhaps you can understand why we never felt we had much in common with anyone so rich they could afford to burn their underwear as a form of political protest."

"The feminists burned their underwear?"

"At one point they did."

"Huh." I remembered underwear, but I couldn't figure out how burning it could be taken as a political gesture. That's the thing about history, I guess. If you learn enough about any culture that you haven't actually lived in, sooner or later it just seems silly.

But Lys was speaking: "Communication. It was the net that brought down the old hierarchy—their desire to increase the power of the net. They needed us to do that."

"The more minds that were connected—"

"Exactly. The 'Third World,' as it was called, didn't have much, but it had a great many people.

"It was really the greatest achievement of the age, integrating the entire human race into one informational system, but they had to know it would change everything—economics, politics, social structures. It certainly gave us the ability to communicate quickly and cheaply. Can you imagine the first time a woman in purdah in, say, Afghanistan, communicated directly with another in Eritrea or Iraq?"

I was trying to remember where those places were. I knew they were on Earth, but that was all. She went on:

"Perhaps if we'd had time to get used to it before we were given open-ended longevity, we could have avoided some of the turmoil." She glanced at another display as we passed it. "Some of the tragedy."

I hadn't thought about it, but it was kind of ironic. The net gave us re-booting, a gift horse that was hard to look in the mouth, but the two of them together were a pretty big package of change for any culture to absorb.

We were passing a holo of one of the prison camps on Alcyone IV. It was near the end of the war, when all political and military goals had seemed to be reduced to nothing more than sadism and sexual anger. It was as if every rejection, every betrayal, every slight and humiliation throughout history was being avenged in one terminal paroxysm of rage. The things women and men had done to each other in that conflict were practically beyond imagining. The rules had broken down. The very concept of inter-gender warfare was so horrific that when it actually happened people just went insane.

I gestured toward the image, "You're saying that re-booting caused ... caused *this*?"

Lys was somber as she studied the scene. She shook her head, "No. Misguided ambition and diplomatic incompetence, unforgivable diplomatic incompetence, caused the war. But re-booting laid the foundation for it."

I didn't get it. "How? I mean—how?"

Lys stopped walking and turned to me. She started to form an answer and then stopped. She didn't seem impatient, it was more like she felt we had strayed from the purpose of our meeting.

I said, "I'm sorry, you don't have to—I mean, I know we're here for some other—These displays are just so ... so ..."

"That's all right," she said. "They were designed to provoke a reaction. A conversation. It's important to discuss these things," she gazed at the holo, "very important." She seemed lost for a moment. "And your question is legitimate. Quite pertinent, in fact. I'll try to answer it, although historians have been chewing on it for centuries."

We started walking again. She thought for a moment and then said, "The net profoundly altered all economic, political, and large-scale social structures in a very short period of time—a matter of decades, perhaps even of years." She thought a moment more, "But the most basic social unit, the 'family', was still intact. It had changed a great deal, to be sure, but it still survived. The main purpose of the family was—"

"To raise children," Alice said.

Lys turned to her, "That's right, Alice. To raise children." She put a hand on Alice's shoulder and went on, "But even as far back as the end of the twentieth century children were starting to be thought of as more of an inconvenience than a blessing. It's always seemed odd to me that this came about in the wealthy nations first, where the financial burden of child rearing could be borne most easily. But after analysis, it makes perfect sense."

It did? I couldn't wait to find out how.

"You see, one had to be rich enough to be concerned with the quality of life, rather than mere survival, to consider not having offspring. Overpopulation and the environmental degradation it caused were only concerns to those with the wealth and leisure to be able to sit back and enjoy the view. To someone living in a dirt-floored hut scratching a living out of a small patch of earth procreation was one of the very few creative joys of life. To the wealthy, other options were open. Why be a parent when one could be a lawyer, an advertising executive, an entertainer? Or fill some other, equally essential social function?"

She had a very subtle irony about her. I was liking her more and more.

"And how did this lead to the war?" I asked.

She smiled. "I'm sorry. Digression is one of the hazards of being a museum curator. Too much information, not enough direction." She pondered. "The war, yes. Re-booting, as you call it—you wouldn't believe where that term originally came from—re-booting gave us open-ended longevity and that very gift took away two things: the need to carry on the family and the chance of a better life after this one was done. The heavenly reward, the wheel of karma, joining one's honored ancestors, these were given up in exchange for not having to lose loved ones, not having to face the pain and uncertainty of one's own physical cessation. In these two ways it struck at the core of the one social adhesive that the net hadn't really touched."

"Religion."

"Yes. And it wasn't as if one moment everyone lived their three score and ten and the next, everyone lived forever."

"Certainly not. Those were long, tough centuries before everyone could afford it."

"And it took even longer to gain the power and techniques to deal with accidental trauma in remote areas, longer still to be able to handle large numbers of people in a short time. If the wreck of the Karachi occurred today, no one would perish, even if there were twice as many people aboard. But during those centuries the forces tearing at the structure of societies were colossal, and the more fundamentally religious a culture was, the more wrenching was the displacement. Religious groups splintered, some grappling with the new set of circumstances, others becoming violently reactionary. Many cultures started oscillating between directionless permissiveness and crushingly orthodox theocracies. You see? If the purpose of life was no longer to 'make a better world for our children,' nor to prepare our souls for the next life, what was left? To make a better world for ourselves? To serve only ourselves and nothing greater? To acquire endlessly bigger houses and better gadgets? More and more toys? More and more wealth?"

"Things got pretty existential there, for a while, didn't they?" I shook my head at the memories. "I guess it was quite a bit easier on Mars. All the social structures there were new anyway. A lot less tradition to fight against."

"Yes. It was the fight against tradition that was so disruptive, so painful for everyone. The Yin rose from the last, most extreme cycle of orthodoxy. It was our fight to end our roles as subservient chattels and vessels of reproduction that ultimately led to the war."

We came at last to the administration area, leaving the horrors behind us. We entered a plush reception room. Floor to ceiling windows looked out to the north, reminding us how high we were. Far below the rolling Serendipity Mountains crowded the coastline clad in golden grasses, sensually folding into branching gullies and narrow valleys lined with sparse groves of acacia trees. Clouds were moving in from the west, their bases close enough to touch. The overcast bathed everything in pewter.

Lys offered Steel and me seats in her office and then took Alice through another door. "This shouldn't take long," she said.

We sat uncomfortably for a moment before I asked, "What's happening in there?" referring to where they'd just disappeared.

"Probably just some tests," she answered, not looking at me. I don't know if it was the lack of fur or just the situation, but Steel seemed very naked, very vulnerable.

"Probably?" I asked.

"Yes."

"I don't understand. We traveled all the way to the Pleiades so someone could 'probably' do some tests? What tests?"

"Well," she kept getting quieter, "we didn't expect to be gone so long, you know, the time dilation. Lys is hoping they've made some progress."

And that was it.

"Progress in what?" seemed to be the next logical question.

"Let's wait until they come back."

"Okay." We waited. Then I said, "That's quite an exhibition they have. About the war."

"Yes. I wanted you to see it." And she looked at me as if to say, 'I guess you understand now.'

I suppose I must have looked back at her with an 'Uh, nope' expression on my face because she went on, "We just want to make the world a better place, that's all. We just want to make the world better."

Maybe I'm slow, but I still didn't get the connection. "Well," I said, trying to keep the conversation going, to fill time if nothing else, "She had some interesting ideas."

"Lys is a crazy old bird. Re-booting didn't cause the war."

Oh. "I *thought* she had a pretty odd take on—"

"Hubris caused the war. The war happened because nobody believed it *could* happen. Men couldn't believe that they'd ever go off with the purpose of deliberately killing large numbers of women, and the Yin, the *freaking* Yin were so goddamned convinced war was a purely masculine failing that they refused to see it coming. Even after they built their 'defense' system. Even after the Karachi. It was stupid. Just stupid."

Passion always takes a moment to absorb. I pondered what to say: "Maybe that's what she meant by—by unforgivable diplom ... unforgivably bad diplomacy— what did she call it?"

"Yes. Probably."

"Are you all right?"

"Yes. I'm sorry. I'll be fine. I didn't mean to ..."

Then it struck me, "Did you fight in the war?"

"What? No. No." She thought. "Why, did you?"

"No, Valhalla was enough for me. I never wanted to see anything like that again. I spent the whole Pleiadean Wa— I mean, the War of Liberation, drunk in the outer arm somewhere."

"Hmm." She seemed distracted. We waited for a while.

They finally came back.

"All right, Alice. Thanks for your patience," Lys smiled.

"Sure," Alice replied. She had a small bandage on her right shoulder.

Steel stood up so I did, too. "Alice," she said, "why don't you go join Tamika and Yuri? I just bulleted them, they're in the—"

"I know," Alice replied, "And I want to do the pandimensional interactive ride, too." She smiled, "Since we're here."

"All right. We'll see you in a little bit."

And off she went.

Steel turned to Lysistrata. Expectation? Hope? No, no hope. If there had been, Lys took no time disabusing it. She shook her head: "It's still getting the better of us. We were hoping to have made some significant advances, but it's still just too time intensive. We just take too long."

"I guess I didn't really expect anything else."

"I'm sorry. I hope you don't feel that you made the trip for nothing."

"No, we had to get the new equipment anyway. And, there was a chance. It was worth finding out."

"Um ..." I said.

Steel turned to me. "Oh, I'm sorry, Mo. Lys, would you mind explaining this to him? I don't think I have it in me."

Lys looked at me, surprised, "Oh, I thought you already knew. Of course. Let's sit down."

Steel walked over to the window and gazed out at the mountains and the ocean. The wind was rising. Fistfuls of fat raindrops spattered against the glass. Lys and I sat facing each other.

"We took some tissue samples from Alice to run some tests on. We were hoping that our procedures had progressed enough to give us positive results, but I'm afraid we were disappointed."

"Why? Is there something wrong with her?"

"Put quite simply," she gathered herself, her feather crest lay back on her head, "if we can't find a way around it, Alice is going to die."

She said it just like that, 'Alice is going to die,' like Alice was an old battery, or a houseplant, or a bad joke. I didn't know what to say. And then an adrenaline rush of panic hit me: "Does she have the plague?"

"No, no, it's nothing like that. Nothing that's contagious. It's a genetic condition. A condition that prevents her from undergoing longevity treatment.

Re-booting."

"Does she need to re-boot?"

"She will eventually."

Of course. "Well, uh, how long does she—How long till—I mean ..." My head was swimming in soup. And not doing a very good job, at that.

"That depends. She's in fine shape. If nothing happens to her she shouldn't need to re-boot for another five or six decades. Maybe more."

"But what's wrong with her? Is this something new, or, or ... I mean, is it a mutation, or something?"

"Well, it's a sort of mutation, yes." She turned to Steel. "Alice tells me you're planning to go back to Eden."

Eden? What did Eden have to do with this? I seemed to remember something ... something at Neuschwanstein. Maybe that's why we got re-worked.

Steel said simply, "Yes."

"Do you think that's a good idea?"

I didn't think it was a good idea. Don't get me wrong, going to Eden is practically a misdemeanor compared with going to Brainard's Planet, but there's a really good reason why it's off limits.

"The trip back took so long ... this may be the last chance she has to see her ... parents. It's been three decades—a little more."

"Wait a minute," I said, "You're saying Alice is from—she was born on—I mean, Alice was ... was born?"

Lys nodded solemnly. Alice wasn't a newbie, she'd never been a newbie. Alice had been a baby. She'd had a father and a ... a ... She was from *Eden*? "But, but Eden's a—the people there, they're a ... *suicide* cult." I turned to Steel. "You were there before? You—you took Alice from Eden?"

"Alice. And her brother."

Lys intervened, "I think suicide cult might be too strong a term."

"Well, whatever you want to call them. They don't re-boot—Wait. Alice has a *brother*?" This was a lot of information to absorb all at once.

Steel started, "She *had*—had a ..." but could get no further.

"Perhaps I should bring you up to date," Lys interjected. "I was under the impression that you had all the pertinent information. Steel, didn't you brief him when you brought him on board?"

"She didn't bring me on board. She picked me up in a bar."

"I see. Well."

"What was I supposed to do?" Steel asked, her voice fiery and defensive. "I needed a replacement for Drake. We were stuck in the middle of nowhere, the engine was out of balance, and we couldn't get home. We were running out of time. We're still running out of time." She turned back to the window, obviously very upset.

"I understand," Lys said soothingly, "I understand. I still think we should fill him in now. Don't you?"

Steel didn't say anything. She didn't nod, she didn't do anything; she just kept staring out the window.

Lys turned back to me, "I'm afraid Steel's gotten a bit attached to Alice. We knew that would be a hazard, doing this sort of research."

"You were doing research on Eden?" I asked. "I mean, it's illegal—you're not supposed to ..."

"I know. It was because of our conflict with Draco that Eden was allowed to go off the net, to become isolated from the rest of humanity. The price that was paid to keep the Pleiades integrated was far too high."

"But," I started, "but what did you want to know about Eden? Aren't they just a bunch of fanatics? I mean—zealots, religious extremists ..." It was starting to make a weird kind of sense to me.

"A half-century ago we were planning to celebrate our millennial," Lys replied. "We made funds available for various projects that would help us bring more depth and meaning to the observance. Archie submitted this proposal. Using her background in bio-engineering and social dynamics, she wanted to study the only remaining example of a mortal society, with its religious rites and beliefs— it's social structures and traditions—and contrast it with our own."

Things were falling into place. "So the skyhook was *her* idea?" I asked.

"Yes," she replied, "that was part of her proposal. The project would have to be carried out covertly because of the legal situation, and she figured out a way to get down to the surface. It was quite ingenious, really."

"Yeah, it sure was," I agreed, but my mind was racing ahead. "So—so you guys funded this project?"

Lys shook her head, "It was far too expensive for us to support on our own. We would have had to abandon many other equally meritorious ideas. So we contacted Steel and she agreed to become involved."

"Hmm," I nodded, "how'd you know Steel?"

"Well—"

"We'd known each other for a long time," Steel said, turning toward us.

Lys stopped saying whatever it was she had started to say and said instead, "That's right. You must understand that this project was very intriguing to us. They still practice child-bearing on Eden. Marriage. Funeral rites. There is murder there, and rape. Spousal and child abuse. It was a chance to re-acquaint ourselves with where we had come from, why we had gone through all that we had."

CHAPTER 17

I cornered Yuri in his compartment when we got back to the Lightdancer. "Did you know we were going to Eden?" I asked.

"Eden?"

"Yeah. You know, religious freaks. Nobody 'boots. Everybody goes to heaven. That sort of thing."

"Wait a minute, wait a minute. What are you talking about?"

"Eden! Eden!"

"The planet?"

"Yes!"

Yuri looked at me for a moment. "We're going to freaking Eden?" He threw back his head and laughed. "I knew those two were insane," he said.

"Who?"

"Steel and Archie. Holy Shiva. Eden." He shook his head.

"That's where Archie was doing her research," I told him. "Alice ..." I didn't know if I wanted to talk about this.

"What about Alice?"

"Did you know she was from ..." I didn't know if I wanted to ask him, if I wanted to find out that he'd been lying to me.

"From where? Alice is from Eden?" Understanding bloomed on his face, "Oh, that makes sense," and faded just as quickly, "I guess."

"What do you mean?"

"Hmm? Oh. Well, it doesn't explain—"

"What?"

He shifted tracks, "Well, I mean, it explains why she doesn't remember anything, doesn't it? Before a couple of decades ago, I mean." He looked at me blandly, "I mean, she wouldn't, would she?"

I studied his face. Jesus H. freaking Buddha on a Musadhi lift, who the hell could I trust on this ship? I stared him in the eyes, "You knew, didn't you?"

"What?"

"You knew about Alice." I guess I must have looked threatening; Yuri took a step back:

"What? I didn't know she was from Eden."

"You knew about Alice. That she was going to—that she couldn't—that she can't—"

"Can't what? What did they tell you?"

I took a couple of breaths. I couldn't say this and look at him. I looked at ... something else. "That Alice has a genetic condition that keeps her from ... re-booting."

"Oh," he scratched his earlobe. "They told you that, did they?"

"Yes. Only they didn't make it sound so pretty." I was so filled with anger and grief and, I don't know, frustration, or something, "They just said she was going to die. Just like that: *Alice is going to DIE.*"

"Hey, hey, hey, settle down. Watch your language."

I raged, "They didn't watch *their* language."

"Well, they should have. Now, just take it easy." He sat me down on his desk.

I tried to take it easy. I think I failed. "You knew, didn't you?" I said.

Yuri contemplated his reply before he made it. "Yeah," he nodded. "Yeah. I knew she couldn't re-boot." He looked at me apologetically, "Sorry. Steel didn't want us to tell you."

"WHY NOT?"

"Would *you* want people to know if *you* couldn't re-boot?"

He had a point.

"But—" I started, "but, why did she tell you?" I sounded like a little kid on a playground: 'no fair keeping secrets.' Allah, Alice had been a little kid just a few years ago.

He replied, "She knows me. She didn't know you. She knew what it would take to get me to go to Brainard's Planet."

"To—What do you mean?"

Yuri sat on the edge of his bunk and looked at the deck. He studied a piece of lint on the carpet, "Steel knows how to work people, you know?" I did. Then he changed his mind, "Ah, it's nothing. It's ... it's nothing. It's stupid."

"What?" I sat down on the chair at his desk tucked into the cubby beside his wardrobe. Crew cabins are small. We were only about three feet apart.

Yuri studied the lint some more and said, "Alice is sweet, isn't she?" He looked at me.

"Yeah," I answered, "she's great. She's a great—" Kid? I couldn't say it. "A great person."

"Bright. Funny. Pretty. She's just about perfect."

"Yeah." I liked Alice. It hurt, it really hurt to think of her being ... not. Not being. Yuri started moving the piece of lint around with the toe of his boot.

"Steel kinda set me up with her at a party she threw in Katmandu a couple of years ago. Well, thirty-three years ago. Depending on your frame of reference." He laughed and shook his head, "Time dilation. Really messes with you."

"Yeah. So what happened at the party?"

"Well, you know, I just—got to know her. We had a great time. Then, a couple of days later Steel bullets me. Says she's got a job for me. A dangerous job."

I let out one explosive laugh, "Dangerous."

"Yeah. Says we can't talk about it over the net. Wants me to come up to Neuschwanstein."

"I've been there."

"You sure have." He'd managed to pick up the lint with his feet. He dropped it. "Anyway. You know how I like old movies."

Old movies? I nodded.

"Well, Steel knows it, too. I guess anybody who knows me knows it." He stopped. This was hard for him. "Anyway, there are all these movies where—ah, this is stupid."

"What?"

He had the lint again; he was rolling it between the edges of his boot soles, spinning it into a tiny piece of yarn. He sighed, "There are all these movies where, you know, the guy would go off and ... you know ... risk his ... risk his life to save the ... you know ... the woman." He shook his head in disgust, "I told you it was stupid."

"What do you mean? What's stupid?"

He stared into the past. "Well, back when I was hatched, women were pretty upset. Pretty ... angry, I guess. They didn't want you to do anything for them. They wanted to do it all themselves, you know?"

I nodded. "Yeah, I remember that time."

"And then ... things changed. You couldn't risk your life anymore." He was looking at a very lonely place. "You just couldn't. You couldn't say, 'I love you more than my life.' It didn't mean anything."

"Oh." We just sat there for a while. Then he said:

"When Steel told me about Alice, I just wanted to ... save her. That's all."

I understood. I really, *really* understood. Something occurred to me, something I wasn't sure I could ask. I said, "You once told me that you'd have to be drunker than I was in Kindu to tell me your story."

"That's still true," he answered.

"I was just wondering ... I was just wondering if it had anything to do with the, uh, the 'War of Liberation.' "

He stared at the floor for a long time. A long time.

Then he looked at me and said, "I don't think I'm drunk enough to answer that question."

We got underway the next morning. We had new ultra-lights, a new cable for the sky-hook and quite a bit of new equipment that Yuri designed for Archie's research into the Brainardians, the Brainardites, the Brainardese—the slugs.

Yuri hasn't been able to figure out a way to make the E-suits impervious to any unpredictable thing the slugs might do, however. That's the hitch—they're unpredictable. He can beef up the joints, thicken the armor, but that increases the power needed to run the suits; they already mass over three hundred kilos and they're having to deal with the robust gravity of Brainard's Planet, almost twice that of Earth. And even if he does beef them up, how much does he need to? Should he make them twice as durable? Three times? Four? We don't know what the slugs are capable of and we don't know when, where, or why they might choose to do something. It's a real problem.

When we got on the nav net to boost for Eden I realized that it's just down the road from Brainard's Planet. I mean, twenty-three light years is actually an incomprehensibly vast distance, but on a galactic scale, or even that of human occupied space, it seems like it's right next door. It got me thinking about something, something I hadn't been able to figure out.

Marcus and I shared the first watch again. When we came off I asked him, "Sir, do you mind if I talk to you about something?"

"What is it?" he replied.

"It's about Drake."

He studied me for a moment and then said, "Join me in my quarters." He led me down the passageway.

After he closed the hatch and offered me a seat he asked, "What's the problem?"

I wasn't sure how I wanted to tackle this. Finally I said, "I was just wondering ... how Drake fit into the engine—after he was sick, I mean. How did you keep him quarantined?"

"He was never part of the engine after he came down with the plague." Marcus stated it simply. Even so, I had a very difficult time accepting it.

"But, wait a minute ... How did you freewheel?"

Marcus smiled ruefully and shook his head. "I put eighty kilos of dead weight in his spot to balance the engine."

I must have looked stunned. "But—but—" I started.

Marcus held up his hand, "I know, I know," he said, "The physical balance is the smallest part of the problem. A seven perspective star is not designed to work with one of the perspectives missing. I just shunted Drake's load onto the rest of us and hoped for the best. I didn't know what else to do."

"And it worked?" I asked.

"After a fashion," he answered wryly. "We only missed Earth by three hundred eighty-two light years."

Thirty light years from Vesper plus the three hundred fifty-two from Vesper to Earth. "So you weren't aiming for Vesper?" That was one of the things I couldn't figure out: there were lots of inhabited worlds closer than Vesper to Brainard's Planet.

"Why would we? Steel doesn't have any holdings there. Or friends. We needed to get home." He mused for a moment, "I'm amazed it worked as well as it did. I was half expecting us to develop some bizarre secondary resonance and end up in another galaxy. Or another universe. I hope to hell I don't have to do anything like that again."

I echoed his sentiment. The math is pretty complex, but theoretically they could have ended up anywhere. Pan-dimensionally anywhere.

But it still didn't make sense. I'd been thinking that in order for Drake to synch in with the nav net his bio-chip interface had to be functional, but if that were the case ... "So you never used Drake in the engine ..."

"Not after he got sick, no."

"Then why did you keep him around? Why didn't you let him— Okay. Let me start again." I studied Marcus' face as he gazed steadily back at me. Then I decided, why not? Ask the big question. Marcus had never lied to me. That I knew of. Still, I kind of led up to it gradually: "I was doing some research into the nature of the plague ..."

"Yes?"

"Did you know that quite a few people survived it?"

"Well, their perspectives survived. Their bodies didn't."

"Right. They uploaded onto the net and waited for new ones to be grown for them."

"That's correct."

I looked at him, "Why didn't Drake do that?"

Marcus didn't speak right away, but he never dropped his gaze; he looked square at me the whole time. He started, "A plague victim has to upload in the first few hours—"

"Before the bio-chip interface degrades. Yes, I know. So why didn't he upload as soon as he knew his suit was holed? Steel told me there's some kind of alarm that goes off right away."

"That's true."

"So?"

"Well, he couldn't very well upload from the surface, could he?"

"Why not?"

Marcus considered this for a moment, then he said, "I'm not sure where your confusion is stemming from, but perhaps this will help clear it up. You understand that he couldn't upload onto Steel's system?"

"Uh, no. Actually, I thought he could."

"No. Steel's system doesn't have near the capacity needed for a comprehensive memory dump. I forget how many people uploaded back during the plague but it was only a few thousand."

"Around five thousand."

"Yes, that sounds about right. Well, how many were on the net back then? Thirty or forty billion, certainly."

"At least."

"Even with that many they were only able to handle those few thousand."

"So Steel's system is just too small."

"It's very capable," Marcus answered, "but it's not that capable." He sighed. "We thought we had a workable procedure to cover the possibility of contamination. Archie and Drake had researched it quite thoroughly. According to their figures a person has about eighteen hours to upload from the time they're exposed. We figured that would give us enough time to get them back up to the ship."

"But why? Why bother to go back up to the ship?"

"We weren't supposed to *be* on the surface. If Drake had uploaded from there that would have been it. The project would have been finished. Draco Traffic Control probably would have confiscated the Lightdancer and sent us all to the trades. Or worse."

I was incensed, "But Drake was—was—" Even after Lys had used the word I didn't feel comfortable with it. "You mean to tell me that Steel kept him from uploading just to save her precious project?"

"No, no. You don't understand. Steel didn't keep him from doing anything."

He was right. I didn't understand.

"It was really a tragedy," he continued. "We should have gotten him up to the Lightdancer in time; we had the procedures in place. It was just—" He looked for words, or words to avoid, "I was in orbit, so I don't know exactly what happened, but I think the pressure was just too great for everyone. We knew this might happen; we'd talked about it, prepared for it, but when it did ..." He didn't want to judge them. He wanted to excuse them, to pardon them. "They were literally staring at ... death. I don't think they were able to handle it. Emotionally, I mean." He shook his head at the memories. "It was chaos down there. They wrecked one of the ultra-lights taking off so we missed the rendezvous. Then Steel didn't want to leave anyone on the surface without a way up to the ship so they all piled into the other one and screamed west to meet up with the hook on the next orbit. It was so overloaded I'm amazed we managed to hook up at all. As it was, the second ultra-light wasn't in any kind of shape to fly again. But it didn't matter, they'd used too much time. Drake was off-line before they'd even made it out of the atmosphere."

Marcus' face grew very solemn, very hard. "Perhaps you should talk to Archie about this. She understands the particulars of the project. Steel tells me that you have been informed of Alice's condition. Archie knows the details of that as well. But in my opinion, what Drake did was an act of heroism, pure and simple. He sacrificed himself so that the project could go forward." He sighed and studied his fingernails. "If there were a medal to award him posthumously, I'm sure Steel would do so, but I'm afraid that sort of practice has passed out of fashion."

It turned out I didn't have time to talk with Archie. Steel had decided that, since I'd been an actor, she wanted to take me with her down to the surface of Eden. She must have decided back on Earth; that's why she'd had my genome re-worked.

The problem was that Eden was a completely insular society. It had been cut off from the rest of the galaxy since just after the Pleiadean War; no one had been allowed on or off the planet. In order to go there and interact with anyone, we would need to pass ourselves off as natives.

That entailed a lot of research. I was spending all of my spare time learning about their culture, their history, and learning to speak a dialect of Systemic that hadn't been used for almost a millennium. More than that: nobody was on the net there. They communicated with strings of graphic symbols that they had to draw by hand, one for each vocal sound they made, and even that wasn't consistent. It was utterly arcane. There were only a couple of dozen of these little squiggles, but sometimes it took ten or fifteen just to form a single word! Madness.

It was a fascinating place, really. Even the name: Eden. Of course there were a lot of planets around with names like that—Heaven, Himmel, Celeste, Shangri-La, Valhalla, the list is endless (it's a long established fact that real estate developers will stoop to anything to sell property), but Eden was named for a different reason.

The group that colonized and developed Eden was led by two people, Edith Stauber and James Wesley Burroughs. Stauber was a geneticist, Burroughs a nano-surgeon. They met while working on the team that developed the bio-chip. Highly respected scientists in their time, they won a lot of awards, had high-powered careers, all that sort of thing. However, after the advances in healthcare they were helping to develop seemed to be heading toward unlimited life extension, they became very concerned. Both were deeply religious—that much is clear—but it was hard to tell from their recorded works whether they objected more to man playing God or to the idea that, by extending our lives forever, we would never get to meet Him. However, this didn't seem to stop them from re-booting several times.

In any case, they decided that humanity wasn't ready for immortality and set off to found a new society based on spiritual, not material, pursuits. They wanted to go off the net, too, just like the Yin. They were another group that thought the only way they could achieve their goals was to remain unpolluted by the hoi-polloi, the great unwashed— basically people like me. However, where the Yin felt they could attain a utopian society only by banishing masculine thought patterns, Stauber and Burroughs were simply afraid that the temptation to re-boot would be too great for their flock to resist if the option were available to them—that envy of immortals would tear their society apart.

Lysistrata had been right about one thing: if it hadn't been for the Pleiadean War, Eden would probably not have been allowed to exist. Power for the net was such an all-consuming goal in the early days that anyone who opted not to hook up was simply convinced to change their minds. The war changed all that.

Although I wonder if the problem would not have eventually faded away by itself. You didn't see people popping off to form insular religious societies these days; everybody was pretty well-adjusted to things. Even people in the trades; they might get upset from time to time—like that man in Kindu when Matessa was taken away—but, for the most part, they accepted things as they were.

Lys was right about another thing, too. They did have a lot of violent crime on Eden. I had listened to Archie's figures. I guess she did a thorough job of researching that aspect of Eden's society—it was pretty appalling. There had been literally thousands of people murdered there—over six thousand, in fact. That was over six murders *per year!* Almost eleven thousand reported rapes—Archie made this distinction because, evidently, there was some kind of stigma attached to sexual activity that caused people to be reluctant to report them.

I started to wonder if it wasn't safer on Brainard's Planet.

But the hardest thing was learning the dialect. It's difficult enough to learn a language when you share all the concepts, but the Edenites' way of thinking was as obsolete as their speech. They'd obviously had to regress to a level of technology much more primitive even than when I was a kid on Mars. All kinds of weird things—I'm still not sure what a 'mailman' is. A guy who delivers letters? You put letters together to form words, I understood that, but why would you need them delivered? I mean, they were just conceptual until you wrote them down, right? It wasn't like you could run out of them. I asked Yuri about it and he gave me the titles to some movies he thought might help.

And speaking of writing, my wrist was sore. I couldn't believe people had to go through this to communicate. Thank Allah for downloading or I never would have learned all this stuff.

It was like going back in time. Take familial relationships. They really threw me for a loop and that surprised me—after all, I'd *had* a family—but I was running into words I'd forgotten a thousand years ago. They kept talking about "our suns and dotters" this and "our suns and dotters" that. What do suns have to do with families and what the heck do dotters dot? Then I learned how to spell and it finally clicked. Sons and daughters. I had been a son. My sister, sister—there's another word—my sister had been a daughter.

It was tough emotionally, as well. When I realized that I had forgotten the word 'sister' I just started crying. I don't know why, but I couldn't stop for a long time.

Steel or Archie and I started to get together for coaching sessions whenever any two of us were off watch together. They were helping a lot, but it was going to be a real challenge.

We'd already freewheeled and were backing down into the Eden system when I ran across something that really worried me—it just didn't look right. I brought it up with Steel at our next cramming session:

"I think this one word is wrong," I said.

"What's that?" she asked.

"Well, it's a word we use, but not in this context. It doesn't make sense to me that they would use it this way. It pre-dates their split with Draco by—I don't know—centuries, anyway. It's really archaic."

"What is it?"

I booted up our training program, called up the glossary and played it for her.

"No, that's right," Steel confirmed. "That's the word they use."

"I just don't see *why*. I mean, why wouldn't they use—"

"Use what?"

I shook my head, "That's just it. I can't think of it. It's the word we used when I was young, you know, when I was a kid—" I looked to her to help me out but she obviously didn't know what I was talking about. "It's what I called *my*—I just can't think of it."

"Well," she said, trying to help, "there are several variations: mommy, mom, mama. Any of those—?"

"No, no. Those are all too old. Way too old, centuries too old. It was something ... something else." It was just beyond reach. I could lead up to it, but I couldn't get there. "Boy, you know how it is when you can't think of something? I'm just afraid I'll remember it when we're down on the surface and slip up and use it instead of this one."

"I'm sure you'll be all right. We've done a lot of drilling."

"Yeah, you and Archie have done this before. I mean, I've done some extended improv, but nothing like this." It worried me. "I'll just have to stay in character. If it happens to occur to me I'll just—It's driving me crazy that I can't think of it!" I shook my head again. "I'll just have to stay in character, that's all."

PART V
EDEN

CHAPTER 18

E den floated below us, huge, round and seemingly barren. I knew it wasn't, but the area that had been cultivated was so insignificant it had been swallowed up by the vast expanse of the planet that was still pristine. The Edenites lived along a narrow strip of land on the western shore of the main landmass, with a few communities tucked into slot canyons that wound back into the high plateau. I could see the plateau off to the west, just coming over the horizon, painted in buff and tawny hues rising to the base of the huge escarpment we were going to use as a landing point.

The escarpment was what had given Archie the idea of visiting Eden in the first place. Half again as tall as Olympus Mons at its highest point, it reached right up out of the troposphere. The barometric pressure at the summit was negligible—the skyhook could literally drop us off. Start at orbital speed, slide down a twelve-hundred kilometer rope, then just step off onto the ground. The concept was fascinating, in theory. Floating in the spool bay, waiting to hook onto the tether, staring at the awesome planetary mass of Eden turning majestically below us, it was exhilarating, to say the least.

No, I'm kidding myself. It was terrifying.

The sensation of being out of control was exacerbated by weightlessness. I suppose if I'd been under gravity my knees would have been jelly; as it was every muscle in my body was trying to run in a different direction—with nothing to push against. Shakes would start, just take me over for a moment and then subside again.

The idea was to keep our cross-section as low as possible, just in case Traffic Control was looking. A crate with our supplies and such was already on the surface; we'd lowered it the day before. Now Steel, Archie, Alice and I were waiting to be lowered with nothing around us but space suits.

Jemal was checking Archie's equipment. Steel and Alice were helping each other. Marcus and Tamika were in control, getting ready to fling us into the night. Yuri floated over to me. I could see his grin through his helmet. "You ready, Big Kahuna?" he asked.

"I guess so," I said with a laugh, "I suppose it's too late to exercise the escape clause in this contract."

"You'd have to talk to Her Highness about that." He tugged on the rigging of my harness, making sure all the hasps and backup hasps were closed. Of course, I'd checked everything three times, myself. "It's a wild ride, a lot different than coming up."

"At least I'm on Steel's system now," I mused.

"That's right!" Yuri affirmed, "If you get a bit scattered across the countryside we'll just put you back together!" I tried to laugh. We both looked over to where Steel was checking Alice. I knew what he was thinking—it was what *I* was thinking: Alice couldn't re-boot. As scary as this was for me, it was just that— scary. For Alice it was dangerous. I wanted to go over there and tell her in no uncertain terms that she *wasn't* going on this date tonight and to go back to her room NOW. But it wasn't my call, or Yuri's.

We pulled ourselves over to where the base of the tether was slowly, almost imperceptibly, rotating around the spool. It was hard to imagine how fast the other end was moving, twelve-hundred klicks away. Yuri backed me up to the tether and clamped me into the armature. Since I was the heaviest and Alice was the lightest we would ride together, with Archie and Steel just over our heads. He went over each connection twice, with Jemal right behind him checking things off. I could hear Steel carrying on a running conversation with Tamika in control, calling and confirming each indicator as it turned from red to green.

Yuri turned back to me and clapped me on the shoulders. "There's a barometric *and* a radar altimeter in this thing. It's designed so it *has* to let go of you at the lowest point of the swing." He touched his helmet to mine so he could talk to me acoustically without anyone else hearing. "The hook works," he said. "I might decide to risk *your* life, but I'd never risk Alice's." He whapped me on the top of the helmet. "KOWABUNGA! Have a good trip," he grinned and floated back over to the airlock where Jemal was already waiting to cycle through.

I leaned over and touched helmets with Alice. "Well, I don't know about you, but *I'm* petrified."

She laughed nervously, "Yeah, it's gonna be pretty strange going home."

"Oh. Right. Actually, I was referring to riding this insane Ferris wheel. But I see your point." I wondered how old she had been when she left. "Do you think it will have changed much?" I was just making conversation—trying to subdue the shakes that kept hitting me every so often.

"I don't know. It's been longer for them than it has been for me."

"That's right." It made me think about the things she had experienced since she'd left Eden. Earth, space flight, freewheeling, the Institute on Circe, things she never would have known about had she stayed on her home world. The fragility of her hit me right in the chest. There she was, cocooned in a suit that protected her from vacuum that would terminate her life irrevocably. I had forgotten what a dangerous place the universe was—a seemingly infinite catalogue of risks started running through my head, and I wanted to protect her from every one. I wanted to say something comforting but I couldn't come up with anything. We'll be okay? No, if anything went wrong I'd be okay, but—I didn't want to think about it.

She must have seen my discomfiture, because she said, "Don't worry. I'm all right." She smiled at me and my heart just broke.

"You sure are, Alice," was all I could answer, "you sure are."

Steel came on the intercom, "Just remember to relax your knees—be ready to drop and roll. The suits should bring you into a soft landing and the gyros should keep you upright, but stay relaxed in any case."

"Roger, Captain," I replied, wondering how I was going to comply. We wouldn't actually step off the hook onto the ground—I guess they weren't *that* crazy—but we'd get pretty darn close. The hook would release us at about ten meters above our landing site. Little maneuvering jets in our suits would cushion our landing—if everything worked right. I started to get the shakes again.

Marcus was timing the start of our descent so that we would arrive at the end of the tether just as we reached our drop off point; this was so we'd have to spend as little time as possible at a full six Gs. We just hung there waiting, strapped to the top of the galaxy's tallest carnival ride, turning ever so slowly around the long axis of the Lightdancer.

We'd made almost a full rotation when Marcus' voice sounded in my helmet: "Descent commencing in ten seconds ..." the shakes started again, "five ..."

The release itself was a bit of an anti-climax. We were already in free-fall so there was no sensation of falling. Just a little thump to get us started and the bulkheads of the spool bay began to move past us. I think the adrenaline content of my blood managed to get even higher, although I don't see how it could have and still leave room in my veins for corpuscles. Then we were out in open space and starting to pick up speed. We were using our own centripetal acceleration to propel us down the tether. We'd reach a speed of over two thousand klicks per hour relative to that super-diamond clothesline before the brakes kicked in.

It was very strange. The only thing close enough to give us any sense of motion—besides the tether itself—was the Lightdancer, and it seemed to be moving away from *us* instead of us from it. Eden kept turning below us, but as yet we couldn't see it getting any closer.

As I slid down the tether, I could feel it pushing against me more and more, decelerating me from orbital speed, but the Gs built up so slowly it was like watching my hair grow. I'd never felt so naked in my life. With as much space travel as I'd done I'd never had a reason to be out *in* it before. Space is really big. When I looked at my feet (it still wasn't *down*) I could see the tether stretching out to infinity. The stars wheeling slowly past weren't getting any closer but the tether kept zipping toward us faster and faster. It looked like we were going to shoot right out through the bottom of reality and into the nether regions. I hoped I was keeping all my Holy Shivas, Allahs and Jesus H. whatevers subvocalized.

As we continued to rotate around the ship it came between us and Eden and suddenly we could tell how far we'd traveled. The Lightdancer was a tiny needle silhouetted against the planet, growing smaller as we watched. Then we swung slowly—achingly slowly—around beneath the ship and we could see the planet swell toward us and I *knew* we were falling, but it swung past and away again. By the time we made it to the top of the next loop, the Lightdancer was too far away to see. The tether just dwindled away to nothing—even Eden seemed significantly smaller—but we continued to swing down and down and down until I was sure we'd smack right into the immense, tawny desert. We weren't even halfway down.

On the next upswing the brakes cut in and the Gs built up rapidly. At first it was nice having weight—it settled my stomach and got rid of the shakes—but all at once I knew how fast we were moving. The brake system, I'm sure, was top-notch and as smooth as Yuri could make it, but as the Gs continued to climb, any vibration at all became more amplified and violent. I had to hold my head perfectly upright to keep from wrenching my neck.

On the third swing down, the horizon really started to flatten out and I could've seen a lot of detail in the landscape if the vibration hadn't been so intense. It was the strangest sensation to watch the passing planet slow way down and then speed up again. Then up and away one last time, farther away, Eden shrinking to a globe—a really *big* globe, but still, you could see it as a ball. The Gs kept building and building as we started our final descent and Eden grew and grew, swelling and rushing toward us until it wasn't a planet at all anymore. It was the ground, and we were flying above it. I could see the escarpment dropping steeply away to our right as what I thought was dust resolved to sand, to gravel, to fields of boulders the size of houses. I could see the large, open expanse of the landing site coming toward us, slowing as it neared. The g-forces were incredible and it seemed like we'd be flung into the rock and smashed to atoms when the hook released us. We would in fact be moving the same speed and direction as the land below us at the bottom of the swing.

I didn't hear the catch release. I was just weightless again for an instant until the braking jets on the suit cut in. I could see them kicking up dust and sand below me, and I tried to keep my legs relaxed, but I couldn't really tell if they were or not after the ride I'd just been on. I was glad the suit had gyros, or I would've fallen right over.

But I didn't. I was standing on bare rock that sloped away into something like a wadi to my left. The glare of the sun on the rock around me contrasted with the satiny, bottomless black of the sky, which faded to the deepest violet right at the horizon. We were still above most of the atmosphere, still in space, really. I could see the inky shadow of a space suit stretching out in front of me, but it took me a minute to recognize it as my own. It was beyond my comprehension that I was in one piece and down on the planet. For a moment I couldn't move or do anything; I just listened to my breathing resonate in my helmet, reacquainting myself with the concept of my continued existence.

Alice bulleted me, [You okay, Mo?]

"Yeah, looks that way," I answered.

[Welcome to my home town.]

"Thanks. Nice place. Where are you?"

[To your left about fifty meters.] I turned and looked. There she was.

"I got you." I started walking toward her. "Captain? Archie? Did you make it okay?"

Steel's voice filled my auditory lobe, [Yes, we're about a hundred meters south of you. Do you see the crate?]

"No. There's a kind of rill or depression not too far from me. It might be down in it."

[All right. Check it out.]

"Right." I headed that way. Alice angled to meet me there. "Yeah, it's here," I said. I could see it down at the bottom of the rill. "Looks like it's in good shape."

[Good,] Steel answered, [go on and fire it up.]

Alice and I made our way down the slope to a winding, flat floor where the crate rested. I palmed the panel on the side and the airlock extended and started to cycle. When the hatch opened we stepped in, cycled it again, and went on inside.

The lights flickered on, and everything looked to be in order: our packs were strapped to the bulkhead, the food lockers were tight, even the bunks were made up. "Home away from home," I said.

We were taking off our helmets as we heard Archie and Steel stamp into the lock and cycle it again.

"Let's get something to eat," Steel said as she, too, doffed her helmet, "and go over everything one more time."

"Right," I answered. I disconnected my gauntlets from my suit sleeves and got some prepackaged meals out of one of the food lockers. A funny thing: the graphic on one of the package covers caught my eye. It was a brand we had sold in Sheila's store back in Spam-town. I stopped what I was doing for a minute and looked at it. Time dilates in many different ways; the fuller it is, the shorter it seems, but the more it separates you from the past. I unconsciously reached up and rubbed my left shoulder where my meteorite used to be. Of course I couldn't feel my shoulder—wearing a space suit is like being encased in medieval armor—but it was only a reflex action anyway.

Archie said, "Is your shoulder bothering you, Mo?"

"Huh?" I looked up at her. "Oh. No, it's fine."

"I can take a look at it if you want." She came over to me.

"No, no. It's all right," I smiled at her, "Let's eat." I fired up the microwave.

Steel and Alice were checking out the smaller crates we would lower with us to set up the camps down the face of the escarpment; we had seven Mount Everests to climb down before we reached the plateau.

The food smelled good, but I have to say that after riding the skyhook I wasn't all that hungry.

Steel started right in, "The first thing we have to do is locate the fixed ropes we left. This has got to be the right place, but it looks different to me."

Archie replied, "I know. Me, too. It's been a long time. We may be farther from the edge than we were. I thought we could see the cairn from the pickup point last time."

"No, I don't think so." Steel took a bite. "Anyway, we'll find it. It may have gotten knocked over. Remember, it's been four decades."

I asked Alice, "Do *you* recognize anything?"

She shrugged and then spoke around a mouthful of hash, "Kind of. I was pretty young. It seems the same."

"We'll find it," Steel repeated.

"I think it's best if we don't start speaking in dialect until we get down to the plateau, same as last time," Archie said.

"Right," Steel agreed, "too much alien technology up here. We'd just confuse ourselves. But when we get down," she looked at Alice and me, "we *must* stay in character." We nodded. "It's not just the way we talk. It's the way we act."

"No public sexuality," I said.

"No public *touching*," Steel corrected, "except handshakes. Women who know each other can embrace when they greet, but we won't know anyone so that won't be an issue. Other than that, nothing. No back rubs, no erogenous massage, no fondling. Nothing."

"If you just think of yourself as constantly tense and frustrated you should do fine," Archie put in.

"And we need to remember that males have the power here. Women are subordinate. Men run the government; men run the families. From church elders to elected officials, the power structure is male."

Alice and I nodded again. It was going to be a challenge putting this over. We had to stay constantly alert, on our toes, concentrating—while appearing relaxed.

I remembered going to an open-air museum on Earth once, in Europe somewhere or maybe North America—no, it had to be North America. It was the re-creation of a colony where somebody had landed on a rock and started some traditional holiday or other and later they named an automobile after the colony (I'm sure I'm getting this all confused)—but anyway, everyone there dressed, spoke and acted as if they were in the seventeenth century. If you asked them a question that required knowledge of later times to answer, they'd just stare at you quizzically or try to answer using only what they would have known in that time. I had been fascinated and amazed at how well they'd pulled it off.

Now *I* was going to have to pull it off.

We finished the meal, suited back up and started hauling pallets of provisions out the airlock. We'd have to stock twelve different camps; it would have been a lot more but we were going to use powered jumars coming back up that would speed up the trip immensely. On the way down we'd be rappelling more often than down-climbing. Still, we figured it would take us about a week to make it to the bottom. The plateau was around two thousand meters in elevation; where we were at the summit of the escarpment was almost sixty thousand. A long, tough climb any way you sliced it.

The cairn turned out to be almost five hundred meters south of us. The little transponder they had left in it had died years ago so we had to find it by casting around. Fortunately we knew it was close to the edge of the cliff, so we were searching a line, not an area.

But what a view! The escarpment dropped in a series of cliffs and scree slopes. We were standing on good, solid crystalline rock (mostly granidiorite and schist) that fell initially almost two thousand meters in near-vertical cliffs, broken here and there by narrow ledges. At the bottom of this first drop, piles of scree descended at a forty to fifty degree angle before the next cliff cut them off. We'd get almost half-way down the escarpment before we started running into any significant amounts of snow; up this high, the atmosphere was simply too thin to support much precipitation. As I looked down past the fifth or sixth cliff band, I could see the atmospheric haze start to build up. Lines started to get a little softer, and the snow and rock took on a bluish tinge. I could easily see the curvature of the horizon out past the plateau and the ocean—I could see the band of atmosphere wrapping around it like a diaphanous halo. It was different than flying or being in orbit; we were actually standing on the ground. We would be walking from where we were down into the biosphere of the planet, descending into the soup of air and water the Edenites called home. I'd never experienced anything like it.

We spent the next six hours or so hauling all the supplies over to the cairn. Landing half a klick away from it had put us behind schedule. Archie and Steel debated whether we should spend the first night on top (putting us even more behind schedule) or trying for the first hut with what we had left of the day. Steel ultimately decided that we should press on. We'd landed in the early morning, local time, so we had another six hours of daylight left.

We were all a little tired from hauling. Even with powered suits, which negated the extra weight of wearing one, you still had to muscle around the mass every time you changed direction. They were well designed, so you really didn't notice it at the time, but after a while it wore on you.

The first drop would be the toughest because we had the most supplies with us. We'd drop off a container at each hut. There were four of us (and I wished Ham were with us, but we had to leave him on the ship for obvious reasons) so we each tied into three containers for the first rappel. They would dangle below us on our way down. The other thing I wished for was a portable Musahdi lift, but high-energy gravitons have such a distinctive signature that Traffic Control would have been all over us.

When we were all rigged up it was time to decide who would go first. Steel took the honors. Alice would follow her down, then me, and Archie would bring up the rear. Steel snapped two carabiners into the descender and her harness and backed toward the edge. After she was in position, we carefully lowered the three containers that were also tied into her harness over the side. She continued backing up until her feet were on the edge and worked her way over. When she had her feet planted on the side of the cliff with her weight below the lip, she waved to us and kicked off.

It was a straight shot six hundred meters down to a nice little ledge about two meters wide. Archie, Drake and Steel had rigged ultra-lines when they were doing their research project—basically just bundles of super-long-chain polymer molecules wrapped in a sheath that's opaque to ultraviolet rays, impervious to cosmic rays, and oblivious to attacks on its character. The stuff lasts forever and you can use it in lengths up to a thousand meters or so. Still, six hundred meters is a long way, especially when it's vertical; Steel dwindled to a speck bouncing rhythmically off the face long before she reached the ledge.

[There's a bump about a third of the way down,] Steel's voice said over her system, [The crates got hung up on it for a minute. I had to swing out pretty wide to clear them.]

[I understand,] Archie answered.

[You can't really see it coming. Just be aware.]

[Roger.]

We waited for about ten minutes before we heard her say, [All right. I'm on the first ledge. Send Alice down.]

So Alice hooked in and we backed her up to the edge, lowering her three crates over the side as she went. She placed her feet wide on the lip and started to lean back, letting the line take her weight, then stopped. Glancing down between her legs at two klicks of nothing she said, [Just a second,] and started to stand back up. She pulled herself away from the edge and turned to Archie, [You're sure I came up this when I was ten years old?]

Archie laid a gauntlet on her shoulder. [You and Jacob both,] she said. I guessed Jacob had been the name of her brother.

[Boy, it's ...] she looked over the edge again, [it's a long way down, you know?] She laughed nervously.

[It's all right,] Steel said, far below us but sounding no farther than our own breathing, [You know how to do this, Alice. Just take it one step at a time.]

[That's right,] added Archie, [As long as you're tied into the harness you can't fall. Even if you let go of the rope, the descender will just brake you to a stop. The worst that can happen is you turn upside down, which is disconcerting but not dangerous. Just grab back onto the rope and pull yourself upright again.]

The image of me dangling upside down halfway down a two-klick cliff face came into my mind. It didn't reassure me, and I wasn't sure why it would reassure Alice, but she said, [Yeah, I know. I'll be all right.] She took a breath and gathered herself. [I guess, if I'm gonna see Dad ...] She took another breath. [Okay. I'm okay] and she started backing toward the edge again.

She didn't make it quite as far the second time. She came back up again and said, [Boy, I don't know if I can do this.] She sounded pretty shaken. [It's not like the simulators, you know? It's—it's ...]

[It's all right, Alice,] Steel's voice again, [just take a minute. We're not in any hurry. Getting over the lip is the scary part. After that it's really fun. You just have to trust your equipment.]

[Right,] Alice answered, trying to sound brave.

[Hey, it worked for me!] Steel said jovially.

Alice laughed, [That's true.] She was still breathing heavily.

[Take your time,] Archie counseled.

"Yeah," I added, "Think of it this way: the longer you put it off the longer *I* get to put it off."

She laughed again. [I guess I am kind of holding up the show.]

[Not at all,] Archie said, [We have plenty of daylight left. If worse comes to worst the Captain can jumar back up here and we can spend the night on top. Try again in the morning.]

[That's right,] Steel echoed.

Alice took a few deep breaths and said, [No, that seems silly.] She looked around for the crate, but it was out of sight behind a low rise. [Let's just do it.] And she turned around again so that her back was to the edge.

This time she got to where she was squatting over the abyss, her weight mostly on the ropes, when she quickly pulled herself back up.

[Boy,] she said, [I just—I just feel like I'm going to fall right over and crack my helmet open on the rock.]

Archie put a gauntlet on either shoulder this time and said, [I wouldn't worry about that. These suits are pretty tough.]

[It just feels so—so—You know? When you're right there on the edge, you feel so out of balance, you know?]

"That's because your rappel point is between your feet," I offered. "I hate rappelling right off the top of something, because there's nothing taller than you to tie off to. You're right; it makes you unbalanced for a minute."

[But as soon as you get over the side, and your center of gravity is lower than your anchor, you're fine,] Steel added.

Archie agreed, [That's right. That feeling of toppling goes away as soon as you're sitting in your harness. Then you're just … sitting.] She laughed.

[Hey, how're you guys doing down there?] It was Yuri.

[We're fine,] said Steel. [Just a little momentary setback.]

[What's up?] Yuri asked.

[I guess I'm being a problem,] Alice answered.

[No, you're not,] said Archie, [You just take it easy. Take your time. You'll be fine.]

[That's right,] Steel agreed.

[Gummin' up the works again, huh kid?] Yuri asked.

[Yeah.] Alice's voice was still anxious, but you could tell she was starting to relax a little. [I'm just being a coward. I'm scared to go over the edge.]

[Well, you know what I always say …]

[What's that?] she asked.

[KOWABUNGA!]

Alice laughed, [Oh, yeah? Then *you* come down here and jump off this stupid cliff!]

[No, thanks,] he replied, [I'm always braver when everyone *else* is in danger and I'm some place safe. But I'll tell you, Tamika and I just had some really great sex, if that makes you feel any better.]

[It does, it does,] Alice replied, [It really does.]

[It certainly makes *me* feel better.] That was Tamika's voice.

[Well, let's just bring *everybody* in on this,] Alice said, [This is getting embarrassing.]

[Sorry,] Tamika answered, [we were just monitoring you. Are you going to be okay?]

[Yeah, yeah, I'll be fine,] Alice protested, [I'm beginning to think it'll be easier to go over the cliff than to continue this conversation.]

[That's the spirit!] Yuri cheered.

[Whatever you think,] Archie cautioned, [If you feel up to it, we go. If not, we can come back and try again tomorrow.]

Alice came to a decision, [No, I can't see this getting any easier if I back out now.] She checked her rigging. [Okay, let's go.] She backed up to the edge again. [See you in the Great Hereafter,] she said, and backed over the lip. She had one bad moment, just at the point where her center of gravity shifted, but then she was fine. She sat in her harness for a moment, getting used to the feeling, then she said, [You're right, Captain! This *is* fun! What a view!] and she dwindled away to insignificance.

CHAPTER 19

Getting down was just a tremendous amount of work. The hardest part was wrestling those damn crates down the talus slopes. After a while it seemed like they would deliberately seek out places to get hung up; we were constantly and endlessly pulling them out of holes. The way a talus slope is structured is determined by the fact that the bigger a piece of rock is, the farther down the slope it rolls. So up at the top (which would be right at the bottom of the cliff we'd just rappelled down) we'd be working on a steep hillside made of stuff the consistency of gravel or even sand. By the time we got to the bottom (which, in this case, was the lip of the next cliff we had to go over), we were working around pieces of mountain, ranging from maybe a meter across up to some the size of buildings. It seemed to go on forever; the only bright spot was that we lightened our burden by one crate with each hut we supplied.

The third day was the worst: the jet stream hit us. Marcus warned us that it was shifting north and we'd probably get a piece of it, and boy did we! It was impossible to rappel; we were lucky to get back to the hut. We had to sit there most of the day listening to the walls ring and hoping the whole hut wouldn't launch into the void. It was so loud you couldn't talk; you couldn't think. Fortunately we were all exhausted so we slept most of the time. The next day the stream headed back to the south and we set out again.

Around fifteen thousand meters we started to hit patches of snow. A little lower the snow covered everything that wasn't vertical and lowering the crates became a breeze; we just glissaded them down the snow slopes and then glissaded right after them. Of course, by that time we'd dropped most of them off at the various huts, anyway.

As the going got easier our spirits lifted considerably. It's hard to describe what it felt like to look up and see the tens of thousands of vertical meters we had descended—glistening, fractured rock faces soaring to the zenith, achingly defined in the harsh, unfiltered sunlight of the stratosphere—and then turn around and see cliff upon cliff upon cliff falling away, fading into the blue haze of the thicker air beneath us. The scale was almost too vast to encompass. We'd get into arguments over whether or not the plateau was looking any closer, pointing out details we thought we hadn't noticed before. But the horizon would be a little nearer after each day's work; more of the ocean would disappear beyond it. The angle at which we viewed the tawny rock tableland below would get a little bit more oblique. The day came when the ocean disappeared all together, dropping below the edge of the plateau, and our impression of the planet changed from one of land defined by water to one of endless, endless rock. Rock defined the world before us; it filled the sky behind us. It held us and dominated us and overpowered us.

A kind of giddiness overtook us when glissading took the place of those back-breaking talus slopes. The ordeal of descending was transformed into a vacation as we went sliding down the mountain on our butts—sparkling, lacy rooster-tails of snow bursting from the pikes of our ice-axes like fireworks celebrating the ease of our descent. What would have been hours of hard labor up above became minutes of exhilarating fun, bouncing and caroming over sun-cupped snow. We just had to make sure and control our descent with the ice-axes, using them as both rudders and brakes.

Each new slope became a new artistic challenge. Another cliff had been negotiated, another danger had been overcome. Nothing to do but sit down and let gravity do the work. As we got more confident in the use of the ice-axes, we took the slopes faster and faster, making up all of the time we'd lost up on top. We were truly playing. Laughing and whooping, catching a little air as we went over small, natural ski-jumps, we flew down the escarpment like mountain sprites, completely at home in our world of precipices and steep snow. We had it licked. The mountain was ours.

Steel and Alice clapped and laughed as I swerved to a stop in front of them, sending up a spray that pelted them from head to toe. We were still up around ten thousand meters, two thousand higher than Everest. The next cliff we had to go over started twenty or thirty meters behind them, beyond a sequined snowfield. The hut we would spend the night in was at the bottom of the cliff, about eight hundred meters below. The wind was calm, and the weather was great. There was a small storm system building to the west, but it wasn't a worry. One more rappel and we'd be done for the day.

As I stood up I looked up the slope to where Archie was descending. I couldn't actually see her; she was lost in the flume of snow her heels were kicking up as she zipped down the hill. She was really moving. There were a couple of little jumps where you could grab some significant air and as she went over the first one we saw her explode out of the cloud she was creating, hurtling out into the void before she bounced back to earth. We couldn't really see, but she seemed to hit the second jump a little sideways. It became clear that she had after she emerged from her snow cloud with her body perpendicular to her direction of flight. She hit pretty hard and started to roll. We waited for her to self-arrest, but she never did. She just kept tumbling down the hill. Then I saw her ice-ax flopping around her.

This wasn't good. Her ax was attached to her wrist by a short piece of webbing, but she'd let go of the ax itself. It was bouncing all over the place and there is no end of an ice-ax that isn't sharp or pointy. I heard Steel yell, [Archie! Arrest! Arrest!]

"She can't arrest," I said, "She's dropped her ax."

[Oh, Shiva!] she answered. [We're gonna have to try and catch her.]

"Right," I said, "She's coming pretty fast." I couldn't see her ice-ax anymore. Had the webbing come off her wrist or had she managed to get hold of it again?

[Alice?] Steel asked.

[I'm here,] she replied.

"Just try and get in her way, slow her down," I said.

[Right,] Alice answered.

[I think she has plenty of run-out,] Steel said, referring to the flat expanse of snow behind us, [but we don't want her going over—NOW!] Archie was on us. Steel and I both managed to get a piece of her, but she just whanged into us and on past. Alice caught one of her ankles and managed to hold on, getting dragged down the hill with her. She and Archie both starfished out, creating enough drag to bring them to a halt just a couple of meters from the edge. Steel and I got up and trundled down the slope to them, as fast as we could move in our suits.

It looked like Archie's ice-ax was sticking right through her chest. "Allah," I muttered and hurried over. Steel got there first. It wasn't as bad as it looked. The pike had actually pierced the shoulder joint of her space suit and was sticking through it, pointing up into the air. I couldn't see any blood on it.

[Archie! Archie, are you all right?] Steel gazed into her helmet. She didn't answer. Then I saw how the handle of the ax had wedged the two sides of the joint apart; there was a gap of almost an inch under her arm.

"Shiva, she doesn't have any air!" I yelled. The air pressure around us was much greater than it had been up on top, but it was still little more than half what it was at sea level. "We have to get her suit closed up," I grabbed Steel, "Look!"

At that point it was more important to get her suit put back together than avoiding the possible harm we might do by moving her. The three of us got on either side of her and I stood on the adz of the ax as we lifted her off it. I still didn't see any blood; maybe it had missed her arm. We set her down, gently but quickly. Steel got into my backpack and got out a repair kit. Those things are amazing; her suit was sealed in about a minute and a few minutes later the suit's compressor had the air pressure inside back up to normal.

Archie still wasn't talking to us, however. Her breathing was okay and we could check her vital signs on Steel's system—everything seemed fine. We hoped she had just lost consciousness from the drop in her suit pressure. We couldn't really tell if she was bleeding; if she'd cut an artery or something it would have shown up on her vitals, but minor bleeding would only show up with time.

[We have to get her down to the hut so we can take a look at her,] Steel said.

"Right," I answered, "we can rig a sling and lower her." It was a long way to lower her. A dead weight on eight hundred meters of line makes quite a pendulum. "Is it a straight drop to the hut?" I asked.

[I don't remember,] Steel answered. So we went over to the edge and checked.

Eight hundred meters never looked so far. We could see the tiny, manufactured shape of the hut glinting in the sun, no bigger than a piece of glitter tossed onto the scree slope far below. The face of the cliff was pretty clean, but about halfway down there was a crumbling lip that slanted steeply to the south, then a clean, narrow shelf about a hundred meters below that, and a wide hump covered with scree and talus maybe a hundred meters from the bottom.

"How the heck are we going to do this?" I asked myself as much as anybody. Archie wasn't going to be able to negotiate those ledges if she was still unconscious. I looked at Steel. "Do you think we'll be able to drag her over them? What if she gets hung up?" Of the three obstacles, only the second looked negotiable.

[Yes,] Steel replied, [We're just going to have to do it in three stages.] She looked up at the approaching storm front, still far off, but looking a lot closer than it had a few minutes earlier.

[I'll go first and get set up on the first ledge,] she continued. [Alice, you follow me down. We'll have to set up some guy lines to steady her with.]

[Okay.]

I didn't know how they were going to be able to work on that ledge—it wasn't really a ledge at all. I couldn't see any level area, just a crumbling, steeply canted mess.

Between the three of us we carried Archie to the edge. We got out two extra light-weight lines, passed one of them through the bolt the fixed line was tied to, and tied Archie into both of them. Then we threw the other ends over, watching them twist and writhe in the rising breeze. Steel and I looked at each other, then back at Alice. The wind would probably get a lot higher before long.

"You two be careful," I said to her, "let's not be in a hurry about this. We won't help her if more people get hurt."

[Right,] Steel agreed, and got ready to rappel. [I'll let you know when I reach the bottom.] She kicked off and disappeared.

I looked apprehensively out at the western horizon, then turned to Alice. "How are you doing?" I asked. "You took quite a hit when you caught Archie. Are all of your parts still working?"

[Yeah, I'm okay,] She answered tersely, [I wish we were back aboard the Lightdancer.]

"You and me." The Lightdancer, fifty thousand tons of fortieth-century technology orbiting above us and we might as well have been in the Himalayas on Earth two thousand years ago. Well, we had space suits; that was something.

We kept checking on Archie as Steel continued down the cliff, but she didn't wake up. We fidgeted. We were in a hurry with nowhere to go. We'd ask Steel how she was doing, she'd reply, then we'd check on Archie and she wouldn't reply. Then we'd stand around and shift our weight from foot to foot and look at the storm and look at each other and check with Steel again. It took forever for her to get to the bottom.

Finally we heard, [There's no place to stand down here. We're going to have to stay tied in.] Alice and I glanced at each other. Then, [Okay, I've set a couple of bolts. Alice?]

[Yes?]

[You're going to have to tie into this bolt *before* you go off rappel. Understand?]

[Yes, Captain.]

[All right, come ahead.]

[Roger], Alice replied and tied into the rope. She didn't hesitate this time. For one thing, she was used to rappelling by then, but I don't think she would have hesitated anyway. She was a trouper. She had more to lose than any of us, but I'm sure she would have risked it all, risked her life, to save any one of us. She was incredible.

I think I was falling in love with her.

Lowering Archie to the first ledge went smoothly. I just had to muscle her and her space suit—a not insignificant mass—over the lip of the cliff. Steel and Alice had taken the other ends of the two lines and spread out on the ledge below. Steel belayed Archie on the line that we had passed through the bolt while Alice steadied her with the other. It seemed to work fairly well.

[Okay, off belay,] came Steel's voice. [We've got her.]

"Roger." I started pulling up the belay line as fast as I could, passing it through the bolt and feeding it down to Steel as I did so. We'd need to rig up the same sort of sling two more times. It was a long rope. I thought I'd never reach the end of it—and the storm kept moving closer as I pulled. When I finally got the end in my hand I dangled it over the edge and said, "LINE! Coming down!"

[Just a second!] I looked over the edge, saw their tiny figures struggle to drag Archie out of the way. [Okay, go ahead.]

I let it go. Steel tried to gather it in as it fell, but she was four hundred meters below me. The wind caught it and blew it all over the place.

They continued to gather it up as I tied into the fixed rope, backed over the edge, and flew down the side of the cliff as fast as I could go. The breeze was freshening; I could hear it whistling past my helmet. The longer I made my jumps the more it tended to twist me around. I banged back into the rock face on my shoulder a couple of times; once I even bounced off my backpack, but I made it down to them.

The ledge looked worse close up. The face had cracked along a wandering vein of intruded quartz, leaving an uneven shelf of granite about three meters wide that had expanded and fractured vertically. It was like trying to walk around on top of a pipe organ. The only place where it was even close to level was right next to the face; it fell off more and more steeply toward the edge. *And* everything was covered with patchy snow, sand, and gravel.

This meant we all had to stay tied in; the chance of slipping and falling was just too high. We were hampered by constantly having to deal with line as we moved around on the ledge, feeding it through our descenders with one hand while we manhandled Archie down to the next drop with the other. Steel had tied her into a bolt, as well, and we would lower her a little, then lower ourselves, then lower her a little more, kicking rocks and snow over the edge as we slid downwards.

After we got Archie in position Steel scrambled back up to the bolt she was tied into, tied herself into the fixed line, and then untied from the bolt. In situations like this it's very important to do everything in the right order. Then she backed down past us and over the lip.

After a couple of minutes we heard, [I'm down on this little, straight ledge. Can you see me?]

Alice and I slid down to the edge, trying not to kick any rocks down on Steel, and looked over. We could see her, on the other end of a vertical football field of rock. The ledge was clean and level, but just barely wide enough to stand on.

[I think we can get her past this, don't you?] Steel asked.

"Looks good from up here," I answered.

[All right, I'm going on down to the next step.] She looked up as a shadow passed over her and then us as well. The storm clouds were moving in. We'd seen the last of the sun that day.

It felt very exposed, huddling there with Alice and our helpless charge, clinging like lichen to the edge of the world. We couldn't even move, for fear of knocking stuff off the ledge to rain down on Steel. She was two to three hundred meters below us; anything that fell off the ledge would be moving the speed of a bullet by the time it got to her.

After an eternity we heard, [All right, I'm down. Come ahead, Alice.]

"Wait!" I said, putting my hand on Alice's shoulder to keep her still. "Captain, you're going to have to get well off to the side before either one of us moves. Every time we twitch up here stuff slides off the edge."

[Don't you think the wind will blow it north of me?] she asked.

"It'll blow the small stuff, but it's not the small stuff I'm worried about."

[Right, of course. All right. Give me a couple of minutes.]

A wall of air slammed into us.

Just like that. One second it was breezy, the next a forty-five knot wind was tearing at us, peppering our faceplates with sand and blown snow.

[Holy Shiva!] Alice said, clinging tighter to her rope.

"Yeah," I agreed, "Jesus, what are we going to do? Steel! The storm just hit up here! How is it down where you are?"

[It's pretty bad—Woah! Wait a minute.] What could we do *but* wait? [I just got knocked off my feet. It's really blowing. On the good side, there's plenty of room to work down here.] The hut was only a hundred meters below her. It was still four hundred below us.

"What should we do?" I asked her.

[What do you mean?] she answered.

"Well, I don't know about the advisability of rappelling in this wind. I had enough trouble getting this far, and it wasn't blowing nearly as bad."

[We *have* to get Archie to the hut. We have to get her out of her suit. Why are you asking me this?]

"But that's my point. We don't have to get her to the hut. What's the worst that can happen? Her brain stops functioning and she automatically uploads."

[What?]

"Archie can't—can't—you know. We get her body back up to the ship and fix her up good as new. Nothing can happen to her. But if Alice ..." I felt funny talking about it in front of her.

[I'm okay,] Alice said. Then she said, [Shiva!] as another gust collided with us. [I think I want to keep going, you know? Get to the hut.]

"Listen," I said to her, "I know it feels scary tied to the side of this rock while the wind howls around our ears, but it's a lot safer than trying to rappel. Lines the length we're using act just like a sail in winds this high. You'll get blown all over."

[Well—]

Steel cut in, [Look, none of this matters! We don't have time for Archie to re-boot! We *have* to keep moving. We *have* to. That's an order.]

"Okay, okay. Just trying to—"

[I know. We're all doing our best.] Steel paused for a minute and I pondered the dilemma. If Archie had to re-boot, that shoved us back three months. We obviously had to have Archie with us (Steel certainly thought so); she was the only one who knew as much, probably more, about the project than Steel. On the other hand, if we didn't move quickly enough, Alice would ... would ... die, anyway. I glanced at her sweet, tough face, saw her clinging microscopically to a colossal, inhuman, unyielding and uncaring anvil of stone, the hammer of the storm poised to crush her. If Archie had to re-boot, would Krupp and Daimler catch up with us? What would happen if they did? Was it really worth risking Alice's life this way, just so she could see her parents again before they ... passed on?

I didn't have any answers. I hadn't been around death in centuries.

[Alice, are you ready?]

I looked at Alice and said, "I guess we're going on."

Alice nodded. [Just a minute,] she said, and started clambering up to the bolt.

"ROCK!" I yelled, as a brick-sized piece she inadvertently kicked loose slid over the edge.

[I'm out of the way,] Steel answered. As it fell I listened, straining to hear over the wind. After a long time there was a crack like a gun going off across a valley, then Steel said, [Okay, I'm going to move a little bit farther out of the way.]

We waited for her before Alice started to move again.

"Rock! ROCK!" I said again, as Alice's climbing kicked off little landslides.

[I'm okay. I think I'm out of the line of fire now,] Steel replied.

Alice had made it to the bolt and started to untie from it. "Alice, no! WAIT!" I cried.

[What?]

"Tie into the fixed rope *first*," I said, "*Then* untie from the bolt."

[Oh, right. Sorry.]

My heart was pounding in my chest, "Just be careful."

[Okay.]

I had an idea. Archie still had two extra full-length lines tied into her: the belay line and the line Alice used to stabilize her. I checked to make sure that Archie wasn't going anywhere, then I untied the stabilizer line. "Here, Alice," I said, scrambling up to her, "tie into this line, too."

[Huh? Why?]

"If we can stabilize Arch, maybe we can stabilize you, too."

[Oh, I see. Okay.] We slipped a second set of carabiners into her harness, over on her side, and rigged up the second line.

"I'll head north along the ledge and find a place to tie into." I didn't want her pulling me off if she really caught a good gust.

[Right.]

I clipped the line into a carabiner on my harness so I could have my hands free and took off, moving as fast as I could, setting protection as I went. I was torn between the need for Alice to get going and the desire to get far enough away to provide a decent angle on her when she got down close to the bottom. A percussion sonata started playing on my helmet. Drops of rain appeared on my faceplate and gathered into tiny streams. Warm front, I thought, southwesterly, moving in from the ocean. It could really dump on us. I looked up at the darkening sky. It would be getting colder again real soon.

"Hey, Yuri, are you guys tracking us?" I asked.

[We have you in our sights,] came his reply.

"Let me know when I'm fifty meters from Alice, all right?"

[You got it.] Fortieth century technology did help. Though the Lightdancer was on the other side of the planet at the time, we were in constant communication through Steel's system. Ain't telepathy grand?

I crabbed my way along the ledge on rock that was getting wetter and slicker with each step. Then, [That's about it,] Yuri said.

I found a tapering granite column to tie myself to and sat down. "Ready, Alice?"

[On belay,] she answered.

I clipped the line into a second, reversed carabiner and took it in both hands. "Belay on," I responded. The air filled with swirling flakes, fat and wet. I could barely see her.

[Descending.]

I talked to her as I watched her dwindle away. "Stay close to the rock. Walk down, don't jump. Try to stay in contact with the face."

[Roger. The wind is heavy, but it's steadier now. Not as gusty.] She vanished into billowing chaos, a seething static of snowflakes, leaving me alone on the rock. It was strangely beautiful, natural, harmonious. Almost mathematical.

As I sat there letting the line slide through my fingers, the snow piled up around me. Fog moved in and I was in a frosted gray-white world, featureless beyond four or five meters. The wind just kept getting worse, slapping me and knocking me around like a prize fighter.

[I'm down,] came Alice's voice not a minute too soon. Then Tamika's voice:

[I think Archie's beginning to come around.] They'd been monitoring her from the ship.

"Is she moving?" I asked.

[Not yet.]

Great. I untied from the pillar and started fighting my way back to where Archie was, removing as I went the protection I'd just set coming up. All we needed was for her to start staggering around in a white-out on the edge of oblivion. Snow was dumping on us now, piling and drifting, making it harder to find good holds.

I heard Archie's moan in my auditory lobe as I brushed off a handhold and carefully moved my feet. "Archie! Archie, do you hear me?"

Nothing. Maybe another groan. Just in case she could understand me, I said, "Don't move! Stay where you are!"

[Where I am?] It was her.

"Hey, Archie! Glad to have you back!" It was hard to talk while I struggled down the ledge, but I didn't want her to wander off, or worse, decide to untie from her protection.

[I can't ... I can't see anything. Ow! Shiva!]

"Don't move! Don't move, I'm on my way."

[What happened? I can't see anything. What's wrong with my eyes? I can't see anything.]

"Just stay put," I panted, "I'll be right there." I didn't know what could be wrong with her vision and I tried not to let it worry me. We'd fix it, whatever it was. I could barely see, myself.

I almost missed the bolts in the cliff face. Snow had covered them and the ropes as well. If I hadn't tripped over one of the lines, who knows how far I would have gone?

When I got back down to the edge I looked around and my adrenaline spiked. No Archie. I couldn't see her anywhere. Where could she *be*? There was no place to go.

"Archie! Archie, can you hear me?" Nothing. Then, right under my feet, a lump of snow moved. I was standing on her. I got down on my hands and knees and started digging her out. I found an arm and moved toward the head. When I had her faceplate clear I said, "Hey, Archie, how're you doing?"

[What?]

"How are your eyes? Can you see me?"

[My eyes? They're fine. Why?]

"Well, you said ..." Great. She wasn't blind; she'd just been covered with snow. "Never mind. We need to get you down to the hut."

[Hut? Where is it?]

Steel asked me, [How does she look, Mo?]

"Well, she's conscious. She's still pretty wobbly."

[Archie? How do you feel? Are you all right?]

[Am I—? I don't know. I guess I'm okay. What's going on? OW! I can't feel my arm.]

I looked into her faceplate. "Archie, we have to get you down to the hut so we can get your suit off and check you out."

[Okay,] she said, amenably. [What happened to my arm?]

[You took a spill,] Steel said, [You're okay. We just need to get you inside so we can take a look at you. We can lower you. You don't have to do anything. Just relax. Let Mo slip you over the edge and we'll do the rest. Okay?]

[Sure. Did I lose my arm? I can't feel it.]

"We didn't see any blood. We think you're okay," I reassured her.

[Just relax and let us lower you. All right?]

[Yeah, okay.]

"I need to tie you into this other line—"

[What the hell happened to the weather? Is it winter? Where the hell are we?]

"Just let me get this tied ..." I was starting to wear out. The wind was brutal and relentless. It obviously had no concern for what *I* was trying to accomplish; it just kept pounding and battering, roaring and wailing. I finally got the knot tied.

"Okay, Archie ... Archie?" She was limp in my arms. "I think she's faded out again, Captain."

[That's all right. We can get her down. Just get her over the edge. I'm already on belay.]

[I'm ready, too,] echoed Alice.

"Okay." I started sliding the two of us down to the edge, scooping buckets of gravel into the void. "Rock! ROCK!" I yelled.

[We're okay. We're off to the side.]

"Okay." I got her right to the edge and started pushing her over when I noticed she was taking a chunk of the cliff with her. It was an oblong piece of granite about the size of my leg—probably didn't weigh more than three hundred kilos—and there was not a thing I could do to get it back into place. I just watched helplessly as it toppled. "Mother of Allah, ROCK! Steel, Alice! Get behind something! This thing is huge!"

[We're on it. Alice! Get down!]

I waited as it fell. I didn't hear it hit the first ledge; it must have fallen clean all the way. It sounded like a cannon going off when it finally reached the second ledge, the hump where Steel and Alice were, hopefully, out of range and undercover. It must have just exploded when it hit; the initial boom reverberated up and down the cliff, followed by the clatter and rattle of smaller pieces bouncing back to earth. Then the roar of the wind once again blew its angry solo unaccompanied.

"Steel? Alice? Are you okay?"

The wind howled.

[I'm all right. Alice?]

[Yeah. A big piece whizzed right above me. I heard it. It was really moving.]

[But you're okay?] Steel asked.

[Yeah, yeah. I'm okay.]

I was shaking from relief. I couldn't stop. I think the cold was getting to me, too. "Okay," I said, "let's get Archie down there."

[Right,] Steel answered, [Belay on.]

I let Archie slip out of my grasp and onto the rope. She hung there for a moment and then receded from me haltingly, vanishing into snow, into fog, into wind, into nothingness.

CHAPTER 20

The snow danced around me, hard and icy, chattering against my suit in percussive sprays. I absentmindedly wiped it off my faceplate from time to time, brushed it from my sleeves, my chest. The external thermometer read minus twenty-six; it had dropped thirty degrees since the storm started. Wind chill probably kicked that down to minus sixty or worse. I sat there in my little person-shaped cabin, watching the storm through the window, watching the uncaring universe continue to unfold, watching the tiny evidence of human endeavor fighting against it—Archie's belay line hissing over the edge. I must have been looking somewhere else when it stopped.

Steel was talking to Alice, [Can you see what she's caught on?]

What now? I thought.

[No.] Effort and worry tightened Alice's voice.

[Try whipping your line around. Every time I look up, my face plate gets covered with snow.]

[Okay.]

[No, that's not doing it. Mo?] It was Steel.

"Yes." I was really tired.

[Mo, Archie's hung up on something. Can you see from up there?]

"Uh, not from where I am. I'd have to scoot down to look over the edge." My breath made little mist flowers bloom on the inside of my face plate before the tiny wind inside my suit carried them away.

[Could you do that?]

"Yeah. I don't want to knock anything down on her."

[I understand. She's just stuck. We can't budge her.]

"Okay. Let me stand up." I got carefully to my feet, trying not to move them unnecessarily. The snow had been thick and wet. It now had a frozen crust just thick enough to make it difficult to kick steps, but not so thick as to solidify the mess of rocks and gravel underneath. I had to wriggle my foot around until I felt rock, make sure the step was stable, and then repeat the process. It took time. The big chunk of granite Archie had knocked loose had left a scar—a nice clean ledge to stand on right at the edge. I worked my way down to it.

I could see her. A trick of wind currents had left a slim shaft of clear air next to the cliff. I could even follow the two lines down, writhing like snakes, and find the minuscule figures of Steel and Alice silhouetted on the snowy ledge, impossibly inaccessible, infinitely removed, but closer because I could see them.

Archie was spinning and swinging in the merciless wind, but I couldn't see anything that would stop her from descending. "She's well past that little ledge," I said, "She's just dangling free. The line looks good."

[Well, she's not moving.] I saw Steel flick the belay line. The wave she caused climbed up the rope, all the way to the ledge where I was standing, reflected off, and descended again, but to no good effect that I could see. The rope wasn't caught on the edge; it was encrusted with ice.

"Just a second," I said, and started working my way up to the top of the ledge where Steel had set the bolt in the cliff face. It took a lot longer than a second. I had to be painstakingly careful when planting my feet because Archie was directly below me with no way to get clear, and fatigue was taking its toll. The leg my weight wasn't on would start to vibrate every time I stopped to rest.

When I got up to the bolt, the problem was easy to see. A big clump of ice was preventing the line from sliding through the carabiner.

"Ice," I panted.

[What?]

"Ice is all over the rope. I'll chip it off." I sidled up to it and readied my ice ax. "Are you under tension?" I asked.

[Yes. Tension.] I saw the line tighten as Steel took up the slack.

"All right, here goes." I started chipping. When I got the first piece knocked off about two meters of line slid quickly through the 'biner—there's only so much tension you can put on three hundred meters of rope.

[Whoa! All right. I've got her.] The line started to flow through more steadily, until it got to the next chunk.

"Hold!" I said, and the line stopped. I cleaned off as much line as I could reach, then said, "Okay, lower away." We went on like that for what seemed forever. Long before Archie reached the bottom, the gloom of the storm had thickened to full night and I had to turn on my helmet's headlamp to see what I was doing.

Even after she was down on the next ledge I kept cleaning until I remembered to simply open the carabiner and unclip the rope from it. We should have done it that way up on top, too, I mused. We should have clipped a 'biner into the bolt and run the rope through that. It would have saved a little time. Too late now. We'd been rushed. 'We need to not rush,' I thought. 'We need to think things through.'

I held the line in my hand. "Line!" I said.

[Ready,] came Steel's reply. I let it go.

The world had reduced to a black tunnel filled with dancing flakes, backed sometimes with glimpses of rock, sometimes with nothing. It struck me that night is much larger than day; night is connected to everything. The universe is night, infinite night, lightless, bottomless, endless, impermeable night. The tiny places that are day shrink to infinitesimal points in a few million kilometers, points besieged by that which is not. Absence. Of heat, of light, of life.

My headlamp made a tiny pool of light that preceded me—my campfire, my hedge against the blackness. At least I was already where I needed to be, at the top of the ledge. I found the fixed rope, methodically tied into it, and readied myself to rappel. Then I untied from the other bolt.

"Ready to descend," I said. "Is everybody out of the way?"

[Come ahead.]

"Descending."

I leaned into the rope and started backing down the pile of rubble that had been my home for the last hour. As I stood out from the cliff, the wind caught me and knocked me off my feet. I slid a couple of meters before I caught myself, sending a small avalanche of snow and gravel sliding into the dark.

"Rock!" I said, with less urgency than I should have. It was all seeming rather surreal.

[We're okay. We've shifted south about twenty meters and are setting up the last leg.] Steel's voice. Or maybe Alice's. It was a really nice voice. Even here. Maybe especially here.

"Okay." That was good, I guessed. Need to keep moving.

I regained my feet and crouched low, trying to stay out of the wind, looking between my feet to see when the edge arrived. The wind was brutal. When I backed over the lip it caught me again, slamming me into the face and spinning me around a couple of times. The rope slipped out of my hand and I toppled over, hanging upside down on my descender. The beam of my headlamp swung chaotically through the driven night.

I grabbed frantically for the line, caught it again and hung there for a moment, resting, breathing hard, feeling the blood start to pound in my temples. Righting myself, I managed to get my feet on the face, fighting the relentless pressure of the wind. I was faced with a dilemma: when I got my feet planted and leaned out into the rope, the wind was just ferocious; it knocked me all over the place. When I stayed in close to the face, trying to stay out of the wind, I'd lose my leverage and my feet would slip off, leaving me dangling in space with no control, spinning and crashing into the rock.

Randomly alternating these two equally unpalatable techniques I managed to descend twenty or thirty meters—where I was stopped cold. The fixed rope had iced up, too. A big chunk of it had lodged in my descender. I tried to knock it loose with my gauntlet, but it was unyielding as a landlord. I wanted my ice ax. It hung from a loop on my belt, but I needed to tie it to my wrist before I got it out; I didn't want to drop it.

"Uh, Steel? Captain?" I snapped the webbing into the clip on my gauntlet.

[Yes?]

I withdrew the ax and started chipping as I spun dizzily in the wind. "Ah, I got a problem up here. It's gonna take me some time to get down."

[What's wrong?]

"Everything's iced up. I have to chip my way down."

[What?]

"The rope. The rope's covered with ice. How are you doing down there?"

[We're ready for the next drop. Can you make it?]

I had to hold the lower part of the rope between my boots to keep tension on the descender while I chipped away, holding to the upper part with my other hand. I finally got the chunk to break loose. It disappeared into black nothing as it fell. "Ice! Coming down."

[We're out of the way. Can you make it?]

"I don't know. The wind's got to be up around sixty knots up here." I slid another few meters down the rope, banging into the cliff face a few times in the process, until I hit the next chunk of ice. "Shiva, this is gonna take me forever."

[We need to get Archie down.]

"Yeah, I know. You go ahead. I'll just keep chipping. How's the rope down there?"

[It's a little icy. Not bad.]

"How's Archie?"

[She's in and out. I think she's asleep now. Her suit's taking care of her. She's stable.]

"Alice? You okay?"

[Yeah, I'm okay.]

Steel said, [The drop from here is really not bad. Can't be more than fifty or sixty meters. We can see the bottom with our headlamps.]

"That's great. How's the wind down there?"

[It gets better the lower we get.]

"You two can get Archie down, then?"

[We're going to have to try.]

"Yeah. Then I'll see you at the hut."

[Right. Mo?]

"Yeah."

[How's your suit power?]

Oh. Good thought. "Um, it's down to about thirty per cent."

[Hmm. You probably better power down everything you don't need.]

I saw her point and I didn't like it. The idea of spending the night out in the storm with nothing but the suit around me was not very attractive, but it was becoming more probable. The suits were designed to last for about eighteen hours before recharging. They were meant to get you from hut to hut. Each hut had a solar generator and storage system. At that particular moment it occurred to me that they could have designed the suits less optimistically.

"Yeah, okay," I answered. I powered down all the instrument lights, everything I could think of but the compressor and the heat. It was *cold* outside; I didn't want to turn off the heat. Communicating over Steel's system used my own metabolic power, so that wasn't a problem, but the headlamp was another matter. I had to see to clean off the rope, but with it on I wasn't going to make it through the night.

The biggest drain was the suit itself. There was no way I could move without the various servo-amplifiers moving the suit for me, it was just too damned heavy, and those little motors drew current like avant-garde theater draws critics. I didn't know what I was going to do, so I started chipping again.

I figured if I could just get down to the big hump where Steel and Alice were now wrestling Archie over the edge, I could at least find some rocks or something to keep me out of the wind and lessen the power drained by my heating unit. Where I was, Eden's atmosphere was carrying away calories as fast as I could make them. The heater had been going full blast for quite some time, now.

[Mo! Mo, we've got her down! We've got Archie down!]

"Great! Alice?"

[I'm descending now.]

Steel again: [If you can make it to the bottom ledge, the rope's pretty clean from there. Here comes Alice.]

In a few moments I heard them struggling to carry Archie into the hut.

[Here it is! Here it is! We're here.]

"Great!" I kept chipping, spinning, descending a little, cleaning some more, banging into the face, spinning, chipping, descending a little more, like a bad mantra.

Steel's voice flowed, sad and warm: [Oh, Archie! Oh, no. Let's get her into the nano-doc.]

[Okay.] Alice was quiet, reverent.

"How is she? Did you get her out of her suit?" I harassed an icicle into the night, dropped a little, started on the next.

[We've got her in the nano-doc.] Steel sounded tragic. [She'll be okay.]

"How is she?"

[She'll be okay.]

"What is it? What happened?"

They didn't answer for a while. When they did, it was Alice who spoke, not Steel. [Mo?]

"Yeah."

[We couldn't get her suit off. We had to put her in the 'doc with it on. It was ... kind of stuck to her.]

"Oh." That sounded bad.

[M—Steel—] Alice stopped, then started again, [The Captain thinks she might lose her arm.]

I kept chipping. I didn't have any other options.

"I think I see the ledge!" It had taken me forever to get to where I was, but I'd just caught a glimpse of something as I'd followed a piece of falling ice.

[Great, Mo!] Alice's voice cheered me, [It's not far once you get there.]

I turned on my instrument lights and checked my suit's power: twenty per cent. Not good, but it might be enough to get me down. I fought the ice a few more meters until my feet touched rock. "This is it, I'm down! I'm down on the ledge." I looked down at my feet. "No, wait—" I stood on a narrow slab of rock, bordered by blackness. I looked for the rest of the ledge—it was wide, covered with scree and talus, I remembered. I thought maybe the snow was just too thick in the air for me to see very far, that the blackness of the night was swallowing up the light from my headlamp. It took me a long time to accept that I had only reached the upper, narrow ledge, that I still had twice as far to go as I had already come to reach the lower one.

"Oh, Shiva."

[What's wrong?]

"It's—It's not the—I'm on the upper ledge. The narrow one."

Alice's voice fell, [Oh.]

The wind just kept beating at me as I tried to think. Fortunately, Steel came online and did my thinking for me:

[Mo, you're going to have to bivouac where you are.]

"Yeah, I guess so." She's writing me off, I thought. She's gonna let me freeze and re-boot me on the way back up. "I guess this is it, huh?"

[No. Listen. You have to tie yourself in. Now.]

"Right. Right." This wasn't going to be fun. Freezing. Jesus.

[Do it now, while you still have power. Tie yourself in and then power down.]

"Yeah, all right." I was pretty lethargic about the whole thing, but I set a couple of bolts. What was better, I thought, freezing? Or just taking a dive into the night and logging off quick and clean? It takes the same three months to re-boot, either way.

And Steel was going to re-boot me. I wondered if she would leave me my past. She had to take the recent stuff, my memories of her, of Alice, Neuschwanstein, Kindu—I understood that, security and all, but I wondered if she'd leave me the rest, or if she'd just make a clean sweep, just to be safe. Mary. Sheila. "Don't take my wife ..." I mumbled.

[What?]

"Nothing. Nothing."

[Mo. I don't want you to hurry, but I want you to keep moving. Tie yourself in.]

"Okay, okay." I clipped into both of the bolts, turned around and sat down on the ledge, my feet dangling into the flurried void.

[Are you tied in?]

"Yeah."

[I want you to lie down on the ledge, on your side, with your feet into the wind and your back to the cliff. Do you understand?]

"Why?"

[Don't hurry, but do it quickly. Now.]

"Okay."

[Your air intake is on your backpack, right between your shoulder blades. Your CO2 vent is back there, too. It lets out a good bit of heat. The air between you and the cliff should get a good bit warmer than the air around you. We need to take as much stress off your heating system as we can.]

"Right. Good idea."

[I want you to lie on your side, with your right arm under you. Your right side, facing out from the cliff.]

"I got it, I got it." I leaned over and pulled my legs back up on the ledge.

[Put your arm between your body and the rock. It will help insulate you. The less surface area you have touching the ledge, the better.]

"Yeah, okay." She was right: rock is a great heat-sink. I squirmed the rigid arm of the suit under me.

[Are you lying down?]

"Yeah. Yeah, I'm there."

[All right, now cinch yourself in tight. As tight as you can.]

"What?"

[You're tied into the bolts, right? Cinch up the ropes as tight as you can.]

"Oh. Right. No, yeah, I did that already."

[Now I want you to pull your arms out of the suit sleeves and into the trunk.]

Another good idea, if I could pull it off. "Uh, right," I said as I struggled to squirm my arms up through the sleeves without dislocating my shoulders. "How the heck am I supposed to do this?"

[It might help to turn your suit off.] That wouldn't have been my first choice. [Turn off the servos. With the suit rigid, it gives you something to push against.]

"Oh. I see." I powered down. All that was left on now was the heater, the air compressor, and my headlamp. I hadn't gotten up the nerve to turn that off yet; it made me feel better being able to see.

With the suit rigid it did give me some leverage; it didn't make it easy, but it made it possible. After a good bit of struggling I got my arms in and folded across my chest. That pushed my back right up against the back of the suit, but I did feel warmer. In fact it made my legs, each isolated in a leg of the suit, feel colder by contrast.

"Done," I said.

[Good. Now close your waste exhaust valves.]

"What?"

[Your urine and fecal exhausts. It may get uncomfortable, but we need to do everything we can to conserve heat.]

Great. I liked her use of the term 'we.' *She* wasn't going to be lying in her own waste all night. I wondered if I could hold it till morning, if I lasted that long.

"Okay."

[You did it?]

"I did it. I did it."

[What else is left on?]

"Well, my headlamp—"

[Turn it off.]

"Right." I didn't want to, but I did it.

Click.

The dancing flakes vanished into thick, heavy blackness, blackness so palpable it pressed on my eyes and made it difficult to breathe for a moment. I felt like I was falling off the ledge. I couldn't tell. My heart pounded and my breathing got heavy and ragged as I waited for the vertigo to pass.

[Are you all right?]

"Yeah. Yeah, it's just ... pretty intense."

[What is?]

"Nothing. I'm fine." I didn't *feel* fine.

A small red indicator flared briefly on the miniature instrument panel in my helmet, then winked out. "Wait a minute. What was that? I got an indicator—"

[I just locked you out of your suit.]

"What? Why? What are you—"

[Mo. Listen to me. You may go into hypothermia before we can get to you. Your thinking may get impaired.] I could hear that beautiful, ironic smile come into her voice. [We can't afford to have you squirming off that silly ledge now, can we?]

"Right." I still didn't like it. Lying on a tiny ledge in a high wind on a huge cliff in the middle of the night on a planet full of religious fanatics ... and now I was trapped in my own space suit. How could things be better? "What if something falls on me?"

[Like what?]

"I don't know, a rock or something." I was wondering if I'd loosened anything up on the ledge above me that was now just teetering in the wind. It was a silly thought, but I thought it anyway.

[Well, if that happens I guess we're screwed and tattooed, Hmm?]

"Yeah, I guess." The blackness was still a solid thing engulfing me. I kept waiting for my eyes to adjust, but there was nothing for them to adjust *to*. Starlight, or even moonlight, couldn't penetrate this storm; I was in a lightless environment. It was all the more disconcerting because the level of noise was quite high. The wail of the wind and the percussive hiss of dry snow hitting my suit had the endless, chilling quality of arctic surf.

Alice spoke to me. [Mo, do you have any food left?]

"Uh, yeah, I do. I have, let's see, five energy bars and some dried fruit."

[We're eating down here. Maybe you should eat something, too.]

"Yeah, you're probably right." I turned my head and pulled a bite of energy bar out of its slot beside my face plate. Then I turned the other way and took a drink of water from the tube on the water tank. I figured that I should drink as much as I could before it froze—and then I thought that drinking a lot would make me have to urinate and I sure didn't want to do that. Eventually my thirst won the argument, but what a weird argument to be having.

For a long time things were just kind of boring, in a hyper-tense, terrifying sort of way. Alice would talk to me pretty regularly, and everyone on the Lightdancer would check in as well. I'd start to relax a little and then a titanic gust would hammer me and I'd jerk into full, adrenaline-soaked, utterly pointless readiness. I tried to do a couple of Realities on Steel's system, but I couldn't concentrate: I was always popping out to check some sound or sensation. Time slowed down as I checked it more and more often; dawn was still a long way off. Sometime after midnight my suit ran out of power and it started to get cold. Really cold. Doing isometrics kept my body heated up for a while, but I couldn't keep doing them for very long. I was already exhausted from the day, and, anyway, how long can you exercise, even when you're fully rested? My feet got cold first, because they were facing into the wind. The cold turned to numbness and started creeping up my legs. After a while I started trembling uncontrollably, and then I got too exhausted even for that. It occurred to me that if I didn't completely freeze and have to re-boot, I might lose some fingers or toes. Well, toes anyway.

I started to wonder how Sheila was doing back on Vesper. I wondered how Shaughnessy's show was going; they would have finished the run on Heaven by now. I couldn't remember where they were going next. It didn't matter, but I wondered where they were.

I wondered if my tax auditor was sleeping soundly, the bastard.

After a while it didn't feel so cold.

CHAPTER 21

I woke up in the hut. I knew it was the right one because I could see Archie sleeping in a bunk half a meter away from me. I was out of my suit, lying under soft cotton sheets. I wiggled my toes—they felt fine. Nobody missing, no frostbite. Everything in order.

I realized that I wasn't alone in the bunk. Arms were wrapped around me and a very warm body was pressed against me, breathing softly, regularly. When I turned to see who it was she opened her eyes sleepily—cat-eyes.

"Hi," I said.

She yawned a feline yawn and said, "How are you feeling?"

"Better than I have any right to feel," I responded, hopefully with suave, sexual undertones. I really did feel great. I didn't understand it. "What happened?"

Steel rubbed my arms and chest and pressed herself into my side. "You lost a lot of body heat. We thought we were going to lose you there for a while."

"What time is it? What *day* is it? I thought—"

"Shh. Let's let Archie sleep. She needs it."

"But—"

"Shh." She snuggled closer. "You need it, too."

I didn't get the whole story till everyone was awake. The short and long of it was that Steel and Alice had rescued me. They'd had to stay with Archie while she went through the operation and then stabilized, and they'd had to wait for their suits to recharge, but as soon as they could—which turned out to be a couple of hours before dawn—they'd suited up again and headed back out into the storm. The ropes had been completely iced up; they'd had to chip their way back up to me. I guess I'd been delirious or unconscious all the way down. I must have been a handful.

When they got me back to the hut they got me out of my suit and both climbed into bed with me, warming me with their bodies. After I stopped trembling Alice moved over to her own bunk and Steel stayed with me the rest of the night.

I didn't know what to say. They'd both taken incredible risks to keep me from going offline, to keep me from freezing. Alice had risked ... everything. I was overwhelmed.

My discomfort was brief, however, as we had to attend to Archie. Poor Archie. The ice ax had bent an interior flange in the shoulder joint of her suit and the flange had pinched closed the main artery going into her arm. By the time they'd gotten her to the hut all they could do was let the nano-doc amputate it. She'd have to wait until we got her to a real hospital before she could get a new one. It made her look smaller. You don't realize how much of someone an arm is until it's missing.

And yet, we'd been incredibly lucky. No one had gone off line. More importantly, Alice was safe.

We took two extra days to make it the rest of the way down. No more goofing around; we were very, very careful. We had to assist Archie in various ways. Anything that took two hands needed one of our hands to accomplish, but we made it.

Our shelter at the bottom was actually a little Buddhist shrine, a destination for pilgrims from a small enclave in the lowlands. It was the first structure pertaining to one of the old religions that I had seen in centuries. Built of flat stones quarried from the talus, it was a small, rude hut—barely more than a pile of rocks—that had been painstakingly covered with illustrations and calligraphy. A large, painted eye gazed benignly from each of the four sides of the base of a small spire on the roof. Small, brightly colored scraps of cloth clinging to lines that radiated from the tip of the spire fluttered in the constant breeze. Archie told me that each one had a prayer written on it.

This struck me profoundly. The people on Eden still asked supernatural beings to intercede for them, to ease the suffering and struggle of their brief lives. They had chosen to eschew physical immortality in their need to maintain their traditional relationship to anthropomorphic spirits, the Godhead, Allah, God. They had chosen to continue dying. They had *chosen* it. All of the studying I had done on the ship had not prepared me for the experience of this one tiny shrine, this little labor of devotion, this place of powerless beseeching, of humble acceptance.

We still had about fifty klicks to hike out before we got to the plateau, still descending steeply but now on the pilgrim's trail that wound down through the eroded piedmont: piled detritus that had broken off the escarpment over the eons. Looking up at that colossal wall I had no idea how we'd ever get back up to the Lightdancer, but Archie, Steel and Alice had done it before.

Breakfasting outside, we polished our plans for getting to Nazareth, the little town where Alice had been ... born. The sun shone in a vivid sky and shattered on the spray of a snow-fed torrent that bounded and raced in the gully beside us. We had stowed our space suits in a small, camouflaged cache a couple of hundred meters up the slope. It was marvelous to be out in the air again.

"My arm will actually help us, I think," Archie was saying to me, lifting a mug of tea to her lips with her remaining hand. "I'd been thinking that we all looked too healthy."

Alice and Steel had finished eating and were off putting their packs together. I glanced over at them working, thinking how lucky I was to be online, let alone healthy. "I hope you didn't lose it on purpose," I said.

Archie smiled grimly. "I'm dedicated, but not that dedicated. Still, we're going to have to degrade our skin on the way down. Alice is okay, she's supposed to look young, but the rest of us need to pick up some sun damage."

"Sun damage?"

"Farmer tans. These folks work outside a lot, and none of them are on the net."

"Hmm." Nobody told me this place wouldn't be strange. "I'm just glad to be down and still functioning. I think I've misjudged our Captain."

Archie sipped at her tea. "How so?"

This was hard to say, but I felt I needed to say it to somebody. "I think I short-changed her." I looked at my hands. Two hands. "When I was up on that ledge ..."

Archie was looking at me, her mug halfway to her lips. When I didn't go on she said, "Thanks, by the way."

"Oh, yeah, that's ..." I started again, "But ... I didn't think—I thought ..." It seemed so unjust to even voice the accusation then, sitting in the sunshine, listening to the rush of the stream, watching the prayer flags flutter urgently in the unaffected wind. Archie waited for me to go on, her remaining hand holding a mug of tea.

"I thought she'd leave me up there, you know? I thought she would just ... pick me up later. Re-boot me when it was convenient. After she was through here. Or something."

Archie watched me for a moment, then gazed out at the sky. "People like Steel are hard to judge," she said finally. "I think we fail to appreciate how profoundly the net affects us."

Steel walked up with her pack already on. "No more talk about banned technology," she admonished. "From here down we could meet natives at any point."

"Sorry," Arch acknowledged.

"There's a small settlement where this trail joins the main road between

Nazareth and New Jordan. We should be able to buy a car there." She handed me a small, flat, folded leather envelope filled with ornately decorated paper. "Here's the money. Christian men keep these in their hip pockets."

"Right. Wallets," I remembered. A funny word. It seemed like it should mean 'little walls,' but it didn't.

Archie rinsed out her mug in the stream. We had to help her get it into her pack. She was working on a technique of using her teeth as a second hand, but she hadn't mastered it yet. Fortunately she had enough shoulder left to keep her pack on.

Steel surveyed us all, "From now on, we're in character." She ended her sweep at me.

"Oh, right," I said, getting her implication. This was it. We were now entering the strange, isolated society that was Eden—a society that had been cut off from the rest of civilization for almost a thousand years. A place of bizarre rituals and ancient crimes: marriages, funerals, births, rapes, murders. I settled the pack on my shoulders, took a stronger bearing, breathed. "Sister-in-law, are you ready?" I asked Archie.

"Yes, Brother-in-law," she replied.

"Niece?"

Alice nodded, "Yes, Uncle."

I looked at Steel. The word stuck in my mouth for an instant, but I don't think it was noticeable. I hoped. "M-mother? Are you ready?" She would be posing as my wife, but I used the higher honorific, just to practice it.

She dipped her head respectfully. "Yes, Father." She returned the gesture.

I bowed my head. "May God protect us on our journey. In Jesus' name we pray." The three women murmured "Amen." I raised my head, looked at my family. "Let us begin," I said.

This was going to be really weird.

CHAPTER 22

Lawson's Crossing shimmered ahead, wavering in the metallic heat. It was still early morning, but already the heat reflecting off the buff slickrock around us was like an over-attentive mate—all over you, smothering you, never leaving you alone. The rock had been scoured into satin by wind and water over endless eons. It undulated softly to the horizon, smooth and sensual as human skin, unbroken by tree or shrub or blade of grass. Compacted umber dust fine as talcum powder gathered in the low spots, traced the paths of empty creek beds, crunched beneath our boots.

Steel had tied her hair up under her hat to keep it off her neck, but a few stray locks adhered to her sweat-slicked skin. Sweat stained our shirt collars and chafed under our arms, gathered under our pack straps and trickled down our spines. We'd been walking five days since we left the shrine and hadn't met a single soul. The escarpment had faded to a purple ghost on the eastern horizon.

Sun-damaged skin, or the lack thereof, wasn't going to be a problem.

"Doesn't look like there's anybody home," I said to Steel.

"They're there," she answered. "They're probably just inside to get out of the sun. I know *I* would be."

"Right," I said. We started walking again. It sure didn't look inhabited. It didn't look habitable. I don't know what I was expecting, but my overall impression was that it had been thrown together slap, dash, and hope it stands up. I had to keep reminding myself that it wasn't because the Edenites didn't care about where they lived, it was simply that they didn't have any time. They couldn't spend decades and centuries working things out and getting them just so. They had only half a century of adult life, maybe a little more, to do everything they wanted to do. Everything. Build a house, run a farm, build a business. They had less than *two* decades, sometimes less than one, to spend educating themselves full-time before they had to enter the workforce. I'd spent longer than that learning how to act, and that was only the latest of my many careers.

The closer we got to the edge of town ("town" seems a rather grand word for that ramshackle collection of hovels) the emptier it seemed: silent, motionless, untouched since the beginning of time. Silly thoughts went through my mind. I wondered how many rapists lived there, how many murderers. Silly thoughts, but the stillness, the silence, the isolation on that vast plain of rock was haunted, haunting. Viscous and sticky and filled with dread.

We neared the first shack, walking along minding our own business, when out of nowhere a huge, black, slavering wolf leapt for our throats, howling for blood! I've never seen anything so terrifying. Its ears were laid back and its hackles were raised. Its yellow fangs were bared and saliva flew from its gnashing jaws. It lunged at us with unbelievable speed and ferocity.

Trying to stay in character, I gathered my family together. I tried to interpose myself between them and certain doom—when Steel whispered in my ear, "It's all right, Father. It's just a dog. He's tied up." At that point he was practically hanging himself on his leash trying to get at us.

"Right, right, a 'watchdog,' I remember," I answered, catching my breath and trying to regain my dignity.

Watchdog. What a stupid concept. But then, these people didn't know each other. They weren't on the net, they'd never melded. Any one of them might rob the other, rape the other, kill the other. Steel had told me that most of the residents of Lawson's Crossing belonged to one of the Protestant sects, Pentecostal, I recalled, which gave them a certain level of trust and security with each other. But one never knew when a roving band of Muslims or Jews or—worse yet—Baptists, might happen by.

We sidled our way past the homicidal hell-hound of space and on into town. It really seemed deserted. "How are we going to buy a car when there's nobody to buy one *from*?" I asked. We'd passed a couple of rusting hulks, but no owners.

"We should try that place." Archie pointed to what looked like the local watering hole. I could barely make out "Sam's Cafe—15 cent Burgers" on a sun-bleached metal sign and "Drink Pokey Cola—the *sloowww* thirst quencher!" on another. There were the remnants of a couple of fueling pumps out front— "Hydroco! Just try five tankfuls—you'll FEEL the difference!" The bubbly enthusiasm of the advertising was woefully overmatched by the silent inertia of Lawson's Crossing. Their happy exhortations vaporized in the desert heat.

It suddenly struck me: "Where do they get all this wood?"

"They have to truck it in from the coastal forests they started back in the twenty-nines," Steel answered.

"Hmm." I looked around at my little troupe of actors. "Well, shall we?" We all seemed a little jittery. Alice looked like she was floating in a sea of undefined expectations.

"Fine with me," she said. Steel and Archie nodded.

We were announced by the rusty whine of the spring on the screen door. Dusty sunlight filtered in through the two large, wavy-glass display windows, making bright trapezoids on the worn wooden floor. The interior was lit from below by those two chrome-white patches. A lunch counter stretched along one wall. There were a couple of shelves sparsely stocked with obscure wares—food, it may have been, and two tables in the back. At one of these sat the first Edenite I had ever seen.

He sat in a chair slightly hunched, his stick legs bent like old hinges in front of him. His spine curved forward at the top and his chest seemed to have caved in, sitting disconsolately on the little ball that was his belly. Thick, purple veins roped across the back of his hands; his fingernails were made of yellow horn. His face hung from his skull like a tired tapestry, longing for the earth from whence it had come. He didn't look at us.

I had a sudden bout of stage fright. I cleared my throat. Steel, Archie and Alice clustered behind me like hens, or bees. "Uh-h, h-hello?—" I started.

"She'll be right back," he rasped, his voice fragile and worn. He still didn't look at us.

"Oh. Okay. Thanks." I looked at Steel and Archie. They shrugged. I turned back to the old man, for that is what he was. An old man. "Um, we were wanting—"

"She'll be right back," he repeated, like a recording of himself.

"Okay. Sorry. We'll ... uhh ... we'll wait."

"Might as well," he croaked.

We stood in the doorway for a few minutes. No one appeared. I didn't know what 'right back' meant in this context. I turned to Steel for advice. She had none, so I risked the old man again.

"Maybe we could sit down?" I hazarded.

"Doesn't bother me if it doesn't bother you." His hand moved to the brim of the hat lying on the table next to him. We rustled over to the lunch counter. More still, desert time blew past the windows. Whoever 'she' was, she didn't seem to be worried about her business.

The four of us carried on a conversation with each other that consisted of shrugs, frowns and questioning glances. I think we were all afraid to speak in front of the old guy. After a while I tried again: "We're trying to get to Nazareth," I said.

"Sounds like you're in the wrong place," he responded.

"Yeah, well, we wanted to buy a—"

"No Nazareth around here," he stated.

That caught me up short. I glanced at Steel. No help. "Right. It's about ..."

"Ninety miles," Steel interjected.

"Ninety miles—"

"South," Steel again.

"South of here. On the Jordan River."

"Nope," he said.

That was it. Just, "nope." I glanced at Steel again. At Archie. They looked back, as puzzled as I was. "Uh, no?"

"No Nazareth down that way."

I looked back at the femmes. I was getting alarmed. I whispered, "Maybe it got wiped out. It's in a slot canyon, right? Maybe there was a flood." Steel shook her head. She was worried, too.

I turned back to the guy. "Was there a flood, or something?"

"Never has been any Nazareth around here. Been here my whole life. I ought to know."

Now what were we going to do? It didn't make sense. I whispered to Steel, "Did we come down at the wrong place?" She shook her head. We weren't even supposed to talk about that. But we couldn't have come down at the wrong place. The fixed ropes were only *in* one place.

"Are you sure? We know some folks down there—"

"You asking me if I know my own home? If there was a Nazareth around here I'd know about it. There's always somebody coming through here that thinks they know where everything is. I met a man once—"

The voice of an avenging Valkyrie emerged from the kitchen: "John Jackson MacDougal, are you lying to those people?" A barrel-shaped woman exploded through the swinging doors. John Jackson MacDougal clammed up. "What have I told you about that? Don't you know lying's a sin? You look at me when I'm talking to you!"

He didn't. He seemed to be contemplating some important appointment he needed to make. She was undaunted. "Daddy, Daddy, look at me," she softened. He still didn't move. "Do you think I want to go through eternity alone? I want you with me up there. Besides, it's bad for business." He wasn't giving an inch.

She turned to us. "He doesn't like me spoiling his fun," she said. "His eyesight's so bad nowadays he can't read anymore—not that my brothers ever write—but he loved his books. I'm afraid fooling people is the only entertainment he has left. God bless him." She turned back to him and placed a hand on his scrawny shoulder. "You got nothing to do all day, do you, Daddy?" He didn't say anything, just jutted his chin toward the window. "Tell you what ..." She leaned down to him. "I just finished some blueberry muffins. Fresh out of the oven. Your favorite.

You want some? Nice, hot blueberry muffins?"

"Don't want any muffins," he grunted.

"Aw, come on now, Daddy, don't be mad." She hugged him from behind around his shoulders, putting her mouth right by his ear. "You know I'm just taking care of you. I want you to get into heaven with the rest of us." She winked at us. He didn't answer. I don't think he liked being old. Old and powerless. Old and helpless. She squeezed him and continued to cajole him in a sing-song, "Blueberry muffins, hmm? Hot and crumbly with lots of butter?"

He was wavering. Dignity demanded he refuse, but accepting would restore peace, equilibrium, normalcy. Finally, "I'll take a muffin," he conceded. "No butter."

"Thaaat's right," she patted him gently, "a nice hot blueberry muffin." She smiled at us. "I'll be right back."

She reappeared with a big bone-china plate stacked with steaming muffins that she placed before the old guy. Then she stepped behind the counter and said, "What can I get you?"

Steel offered no cues, so I said, "Oh, I guess we'll have four burgers and four Pokey Colas."

"Burgers and Pokes all around, eh? You got it." She turned to the grill behind her and started slapping discs of ground meat onto the hot metal.

Steel poked me in the ribs. "And we're looking for a car," I added, under duress.

"Why? You lost it?"

"No, no. We want to buy one."

She turned back around to me. "You came all the way out here to buy a car?" she asked, reasonably I thought.

I went into the story. "I'm afraid ours gave up the ghost ..." (I was pretty smug about working that expression into the improv. It gave it an authentic ring. I hoped.) "a few miles back."

"What were you doing clear out here?" She flipped the meat discs over.

"We're on our way to Nazareth to look up some relatives."

"On your way to Nazareth? From where?"

The next part of the story: "We've been on a retreat."

"Oh, I see." She slid the discs onto round pieces of bread. "What are you, Methodists?"

"That's right."

She placed plates in front of us and turned to a dispenser to get our 'Pokes.' "You Methodists are always going on retreats. Don't you guys ever advance?" She laughed at her own joke.

I echoed her laugh, and Steel and Archie echoed me, each echo getting fainter until Alice just smiled. "Well," I answered, "somebody's got to choose the songs for the new hymnal."

She raised her eyebrows. "Are they fighting over that again? I thought they just finished working all that stuff out."

The rush of being caught out surged through me. Lying is different than acting. We knew this would happen, little parts of the story might not jive with recent events we didn't know about. I tried to look normal—whatever that means, and wing my way through it. "Oh, there's always a few last minute changes."

"Ain't *that* the truth," she agreed.

Made it through that one. "Anyway, our car just finally ran out of steam about twenty miles north of here."

She looked at me skeptically. "What'd you do, miss us?"

"Pardon?"

"I saw you walking in on the Shrine trail. I thought you might have been some of those damn Buddhists. 'Scuse my language."

Another rush. This was like the last watch before freewheeling—stuff was coming at me faster than I could handle it. The Shrine trail, of course, approached Lawson's Crossing from the east, not the north. "Yes, we must have wandered off the road somewhere out on the rock."

"Easy to do. So you need a car, huh?"

Made it through that one, too. If it kept up like this I wasn't going to live long enough to die horribly on Brainard's Planet. "That's right. Nothing fancy. Just something that'll get us where we're going."

"Twenty miles. You folks have had quite a walk."

At least *that* was believable. We looked like the refugees that the other refugees didn't want to be seen with.

"Yeah. Fortunately we had our packs with us." I bit into my burger. I don't know what it tasted like—old memories, maybe. "Do you know anyone who might have something we could buy? It's a long way to Nazareth and we have some important business there."

"Well, let's see," she wiped her hands on her apron. "You might try Bob Wyllis. He usually has a few extras around. He likes working on them. Sort of a hobby, I guess."

"Great! And where might we find Mr. Wyllis?" 'Mr. Wyllis.' I was really cooking.

"I think you met his dog. I heard him barking just before you walked in."

Wonderful. "Oh, yes. A fine animal. Bet he doesn't get many visitors."

"What do you mean?" She didn't get it. I backtracked:

"Nothing, nothing. How much do we owe you?"

"Hmm. Four burgers, four Pokes. A buck even."

"Okay." I got out my 'wallet' and gave her one of the pieces of paper.

"So how'd you like your burgers? You wolfed them down fast enough."

"Oh, they were—" I looked around at the girls. They looked like I felt. My stomach seemed to be wandering around my midsection, trying to find a comfortable position. "They were just fine."

"Hey!" She stopped, looking at the bill. Another rush of adrenaline.

"Anything wrong?"

She turned around holding the bill out to me, "You don't want to spend this. Look here: it's an old Gold Certificate. I haven't seen one of these in twenty years. Bet you didn't even know you had it. You'll want to keep this." She handed it back to me.

"Oh, yeah, look at that, Mother." I looked at Steel significantly, "It's an old Gold Certificate." Steel looked blank and said, "Hmm." I got out another bill and handed it to the woman.

She took it, then stopped. "Well, here's another one! Where'd you get these?"

"Oh, uh—" I looked through the wallet. All the bills said *Gold Certificate* in florid lettering right across the top. "My, uh, Grandmother stuffed these in an old shoebox she kept out on a rafter in the barn. You know, saving for a rainy day." I plastered what I hoped was a jovial smile across my terrified face.

The woman looked at me like I was from another planet.

"She didn't trust banks," I added.

"Smart woman," the old man said.

"You would say that," the woman said to him. "You just eat your muffins and mind your own business." She turned back to me. "Well, I hate to take it off you, but if it's all you've got—"

"I'm afraid so. We've sort of fallen on hard times lately, and, you know, had to break into the old shoebox." Once you start an improv, it's hard to stop.

"Oh, that's too bad," she clucked. She seemed to consider this information, then spread her arms magnanimously. "In that case, it's on the house," she said.

Well *that* wasn't what I'd intended. "Oh, no, no! We couldn't do that." Steel could probably afford to buy her whole planet, and here she was offering us charity.

"I insist," she said. "One dollar won't make much difference to this place one way or the other. But it just might get you folks through a tight spot. When you get back on your feet, you just pass that dollar along to somebody else." She smiled.

I was nonplussed. I finally said, "Well, that's awfully nice of you. I won't forget it."

"Trust in the Lord. You'll be all right." She waved to us as we filed out the door. "Oh, and one more thing."

We turned back.

"You might want to know that the Methodist retreat up north burned down about eight years back. Nobody's been up there since then."

I froze. "Uh—" I said.

She held up her hand. "That's all right. You don't have to make up another story. I just want you to know that, whatever it is you folks are going through, the Lord is with you. You remember that, okay?"

I nodded. "We, uh, we will."

She thought of something else. "You're not heretics, are you?"

"No, no. Nothing like that."

She measured us, skeptical but indulgent, like we were errant children. "Well, I hope you find who you're looking for. The folks down at Nazareth will treat you right. Presbyterians, mostly, but nice people."

When we got a little ways down the street I turned to the rest of them. "Well, *that* went really well. Are you guys ever going to talk? I felt like I was all alone in there."

Steel said, "Well, what about you? 'My grandmother kept them in a shoebox ...' Where did you get *that*?"

"Where did I get it? I don't know, from one of Yuri's old movies, I guess." Then I got huffy: "What do you mean where did I get it? I pulled it out of my butt. I was making it up as I went along. What did you want me to say—'Sorry, my wife forgot to take into account the effects of time dilation when traveling close to the speed of light for thirty years'? That would have gone over real well."

"Keep your voice down!"

"I am keeping my voice down!" I whispered. " 'The Methodist retreat burned down,' " I quoted. "Is there any part of our cover story that holds up? How the heck did you pull this off last time?"

Archie leapt to Steel's defense. "Last time we spent two whole years observing these people before we ever made contact."

"We just didn't have time this time," Steel added. "I was just hoping it would work out."

"Great," I said, shaking my head. Then I noticed Alice looking kind of defeated. "I'm sorry, Alice. We'll find your parents. I know we will. We'll make it work, one way or another."

"I know," Alice smiled at me. "I know." But she didn't look convinced.

"That woman didn't believe us," Archie put in, "but she didn't try to stop us either. I think she felt sorry for us."

"You don't think she's calling the cops right now? Or the Synod or the Star Chamber or whatever it is they have around here?"

"I don't know." She looked crestfallen. So did Alice. So did Steel.

I regretted taking the wind out of their sails. "Well," I tried to buoy things back up, "Let's go see what Bob has to say."

We headed down the street.

CHAPTER 23

Bob had a car and he took our money. If he thought anything strange about it he kept it to himself. Maybe the woman at Sam's Cafe called ahead about us. Maybe he was a collector, who knows.

The car was quite something. I recognized the design. It was a BuckyMobile: a six-meter long teardrop with the blunt end serving as the windshield, two wheels set far apart up front, two little wheels set close together behind. Based on a two millennium-old design by a quirky architect and mathematician, it was huge. We could have fit ten or eleven people in it.

An alcohol-fueled reciprocating engine powered it: hundreds of moving parts, valves and pistons flopping back and forth. It sounded like a big flatulence when we started it up. The clutch took a while for me to master (I told Bob that I'd always driven "an old four-banger with automatic transmission and good rubber") but I eventually got the hang of it and we lurched off across the rock.

From the comfortable confines of the BuckyMobile the desert was entertaining rather than daunting. Still, the vastness of it pointed up the scale of the challenge these people had taken on. Terraforming a world is hard enough when you have the full resources of an interstellar civilization behind you. To cut themselves off the way they had and then try to carve out an ecosystem, I didn't know how they did it. Even considering that the planet had started with a nitrogen-oxygen atmosphere, a twenty-six hour day, and gravity that might as well have been the same as Earth's—I couldn't tell any difference (hence the name 'Eden')—it was a planet where an isolated population could just barely hang on by its teeth and toenails and create a world, a home.

The road wasn't much—we just rolled across the rock from cairn to cairn, trying not to get lost. Late in the afternoon we saw the windmill fields poke up over the southern horizon and we knew we were getting close. Steel and Archie got more agitated; Alice got quieter.

On either side we passed windmills, arms turning lazily in the afternoon, like a colony of hydras. Even then we couldn't see any interruption in the endless rock. Slot canyons are a rather unique geological formation. They can be two hundred meters deep and only two meters wide all the way to the top, caused by water slowly eroding downward through rising sandstone. I've never seen the ones in western North America, but I hear they're very beautiful.

We pulled into the parking lot at the north rim of the slot; at that point it was nothing but a narrow, sinuous gap in the softly rolling rock. There were several other cars there, but no people. Nazareth was below us but unseen, protected from the blistering sun at the bottom of the slot.

"Has it changed much?" I asked, more to break the tension than anything else. No one answered. No one moved. "Are we sure we want to do this?" I added.

Steel said "Yes" as Archie said "No." Alice looked out the windshield at the sinuous ripple in the rock and said nothing.

"It'll be all right," I said. I had no idea if it would be all right. "I mean, we came by car on the same road anyone else would take. It won't be like Lawson's Crossing. We're—we're—"

"Let's get going," Steel said, steely determination adding extra percussion to her consonants. Then more lightly, "Come on, Alice. Let's go find your—" She rose out of her seat and opened the door, then turned back to us. "Let's go."

Alice followed Steel out the door. Archie still hesitated. When they were out of earshot I asked her, "What the hell happened the last time you were here?"

She turned and looked at me for a moment before she said, "You'd better watch your language. Around here." She got up and walked out into the heat. I followed her.

It was hard to believe we were just a hundred meters above a bustling village. The rock was as barren as a fashion model's smile. The slot itself was no more than two or three meters wide, winding and twisting across the fleshy skin of the planet—capricious, unhurried, wandering tunelessly to a sea it could not conceive of.

Steps were carved into the side of the canyon, descending from the merciless glare of the desert into soft, rose-colored coolness. Eons of water had carved the sandstone into fantastical swirls, bowls and hanging sculptures. Its color varied from a golden buff to the deepest, bloody maroon. The stairs wound down deeper and deeper in their own carved groove, open to the sinuous twists of the slot through hand-hewn windows, suffusing us in the pink light of a primeval womb.

Reaching the bottom was like entering another world. Just a few hundred steps away from a boundless, baking plain, we stood beside a golden brook that gurgled gently over rounded stones. We could have leaned across it and touched the other wall, glowing sensually, inviting caresses. The air was cool and moist. The cobalt sky was a banished memory, reflecting down the swirling stone walls and transformed into soft kisses. Everywhere was soft, smooth, curving—the arms and breasts and lips of an infinitely forgiving lover who existed only to enfold and nurture. I found myself constantly placing my palm on the rock. It was dry and cool, its granular surface tickling each individual nerve ending in the mated swells and recesses of my flesh. As I touched it to more intimately grasp its texture and shape, it informed me of my own. It was my teacher, my mentor, my mirror.

A few meters of winding through the narrow, twisting passage deposited us abruptly in a wide amphitheater. It had been carved out by the gushing plume of a tall, narrow waterfall we could make out at the upstream end. A blue banner of sky hugged the vertical north wall of the canyon, allowing a thick slab of sunlight to bounce off its capstone layer of rich, red rock, flooding the amphitheater with soft reflection. The south wall arched over so far that it almost met the north, turning the amphitheater into a cavern, a rose cathedral. Above the waterfall the canyon was wider and shallower. There it was flooded with sunlight: slanting onto the walls, buff, white and rust, illuminating them like stained-glass windows.

The floor of the amphitheater was an unexpected garden—a rich green jungle shockingly out of place in this womb of rock. Feathery tree ferns and thick bamboo sprouted from the sandy soil. Vegetable gardens and dwarf fruit trees intermingled with dusty herbs and rambling berry patches. Sandy gaps were connected by wandering trails. An arched footbridge crossed the stream at one point, leading to a small wooden gazebo.

Half the village was carved into the rock itself. Ovate doors and windows looked out of the rock walls in tiers reached by wooden ladders or steps carved in stone. Other wooden and stone buildings were scattered along the edge of the garden, modest bungalows clean of line and devoid of ornament. A steeple topped with a wooden cross rose above the other roofs not far from the waterfall. As we walked farther we could see that a second canyon branched off at the upper end of the amphitheater, leading to more dwellings, more garden. The entirety was bathed in the rose-golden glow of light reflected off rock—the light you glimpse through the flesh of your fingers when you hold your hand up to a bright lamp.

The light reflected off Alice's face and she returned the favor. This was where she'd been born. Where she'd spent the first part of her life. Recognition flickered across her features as she pointed out familiar things to Archie or Steel, things they recognized too. But she remained reserved; she seemed reluctant to commit to this place as being hers or representative of her. She seemed glad to see it again but distant. Not judgmental, perhaps waiting for someone else to be.

"Is it good to be home?" I asked.

"Well, this isn't really my home," she hedged. "I mean, I haven't lived here in a while. I was pretty little when we left. But, yeah, it's—it's—it's pretty weird, I guess." She laughed in a small expression of self-deprecation, maybe embarrassment. More even than in Lawson's Crossing she seemed to be floating, detached from the ground, detached from her own history, as brief as it was.

Above the distant rush of the waterfall and the soft babbling of the stream another sound came to us, as if out of a half-remembered dream. High-pitched and complex, it echoed around the curving walls. It reminded me of something— birds, maybe, or wind chimes. It pulled at me. There was something primal about it, as though I had always known it. It brought back memories of my earliest life, of schools, teachers, scraps and contests, bloody noses and scraped knees. As we got closer it resolved into a gentle mosaic of small voices: squeals and shrieks, shouts and laughter—but small shouts, small laughter, pealing and cascading, getting lost and then returning, rising and falling in response to its own internal rhythm.

Emerging from behind a stand of bamboo, we came upon its source. My chest ached at the sight and unbidden tears shocked my eyes. It had been a thousand years. More. Not since the corps had taken over production of the labor pool had I seen anything like it.

Miniature people frolicked and played on swing sets and slides, ladders and matrices of pipes, patterns laid out in the sand by means of chalk dust or the dragging of a heel. They were watched over by attentive women—stern, casual, alert, relaxed.

I couldn't move. I stood and watched, amazed, enchanted, frozen in time— time that was sixteen centuries old. I looked at Steel and tried to speak. I could not. Emotion filled my chest and clogged my throat. I looked back at the playing children. The little playing children. The tiny, uncivilized, immediate and unedited motions and emotions of children.

Alice and Archie caught me under my arms as my knees buckled. Steel soothed me, caressing my forehead with her hand. "It's all right," she said, and Archie echoed her. "It's all right. It struck me the same way the first time. Let's just sit down over here and collect ourselves. You'll be all right."

She kept smoothing my hair and face as they half-carried me to a nearby bench. We sat looking at the children as my chest heaved and tears rolled down my cheeks. Alice hugged me and put her head on my chest. Archie rubbed my shoulders with her remaining hand. Steel kissed my temples and hugged my head.

"Mo, oh … Mohandas. It's all right," Steel sighed, almost singing, her tears wetting my temples and joining my own. "It's all right." And even though she was right, even though it really *was* all right, the ache in my heart wouldn't subside. Archie's tears fell on my shoulders. We grieved the ancient loss of families.

Alice rested quietly on my chest, her arms around me. She held me, but when I looked into her eyes they were dry. She looked uncomfortable, awkward. She didn't know how to act, what to feel. She knew we were upset. Perhaps she was upset, too, but her features remained blank. Whatever she was feeling was too expensive for her to reveal—to us, to herself.

A teacher had noticed us. She came over to the edge of the playground. "Are you folks okay?" she asked.

"Yes, we're fine," Steel responded. "We lost a child not too long ago, that's all."

"Oh, I'm so sorry," the teacher said, and I grieved that we were lying to her. "A boy or a girl?" she asked.

"A boy," Steel responded. "Jacob. He was only thirteen." Looking into Steel's sad eyes I knew we weren't lying after all.

A little girl (What a marvelous phrase! 'A little girl.') came over, transcendentally beautiful. She walked like a tiny goddess, her posture defying gravity, bolt upright, perfectly balanced. Her hair shone like spun ebony and her blue eyes were absolutely clear, unclouded by history or pain or anything at all, expressing nothing, expressing everything. In a small, shy, bell-like voice she asked the teacher, "What's wrong with those people?"

The teacher patted her hand. "They're just sad, that's all. Just sad. Let's leave them alone, okay? Go back and play." She herded the little girl back to her friends, but the little one kept looking at us. She stared unblinkingly over her shoulder at us as she went, before turning and running back to one of the games.

I didn't want her to leave. I wanted to talk to her, ask her things, teach her, protect her, bathe in her innocence and purity of desire. There must have been twenty-five or thirty of them—riches beyond measure: thug-like little boys harassing and laughing, bossy little girls prescribing and posing, innocent little angels hesitating on the sidelines, brooding misfits spoiling for a fight. Potential people, future people, *little* people.

Who had this experience anymore, besides professional caregivers? Newbies were protected and isolated from the capricious malevolence of adults. They were far too valuable to the corps to risk being psychologically damaged by untrained amateurs. They were painstakingly raised, instructed and nurtured by people who knew how to do it best. It made me wonder when it was we started to think that we weren't good enough, just as we were, to raise children. But it didn't matter: no one could afford it anymore. There were too many other things to pay for, too many other things to do.

It struck me that the corps raised newbies to be good workers, not necessarily to be good people. I thought about it. The SyndicEnts in New Spanaway weren't people at all, not in the fullest sense of the word, yet the people of Kindu, at Matessa's party, at the dock on that river of luminescent flowers, they certainly *were* people, wonderful people. Kind, expansive, creative. Yet Matessa wasn't one of them anymore; she had been altered, diminished, made pliable and docile, less than herself: an unthinkable crime. But that crime made it possible for her to live forever. And so my thoughts went, circling and circling and finding no rest.

Eventually I came to realize that we couldn't stay sitting there forever, although I wanted to—to simply sit, watch and absorb. We got out handkerchiefs, blew our noses and wiped our eyes. The amazing thing about crying is that it really does address grief. Somehow squirting out some salt water makes your chest feel better. I wonder if anyone has ever figured out how it works.

Archie called to the teacher, "Ma'am?"

"Yes?"

"We haven't been in Nazareth in quite a while. We were looking for a place to stay. Is Mrs. Fogarty still running her boarding house?"

"Her daughter runs it now, but she's still there. We keep trying to get her to retire and let one of us take care of her, but she won't hear of it. She's just as independent as she can be." She smiled.

"Is that right? Is it still in the same place?"

"No reason to move it. Just on the other side of the river."

We set off, but in a different country than I had been in just moments before: a country where people spent the few decades allotted to them raising children, knowing those children, too, had only a few decades to live. They did it all in the hope and belief that they and their children would go to a better place when they died. It struck me again that everyone here died. They *died*. They lived for a little while and then they stopped living. All those beautiful children I had just seen would be dust in only a few short years. And their children and their children, generation after generation until the end of time.

My wife appeared before me. My heart stopped. She was young and healthy, radiant and serene. No, she was radiant and kind of feisty, like she'd always been. She spoke to me. She told me that the children were with her now, that they were fine, they were happy. I wanted to ask if *she* was happy, but I couldn't get a breath to speak. I wanted to ask her where she was, if my father was there, my sister, my mo- my mo- I couldn't. She smiled at me. I was unworthy of her smile. She smiled again. I was still unworthy. I tried to reach out to her, but my arms were dead, inert. Did she look sad? I couldn't tell, but she had to leave. She turned, glanced back over her shoulder, and ...

"Mo? Mo, are you all right? Mo!"

"What?" Steel had cupped my face in her palms. She was looking into my eyes. Archie and Alice were behind her. "No, I'm okay."

"Are you okay?"

"I'm okay."

"Are you sure?"

"I'm okay."

"You kind of faded out on us."

"I'm okay. I— uh—" I couldn't think of how to explain. "I'm okay."

They were still concerned. They didn't need to be. "You don't need to be," I said. "I mean, I'm okay. You don't have to—Don't worry. You don't have to worry."

"We all need some rest," Archie said.

"Yeah," Alice agreed. "We should just go to the hotel, the rooming house."

"Right." Steel was still looking into my eyes. "You're all right now? You can walk?"

"Yeah, I'm fine. I'm okay. It's all right. I'm fine."

We set off, Steel on my arm (but in reality making sure I didn't fall over) as I wondered what had just happened to me. In my heart there was no doubt—I had just had a brief conversation with my wife, my wife who had died twelve centuries ago. That had been my experience. It didn't feel like I was lying to myself or fooling myself. It didn't feel like I was making it up. My head was already saying something different, coming up with explanations: I had been overcome with emotions, fatigue, the strangeness of the place, the stress of our mission here. Neither side won; my heart supplied its certainty, my head its skepticism.

We continued walking through Nazareth.

By the time we crossed the footbridge and walked up the sandy trail to Mrs. Fogarty's place I was feeling pretty normal again—puzzled, but normal. The rooming house was a two-story structure nailed together from rough-cut lumber. Brightly colored flower beds lined the walk and the generous porch with its heavy, overhanging roof. Baskets of flowers hung from the eaves. Mauve sandstone streaked black by water soared above it and arched over it. Beside the open front door was a sign that said simply, 'Rooms.'

As we entered through the front door we were greeted by a shriveled, silver-haired elf. "Mrs. Fogarty?" Steel inquired, a little shaken.

"That's me," said the elf.

Steel seemed taken aback by something, so I took over. "We're going to be in town for a few days and were wondering if you had a couple of rooms."

"Two?"

"That's right. One for my wife and me and one for my sister-in-law and niece."

The elf looked around at the four of us. "Yes, we have rooms."

"How much are they?" I didn't care, but it seemed like an Edenite would ask.

"Two dollars a night. That includes breakfast and lunch. It's fifty cents extra for sit-down dinner. Fresh bread every day. Still do all my own baking."

"That's great," I said. I was already looking forward to a meal. "We'll take them." I got out my wallet, did some quick arithmetic and handed her a twenty. "Here's for four days in advance."

"All right. I'll just need you to sign the guest book." She took the bill and tottered back behind a small desk, turned the flat, open book to me and watched me sign. "Glad to have you here," she read my writing, "Mr. and Mrs. McGavin. Do you plan to be staying on awhile?"

"We're not sure," I answered. "We're trying to find some relatives, if they still live here."

"Oh, that's nice," she said. She opened a drawer and took out a small, metal box, placing the bill I'd handed her on top of a stack of others. "Well, look at this!" she said at the sight of the bill. "It's one of the old Gold Certificates! I haven't seen one of these in years!"

I looked at Steel. She started and said, "Oh, yes. Our, uh, our old Granny kept all our money on some old rafters in a barn. In—in the old shoebox, I mean, in the barn. She kept the shoebox on the rafter," she faltered, "with the money in it …" She looked for a way out of the improv. "She didn't trust banks," she finished.

"Oh," Mrs. Fogarty replied, blinking. She seemed to accept it, or decide it was none of her business. As she led us up a creaking staircase to our rooms I leaned over to Steel and whispered, "I liked my version better." She elbowed me in the ribs.

That night the nightmares started.

CHAPTER 24

If you want to learn about a culture, stay in a boarding house. What a collection of characters. We met Mrs. Fogarty's daughter, Ruth Hudson, and her husband, Matthew Hudson. The last names confused me at first. I had assumed that Ruth's last name would have been Fogarty, like her mother. Of course I hadn't dealt with anyone who had more than one name in centuries, so I was rusty. I asked Archie about it and she muttered something about "capitalist patriarchy" and "inheritance." I tried to remember if my wife had taken my last name when we got married, but I couldn't remember what it had been. I must have lost it on some re-boot or other. It must not have seemed important to me at the time. I wondered if that would have upset my father.

Ruth and Matthew looked about the same biological age as Steel, Arch and me, but they were shaped quite differently. I had forgotten human beings could take so many different shapes. Matthew was long and so thin as to be almost skeletal. Time or shyness or both had collapsed his posture into a triple ess-curve—he was preceded by his knees and Adam's apple wherever he went. Ruth was a compact pile of a person: her plump head was piled on her plump neck and shoulders, her plump breasts were piled on her plump belly, which was piled on her plump hips, and the whole assembly sort of plumped around the room together, various parts oscillating in their own rhythms, her thick skirt sweeping the rugs on the foot-polished floor. It seemed there was nothing Matthew could say that Ruth couldn't say better, or so she thought, so she usually did—in a voice that assumed volume made up for any other deficiencies. She seemed to be of the general opinion that her life was not all it might have been, largely because her husband wasn't all that he should be. She ran the place while Matthew maintained it, but never to the level of proficiency Ruth expected or deserved. "Nails cost money!" was about the most supportive thing I ever heard her say to him.

In fact, she was so unquestionably in charge of the whole operation that once I was moved to remark to Steel, "I thought you said this culture was male-dominated."

"It is. Why?"

"Well, it seems to me like Ruth is telling Matthew where to go, what to do and how to do it."

"Oh," she said. "Well—" and that was as far as she got: "Oh. Well–"

Oh, well. Matthew didn't seem to pay all that much attention to Ruth's continued instruction, anyway. He pretty much did things the way he thought best, with Ruth looking over his shoulder, asking him why he was doing it this way and why didn't he do it that way and how was she expected to keep the place open if he couldn't take care of it any better than that?

They were an interesting couple.

Mrs. Fogarty, herself, (and this, I came to find out, is what had shocked Steel so when we first met her) consisted of what was left over after her DNA had finished with her. She must have been about five decades old when Steel and Co. had last been in Nazareth; she was well into her eighth decade now. The change in those three decades must have been profound. There was no fat left in her skin; it was dry and transparent. Her little, bent elfin body was carried on her pelvis like fruit in a basket, her twig legs stiff and bony. She held her blotched hands in front of her like she was praying all the time, and maybe she was. Her hands were the most painful part of her for me to watch: they looked crisp, like they'd been deep-fried. Arthritis had swollen her knuckles and bent her fingers into little paws; palsy made them shake. It was hard to imagine them as they must have once been: useful, dexterous tools capable of playing a musical instrument, drawing a picture, building a civilization. She didn't seem to mind. She'd do what she could and let Ruth or Matthew do the rest.

She tried to be the attenuator on Ruth's exasperation, but her little, frail voice wasn't up to the task. The three of them had achieved an odd, tripodal balance: the louder Ruth got, the quieter Matthew would get, and Mrs. Fogarty would flit back and forth between them, trying to grease the wheels.

I suppose Mrs. Fogarty had a first name, but I never learned it. Ruth called her 'mom,' Matthew called her 'mother,' and everybody else just called her 'Mrs. Fogarty.' There was a certain respect offered in the honorific; it would have seemed too familiar, somehow, to call her 'Maggie' or 'Flo' or whatever her name might have been.

We met the other guests at dinner that night. (And what a dinner! The best fifty cents I ever spent.) There was Mr. Keebler: a quiet man with a fringe of hair around the sides of his head but none on top. He was a bachelor, and had lived at Mrs. Fogarty's since moving to Nazareth from his parents' house in New Jerusalem. He had a trade, bookkeeping, and was hoping to find a wife, so far without success. The Courtney sisters, Abigail and Patience, were hoping to find husbands, but there didn't seem to be any electricity between them and Mr. Keebler. I got the idea that if there had been it would have broken a taboo—that if a courtship had started, either Mr. Keebler or the courted sister would have had to move to another house. Archie and Steel were right: sexuality was a closely and constantly monitored activity in this place.

I was never entirely sure why the sisters lived with Mrs. Fogarty. I had the impression that most young women stayed with their parents until they were married. For some reason these two were out on their own. They had jobs in town to support themselves, but nothing they hoped to turn into careers. Women gained prestige and power on Eden by raising children.

Then there was the Morgan family. Mr. Morgan ("Call me Samuel") was a large man with large hands and a large, stern face carved by harsh sunlight and hard work. His wife, Theresa, was scrubbed and pink, and would have still been pretty if life on Eden hadn't been so wearing. Her eyes and smile were still bright, but her face had been creased by the strain of bearing and raising her family, and she had quite a family. Michael was seventeen and earnest ("Hello, Mr. McGavin"), Rebecca was sixteen and flirtatious ("Pleased to meet you, Mr. McGavin"), Aaron and Elizabeth were fourteen and taciturn ("Say hello to Mr. and Mrs. McGavin. Aaron, Elizabeth, say hello." "Hello."), Esther was twelve and shy ("Hi"), and Isaac was nine and boisterous ("HI!").

Then there was "our little surprise package," as Theresa put it, Sarah—tiny and wide-eyed and not yet two years old. Theresa managed this horde like a CEO runs a corporation: with motivational speeches and long-range strategies, bonuses, penalties and hard-ball negotiations.

The emotional lives of the children fascinated me; they seemed to be constantly careening from ecstatic victories to bitter disappointments and back again. The tiniest things would send them dancing and shouting with unbounded elation or crashing down into heart-wrenching tears. It seemed to be Samuel's job to install governors on these emotions; he was always admonishing the children to moderate them: "There, there, now, it's nothing to cry about. Chin up. Be a man." or "All right, all right, settle down. The river will still be there when we get there. Theresa, do you have everyone's bathing suits?" Following an individual child's path in the movement of the family was like watching a particular drop of water in a complex cascade—you knew all the drops would reach the bottom, but how they got there was always surprising and unique.

Meals were served by Matthew and Ruth and presided over by Mrs. Fogarty. Conversation was allowed a fairly free range except for three topics: politics and religion were frowned upon (only as topics of dinner conversation, not as activities) and sexuality just never came up. Well, it wasn't brought up by adults. One time Isaac asked what 'jacking off' meant (Archie told me later that it was an archaic expression for masturbation) and the reaction around the table was immediate and profound. It was as if a terrible pestilence had been spotted on the horizon and all able bodies were needed to stem the tide. Everything stopped while Samuel dealt with the situation:

"Where did you hear that word?"

Isaac squirmed. "I dunno."

"Where?"

"I dunno, somebody said it. What's wrong with it?"

"That's not the sort of language we use in polite society, and I'll not hear you say it again."

"But what's it mean?"

"You don't need to know what it means because you won't be using it, will you?"

Isaac looked darkly into his pudding with his chin in his palm.

"Elbows off the table," Theresa said gently. Isaac heaved a huge sigh of unendurable oppression and complied.

Whenever either of the other two topics was strayed into, Mrs. Fogarty would guide us back away from the danger areas. It seemed that each meal would start as one big conversation, the women offering views based on their experience, feelings and impressions, the men occasionally inserting Solemn Pronouncements of Established Fact. These pronouncements would be considered in momentary silence and then the conversation would resume, largely ignoring whatever Established Fact had been brought up. After a few of these occurrences, the conversation would gradually split in two, the women discussing one topic, the men another.

The structure of these conversations was very revealing. I don't claim to have ever come to understand the culture of Eden, but my impression of it was that it was not so much male-dominated as it was sexist. Each of the genders seemed to regard the other as alien, incomprehensible, and incapable of understanding the utterly obvious. This mutual mistrust engendered a complex set of checks and balances on economic and political power. If men made most of the money, they were expected to spend most of it supporting women. Men who failed to do this were ostracized and shamed by everyone, men and women alike. Women, on the other hand, wielded a great deal of power within the home and were expected to use that power wisely for the benefit of the children in the home. This was the trump card. I saw Theresa play it more than once. A wife might disagree with something her husband wanted to do, and there was certainly friction while the difference of opinion was worked out, but if the wife could show that what she disagreed with was bad for the children, the husband would invariably acquiesce.

If anything, Eden's culture was child-dominated.

We only spent meal and sleep times at Mrs. Fogarty's, though. The rest of the time we spent searching for Alice's parents. We couldn't tell anyone they were her parents, however. Because of the time slippage on the voyage back from Brainard's Planet, Alice was thirty years too young. We told everyone we were looking for her grandparents. The morning after our first night at Mrs. Fogarty's (and my first nightmare) we went to the house where Alice grew up: no luck. We spoke with the people who lived there, but they had bought the place from someone else. They didn't recognize Alice's last name.

That was another little shock: Alice had a last name. Her full name was Alice Louise Cheatham. It was a pretty name, but, I don't know, it just felt strange to think that she had all those names. It seemed to connect her to all sorts of things: ancestors, traditions, social structures, belief systems. But anyway, the people who owned her house had purchased it from somebody named Harrison, so that was a dead end.

We checked with the people who lived in the surrounding houses until we finally found someone who Steel and Archie recognized—they recognized his name, anyway, a Mr. Murray. I guess he'd changed as much as Mrs. Fogarty had. If they recognized him, he certainly didn't recognize them. He was friendly enough, though, until we mentioned who we were looking for. At that point he clouded over and became reserved.

"What do you want to dig that stuff up for?" he asked. I explained that Alice hadn't ever met her grandparents. He grunted. "Didn't know they had any grandchildren. You the son?"

"No," Steel answered for me. "The son, Jacob, died in an accident."

"Oh, that's too bad."

"Do you know—" Steel started again, "Do you know where they went?"

He shook his head. "It was a sad business. After the wife ran off everything sort of fell apart. How did you know them? That was a long time ago."

"We—we've been taking care of Alice since she was a, a baby." Steel was working hard to conceal her emotions about something.

"Hmm. So your name's Alice, too, huh?" he asked Alice.

"Yeah."

"Alice was the daughter's name, right?"

Steel nodded. He asked Alice, "Was she your mom?"

Alice glanced at Steel, then nodded.

"What happened to her?"

Archie stepped in. "We're not sure. We're just looking for her grandparents.

Mr. and Mrs. Cheatham."

"Oh." He eyed us all like he wasn't sure he wanted to be involved with us, even tangentially, "Well, they probably have something about them down at the City Hall. That's all I can tell you."

We thanked him and started to leave, but he said, "I don't know that I'd go to too much trouble to find them." We turned back. "They were heretics, you know. Never proved anything, but we all knew they were. Especially the wife."

We thanked him again and headed for Mrs. Fogarty's. It had been a long day.

The only time we could really talk to one another was in the evenings, in one of our rooms, with the door closed. The talks really helped me, because I was struggling trying to figure out how the place worked. Every time I turned around, something else strange and incomprehensible would confront me.

"What did he mean, 'heretics'?" I asked after we'd retired from another interesting dinner.

"There's only one heresy on Eden," Archie replied. "Wanting to get back in touch with the outside world."

"Oh."

"I think they've institutionalized the taboo because the temptation is just too strong for individuals to deal with. Every time someone gets sick, or injured, or just old, the temptation is to think, 'If only we could cure this one disease, save this one person.' It's really fascinating from an anthropological viewpoint. People rarely ask it for themselves."

"What do you mean?" I asked.

"If a person is dying, he or she accepts it with surprising grace and dignity. It's when a loved one is suffering or dying that the temptation to intervene comes up. But it really doesn't come up that often. These people are pretty secure in their beliefs."

"Not *that* secure," said Steel.

"I really don't think they know about that," Archie answered, "We would have found out. There would have been documentation somewhere. We would have learned about it before we left Eden."

"What?" I said. "Found out about what?"

Archie examined me for a moment, then got up, walked to the door and checked the hall to see if anybody was around. She shut the door again, came back over and sat down. When she started to speak again it was with a quieter voice:

"You know that the two people who started this place were involved in genetics and nano-technology."

I thought. "Yeah, right. Edith somebody and John—"

"James. James Wesley Burroughs and Edith Stauber. She was a geneticist, he was in nano-surgery."

"They helped develop the bio-chip."

"And had serious second thoughts about it."

"Right."

Archie glanced at Steel, at Alice, and then back to me. "We're pretty sure they worked out a kind of insurance plan to deal with backsliders."

"Backsliders?"

She thought for a minute. "You probably remember what it was like when not everyone could afford to re-boot. You were there, right?"

"Yeah," I said, "Yeah, I was there."

"I think the two of them knew, instinctively, that the only way a sub-culture like this could hold together was if there was no going back."

"How so?"

Arch glanced at Steel again. Steel put her hand on Alice's knee and took over: "We know the original pilgrims— the first ones to colonize Eden—were required to undergo a medical procedure. At the time it was thought to be nothing more than a standard, broad-range immunization treatment, just in case there were any indigenous microbes here that might present a problem."

"Yes?"

"We think they did something else. Something more invasive."

"What?"

Steel patted Alice's knee again. Alice looked like she wished people would stop paying her so much attention. Steel said, "You know Alice had a brother."

"Jacob."

"Yes, Jacob." She paused. "After we brought Alice and Jacob back to Earth, he ... was involved in an accident."

"What happened?"

"It was—It was so—"

Archie stepped in, "He was skiing in Gstaad. In Switzerland. On Earth. He evidently wandered off the main slope and into some trees. There was some trauma to the cranium and brain. Nothing that re-booting couldn't take care of, just normal trauma. But when we tried to re-boot him, tiny cancers started in every single cell we touched. In a matter of hours, he was gone."

"Did you try uploading him?"

Archie thought hard thoughts about a hard past. "It was a difficult decision. There wasn't enough capacity on Steel's system to upload. We had to go online. Nobody knew about either of them. Jacob or Alice. Nobody knew we'd been to Eden. It meant breaking security and opening up everything to Traffic Control."

"But we did it," Steel interrupted, "We decided to do it. We did everything we could—"

"So—but, wait –," I was confused, "So people know about Alice now? I hadn't heard—"

"No. No one knows," Arch answered. "Jacob never made it onto the net. When we started the upload his memory structure just fell apart. He was with us one second and the next second he wasn't anywhere. He was just gone. We shut down as quickly as we could, but it was too late. We couldn't find him again. That's what convinced us it was a manufactured condition, not just some random genetic mutation."

"So it was—"

"We think," Archie said, "we *think* the original pilgrims knew what was being done to them, that they were being implanted with a chromosomal trigger that would make it impossible for them to re-boot. But the knowledge seems to have faded into myth over the generations. We've never been able to find any reference to it anywhere."

I made a connection. "But the symptoms resemble Brainard's plague—the cellular destruction, the widespread—"

"It bears a superficial resemblance, yes."

"Is that what made you think—"

"It's what made us hope," Steel interjected. "We hope to find an answer on Brainard's Planet. Something we can use."

Archie said, "After we lost Jacob we ran some tests on Alice. We basically did a biopsy. We took a little tissue and tried to re-boot it."

"And that's when you knew ..."

Alice said, "Could we stop talking about this? Please? *Please?* I mean, I know everybody's trying to help me—"

"I'm sorry, Alice," Steel said.

Alice got up from the bed where she'd been sitting. "I just don't see why it has to be such a big PROBLEM! I just want to find my—I want to see my—" She glared at Steel and then kind of deflated. She looked at something, something hopeless and distant and unattainable. "I'm going to bed. I—" She stopped at the door and looked at Steel again, but whatever it was she wanted to say, she must have decided against it. "I'm going to bed."

"I'm sure we'll make progress tomorrow," Steel entreated, "We'll find them."

Alice glared at her again. "Yeah, sure," she said, and walked out the door.

Archie stared after her. "I guess I'll get to bed, too." She started to walk out. When she got to the closed door she stopped. She didn't look back at us; she just spoke to the door. "This research keeps getting more and more expensive," she said.

"Don't worry," Steel answered. "I've got plenty of credit. We'll keep going till we find an answer."

Arch put her hands behind her neck and looked at the ceiling. She sighed. "You can be really obtuse, sometimes; you know that?" Steel didn't answer and Archie didn't wait for her to. She just said, "Good night," and walked out the door.

After a while Steel said, "You make things really difficult."

That hit me out of the blue. "Me? What did *I* do?"

She shook her head. "Nothing, nothing. I just—I just wish we hadn't lost Drake. Things would have been so much simpler." The stress was really getting to her. I started rubbing her shoulders.

"I'm sorry if I ask too many questions." She leaned her head back as I dug into her traps. "I just feel like I'm being asked to do this with one foot in a bucket and a bag over my head. Wouldn't it be simpler if you just told me the whole story?"

She let her head fall forward again. "You know the whole story. Alice is dying. We have to save her. *I* have to save her."

I thought and I thought. Theories were racing around my head in a surreal steeplechase. Steel finally sighed and said, "What do you want to know?"

If you ever want to keep a person in total ignorance, ask them what they want to know. Where to start? What question to ask? "I don't know," I said, defeated. "Whatever you want to tell me."

Steel breathed for a while. I'd stopped rubbing her shoulders and was just holding her. She leaned back against me and snuggled her forehead into the cavity above my collarbone. She breathed some more. Then she said, "I'm too tired. I'm just really, really tired. Can we just go to bed?"

So we did. That was something else that was getting to me: sharing a bed with one of the most beautiful women I'd ever known, one who'd practically seduced me into joining this crazy voyage, and just sleeping in it. It was a small thing, but it was starting to build up. I didn't understand it. Steel was tense and under pressure. We all were. The easiest, most natural way in the world to deal with it was to have sex. It was practically assumed nowadays—if someone seemed troubled or uptight, you had sex with them, or at least offered. That is, a woman would offer. Men didn't initiate sexual intimacy anymore, except with each other. I forget why. It was just the way it had worked for a long time. Except here on Eden. I didn't suppose it mattered, as long as *somebody* initiated it, but I certainly wasn't going to initiate it with Steel.

I wondered if Archie and Alice were having sex next door. No reason not to. Alice was upset and Archie was tense. It was the perfect way to reassure each other they were still on the same side, still supporting each other, still with each other. But maybe they weren't. We *were* on Eden; there were taboos. Maybe that was why Steel—but *we* were supposed to be man and wife. We were in our own room, with the door closed. I couldn't see any taboo we would be breaking.

Mr. and Mrs. Morgan were probably having sex.

Why was I thinking about sex? At a time like this? With all that was going on? I glanced over at Steel. Her eyes were closed, her breathing regular, her soft breasts rising and falling under the thin, cotton sheet. I rolled over and tried to go to sleep.

I had another nightmare that night.

CHAPTER 25

Things kept getting stranger. It was like the Cheatham family had never existed. We went down to the City Hall and found nothing. There were lots of records about lots of people: marriage licenses, birth certificates, death certificates, criminal records. All sorts of things, all on little, yellowed, brittle pieces of paper that were stored in dusty cabinets in an ill-lit basement. But nothing about the Cheathams. Our Cheathams, anyway.

People were always helpful. All the civil servants were men and they seemed to fall all over themselves trying to help us. This was for a very old, very obvious reason. There might have been one or two women somewhere in the galaxy more beautiful than Steel, but no one on Eden even came close. Archie's worry had been warranted: even after our trek through the desert we still stood out. We just didn't look nearly as worn, as beaten up. Combine the lifestyle we enjoyed with who knows how many re-boots of genetic nips and tucks and 'I've always thought my nose was a little too long' and 'if only my hips were a little more this and my breasts were a little more that' and—well, the local talent didn't stand a chance against Steel, Alice, or even Archie with her missing arm.

Me, too, I guess. I mean, take teeth, for example. Everyone on Eden seemed to take fairly good care of their teeth, but *our* teeth were *perfect*. Crooked teeth tend to collect food and be hard to clean. That increases bacteria in the mouth and the risk of infection, even things that can cause heart disease. Dealing with those things costs money. If you have to re-boot every fifty-five years instead of every sixty it can really impact your financial situation, so people just don't have crooked teeth anymore.

In hundreds of tiny ways we were just more attractive than the Edenites.

Steel used this power judiciously, but she used it—I'm sure we got to see every file that might have pertained to our search, and quite a few that didn't. It got annoying, and a little embarrassing sometimes, watching these innocents deal with this rare concentration of sheer physical beauty and irrepressible sexual attraction. The older men tried to maintain some dignity; the younger men had no dignity. All of them were betrayed by their eyes, their hands and feet. They stumbled, they stammered, they knocked things over. They tried not to stare, or they just gave up and stared.

It was becoming a problem at Mrs. Fogarty's as well. Mrs. Morgan was becoming visibly uncomfortable whenever her husband looked at Steel. The Courtney sisters seemed to consider her a threat, or at least unfair competition. It was rare that Mr. Keebler could get through a meal without spilling something on himself. It made me wonder about the nature of power. It seemed to me that, given the briefest amount of time, Steel could have become the most powerful person on this planet without voting in a single election, let alone running in one.

But no amount of attractiveness could conjure up documents that weren't there. No John Jacob Cheatham, no Alice Cheatham, no Jacob Cheatham. Nothing about Alice's birth—or Jacob's. No deeds or titles. No information, nothing. I asked Steel if we might check under the wife's name, but she brushed me off. She was dealing with a lot of emotional stress, I could tell, and I don't think she wanted my help.

One clerk suggested we try at the newspaper office, so that's where we went next. It started becoming clearer what had happened. Arch and Steel knew quite a bit about the Cheathams, so we knew what dates to check for marriage announcements, birth announcements and so forth. They had been on Eden when the Cheathams got married—I got the impression they'd actually attended the service. In any case, we could go right to the correct issue and check the community calendar for the announcement. But there was no announcement.

In the city files there just hadn't been any documents. In the newspapers you could see where things had been removed, cut out, leaving neat, rectangular spaces in the pages. The Cheathams had been removed from the collective consciousness of Nazareth as neatly as if the whole community had re-booted and had all memory of them erased.

"I don't want to see her."

"What other choice do we have?"

Steel and Archie spoke quietly, intensely to each other as Alice and I sat on the bed in our room that night.

"I don't care," Steel answered, "She was—I don't want to see her."

"*I'll* go see her," Arch offered.

"No."

"It's been over forty years—"

"Not for me, it hasn't. She—she—if it hadn't been for *her*, none of this—" Steel fumed, unable to finish.

I glanced inquisitively at Alice while Archie tried a different tack. "They've wiped the record. It's all gone. How else can we find them?"

Steel looked at Alice with a desperate grief in her eyes, imploring, asking— what? Forgiveness? Grace? Reprieve, maybe. I think Alice would have given it had she known how, but she didn't. She tried. She started to say many things, but settled on: "I want to find my—I want to see—I want to be a family again. I just want—Is that so bad? I just want to be together again. To visit. To remember ..." She faltered.

"Of course you do, Alice," Steel reached out to her, to touch her hair. Alice recoiled.

"No," she said, "don't. I don't want to be nice. I don't want to just go along. I don't want to do what you think is best. I want to see my f- my f- I WANT TO FIND MY FATHER! OKAY? I want to find my father." She stood and crossed to the door, then turned back. "I'll stay here by myself if I have to. You can't make me leave again."

Steel looked stricken. "But—but, Alice, sweetheart, you can't live here. You— you'll die if you stay—"

"I DON'T CARE. All right? I don't care." She looked at Steel for a moment, but there was nothing else to say. "I don't care," she repeated, turned, and walked out, closing the door quietly behind her.

The next morning I stood beside Archie on the porch of the Lockridge house, hoping to find Louise Lockridge, née Cheatham, at home. Alice stood a little behind us. Steel was back at the rooming house, having refused to come.

It had been a little while since I had knocked on the door and we were just about to give up when a ghostly figure appeared behind the lace curtains. The door creaked open and we faced a handsome, older woman, her face jowly, her once black hair mostly gray.

"Yes?" she said.

Archie picked up her cue pretty quickly. I think she was getting used to the change that all the Edenites had undergone while she'd been off flitting about the galaxy. She looked at the woman for just a moment and said, "Louise?"

"Yes?" the woman answered.

Archie waited, then she said, "Do you remember me?" She turned and brought Alice forward. "This is Alice. Alice Cheatham. Your niece."

Alice said, "Hi, Aunt Louise."

The woman put a hand to her breast, her face opened in wonder. "Alice ..."

Alice replied, "It's me. I'm all grown up now."

Aunt Louise looked for words. Her glance shifted to Archie, to me, back to Alice, searching, unable to comprehend, to accept. "Alice?"

"It's really me," Alice replied, naked, unassuming. "Can ... Can we come in?" she asked.

Louise's eyes kept dancing between the three of us. She didn't recognize me, of course, but I could tell when she recognized Archie. I'm sure Alice had changed so much that she had to simply accept that it was her and not some impostor. Finally custom overcame confusion and she said, "I'm sorry. Of course, come in, come in." She stood aside and ushered us into her foyer. A sitting room stretched through an archway to our right, a dining room opened to our left. Wooden stairs ascended to a railed balcony on the second floor. She led us into the sitting room and then turned to face Alice once again.

She reached out and touched Alice's cheek. "It really is you?"

"Yeah, it really is." Alice gave a little laugh and shrugged.

"But you're—wouldn't you be—? It was true, then." She turned to Archie. "What you and Mr.—I'm sorry, I've forgotten your last name."

"Drake," Archie replied.

"Yes, you and Mr. Drake. What you said. It was true." She gazed back at Alice in open awe. "You went away, off the world."

"We did, Aunt Louise. I've been all over. You wouldn't believe some of the things ..."

Aunt Louise looked pale and unsteady. "I'm sorry," she said, "I guess it's the—I need to sit down." I led her to an upholstered settee and helped her sit. "Won't you all sit? Please." Alice sat beside her. Arch and I pulled up chairs. "Just give me a moment to collect myself."

"Of course," I said.

She looked at me. "Who are—I don't remember you. Are you—?"

"I'm just a friend of the family," I said. "We've never met."

"Oh." She turned back to Alice. "But, Alice, you—you're so young." She turned to Arch, "It really is true, what you said, that people don't, don't get old? Don't age?" She turned back to Alice. She didn't know where to turn, who to look at. "But you've grown up. You're so pretty. I knew you would be."

"Thanks."

"Where's Jacob?"

"Um—" Alice looked to Archie for support, but then turned back to Louise, "Jacob's gone."

"Gone?"

"He, uh, he died."

"Oh, no."

"It was an accident. He was—" I guess Alice elected not to explain skiing to her. "It was an accident."

"But—but—" Louise turned to Archie, "You said people don't die. If you left, and took the children, they wouldn't—"

"That's what we thought," Archie answered.

"But—"

"It's a long story, Aunt Louise," Alice said gently. "There are some problems."

"But are *you* all right? I mean, are you—Oh, poor Jacob. He was—How old was he? When—"

"Not very old—"

"He was thirteen," Archie interrupted.

"Thirteen. But that must have been right after you left. Oh, my goodness. Where ..."

"He died on Earth. In a place called Switzerland."

This was all way too much for poor Aunt Louise to ingest. It took us a long time to get her settled down and brought up to date. Some of the story I don't think she ever really understood: time dilation, for example, the reason Alice looked about twenty instead of fifty. But there were so many wonders in the story that the idea that "time slows down when you go really fast," as Alice put it, seemed the lesser of many—when there was Alice, Alice who'd been to Earth, who'd grown up in a fairytale castle surrounded by riches and servants, who'd flown among the stars, Alice sitting there beside her. Alice who was thought to be lost forever, along with her brother, lost to the infinite void.

And when we finally did get her caught up, she looked around at all of us and then just broke down, hugging Alice to her bosom and rocking back and forth, crying, crying. Then she'd dab her eyes with a tissue, apologize, sniff, and start all over again. "It's like you've come back from the dead," she said, gazing into her eyes, then, hugging her close again, "We thought we'd never see you again. Never, ever, ever." And she'd rock and rock.

But finally she said, "But why are you here? Why did you come back? Are you going to stay with us for awhile?"

"I can't, Aunt Louise," Alice answered. "Like I said, there are some problems that we have to figure out. But I wanted to come back to see everybody again."

"Of course. Everyone will—Oh, no. Most of your relatives have passed on by now ... Your grandparents—"

"What about dad? I really came to see dad."

"Oh, yes." Louise suddenly looked concerned.

Alice's face immediately hardened and she said, "He's dead, isn't he."

This chagrined Louise: "No, no. I'm sorry. I didn't mean to—No, he's fine. Well, not fine, maybe, but he hasn't died. Not yet."

I could see Alice's hopes soar. "Is he—I mean, where is he? Is he here? In Nazareth? We haven't been able to find any—any ..."

Louise took Alice's hand and patted it. "He's here. He should be coming back from the store any time, now."

"He lives here?" Alice asked.

"Oh, yes. John—you're father, I mean, has lived with us since that, that (witch)," she whispered the word, "if you'll pardon my language—Oh, I'm sorry, Alice. Your mother had many fine qualities, I'm sure, but she ruined my brother's life." This last was to Archie.

"How?" Archie asked.

"Well ... Oh, we shouldn't talk about sad things now," responded Louise. "This should be a happy time. John is going to be so thrilled to see you. I mean—well, that is—Oh, dear. Maybe we should ..." She looked seriously at Alice, choosing her words. "You understand that John, I'm sorry, I mean your father. It's just been such a long time."

"Yes," Alice said.

"You understand that he's changed quite a bit since you last saw him. He's an old man, now. Very old."

"I know," Alice nodded. "Do you think he'll remember me? I've changed a lot, too."

"Oh, I'm sure he'll recognize you. You look just like your mother."

Alice smiled a kind of strange, half-wistful, half-cynical smile. I don't know what it meant. I was trying to imagine her mother. Mother. The word still felt empty to me, detached. Not at all like I felt it should feel. An arbitrary label, something somebody made up.

Louise continued, "It's just that—well, it's not only that John is old now. He's had a—he had a pretty hard time of it for a while."

"What happened ... after we left?" Alice asked.

Louise shook her head sadly, "Oh, it was just so hard on him back then, losing all of you so close together. First Estelle ran out on him and then you folks came," she looked at Archie, "and took the children."

Alarm bells were going off in my head. Where had I heard the name 'Estelle' before? But Archie was speaking:

"We thought—we thought it would be best ..." Archie didn't seem to believe what she was saying even as she said it.

"I know, I know." Louise looked at the floor. "Things were so ugly back then." She turned back to Alice, "I don't know if you were old enough to understand ..."

"I remember everybody yelling and stuff. And a fire. Windows breaking. Things like that. Dad never told us why. He just said people were angry."

"Yes. Yes, people were angry. And frightened. Maybe more frightened than angry, but sometimes those two things go hand in hand."

"Why were they frightened?" Alice asked.

Louise looked back on painful memories. There was still anger there, too, but mostly pain. There was more anger in Archie—a detached, observational anger. Her face was stone as Louise spoke.

"Well, we tried to keep this from you children, but—but your mother," this with great reluctance, "Your mother was a heretic. She ran off before we could try her, but she was. We all knew it. She tried to poison your father's mind, too, and she almost succeeded." Something occurred to her and she turned on Archie. "It was you people, wasn't it? You came from somewhere," she waved her hand at the ceiling, "out there. Earth or somewhere. You got to her, got her thinking about ... sinful things. Evil things. I never believed you before. I thought you were heretics, too." Archie didn't respond. Louise regarded her for a moment but, receiving no answer, turned back to Alice. "But John knew," she dropped her eyes to her lap, "I knew, too, that we had to get you children away. The only way we could do that was to let Mr. and Mrs. Drake have you. John thought they'd take you someplace safe, someplace ..." Archie shifted in her chair, her anger rising, but still distant, somehow.

"Mom wanted to take us off Eden, to make contact with the outside," Alice said. It was a statement, not a question.

Louise thought a long time before she spoke: "A person can love someone too much. A mother can love her children too much. She can want to possess them so much that she's willing to take them away from God."

"She didn't want us to die."

Louise looked earnestly into Alice's eyes. "No one wants anyone to die. Only murderers want someone to die. I certainly never *wanted* you children to die. Death is something we accept as part of the great gift of life. It is God's way of calling us home, to His home, His heavenly home. All of us here, of any faith, Muslim, Jew, Hindu, every one of us accepts death as a natural part of the cycle of life. An inevitable part. A necessary part. Whether you call it the wheel of Karma or the Will of Allah or God moving in mysterious ways. We believe that God is a good and just God—that His plan for us is wise and wonderful in ways we can't conceive of." It sounded like Louise had said all this before.

Alice took it in, then answered, "But, but didn't God give us the ability to learn how to cure disease, how to stop people from dying?" Alice asked.

"Oh, yes. God has given us many abilities. To cure death, to cause death. To rain fire on people by the millions. We don't have to use every ability God gave us. He also gave us the ability to choose between good and evil."

Alice was thoughtful.

Archie said, "He only seems to have forgotten to give us the ability to agree on which is which."

There was what I think could only be described as an awkward pause, then Louise said, "Well, this conversation certainly has become serious, on a day that should be spent in rejoicing. I'm sure we can put aside our differences long enough for—"

We heard the front door open.

"Oh!" Louise hopped up. "That will be John. Please, let me try to prepare him for this. It's going to be quite a shock." We nodded in agreement. "John?" she called out.

"Yeah?" a gruff, ruined voice answered.

"John, there are some people here to see you—"

"Who the hell would want to see me?"

Louise went out into the foyer. We could hear their voices through the archway. "Now, John, please watch your language. These—"

"I don't have to watch my fucking language. Who gives a rat's ass what I say? Who the hell are these people?"

"Please, John, these are people from long ago. Long, long ago—"

John Cheatham strode angrily into the sitting room. "What the hell do you people want? Huh? Haven't had enough? You want to rip out my guts, too? Fucking pious assholes—"

"John! John, please!" Louise implored. "Don't you recognize them? This is Mrs. Drake, remember? Remember Mrs. Drake?"

John Cheatham, or what was left of him, stood staring at the two femmes. A once handsome face was creased and weathered, the skin thin as paper. A white frost of stubble covered a strong jaw, but the teeth were worn and yellow. Blue eyes had faded almost to grey, rheumy and vague. A shock of unkempt white hair hung over his forehead. He was tall for an Edenite, even old and collapsed as he was. He had been a large man, once, but his frame now was gristly and vacant. His clothes shone with ancient grime. He uttered just one word:

"Estelle ..."

"No, dear," said Louise. "I made the same mistake."

"Estelle ..."

"No, this is Alice, John. Alice. Do you remember? This is your daughter, Alice." Louise led him over to her.

"Alice?"

Alice stood. "Hi ... Dad. Daddy. Hi. It's me." She started to hold her arms out to embrace him, stopped, started again. He looked down at her arms uncomprehending, then back at her face.

"You look like ..." he croaked.

"I came to ... see you," Alice offered. "I came back. To see my ... to see my father."

He looked confused, uncertain. He looked her over again, then said, "You grew up."

Alice laughed, "Yeah, I guess I did." He reached out and touched her hair. She let him. She asked, "Do you remember me?"

"You look so much like—where is she? Your mother, is she—do you know where she is? Is she with you?"

Archie said, "We don't know where she is, John. Didn't she run off to New Jerusalem?"

John's expression hardened when he looked at Archie. "You look the same," he said, his voice cold, guarded. "What happened to your—" He was looking where Archie's arm used to be.

Archie smiled ironically. "I actually lost it getting back down here," she said.

"Oh." He measured her. "Why did you come back?"

Alice looked like she'd been slapped, but she hid it immediately. "I just ... wanted to ... see you, and—that's all. I just wanted to see you again. I ..." I think she might have wanted to tell him that she loved him, but I'm not sure.

He seemed to soften a little. Louise said, "Let's sit down, John. Hmm? Let's all sit." She led him to the settee, then stood behind it. John kept staring at Alice.

"I can't believe how much you look like your mother," he said, shaking his head. "I think you're even more beautiful than she was." His voice tore and flapped, a painful scraping.

Alice blushed and looked at her feet, "Oh, I don't know."

"She's not with you? I thought she might have—"

"We don't know where she is, John," Archie repeated. Alice shook her head, too.

"How old are you now?" he asked.

Alice said, "I'll be twenty-one pretty soon. Well, that is, it depends on how you look at it ..." And she told him of her travels.

"Isn't that something," he said when she had finished. "Have you heard from Jacob? How is he? Do you still keep in touch?"

Louise's eyes opened wide in alarm behind him and she shook her head urgently. Alice picked up the cue and said, "Oh, he's, he's fine. He's doing really well."

"Did he travel around with you?"

"No, no, he, uh, he has his own things to do, you know."

"Uh-huh. So he's a lot older than you now, is that right?" He shook his head in wonder. "That's something, that's really something." He leaned toward Alice, his hands trembling. "And he's just going to keep on living forever, isn't he? Both of you, I mean, you'll get to keep living?" His old eyes searched her young ones, fervid, imploring.

Alice said, "That's right." But she didn't want to, I could tell.

"That's good." He sat back. "That would have made your mother happy. Everything would have been so pointless, otherwise." Sudden water spilled from his eyes, wetting sallow cheeks. "I missed you all so terribly for so long. I— sometimes I—it was ... I didn't know if I—"

"Oh, Daddy!" Alice's eyes were swimming, too. "I missed you! I cried and cried, every night when I went to sleep. Forever, it seemed like." And they moved closer together on the settee.

They talked and talked for a long time. John wanted to know everything, and there was so much to tell. At one point he said, "I'll never look at the night sky the same way again." Then he asked, "Can you stay for dinner? Louise? We can whip up some dinner for everybody, can't we?" He didn't wait for her reply. "Sure we can. Then we can go up out of the canyon tonight and you can show me where you've been. Could you do that? Could you show me Earth and— What were all those places?"

"Sure, Daddy," Alice answered, "I mean, some of them might not be above the horizon, but—"

"That would be something! Wouldn't it, Louise?" Louise didn't look like she entirely agreed, but, once again, John didn't wait for her reply. He was gazing at Alice. "Alice has been all over the sky! My little girl has been all over the sky!"

The day was a difficult one; sometimes things went well, sometimes not. John would focus on the present for a while and then drift off into the past. Alice just tried to put it all together into some kind of coherent memory, the story of her family, of her life, of her father's life.

At one point John asked Archie, "You don't really think Estelle is still on Eden, do you?"

"What do you mean?" she answered.

"I mean, that's just another story, right? Like all the other bullshit you gave me."

Louise blanched at his language. Archie stammered.

John cut her off: "I never let myself believe," he said. "All the clues were there; I just never let myself believe."

"Believe what?" Archie asked.

He eyed her like a prosecutor. Then he turned away and said, "I'm not sure I want to believe it now. I always let it be enough: enough that she loved me, enough that she was the most beautiful thing I'd ever seen, that she wanted to have my children, be my wife."

"I'm sure she did," said Archie. "I'm sure she really loved you. It was—"

"All that crap about visions and talking to people from outer space." He turned back to Archie. "She was one of you, wasn't she?"

"What, what makes you think so?" Archie asked.

"Or if she wasn't, you put her up to it."

"I swear to you I didn't."

He pounded his fist on the arm of the settee suddenly, violently, and just as suddenly was calm again. He laughed a little. "You know, everything was fine for a long time." He gazed at Alice, "You have to know, sweetheart, that your mother and I were very happy. She made me *very* happy. I hope I made her happy. But she started worrying about you kids, you and your brother. I mean, everyone dies. Around here, I mean. Everyone. No one thinks about it much; it just happens every so often. But your mom couldn't take thinking about it happening to you after a while." He turned back to Archie. "That was what I didn't get," he said. "I didn't understand why it would start bothering her so much." He bored into Archie's eyes, trying to pull the truth out through them.

Archie said, "I don't know."

He pointed a bony finger at her. "You look me in the eye and tell me you didn't convince Estelle that you could save the kids. By taking them away."

Archie shook her head, "I suppose—we knew we could—But I didn't, Drake and I, I mean my husband—"

"You don't have to keep up that crap for me. I don't care if you were married. I don't imagine anybody gets married out there, do they?" He gestured at the ceiling.

Archie sat still for a moment, then shook her head. "No, no one gets married. It's a ... It doesn't really make sense for anyone to. Anymore."

"Why the hell did you people come here in the first place?"

Archie looked at her feet. When she raised her eyes to meet John's again I could tell that she wanted to be straight with him, to make amends for whatever had happened, to take responsibility, to atone. "We just wanted knowledge. I—It was *my* project. I brought Drake in on it but it was my project. I wanted to know ... what it was like. In the old days, when people died. When people married, had families, raised children. I wanted to learn from you."

"You wanted to study us."

"I—Yes, all right, yes. That's fair. We wanted to study how you did things, how you lived. But not in any condescending way. Not like studying ants in an anthill or anything like that." It was touching to see Archie so passionate, so desperate to convince this old man that he was something more to her than just an experiment. "I wanted to learn what we'd given up to get to where we were."

"To get to where you were?"

"We've done marvelous things. Impossible things. Traveling from star to star is the least of our accomplishments." Her gaze was intense; she leaned forward on her chair. "We don't hate each other anymore. We can communicate in ways that are so intimate, so utterly revealing that it's possible to actually experience another person's perspective, another person's point of view. Can you imagine what that's like? I don't think *I* could if I hadn't experienced it."

"It's true, daddy," Alice said. "I've done it. It's wonderful."

John sat back, taking it in, his suspicions supplanted by wonder. "I imagine it is, sweetheart. That is, I can't imagine. But it must be. It sure would have helped me understand your mother. What she was going through."

Archie continued, "But things had to change when we gained these new abilities. Conquering death changed us, made us more independent of one another. Gave us less reason to depend on each other. We don't have families anymore. Romantic love is ... unknown. Lots of things. I wanted to see what they were like in the context of ... a coherent ... a coherent social fabric ..."

John's skepticism had returned. "And where did Estelle and I fit in? In all this."

"You weren't part of it. You were not any part of it. I swear. It just—"

"I don't suppose it matters anymore," John said.

"But it *does* matter," Archie answered. "To me, it matters." Anger drove her now. Anger at whom, I didn't know. "I didn't want to come back here. I thought it ill-advised, but now that I'm here I want you to know that I never intended to interfere in any of the indigenous population's private lives. That was *not* part of the research. It was *not* part of the plan in any way."

" 'Indigenous population,' " John scoffed. "I don't think I've ever been one of those before."

Archie started to respond, but Louise jumped in first: "I told you!" she said to John, "I *told* you you shouldn't have had anything to do with those people! You see how they think of us? I told you they'd ruin your life and send your children to hell—"

"Louise, what are you talking about?" John asked.

"I knew all along what that woman was up to! I could see it in her—"

"WHAT ARE YOU TALKING ABOUT, LOUISE?" John shouted. "What the FUCK are you talking about?"

Louise looked at John, shocked, her mouth moving. Then she gathered herself and said, relatively quietly, "How DARE you speak to me like that! In front of these people! After all I've—We took you in when NO ONE else would have you. No one!" Shaking with anger, her eyes brimming with tears, she turned and left the room.

John looked after her for a long time. The rest of us looked for something to say. I wasn't sure what I had just witnessed. A fight, but about what?

"None of this ever made any sense to me," John finally said. He turned and looked at Archie, "I'm sorry, maybe you better go."

"Daddy—" Alice began.

"I'm sorry, honey." He turned to her. "I—I'm sorry you had to see me like this. I didn't used to be this way, I—I'm sorry."

"Could we—could we come back later? Maybe? When things have … When you're feeling …"

"Yeah, maybe that would be best." He hung his head. "No, maybe you'd better not. I don't know. Louise—she, I don't know what she might do."

"What?" Alice asked.

John looked at Archie. "Louise—"

"Your aunt was the one who turned you in," Archie said. "She told the authorities about your mother—what she wanted to do."

"Oh."

"Maybe we'd better get going," Archie said. "I think your father's right. I don't think it's wise for us to stay."

"But I—" Alice balked. Then, "Okay."

We started to go. At the front door Alice turned back to her father. "Would you like to see mom? I mean, if you could, if she were around? Would you like to get back together?"

"Alice—" Archie admonished. Alice waved her off and took her father's hands in hers.

"Would you?"

John Cheatham looked at his daughter for a long time before he said, "I don't think she'd want to see me. The way I am now." He shook his head, "No. I think I'd rather have her remember me the way I was, not this filthy, crazy, broken down old coot." He looked at the floor. "Louise was right to get mad at me. I'm not worth anything to anybody anymore." He looked back into his daughter's eyes. "But I sure am glad you came to see me. I surely am glad."

"Me, too, Daddy."

"Just to hear you call me that," he smiled. "I know I probably smell bad, I—I should have taken a bath—"

Alice shook her head. John asked her, "Do you suppose I could just … hold you for a minute? Just for a minute."

Alice put her arms around him and laid her head on his hollow chest. He rested his head on hers. They stayed that way for a time—forever, maybe, or maybe not long enough. Then they parted. He looked at her and said, "I want you to go out there and take the world by the tail and shake it till it makes you happy. Don't take no for an answer. Don't you ever settle. You understand me?"

Alice nodded.

"I love you, sweetheart. I always have and I always will."

"I love you, too, Daddy."

"Every time I look up into the night sky I'll think about you, what you're doing, where you might be."

"I'll think about you, too."

They looked at each other. Then he said, "You go on, now. Remember what I said."

We turned and walked down the wooden steps, down the sandy path. Just before the path curved behind a stand of cane, Alice turned to wave to her father one last time. He waved back.

"We have to get out of here," Archie spoke quietly but urgently. "We have to get out of here *now*."

I leaned against the door of our room, making sure that no one outside in the hallway could hear us. Alice sat on the floor in the corner, withdrawn and stony. Steel sat on the bed, fighting to keep her composure as she said, "Did he ask about—"

Archie had had enough. She cut her off, "Look, we did what we came here to do." She turned to Alice. "Didn't we, Alice? We found your father. I never thought we would, but we found him." Alice nodded. Archie drove on, "Louise is going to turn us in. She did it before; she'll do it again. It was a risk we took, going to her, but I just couldn't think of any other way to find him. We found him, but we *have* to leave now. John will try to keep her from going to the police, but I don't know how much fight he has left in him."

Steel was in really bad shape. She looked at Alice, she looked at Archie, she looked at the ceiling. She put her head in her hands. "I don't know ..." she started.

Archie sat on the bed beside her. "Captain, this is your expedition. We've come a long way toward our goals, but we still have many things to accomplish." She looked at Alice again, but Alice was still stoic. "I completely understand why Alice wanted to come back here. Of course she would want to see her family again. It was something that needed to happen—"

"I don't think I have a family," Alice said.

"Alice!" Steel implored, "Of course you have a family. You grew up in a family, more than any of us did."

"That's what makes it easy for you," Alice replied. "You don't have anything to lose. You just fly around doing experiments on people—"

"Now, Alice, that's not fair. We didn't experiment on anyone, we simply observed—"

"What about me? Aren't you experimenting on me?"

"We're trying to save your life—"

There was a strange popping sound that seemed to come from far off somewhere, followed by a thundering echo. It brought us up short, but we'd heard other things like it in the past few days. The acoustics of Nazareth's unique setting occasionally made it sound like something was happening next door when it was actually happening across town. The echo died away but there was a pause in the conversation. I took the opportunity to jump in.

"Maybe Alice doesn't want us to save her life," I said. Everyone stopped and looked at me. "It's her life, I mean." Alice looked so ... small. So vulnerable. I couldn't imagine the universe without her, but still, maybe it was her decision. Maybe no one had really given her the opportunity to make it for herself. "What do you say, Alice? Do you want us to leave you here? Do you want to stay?" I couldn't believe I was asking her these things. Staying meant suicide, but it was a strange suicide, one that would take decades to play itself out. On the other hand, maybe she was right. Maybe the experiment had gone on long enough. I just didn't like seeing her so unhappy.

Steel stared at me like I'd committed mutiny on the high seas, but then her expression softened. I think she realized that these were questions that had to be asked, that only Alice could answer.

There was another pop followed by another roll of thunder. "What *is* that?" Archie asked. "What's going on out there?"

Steel shook her head. "If the place is caving in, I'm sure they'll send someone to tell us." She turned back to Alice, calmer, softer, determined to do the best thing, the right thing. "Alice," she started, "I've tried to—We, we've tried to ... to educate you, to integrate you into the world, the ... the larger world out there, to make you feel ... feel welcome. Loved. We ... we all ... care deeply for you and your happiness and—not just me and Archie, but Yuri and, and Marcus and all of us. Even Ham." She smiled.

Alice smiled at her shoes, "I think Ham understands me better than any of you."

Steel allowed herself a small laugh. "Maybe so. Maybe so. He's a pretty understanding guy." She became serious again. "I don't think any of us really remember what it was like being only a couple of decades old. We've lived for centuries. Mo has lived for more than a millennium. We are looking at living for many, many more centuries. Millennia. We don't know how long. We may never d-die, but maybe, someday, we will. We don't know."

"It's a fetish with you people, you know?" Alice shot back. "Avoiding death. It's like this sick fixation you have. People around here don't have it. They accept things the way they are. They live their lives and don't worry about it."

"We don't worry about it either," Steel answered. "We've fixed it. That's all. We've solved the problem."

Something occurred to me. "I don't think this is about death. I don't even think death is about death." They turned to me. "I think it's about losing people."

"What do you mean?" Archie asked.

"We don't like to lose people. Nothing hurts worse. Nothing scares us more. Not even the prospect of our own death." I thought of Yuri, I thought of Drake. I thought, of course, of my wife. "We'll sacrifice ourselves to keep from losing other people. We'll sacrifice everything." I looked at Alice. "Steel and Yuri and all of us are willing to sacrifice everything we have to keep from losing you. Everything. We're willing to go to the one place we know of where we might die just to keep from losing you. You're that important to us. The problem is—" I laughed. "The problem is that in order for us not to lose you, you have to lose everyone here. On Eden. Your father, your aunt, your mother, wherever she is. Your culture. And I know, it hurts. It hurts to lose people."

An orphan's tears came to Alice's eyes and I could tell, in that moment, that she knew she was loved. By all of us.

"I don't mean to be such a big problem," she said, her voice squeaky from her tears.

"Oh, Alice," Steel said as she melted on to her. But she was just an instant ahead of the rest of us. We all collapsed on her and held her like, indeed, like we would never let her go. We stayed that way for a while, a puddle of people on the floor.

Finally Alice said, "It's just so hard. I don't think Dad will be alive the next time I come here. If I ever get back here."

This was progress. It was the first thing she'd said that sounded like she was adjusting to the idea of leaving.

"I don't know, sweetheart," Steel answered. "We don't know how long it's going to take us to finish up, to get you well."

" 'Get me well,' " Alice snorted. "I don't feel sick."

"Well, to find a way to ... to fix it, to fix you. I don't know how you want to put it," Steel replied.

"It doesn't matter," Alice answered, "That part doesn't matter at all." She looked at her Captain, her guardian. She was a member of the crew again. "I'll be all right. It's just hard to say goodbye. That's all."

I knew how she felt. I think we all did.

"I guess we'll leave in the morning, huh?" she asked.

Archie and Steel referred to each other. Archie said, "The sooner the better." Steel and I nodded in agreement, then looked back at Alice.

She dusted her hands and got up off the floor. We did the same. "Okay," she said. "Okay." She started for the door. As she reached it she turned back to Steel and said, "Let's go fix me." Then she opened it and was gone.

It was maybe a couple of hours later when a knock came at the door. Steel and I had just drifted off to sleep when we heard it.

"Now, who could that be?" Steel asked.

"I'll see," I said, playing the role of the Edenite patriarch. I pulled on my pants and went to the door.

It was Samuel Morgan, the man with the pretty wife and eight or ten or a million children. He looked concerned about something, not worried, really, but concerned.

"What can I do for you, Samuel?" I asked.

He said, "Sorry to wake you. Do you suppose I could talk to you for a minute?"

I looked around at Steel. She had her robe on and was getting out of bed. "Uh, yeah. Where do—uh, would you like to come in?"

"No, maybe we'd better talk out here in the hall." He glanced over my shoulder into the room. "No need to concern the womenfolk."

What a strange culture, I thought for the thousandth time. I turned to Steel. "Excuse me, mother, I'll just be a moment." I stepped out into the hall and closed the door, my mind racing, trying to think of any taboo we might have broken, any slip we might have made. "Anything wrong, Sam? I hope we haven't disturbed anyone, done anything—"

"No, no, nothing like that. The, uh, the sheriff is downstairs."

Sheriff! Oh, boy, now what?

Samuel went on, "There's been a—well, you said you and your folks went to see a Mrs. Lockridge, right? You were telling us at dinner."

Adrenaline surged through me. I tried to look calm. "Yeah, we went to see her. We stayed over there most of the afternoon. Why? What's the matter?"

"Well, that's what I thought you said. I told the sheriff I'd come up and get you. He just wants to ask you some questions. I guess something bad happened over there this evening."

"What? What happened? We've been here since supper time."

"Yeah, I know. That's what I told the sheriff. I think he just wants to talk to you. Sorry to be the bearer of bad news ..."

"No, no. That's all right. Just let me get dressed and I'll be right down."

"Okay, I'll tell him you're coming. I just thought it might be nicer if I came up and got you, you know. No need to upset everybody."

"Yeah, yeah, thanks." I let myself back into the room.

"What's wrong?" Steel wanted to know.

I started getting dressed as I answered, "I don't know. The sheriff is downstairs. He wants to talk to me."

"What did you do?"

"I don't know. I don't think I did anything." The culture of Eden was infectious.

I found myself wanting to protect Steel from any unpleasantness, to keep her home and safe while I went out to do battle. "He just wants to talk to me."

"I'll come with you."

"NO." I stopped her. "I don't think that would be a good idea. I'm the head of the family, remember?"

She nodded, but she didn't like it.

"I'll go down and see what he wants. If it's something that you need to deal with, I'll come back and get you. Let's not turn this into anything bigger than it is."

"You're right," she agreed. I turned to go. "Wait!" She stopped me, "Do you remember where we're from?"

"What?"

"Our address. He's a policeman, he'll probably want to know where you live."

"Oh, right, right. 17 Forest Avenue, New Bethlehem."

"Good. He just ... might want to talk to the rest of us. I want our stories to mesh."

"Good idea. All right, I'll be back. Try not to worry."

"Don't volunteer any information, just answer his questions."

"I'll be all right. I've dealt with police before." I slipped out the door before she could give me any more advice.

I spoke with the sheriff maybe fifteen or twenty minutes. He asked me how I knew Louise Lockridge and John Cheatham and I told him who we were, our version of who we were. When I finished the story he nodded and said it made sense and I asked him what had happened. He told me.

A couple of hours earlier John Cheatham had killed Louise Lockridge and then taken his own life. "He shot her once in the chest and then turned the gun on himself," the sheriff said. "You might have heard the gun shots."

Disbelief and bottomless sadness dragged me into a chair. John and Louise ... Alice's father ... What was I going to tell Alice? *How* was I going to tell Alice? Then realization pulled me back to the sheriff's face.

"The gun shots—" We had heard them—those popping sounds, followed by thunder. I had heard Louise Lockridge die. Then John. Alice had heard it. "Oh, no ..." was all I had in me to say.

"I'm awfully sorry," he said.

"We were—It was an upsetting visit. They—I hope we didn't—I mean Alice ..."

"Alice Cheatham."

"She just wanted to see her fath— her fa— her fa-family. She just ... she just wanted to ..."

"I wouldn't blame yourselves for this. Old man Cheatham has been crazy for years, ever since that bad business. I guess we all expected something like this to happen someday. I'm just sorry it had to happen when you folks were here."

I couldn't say anything. I just stared. Stared at the past. But the sheriff had something else on his mind:

"You and your family weren't planning on staying here, were you? In Nazareth?"

I looked up at him. "No. No, we were going to leave tomorrow morning."

"I think that would be best," he said.

CHAPTER 26

I don't know how I made it back up the stairs. My legs felt useless; my soul was in free fall. I felt complicit. I felt used. I felt stained, assaulted, ashamed, outraged. How many, I thought? How many human beings would cease to be before we were done? Drake: incinerated. Jacob: lost in Switzerland. Now John and Louise. Dead. Dead. The word kept ringing in my head like a church bell. What disease were we spreading in our quest to cure Alice? What had set this lethal juggernaut in motion? With each step I mounted I became more resolved: I would not go another hour, another step, I would not perform one more dance for Steel without knowing.

I can't say what I looked like when I let myself into our room but Steel recoiled from me before I spoke. "What's—What—," she started. She gathered her robe around her, kneeling on the bed.

I tried to still the hurricane howling in my head as I closed the door and leaned against it. With my eyes dark and my jaw clenched I asked her one of the first questions I'd ever asked her, one of the first she hadn't answered. I asked, "What is your name?"

She pulled her robe tighter. "What? What do you mean? What happened?"

I tamped down my anger but I didn't know how long I could restrain it. "You have to tell me what your name is. Now." My head felt like a nest of spiders—little strands of thought running in every direction but none of them making any sense. They couldn't make any sense. It wasn't possible. Where did she get the eggs?

Steel hadn't lost her touch; she looked genuinely confused, innocent, as she responded. "You know my— What are you talking about? My name? Tell me what happened." She started to stand. I took a step toward her and she stopped, paled, collapsed back on the bed—ceding the room to me, searching my face, my eyes.

"No," I shook my head. "No. You answer my question. You answer my FREAKING question."

I could see it now. Fear haunted her, but not fear of me. "Mo, please, tell me what's wrong!" She reached out to me— her long, tapered fingers caressed the air, offering, seducing.

Crossing to her took no time. She huddled against the headboard as I loomed over her, balancing. Fear I saw, yes, and profound sadness, but still that iron determination. I think my determination finally matched hers. I knew the consequences of what I was about to say, but I meant every word: "You will tell me what your name is or I swear to you that I will go back downstairs and tell the sheriff everything I know about you."

That shocked her into action. She grasped my wrist with one hand, reached to stroke my cheek with the other, her eyes imploring, "Mo, Mo, my hero, my—my friend and protector! What has hurt you? Tell me—"

"STOP IT!" I hissed. She took her hands away as though the touch of my skin had burned her. Sitting on her feet, hands in her lap, she was neutral, attentive, unthreatening, but unyielding. Never yielding. "All right," I breathed, "if you won't tell me, I'll tell you." She waited, just waited: her eyes clear, an artery pulsing in her slender throat. Would she answer me? Would I be able to believe her if she did? I had no other option; she was my only source of information. In a voice that was probably too harsh I asked her, "Your name is Estelle, isn't it?"

I could see her react to the sound of that name: a small withdrawal of her head, a tension in her shoulders. I thought she was going to deny it but she just stared up at me, unable to respond, unable to move. Fear now overwhelmed her, paralyzing her. I didn't want to threaten her; I didn't want ... I had to get her to talk to me. Trying to calm down I sat beside her and took her hand in mine. Quietly, gently I repeated, "Isn't it?"

"What—" tears stopped her voice. "I don't—People ... some people ... I've, I've ... yes, I've been called that—"

"By whom?" My anger was being replaced by fear. Terror not of the plague or death or anything the future held, but of what I might already have done, or abetted. "By whom?" I urged her, coaxed her, demanded that she tell me the truth at long last.

She was trembling now. Tears shook off the ends of her beautiful lashes. "Mo, I—I—" Her voice broke. "Oh my god, what has happened? What could have— Why are you—"

I put my arm around her shoulders, pulled her to me and held her hand, smelled her hair as I placed my lips by her ear. "You have to tell me. Everything. Now. I have news and I'm afraid it's not good news and I will give it to you. But first, you have to tell me who I'm giving it to. I have to know who you are, *what* you are."

The trembling got worse. I stroked her arm as she tried to speak, "I—I—I don't ... know what, know what you want ... I—Please, Mo, just tell me—"

I placed my hands on her shoulders and turned her to me. She was smaller than I had ever seen her. Trapped, alone, she quailed before me, her chin quivering, her eyes liquid, lost. "All right," I said, "All right. It's all right. I'll tell you what I think; you tell me if I'm wrong. Okay?"

She nodded. And waited. Once I said this it couldn't be unsaid. Once I knew it, it couldn't be unknown. But I had to know. I had to. "You're ... you're Alice's m-mo-moth—" I hated that word. It tasted like cardboard, like ... nothing. The very idea that Steel could be Alice's ... Alice's ... It was just so bizarre, so unthinkable. I changed tacks, "Alice is ... is your daughter, isn't she?"

There it was. The question had been uttered. Steel, Estelle, sat before me motionless, not denying it. The next incredulous question followed inevitably: "You *married* John Cheatham?" Once again, she didn't deny it. She looked at me, looked for condemnation, recrimination. I was too stunned to offer either. All I had was, "W-why? How?"

She trembled in my grasp, tears running down her cheeks. Tears of shame? Of loss? Of relief? I couldn't tell. She pulled away from me. "Okay," she sniffed, that thick curtain of poise trying to descend again, hiding her. She wiped her face with the back of her hand, straightened her robe, "Now you know. Now ... now tell me what's happened. Please."

"Now I—? What do I know? I don't know anything!" I kept falling into rage and I didn't want to. "How could you—Why did you— What the hell were you thinking? Why? Why did you marry him? Do you know what you've done to him? Do you understand what effect you've had on this poor ... this innocent, this—this child, this mortal infant?"

"I— I know ... Mo, please—"

"I don't think you do! I don't think you have any idea what you've ... How could you be so ... so—"

"Mo, please! Listen to me. You don't understand. I don't know what you're thinking, but you have to believe me. You weren't there. You don't understand!"

I squeezed my skull between my palms, pressed my eyeballs into their sockets with the heels of my hands. "Well, then I guess you better explain it to me," I said. The ground wasn't under me. I had no compass. "What was it, some part of the experiment?" I asked, "Some part of Archie's project?"

"No! No, it— It was—" she looked for words, but I couldn't imagine what words she'd find.

Angrily I turned on her, "That's it, isn't it? Archie wanted to know what it was like to be married, didn't she? See what it was like from the inside? Get the straight dope? Record it in her report?" A waterfall of anger poured over me. "GODDAMN IT! *I* was married! You can't— You can't ... HOLY SHIVA!" Everything that I had kept protected within myself for the twelve centuries since I'd lost my wife was being attacked, soiled, demeaned.

"Mo, Mo, please. Calm down. Lower your voice. You can't talk— You can't talk that way here. Please."

My elbows on my knees, my head in my hands, I seethed, I reeled. I lowered my voice, "God ... DAMN it. Goddamn it. Who are you people? What the hell do you think—Goddamn it." I was lost. I didn't know how I'd find my way back.

Steel spoke quietly, hesitantly. She kept her hands in her lap, "We, we didn't— Don't blame Archie, please, Mo. She didn't want us to ... I mean, she wanted us to interact with the Edenites, to, to join their culture, be part of them so we could, could understand them as best we could. She didn't want to judge them from the outside. She wanted to characterize them by their own standards, not by ours—"

"Yeah, yeah, all right. I get it. She wanted to get close. So what did you do? Join a dating service?"

"A what?"

Another archaic concept. When was the last time anyone went on a date? Except on Eden. "Never mind. Go on."

"Please listen, Mo. Please." She risked touching my shoulder. I didn't pull away. Where would I go if I did?

"I'm listening."

"Try not to—" she gathered herself, "Okay. Okay. I met— we ... met, John and I, I mean. I met John at a ... a church social."

"Oh, Shiva," I couldn't help laughing.

"Mo, *please.*" She looked to the door. "We're supposed to be Methodists. You can't use that kind of language—"

"Sorry." I shook my head in utter bewildered despair. "Sorry. You met at a church social."

Steel examined me closely before continuing, "Archie and Drake were posing as a married couple. I ... I was supposed to be Archie's spinster cousin from New Jerusalem." She didn't go on.

"Okay," I prompted. The language of this strange place was almost too much to handle: spinster cousin. Allah and Buddha and fricking Mohammed on a crutch.

"It was, it would have been strange if we hadn't ... hadn't gone to these—It's what they do here. We were *here*, in this place, this culture. We were new in town. People assumed we'd go ... invited us. Thought we could ... meet people, get to know—" I could see the whole thing in vivid detail in my mind. A room full of Edenites dressed in their Sunday best, plain, sunburned, battered, worn ... and

Steel: exquisite, almond-eyed Steel. I tried to keep listening to her, but it was hard. "When we got there a woman introduced John to me. It was like ... it was like her *job* to make sure everyone met someone. John ... offered to get me some punch. He, he asked me to dance. We—"

I couldn't believe she was telling me this—this freaking high school romance. "What are you trying to tell me? What are you saying? Okay, you met, you danced, what freaking difference does it make?"

"I'm—I'm trying to explain—"

"Explain what? How you seduced him? How you lured this, this child—"

"He wasn't a child. He was almost thirty years old!"

"Oh, excuse me. This mature being of almost three whole decades—"

"And I didn't seduce him! I didn't do anything to encourage him, I was just ... polite. Friendly." And spectacular, I thought. She went on, "You have to remember: no one has sex here. I mean, almost never. They, they only have sex when they're married, when they're alone, when no one can see them. Archie and Drake and I weren't having sex. We hadn't had sex since we'd gotten down to the surface. I suppose Archie and Drake could have but they weren't. We wanted to experience the tension these people deal with."

I couldn't believe this. "So you were randy? Is that what you're saying?"

"No, no! I mean, I was, but that's not—I mean— Everyone here is randy to some extent or other all the time. That's one of the things we wanted to research. How they dealt with it, how it affected them—"

I shook my head in amazement, "What chance do you think he had against you? I mean look at you! You have an entire—" I couldn't talk about that here. I couldn't speak of the interstellar cosmetic medical system that made her what she was.

Her response was defensive, desperate, "You're not listening! It was *me*, not him. *I* didn't have a chance. *I* fell in love with *him*. When he asked me to marry him—"

"What are you talking about?" This strained my credulity beyond the tatters it was already in.

She was crying again. "We didn't know, we didn't know. We were so ... naïve. We'd never—" She turned to me. "You *lived* in a culture like this. You spent centuries around married people, around children. We—Archie and Drake and I—we'd never met anyone who was married, never knew anything like it. It was totally alien to us." She pushed her hair back from her face. "Don't you see? The Edenites don't *know* each other. They've never melded; they've never experienced any point of view but their own. Each one of them is separate, disparate. They're utterly, totally, achingly alone. When they marry, when they approach each other in any way at all, they have to do it on *faith*. They have to *trust* that the other won't hurt them, rob them, murder them, rape them."

I knew all this, but I didn't know where she was going with it. She thought for a moment. "They ... they have a phrase here, a—a concept; I don't know if you've heard it since you've been here, but they say it a lot. They call it breaking someone's heart. They say things like, 'He broke my heart,' or 'Please don't break my heart.' They sing songs about it. It seems like all of their songs are either about religion or breaking someone's heart. We didn't know what it meant."

"I know what it means," I said, my voice ashen and dry.

"Do you? I thought you might." She sensed my grief and put her hand on my arm. "I thought you might. How could I break his heart? How could I break mine?" She turned to me with new conviction, "And anyway I *know* you understand. I know you do. I've seen how you look at Alice."

"Alice?"

"These people ... these people are *dying*. All of them. John, even when he was dancing with me that first time, was dying. He was facing his own death. When he asked me to marry him, how could I turn him down?"

"So you married him out of pity?"

"No! No. Think for a minute. Do you pity Alice? You don't. You love her. You admire her. You admire her for what she has to face every instant that she's alive. You respect her for the courage she has to have just to do the things that we take for granted. What if Alice came to you and told you she wanted to spend her life with you, her whole life, with you and no one else? What if she told you that she loved you and you knew it was true? What if she asked you to marry her?"

This didn't seem fair, somehow, but I sure didn't have an answer for it. "I—I—" was as far as I got.

"How would you turn her down? You tell me. How? I had never experienced anything like it. John was offering his entire *being*. To me. As a token of love. If Alice offered that to you would you marry her out of pity?"

New emotions were flooding me now, or maybe very, very old ones, so quickly I couldn't identify them: love, grief, longing, fear. Could I afford to lose anyone else? Could I lose Alice and still ... still be ... be anything at all? "Alice," I finally said, "I— I don't—"

Steel drove on, "He was offering me an honor, an honor greater than any I'd ever known. What gift could I give him that would be great enough to honor his gift to me?"

I looked into Steel's eyes. What I saw there was suddenly, warmly familiar to me—ancient, but familiar. I saw in her eyes what my wife must have seen in mine on our wedding day: that my eyes no longer belonged to me. They weren't mine anymore. They were hers. They belonged to her. And now so much of what I had never understood about Steel finally fell into place. Why I had never been able to read her. I hadn't known. I could never read her eyes because I hadn't suspected in my wildest, most improbable fancies that she had given them away as I had given mine. She had given them to John Cheatham, to her ... to her husband. Her eyes, her heart ... everything.

But her question about Alice wasn't fair, and I'd finally figured out how. "Did you tell him?" I asked.

"What?"

"Did you tell John Cheatham who you were? Where you were from? How long you'd lived, how long you expected to live?"

"Mo, listen—"

"Did you tell him that he was going to spend his whole life with you but you were only going to spend the tiniest fraction of yours with him?"

"Mo, I—" she looked at me for a moment and then collapsed, crushed under inescapable culpability. When she spoke again it was in the thinnest whisper. "No. I— I couldn't, we were ... under cover. We couldn't—"

"Yes. Yes, I understand the stringent demands of field anthropology." What was I going to do? How could I deal with this and still keep my ... keep my ... If only, I thought for the first time in a long time, if only I hadn't re-booted early. If only I'd been stronger, truer. I would still be married. I would still have my wife with me. She would know what to do with this, how to help, how to make things ... better.

No, that was wrong. If I hadn't re-booted early I would have died about the same time she did. But I might be with her now. The vision of her that I had in the schoolyard hit me again with physical force.

Steel took my hand in both of hers and brought it to her cheek. "Please, Mo. Please try to understand. I gave him everything I could, everything I had to give. I loved him. He was going to die. I didn't know what else to do."

I tried to put it all together. She, Archie and Drake had come to this place to study it. When they got here they were profoundly affected, as I had been, by the children, the families, the courage in the face of death. They had joined the culture, become part of it—got jobs, maybe, a place to live, made friends, acquaintances. Steel was introduced to John Cheatham and, to her complete surprise, fell in love with him. They married; she bore Jacob, then Alice. When it came down to staying with her husband or saving the lives of her children, maternal instinct— which Steel couldn't have been aware she had or even identified—took her over, and she elected to save her children, to take them with her back to Earth. Maybe she wanted to take John with her, too, I didn't know.

But something had gone wrong; word of her plan had gotten to John's sister, Louise, and Louise had called the cops. Steel had to flee or be tried for heresy. She then enlisted Archie and Drake to get the children and follow her. But Jacob had been in an accident and they discovered that the children couldn't re-boot. And here we were, still trying to pick up the pieces.

I don't know if I could understand everything, but I understood a great deal more than I had: the lack of sex, for instance, between Steel and me. I didn't even have to ask her now. I knew. She hadn't had sex since the last time she'd been on Eden. Since the last time she'd had it with John Cheatham. She'd denied herself to be true to him, to her vows.

Only now she had been released from her vows, and I was the one who had to tell her. How was I going to do that? I had no idea. I looked at the floor as I said, "Thank you. Thank you for telling me—for trusting me with ... Okay. Okay, now I have something I have to tell you and I ... I don't ... Okay ..."

I turned to face her and she looked into my eyes and I could see that she didn't know. I could see that she thought she was still married, that she couldn't even conceive of any other state of things. Even after losing Jacob, even after losing Drake, even after living on Eden, it was just too alien: utterly beyond the realm of possibility.

I started again, "Okay, I think what probably happened was that ... that Louise ..." I faltered.

"Yes?" she asked, still not knowing.

"Louise, I think, probably was going to go to the police and John ... I think John tried to stop her."

"Oh, no! Do we need to—" she started.

"Wait. Wait, just ... she didn't get to them—"

"Did John stop her? What—"

"Please, just let me ... let me ..."

"What happened? I know what Louise is capable of. Mo, if we need to—"

"Captain, Steel, please, let me tell this. Please." I thought for a moment. "Do you remember those two sounds we heard? A couple of hours ago? Those two ... pops that reverberated while we were talking with Alice and Archie here in the room?"

She nodded, "Yes. I remember. What—"

"That was ... I think John tried to talk her out of going and he couldn't and the first pop was John ... They were gun shots. The pops. The first was when John ... shot, killed Louise. He shot her. In the chest and ... and she, she died. And I think, then, that John couldn't, couldn't face ... I think he just couldn't take it anymore." I looked into Steel's eyes. She still didn't know. "He'd killed his sister, you see? He just couldn't ... the second sound, the second gunshot was John ... He—I'm so sorry, Captain—"

"What? I don't understand."

She still didn't know. She wasn't taking it in at all. "Steel, Steel, John shot himself. He killed himself. The second sound was John shooting himself. He's ... he's gone. He's gone."

"But ... but ... is he okay? Is he—"

"Captain. Captain, he's gone. The sheriff told me that John killed Louise and then took his own life. He's gone. Your ... your husband is, is ..." None of the old religious descriptions seemed right to me, somehow. I couldn't use them. I fell back on the only language I had. "His perspective is lost to us. We don't have him anymore. You're not ... you're not married anymore. Captain?" I searched her face. "Steel?"

At that moment her eyes broke. One instant they still belonged to John Cheatham and the next they didn't belong to anyone, not even herself. They were broken eyes, unable to see, unable to be in the world at all: shattered like glass on pavement.

She sat inert, silent, still, but falling. I couldn't catch her; I couldn't do anything but watch her fall. She looked at a spot on the wall, or through it, or at nothing and said, "We have to ... we have to tell Alice." She looked back at me. She hadn't seen her husband in over a decade of her time but she had been married to him nonetheless. "Would you—I think I need to ... would you mind telling ... I need ... I need to be alone for a little while. Could you tell Alice? I'm sorry, is that too much to ... I don't know what to ... I just need a little time—"

"Yeah, I'll tell her," I said. "I'll tell her. You just ... try to ... I'm sorry, Steel. Estelle, I mean—"

"Don't call me that."

"I'm sorry. I—"

"It's all right. Just ... just don't ..."

I watched her fall. "Okay," I said, "I'll be back in a little while." And fall. And fall and fall and fall. I let myself out of our room.

PART VI
IN TRANSIT

CHAPTER 27

I didn't know what to tell Alice. I couldn't tell her the truth, not the whole truth. I didn't want her to feel responsible in any way. She wasn't, I knew, but I was afraid she'd blame herself somehow: for upsetting her father or for coming back to see him, and I knew that her returning was probably the best thing that had happened to John Cheatham since Steel had left him. Alice and Archie were asleep; as I stood outside their door I thought maybe I should just let them sleep and tell them in the morning, but it seemed like Alice had the right to know.

Archie responded to my knock, and the three of us sat on their bed. As gently as I could, I told Alice that her father was gone, but I didn't mention Louise at all. I didn't mention the popping sounds. When she asked me what had happened—I lied to her. I hope I lied well. I told her simply that his heart had been weak for a long time and it had finally given out. I said how fortunate it was that she had been able to get back in time to see him—to see him before he passed away. I told her how clear it was to me that he loved her, that it meant everything to him that she had come back.

She didn't question me. She didn't doubt. Her reaction was immediate and pure. A sad, small sound started deep within her, her chest convulsed and tears poured down her face. She collapsed against me, her sadness filling her and flooding out of her. I held her and Archie moved in and held her, too. Alice snuggled into both of us and cried and cried.

I spent most of the night with her and Archie. Archie and I made a nest of our bodies with Alice curled up in the middle. Whenever one of us moved Alice would grab us and pull us back around her. Eventually she exhausted herself and fell asleep.

In the small of the morning I went back to my own room. It was dark and

Steel lay in bed, still and quiet. I got in beside her and could tell she wasn't asleep, but she made no overture to me, no movement or sound. I didn't know what to say to her anyway, so I let her alone and tried to get some sleep myself.

We left Nazareth early in the morning, before anyone else was up. I didn't want Alice to hear any news about her father or her aunt. Steel and I didn't talk much as we packed in the room, but I did tell her how I had explained John's death to her daughter and she seemed to accept my handling of it. I don't know if she got any sleep at all.

On our way out of town we passed the schoolyard where I had first seen the children. It was empty, but I could see small footprints in the dust; I remembered the echoes of their laughter. We continued through town, into the narrow slot and up the carved stairs. Emerging from the soft rose light of that stone womb into the metallic brightness of the desert morning seemed more spiritual than physical, more psychological than spiritual: painful, abrupt, silent, terrifying.

Conversation was sparse and laconic as we drove across the rock. I left the road and turned the Buckymobile northeast, angling toward the Buddhist shrine at the base of the escarpment. I wasn't worried about getting lost; Marcus was tracking us from the Lightdancer every inch of the way.

We left our car in a shallow gulch out of sight of the shrine trail and hiked the last few klicks. The shrine itself, my entrance into Eden's culture, was unchanged. Serene painted eyes still stared benignly at the cardinal points of the compass. Prayer flags still fluttered in the wind, offering their silent supplication. Would the Buddha they spoke to intercede for John Cheatham, for Louise? Even though they had prayed to a different being? Did those questions have any meaning at all?

Above the shrine we found our space suits. Putting them on was comforting and familiar, but donning the helmets and sealing them was another leaving. We were insulated from Eden's ecosystem now, as alien technologically as we were spiritually. We said goodbye to Alice's home one more time.

Then cliffs and talus and scree and cliffs. Powered jumars lifted us up colossal walls of rock: into the future, into the past. On the third night we stayed at the hut where Archie lost her arm. The next day we jumared past the ledge where Steel and Alice saved me from freezing. It was a bright, sunny morning; I barely recognized it.

As we ascended into the heavens I thought about John Cheatham's brief, ruined life. Steel's husband. Our captain was a widow now, as I was a widower. I knew we shared a crime. Both of us had betrayed the one we loved. I didn't want to minimize what I had done, I don't think I did, but ... but when I remembered John's face as he said goodbye to Alice, to his daughter, I thought ... I thought— how? How could anyone take a person's children? How could Steel contemplate such an act? How could she carry it out? If she had ever loved John Cheatham as I had loved my wife ...

Twelve centuries ago, on Valhalla, I was with her when she—when she—I was in the room with her. It hadn't been easy to get to her. There had been fighting in First Landing. The newbies had taken the corporate offices and taken control of the spaceport, but I'd told them she was ill, she was dying, maybe, and they let me hop a shuttle so I could fly halfway around the planet to be with her. I got to her a few days before she left me forever. We had those few days.

Through the window in her hospital room we could see the forests she had started. She was so small. Lying in the bed she didn't look like she weighed enough to keep it from floating away. Her hair had turned white, but her eyes still mirrored my soul. She was glad I'd re-booted early. She thought the troubles would be resolved before I needed the treatment again. I told her I didn't want to re-boot again, that I never would. She told me not to be silly. There was so much work left to do, she said, so many stars to visit, so many planets to find, to shape, so many homes to make. We'd never had children but she felt that every newbie on Valhalla—if not every newbie everywhere—was our personal responsibility. All I could tell her was that I loved her. I laid my head on her breast and said, "I love you, I love you," over and over again. As I lay there holding her, I found myself wanting everything to stop, just ... stop. I wanted time to cease being time and become something else, something softer, more merciful. I prayed for it to stop, to just leave me there with her and her with me. My soul ached and screamed and begged for it to stop but it wouldn't stop and I knew I had one other thing I had to tell her. I had to tell her why I had 'booted without her, I had to explain to her, had to ask her to, to forgive me ... but I couldn't. I couldn't. I—I didn't. I couldn't.

She tired and needed to sleep. I held her hand for a long time but eventually I fell asleep, too, in the chair beside her bed. A nurse woke me to tell me she was gone. She was gone and there was nothing I could do to bring her back.

I've never forgiven myself for falling asleep. Of all my failings, shortcomings, weaknesses, losing those last hours with her is what costs me the most.

I wondered if Steel could forgive herself. I wondered if she felt she'd done anything wrong.

She dealt with John's passing much differently than Alice did. It was heartwarming and heartbreaking to watch. Alice was like a young willow: bending to the ground whenever the winds of grieving buffeted her, but springing back as soon as they had passed. Steel was more like an old oak, standing straight and tall against the storm. But what could bend in Alice broke in Steel; Steel would live with the scars much longer.

What was I going to do about Alice? None of this was her doing and our problem hadn't changed: Alice was still unable to re-boot. I tried not to treat her any differently, but I'm not sure how well I did. Being confronted with the unyielding finality of her father's cessation—of her aunt's— had changed me, had reminded me of the old days. Mortality was with me now. It never left my side.

Still, we made it to the top. Finding the crate at the bottom of the rill on that rocky plain above the world was like coming home. Under the black, star-filled sky that simple piece of fortieth century technology suggested that our time in the culture of Eden had been imagined. As we prepared to be hooked into space, to be captured by an orbiting starship, the experience of Eden seemed so dissonant, so strange and removed, it became hard to believe that we had gone through it. But we had changed Eden by our visit and it had changed us.

I lost myself in the work at hand. We would leave Eden as we had left Vesper, only this time none of it was improvised. Every element had been tested and used before. One end of the crate detached and became a tiny chariot, just big enough for the four of us to clamp onto. A small, liquid-fueled rocket motor—primitive but reliable—would boost us the few meters we needed to meet the skyhook and let us hover there until the hook grabbed us and threw us into the void. Tamika would cut in the graviton impellers and scoot out to pick us up and the planet of Eden, the religions of Eden, the children, love and death of Eden would be in our past.

Brainard's Planet was still in our future.

The crew welcomed us back aboard—four people who were subtly and profoundly different than those who had left the ship a few weeks earlier. They wanted to reconnect with us, to know what we had been through. It was odd not wanting to tell them. It wasn't that we wanted to keep it secret, and we didn't. We told them the basic facts, the pertinent ones, anyway: we had found Alice's father; he had passed away before we left. But the deeper things—the fear, the pain ... the anger ... I didn't want to share any of that with them, or burden them with it, perhaps. They regarded us quizzically, but with compassion, respect. Patience, overall. We knew each other in ways the Edenites never could. We knew we could never really be separated, and we had all the time in the world to bridge any distance that had opened between us.

But we had more immediate problems. Marcus asked us to convene in the common room after we had recovered from our ascent. We needed to decide where we were going next, and Marcus had other news for us as well. As we sat around the table he spoke first to Steel:

"While you were incommunicado on the surface Jean-Léon bulleted me from Neuschwanstein. He wanted to talk with you but I convinced him you were unavailable."

"Yes?" Steel responded. "What did he want?" Loss and grief had eroded her voice, leaving it hollow and tired. Archie looked tired, too. Of the four of us who had visited Eden, only Alice seemed stronger somehow, or perhaps just more substantial.

Marcus was measured and concise, but his news was rather disturbing: "Krupp has finished re-booting. He's determined to find out where we are and where we're going."

Krupp. Wonderful. I'd almost forgotten about Krupp. I thought I'd finally gotten Steel to fill me in on everything and then *this* super-juiced maniac comes back into the picture. It was too much. I had to speak. "Who is this guy?" I asked. "I mean, I never really got to meet him before he threw me off a bridge. Does everybody know him except me?"

Steel sighed wearily and looked at the tabletop. "No, Mo. No one really knows Krupp except me." Alice looked at her m– her m– looked at Steel and shook her head in tired exasperation. She wanted to speak but she didn't. Steel raised her head and found my eyes, "Krupp is my problem, not yours. It's a syndicate matter. I'm afraid that's all I am at liberty to say on the subject."

My reply was not as temperate as I would have liked. "Well that's just freaking great," I yelled. I slapped my palms on the tabletop, stood up. "What the hell does a person have to do to get into the inner sanctum around here?"

Marcus gestured to me, "Please, sit down, Mo—"

"Why?" I said, "Why should I sit down? This guy beats me up, rips off my, my—" I turned to Steel, "Do you even know what he took from me?"

Steel looked alarmed. "What?" she asked.

I didn't want to say it, not in front of the crew. I didn't want to upset them. I didn't want them to worry. I hadn't told anyone about it except Archie. It's funny and painful how fragile we feel ourselves to be even in this age of immortality. The thing that's the hardest to hang onto is the past. We've become accustomed to floating free in the river of time, to watching the centuries pass by us in an endless dance, but we still seek an anchor, some structure to inform us of who we are, who we've become, who we used to be. The number of times I'd held that little meteorite, thumbed its pitted texture, was beyond counting: remembering my childhood, my family, my earliest home. I'd had it when I'd taken my degree in architecture. I'd had it when I got married, but I didn't have it anymore. What Krupp had torn away was a souvenir, a trinket, but it had been me.

Archie finally said what I could not, "Mo had his first talisman mounted on his shoulder. When he was injured, the talisman was lost." She spoke in a quiet, calm voice, but the effect her words had was immediate and profound.

Were we a cursed ship now? To look at the faces of the crew one might have thought so. Our experience of the universe was too vast for us to really be superstitious, but still, I knew how they felt. Not just any talisman—my first talisman.

Tamika asked me, "What ... what was it? What did you—"

"It was just a little, a little ..." I felt funny naming it, but there was no reason they shouldn't know. "It was a little piece of meteorite I found on ... found back when I was a ... on Mars. When I was ..."

"Your first life?" Jemal asked.

"Yeah," I said, "Listen, it's—I'm sorry. I didn't mean to ... I mean it's just a ... just a little piece of ... I didn't mean to make everybody ..."

Yuri caught my eye. He cocked his head to one side and tried to smile, but I could tell it was forced. The joviality in his voice was forced, too. "Hey, it's a rock. There are lots of rocks. We'll get you another one."

"Yeah," I nodded, "Yeah."

"Mo, I'm so very sorry." Steel's rich voice poured out like scented oil and I was amazed at how, even now, even after all that had happened, it could warm me, soothe me, flow over me and into me. I looked in her eyes and saw a sea of tears trembling there, threatening to spill over. "I owe you so much, and now this. I can't—I don't know how—I'm so very, very sorry."

I looked at the floor, at my feet, anywhere but into her eyes. "Yeah, well, let's— It's okay. I'm okay. Let's just—" I sat back down. "So you can't tell me anything about Krupp. Okay. Maybe I already know everything I need to know about him. What's next on the agenda?"

The exigency of the present overcame the injuries of the past. We all took a collective breath and tried to move on. Steel looked at the table, at her hands, maybe, or maybe her sins and said, "Well ... well. Krupp wants to know where we're going. So do I." She turned to Yuri. "What have you come up with, Yuri?" she asked, "Where are we going?"

Yuri looked up from a doodle he'd been pulling out of a water ring on the table. "What? Oh, where are we going. Right." He seemed to put thoughts of lost talismans aside and turn to thoughts that didn't feel any more pleasant to him. "Well, um, I've been thinking about the problem. You know, the, uh, the behavioral problem with the Brainardites ... the Brainardites ..." Yuri was definitely darker somehow, not his normal fatalistic self, and his reference to 'Brainardites' seemed kind of formal. We'd been referring to them as 'the slugs.'

"Yes?" Steel prompted.

Yuri looked back at his doodle. "Yeah, it's ... it's not so much an engineering problem as it is a, you know, question of policy. Of procedure."

"Procedure?" Steel queried.

"Well, yeah. More like, I guess, what they used to call 'rules of engagement.' "

"I don't follow."

Marcus said, "It's an old military term."

"Military ... law enforcement ..." Yuri offered.

"We know what the phrase means," interjected Archie, "How does it apply?"

Yuri glanced at Archie, then exchanged looks with Marcus, Tamika, Jemal. He spoke, "Well, I was thinking that you could call the incident with Drake their first interaction with us. Sort of."

Steel looked around at the rest of the crew, looked for attitudes, thoughts, opinions. Tamika said, "Maybe they *have* noticed us."

Archie said, "How? How would they have noticed us? We haven't found any sensory organs—"

"Heat, vibration, I don't know," Yuri interrupted, "maybe the stuff that causes the plague lets them know that something new has entered their environment—"

"But why now?" Steel asked, "Why would they wait so long—"

"I don't know," Yuri answered, "I don't know. It's just ... It's just ... what if it *was* a response to us? A, a directed action? Rational? Pre-meditated?"

Jemal said, "What if they don't want us to be there?"

Steel studied them all for a long time. But it was Archie who spoke, "I'm sorry. I just can't accept that. You're conjuring up an animosity that we have no evidence for."

Marcus started to respond but Steel held up her hand to silence him. She said, "I know that in Drake we lost a colleague, a friend. It was a tremendous shock to all of us. But to extrapolate from that one event—"

Archie interrupted, "Brainard made five sorties to the surface. *We* made over twenty. None of the slugs so much as changed direction. Draco and the Pleiades have observed them for half a millennium from orbit. They've seen nothing that could be interpreted as conflict. No violence, no predation, no—"

"No rapid motion of any kind," Yuri broke in, "I know. Until our last visit to the surface."

Archie and Steel contemplated that for a moment, then Arch said, "But ... but what's their motivation? Why would they be mad at us? We haven't, we haven't done anything to them—"

"Sorry," Yuri said, "I didn't mean to say that they're mad at us. I have no idea how they feel about us or if they feel about us. But suppose ... suppose they're starting to notice us, to respond to us. Maybe they're mad at us, maybe they love us and the slug thought it was shaking hands with Drake. I don't see that it makes any difference. The point is that their behavior has become dangerous to us. We can't communicate with them. If they start to do something that will compromise the E-suits we can't ask them to stop."

Archie asked, "You want us to learn their language? How? We've been trying to do that for five hundred years."

Yuri didn't respond. He just kept dragging his finger through the ring of water on the table, stretching it into a reclining eight: the symbol for infinity.

As Steel observed this she softened. Her countenance changed to one of concern, almost compassion. "What is it, Yuri," she asked. "What are you thinking?"

He continued to trace his finger around the symbol, his eyes focused on something very far away and very sad. Marcus eventually spoke for him: "We've been discussing this regularly while you were on Eden, Captain. Trying to come up with some way to deal with this. Manufacturing environmental suits that are somehow infinitely durable or impenetrable is simply not possible. To make them even incrementally tougher than they already are sacrifices mobility, dexterity. Never mind knee joints or hip joints, how do you design gauntlets that could withstand unpredictable amounts of force? We'd end up in hardened barrels with walls a foot thick. We couldn't move."

"Robots?" Steel asked.

Yuri spoke, "Same problem we had last time. We can't send robotic machines down to the surface. Anything quick enough, agile enough, adaptive enough to handle the environment down there, the tasks we have in mind, would have to be organic. It would have to have at least a rudimentary Farrellian brain. It would have to be conscious of itself. And we'd have to shield it as thoroughly as we would ourselves or the plague would simply destroy it."

"But, Yuri," Steel responded in her gentlest voice, "we have to go back there. Our work isn't finished—"

"I know, I know," Yuri said. "I have an idea that might—I mean, I know a guy who ..." Yuri thought for a moment, "There's this place. It's a kind of sculpture garden—"

"A *sculpture* garden?" Archie asked.

Tamika replied, "Have you heard of Plato Park?"

"In the outer arm," Jemal added.

"The far outer arm," Yuri amended. "New Moorea."

"I don't think I have," said Steel.

"Well," Yuri responded, "New Moorea has five small moons, tiny. They're all clustered together. They probably started out as a single moon that was torn apart by tidal forces. The largest is only fifteen or twenty klicks across. This guy I know noticed that the smallest was kind of tetrahedral, you know, like a pyramid? Another was vaguely cubical. The other three were more spherical, but it gave him an idea that he's been working on for the last century or so."

"What?" Steel asked.

"Well, he's into the history of mathematics and philosophy and stuff and he thought it would be fun, or funny, or ironic or something if he carved them into the five Platonic solids. You know, tetrahedron, cube, octahedron, dodecahedron ... what's the other one?"

Marcus answered, "Icosahedron."

"Right," Yuri went on, "anyway, you know, ideal shapes floating in space and all that. That's the joke. Just another one of those ideas that started as a bar bet."

"Okay, Yuri," Steel said. "Once again I'm way behind you. What does this have to do with our mission?"

"Well ..." He didn't go on. Marcus stepped in:

"Yuri told us that this person ... What was his name?"

"Eddie," Yuri answered.

"Yes," Marcus went on, "He's developed a very powerful, compact tool for doing the sculpting: a high-powered laser, but small, portable." Marcus checked out Yuri's attitude; Yuri was staring at the table. "Yuri thinks we could use these lasers as defensive ... um, defensive ..." Marcus cleared his throat, "defensive weapons."

"Weapons?" Archie asked. " 'Weapons'? We don't want to fight them—"

"Of course not," Yuri responded. "I was just thinking that ... that if we had had something like this when Drake went down we could have ... we could have cut through the slug's pseudopod before ... before his suit was holed."

No one spoke for a time as Steel and Archie digested this idea. I understood why. 'Weapon' was another concept that had just faded away after the war. We didn't have weapons anymore. Why would we? What would we do with them? I had just been reminded of what people did with weapons.

Yuri went on, "The cutting rate and accuracy of these things are very high. Better than any construction tools I know of." His gaze went back to his doodle on the table. When he spoke again it was in a quieter voice, "I thought about modifying ... modifying surgical ... you know, surgical ..." He stopped.

"Yuri, are you all right?" Steel asked. He was looking a little pale.

"Yeah, I'm fine. I'm fine." He looked around the table, "If anyone can come up with a better idea, I'm open. This is the best I've got."

CHAPTER 28

Alice continued to be a little distant from everyone—not surprising after what she'd been through—but still, I was glad when she came up to me after the third boost watch and asked if I wanted to have some sex. She did it in a very fortieth century way. As we left the control room I noticed she was walking a little stiffly. She stretched a little and said, "My back is killing me. Hey, Mo, you want to have some sex?"

I answered, "Sure. How about I give you a massage first?"

She said, "Sounds great," and we headed for her cabin.

As we walked down the corridor I couldn't help but think how different she would have been if she'd never left Eden. If we'd both been Edenites, she never would have asked me and if she had I would have said something like, 'Get out of here! I'm old enough to be your father.' Which wasn't true. My having sex with Alice was more like Eleanor of Aquitaine having sex with me—I mean, you know, if Eleanor had taken better care of herself. But following her around the curving hallway on Steel's personal starship boosting for the edge of the galaxy it didn't seem racy or ribald; it just seemed, I don't know, reasonable.

As we entered her room she stripped down and jumped on her bunk, lying face down. I sat beside her and started to rub her back.

After a little while I asked, "How're you holding up?"

My thumbs tracing up each side of her spine expelled the air from her lungs. She answered, "Okay."

"Yeah?" I pulled down the sides of her ribcage. "You've had quite a ride."

"I suppose. It's the only one I've ever been on." Laying my palms on her glutes, my thumbs on her sacrum, I ploughed a little pile of skin and fat toward her shoulders. She sighed, "I really thought he'd be gone when we got there. You know? After it took so long to get back from Brainard's Planet I ... I thought we'd be too late. I never thought I'd get to see him again."

I walked my fingertips up her traps from her shoulders to the base of her skull. "Yeah, I'm glad you did." Splaying my fingers, I raked down from her shoulders, across her glutes, down the back of her thighs and calves, over her heels and the bottoms of her feet, finally grabbing her toes and pulling, lengthening her. "It must have been tough, though. Emotionally, I mean."

She thought for a moment. Then, "It was just so *sad*. He'd never been anywhere, never seen anyplace but Nazareth. Except for that one camping trip we took when I was little, out to the coast to see the forest—he just, he just lived in his little town. You remember when he wanted to go up and look at the stars? To see where I'd been?"

"I remember." I pushed back up to her neck and into her hair, kneading her scalp.

"That was just so sad."

I worked on her a little longer, until she seemed ready to move on to other things. She flipped over on her back and said, "Hey, you want to log on while we do it?"

"Sure," I smiled. Melding telepathically while you're melding physically can be very intense, but it produces an incredible sense of intimacy, of closeness, maybe safety more than anything else. It can be really hilarious—you can't control what you're thinking while you're in the throes of passion and some of it can be downright funny, particularly in light of what your partner is thinking. But it's also very erotic. We logged on and got comfortable:

The first thing ... the first thing is the infinite mirror of her eyes: reflection upon reflection, thought upon thought. I see her eyes being gazed into by mine being gazed into by hers being gazed into by mine ... her beautiful eyes, almond shaped like Steel's, Steel's eyes that she gave to John Cheatham that John and Steel gave to Alice. That they gave to Alice's brother. I see Jacob Cheatham's face laughing on a ski slope in Gstaad: Alice's brother, her older brother, lost—no. Happier times. Happier times. Bavaria. Motes dancing in shafts of sunlight that bounce off columns of porphyry in a golden hall. Living in a castle! The tallest spire reminds her of an erect penis. We laugh. We caress and feel the skin of the other feeling our skin. And time passing and all the time in the world and not enough time and no time at all as I enter her and feel her being entered as I feel her experience my experience of entering. And she is so young, so new, as I was, as my wife was as I first entered her as I gave my eyes to her, my heart and all that I was and the love that transcended and could not end, would not end, didn't have to end, but—no. No. Happier times. Alice's first time. Her first time with the servant on the Marienbrucke behind the castle with the falls thundering underneath. The Marienbrucke where Krupp had ripped my past away and Steel had ripped Alice's past away and I lost my youth and she lost her youth, her childhood defined by endless desert and my childhood defined by endless desert, only her sky was blue and mine was pale salmon. But time, time was passing and the end was waiting, looming. The party in Katmandu and lights and dancing and Yuri, Yuri who made her laugh who made me laugh and we laughed at Yuri or with him or of him and FREEWHEELING! to Circe and seeing Aunt Archie and Uncle Drake again—only they weren't aunt and uncle on Circe, only on Eden.

This went on for some time. We roamed and frolicked within each other and enjoyed each other and discovered each other. Who knows what all we thought. Passionate minds are kaleidoscopic. After a while we were sweaty and panting and lying side by side.

In time Alice spoke. What she said made me sad and made me smile. Her voice was creamy and relaxed: post-coital. What she said was, "You're wife was very pretty. I don't think any woman can be as pretty as she looks to a man who loves her."

"I don't know ..." Exposure is always a tricky thing for me. I never know if what people are seeing is what is actually there.

"I like looking at me through your eyes," she continued. "I'm not as pretty as your wife, but I'm a lot prettier than I think I am."

Like Matessa in Kindu who was leaving life, I didn't want to deny Alice anything, just in case she was leaving, too. "My wife wasn't pretty," I said, "she was beautiful." I looked into her eyes, just *her* eyes, now. "You're beautiful, too."

She dropped her gaze to my chest. "Hmm," she said, "'beautiful' seems like such a big word for a face."

"I'm not talking about her face. And I'm not talking about yours."

"Oh." And we lay in each other's arms for a while. Then, "So ... Mom told you—I mean Steel told you—anyway, you know that I'm— that Steel is ..."

"Oh," and I remembered remembering, "you picked up on that?" Like I said, you can't control what you think in the throes of passion. "Yeah, we had quite a conversation."

Alice ran her fingers through the hair on my chest—hair that had been scales when she first met me. "She can be pretty difficult at times. I'm not really sure what her relationship to the truth is."

This brought a completely unedited response from my diaphragm; I think it was a laugh, or something like one. Alice laughed a little, too. But then I said, "It was startling seeing Steel through *your* eyes, I mean, back when you were little. I thought I was looking at you, at first, but then I realized I couldn't be." Which brought up heredity, which reminded me of something but not something I could ask Alice. "I wonder how often she changes her appearance."

"Probably too often."

"And seeing John, I mean, your dad ... when he was younger." I looked down at her. "You really loved him, didn't you?"

"He was my dad." She said it simply. I thought of my father and knew what she meant. She seemed to ponder something for a while. I waited. Then, very quietly, she said, "He shot himself, huh? And Aunt Louise?"

My heart sank, "Oh, no." Why had I agreed to go online with her? Damn it. DAMN it! Can't I do anything right? "I'm so sorry, Alice. I shouldn't have—I didn't want you to—"

"It's okay." She lay her head on my chest. "It's okay. I'm glad I know." She made no sound but I felt tears. "You think he did it so we could get away? So I could get away?"

"I—" I remembered something Yuri had said, "I think he loved you more than life. I think he would have done anything for you. Anything he could. This was the best he could come up with."

She thought for a while. Finally she said, "People keep doing things for me."

"They want to help," I responded.

"They all want to keep me alive. Mom—Steel ... You know, she wouldn't let us call her mom anymore when we got to Earth? We had to call her Steel. Everybody acted so crazy there, on Earth, at Neuschwanstein. So strange." She rolled away from me and stared at the overhead. "Or maybe everybody acts crazy on Eden. I don't know. I don't know anything anymore. It seems like the more I learn, the more places I go, the more confusing the whole thing is."

You've got that right, I thought, but what I said was, "I don't think it gets any easier as you get older."

She looked up at me with one of her wonderful lop-sided smiles, so much like Steel's. "Well, I guess *you* should know," she said, digging me in the ribs.

"Nice!" I answered, "Age jokes! After that back rub I gave you!"

She laughed and started tickling me. I don't think I'd been tickled in a thousand years.

I slept well that night, better than I had in a while. No nightmares.

My intimacy with Alice had an unexpected effect on me. It threw into contrast the distance that had opened between me and the rest of the crew. It made me angry. Steel had finally sucked me in—into her world of equivocations and secrets. Yuri seemed upset about something but I didn't feel I could talk with him about it for fear of what *I* might reveal in return. Who could I tell what? Steel's maternity was so bizarre in modern terms yet so sacred in ancient ones. Her marriage, her betrayal. The entire effect Archie's research had had on the little town of Nazareth. How could I talk about any of it? What would I say? Like Steel had said, I had been there in the old, *old* days. I had experienced families and children but even so the idea that she had been *pregnant*, that she had delivered Alice and her brother into the world and then—and then taken them away from their father ... I didn't know how to handle it. It ate at me the whole trip.

I could see the effect it had on everyone else, as well. There weren't any more free-ranging bull sessions in the common room when we came off watch, and I don't think it was just thoughts of my lost talisman that darkened the mood. We were still jazzed coming off the nav net—you couldn't help but be—but our conversations struggled and died; there were too many places we couldn't go, things we couldn't say. We had broken into two camps: Marcus, Yuri, Jemal and Tamika in one, Steel, Archie and me in the other. Alice was the only one of us who seemed to be able to travel freely between the two.

I finally corralled Archie as we came off the last watch backing down into New Moorea. We had a few days before we docked at Plato Park and I *had* to talk to someone. I'd been spending most of my off-duty time alone in my cabin.

Before Eden we might have just stopped for tea in the common room, but now she took me to her quarters. As she closed the hatch behind me she asked, "What's on your mind?"

I looked at her face. She looked so tired. Her eyes looked like they were made out of sand. Or salt. "I need to ... I need to talk to somebody ..."

"That's why we're here," she sat on her bunk, "unless you want to have sex. Or we could do both. Simultaneously or consecutively. You could give me a hand." I looked at her missing arm and tried to laugh at her joke, but I couldn't. "What's up?" she asked.

"What's up," I echoed, rubbing my forehead. "What's up. I'm having trouble, um, I'm feeling kind of isolated. Feeling kind of isolated ..."

"From who?"

I looked up at her. "Haven't you noticed the change in the crew since we got back? I ... I ..."

Archie sighed, "I think the stress is starting to take its toll. We're facing some pretty dangerous times—"

"It's not that. It's—" Then I thought, maybe she was right. The Brainardites. Krupp. Dangerous times. We were looking at the possibility of losing a lot more than a limb. But that wasn't it. "It's the secrecy, the, the—" Shiva. Secrecy. I realized I hadn't even told Archie the truth about John Cheatham's passing. Had Steel? Who knew what? This was insane. I started over: "This, this ... crew. They aren't the crew you had the first time you went to Eden?"

Archie studied me before she responded. "No. Steel put this group together when we decided to go to Brainard's Planet."

"So they don't—none of them know ... what happened, what you did on Eden?"

She studied me longer this time. "No," she said.

I sighed, "Well, I do know, and it's tearing me up. I don't feel like I can talk about it with any of them."

"Talk about it? What do you know that you can't tell them?"

I looked into her eyes. "Steel, or should I say 'Estelle,' told me ... told me about her marriage, her children ..."

Archie inhaled, looked at the deck, exhaled. "I see."

What did I want to ask? "Is—is—Why did you—Is she some kind of amateur anthropologist or something?"

"What? What do you mean?"

"I mean why? Why did you want Steel with you on Eden? The first time you went. Why was she down there in the first place?"

"What makes you think I wanted her down there?"

"Well, it was *your* project—"

"She was the money. She wanted to come." Archie didn't disguise the anger in her answer, "You think I didn't know it was a mistake? A risk?" Words poured out of her now. "I had a solid approach, a well thought-out methodology. Drake and I were a team. We were going to infiltrate Eden's culture posing as a married couple. A. Married. Couple. A stable social unit. Eden's elaborate sexual taboos would have kept us from having intimate entanglements with any of the natives. We didn't have children, of course, but that wasn't unheard of there. We knew we'd be the objects of mild sympathy, nothing more. We had a good chance, a *good* chance, of living among them for decades. Enough time to really understand them."

"So ... so ... What? It was just a, a lark? A whim on Steel's part? She just—"

"No, no," she sighed and rubbed her forehead. "I don't want to misrepresent her. She was definitely interested in the research. Very interested. Profoundly so." She shook her head, "That was the problem. Once she got involved there was no keeping her out of it."

"What did she want to learn?"

"What did any of us want to learn? How it worked. What it was like. I don't know, ask her."

I looked at the bulkhead, but what I saw was Alice waving goodbye to her father. "It all seems so pointless."

"What?"

I raised my head to look at her tired eyes. Did I want to tell her? I guess I did: "You know John Cheatham didn't have a heart attack."

"He didn't?"

"He shot himself. He shot Louise and then he shot himself."

I guess I wanted to shock her, and she was shocked, I could tell, but only for a moment. Then I could see her mind working, processing something. When she finally spoke it was to herself, "Murder-suicide. Classic." Then to me, "He thought Louise was going to the police?"

"That's the way it looks to me."

She mulled that over for a while. "Classic," she said, again more to herself than me, "classic male aggression response."

I was stunned. "That –?" I started, "That's what you think is important? His response?"

"I'm sorry," she answered, "I don't want to seem cold. Of course it was an awful way for Louise to, to die. I know I was angry with her, for her prejudices and her behavior, but those weren't really her fault. She certainly didn't deserve *this*. She was subjected to incredible pressures from the culture she was in." She sighed, "Unfortunately, it was precisely this kind of behavior that we went to Eden to study."

"What kind of behavior?" I wasn't sure I wanted to know.

She answered me as though the answer was too obvious to require stating: "The violence inherent in a male dominated society."

I couldn't say anything. I couldn't respond. I just sat there and stared at her, amazed. Dumbfounded. She finally said, "What? What's the matter?"

"You," how could I put this? I didn't know how to put it. It just came out: "You destroyed John Cheatham's life."

"Mo," she said, "you just told me that John destroyed Louise's life. Remember? He shot her. He murdered her. That's what you said. I didn't put the gun in his hand. I didn't tell him to pull the trigger. That was his decision. He made it. And he made it in a classically male fashion."

I felt like I was talking to an alien from one of Yuri's old movies, like Arch was made out of silicon, or, or dark energy or something. "Did *you* make any decisions?" I asked her, "In a 'classically' female fashion or otherwise?"

"What do you mean?"

"Did you decide to go to Eden? Did you decide to take Steel with you so you could use her money to fund your research? Did you decide to destroy John Cheatham's family? To take his children away from him?"

Archie hung her head in exasperation and exhaustion, "Mo, Mo, listen to the terms you're using. *His* children. *His* family. These are archaic concepts."

"They weren't archaic to *him*."

"Okay," she nodded, "Okay, that's fair. But in order for the project to go forward compromises had to be made—"

"They didn't *have* to be made. You chose to make them."

She looked at me hard. Then she said, "Do you really think the research we did on Eden wasn't worth it? You were there. You saw the children, the culture. You think it wasn't worth the price?"

I stood up, "You didn't *pay* the price! John Cheatham did. He's *dead*. At his own hand. Do you understand what has to ... what has to happen to a person to motivate them to do something like that? Steel married him, left him. You took his children." What could I tell her? What could I say that would get through to her? "When you did that his culture turned on him. He was a pariah. He had no one. You destroyed his *life*."

"Mo, if Steel wanted to leave him she had the right to do it. And even if he hadn't ... hadn't committed suicide he only would have lived a few more years. He was going to die anyway—"

"That's the point, Archie. He had only a few decades to live. Only a few, precious decades and *you* destroyed them."

"How?"

I couldn't believe she didn't understand this. "He lost his wife, his children, everyone he loved." Did she understand love? Did she think men didn't love? How could she be this disconnected? "You made it impossible for him to be a part of his own community. He had no friends, no family, no loved ones, *nothing*. I know they're not on the net there but they still have a ... a common, a common sense of ... of each other. You took that away from him. What did he have left? Didn't you see the man I saw when we were there? Didn't you see that broken, empty, lonely, lost human being?"

Did this finally touch her? I didn't know. She thought a long time before she responded. When she did her posture changed. She was softer, less belligerent than before: "I saw him. I ... I knew time had changed him but ... I ... I know what you're—I mean I ... I saw him."

"Do you really think your actions didn't have an effect on him? I mean, what do you think he is?"

"But, Mo, men don't—I mean, he was—Wait a minute. Wait a minute." I could see ideas tumbling into each other behind her eyes. "Our actions, of course our actions affected him. But he—he was ... I mean, do you really think he was, he was—?"

"He was what? In love with Steel? Missing his family? Distraught over saying goodbye to his daughter again? Archie, he's a human being, like you or me. Or at least he was. And I'll bet you that if he hadn't shot Louise we'd all be rotting in a Nazarene jail right now."

"Just because we benefited from a criminal act doesn't mean it wasn't criminal."

"I'm not saying that! But, holy frickin Buddha, you act like he's some ... some specimen ... some, some sub-human form of life."

I saw anger boiling up in Archie, but the anger was checked by doubt. The anger was old, ancient, but the doubt was new. She warred with herself for a moment, but something occurred to her, something she hadn't thought of before. I could tell it bothered her, scared her, maybe. I took a chance and said one more thing to her, "More importantly, Archie, you act like you had no part in this crime. In a very real sense you did put the gun in his hand. If you and Steel and Drake hadn't gone to Eden, none of this would have happened. Can't you see that?"

She looked at me like a defendant staring down a prosecutor, but her doubt was still there. When she finally spoke it was haltingly, hesitantly, but with the determination of a scientist gnawing at a difficult problem. "The net," she said, "No one's on the net there. Maybe ... maybe we didn't ... Maybe we weren't able to feel ..." Something crossed her face, opened her features. When she spoke again it was in a quieter voice, but one of discovery, of wonder. "I never felt that John was ... We couldn't, we couldn't relate to them the way we ... I mean, I never thought of John the way I think of you or Yuri, Marcus or Jemal. I didn't think of him the way I thought of Drake. I think of you as people. I thought of John as ... as a, a man, a male, different from me, separate from me ... dangerous to me. The other, the, the enemy, even." Her face opened in wonder, in horror. In an even quieter voice, she said, "Oh, no. Oh, no. That's the other behavior we went there to study."

"What behavior?"

Archie put her remaining hand on her head, closed her eyes. "Shiva. *Shiva*. I missed it. I missed it."

"What, Archie?" I sat beside her, "What did you miss?"

"Assumptions. Assumptions." She was really beating herself up.

"What are you talking about? What assumptions?"

She stood up, "Why we were there! Why we told ourselves we were there." Her face closed in anguish. There wasn't room to pace in her cabin, but I could tell she wanted to. "We told ourselves we were going to Eden to help figure out why the war started."

"The Pleiadean—I mean, the War of –?"

"But that wasn't quite the truth. Oh, *Shiva*! I missed it!" She pounded the heel of her hand into her forehead. "The truth was we assumed we *knew* why the war started. We were only going to Eden to confirm our position. We 'knew' ... we 'knew' ..." She turned to me for solace, for grace.

"You thought Draco started the war?"

"We ... we assumed we 'knew' ... that the war started because of male aggressiveness. Behavior that was inherently male. But, you see? That's ... that's a perfect example of the other behavior we went there to study."

"What, sexism?"

She collapsed into herself. "Yes. Gender bias. But *we* defined gender bias as *male* gender bias. We didn't say it, or even think it, but that's how we defined it. It was so ingrained in our way of thinking we just ... we just didn't look for it in women. And I missed it. I missed it in *us*." She was rocking now, her hand to her mouth, her eyes blurry with water. "We, we got to Eden and the old ways ... the old ways were everywhere. The mistrust. The fear. Fear of violence, fear of rape ... fear of men. I—I identified with the women. But that's why I had Drake with me, to, to balance our perspective." She looked really puzzled, "But he didn't ... he didn't seem to—"

I hung my head and laughed like a condemned man. "Drake was just as willing to blame men for everything as you were. Right?"

Surprise brought Archie's eyes to mine, "That's right. He ... How did you—"

"After all these centuries," I said, and I felt like every one of them was piled on my back, "All the pain, all the fighting, the posturing and rhetoric and vitriol and, and Jesus, even the war. The freaking war and everything that happened and sexism is still too precious to give up."

"Precious? Precious to whom?"

I stared into the abyss of human folly. "To us. You, Drake, men, women. All of us, every freaking one of us."

"I don't know what you mean."

"Without sexism," I looked at her with true sadness, "we are forced to face the horror of equality."

"Horror? We've known for centuries that women and men are equal, millennia—"

"Have we? Is that what we've known? If women are equal to men they're equal in venality as well as nobility. In stupidity as well as wisdom. In weakness as well as strength. That's the horror. If women are merely *equal* to men, there's no safety anywhere. The world won't be a better place if women run it; women are just men shaped a little differently. There's no one to run to, no bosom to hide in. We human beings are all we've got. Better to think that women are just 'kind of' equal to men. Equal but different, equal but better, more sensitive, less aggressive, just plain nicer." I simultaneously grieved for our foolishness and wondered at our ability to survive, "So you identified with the women and Drake identified with the women, too, huh?"

"I ... Maybe ... maybe you're right. I don't know. I think he did identify with the women. Or if he didn't he certainly didn't, didn't identify with— I mean, I assumed it was because ... because he *knew* that men were—Oh, Shiva. You're right. You're right. There it is. We assumed ... I brought Drake into the project *because* he agreed with my assumptions. I wouldn't have brought him in otherwise. It wasn't just Drake. I didn't realize they were assumptions. I thought they were facts because everyone around me thought they were facts." She collapsed back on the bunk beside me. "I missed it, Mo. I just *missed* it."

I put my arm around her. I think she needed the contact. She leaned her head on my shoulder as she said, "You have to understand, Mo, the war ... the war was horrible. Horrifying. Women had never started a war before. It became vital to our ... our image of ourselves that we hadn't started this one."

I remembered talking with Lysistrata-24 as we walked through the archives on Circe, "It's pretty hard to say who actually started the war—" I think I was trying to make her feel better.

"It doesn't matter," she cut me off, "It doesn't matter who fired the first shot." She turned to me. "We had created our own culture, our own nation. A purely feminine nation. No men in government, no men in any positions of power. We were in the process of deporting all men, purging ourselves of what we called 'masculine energy.' But even so, the first time we came into conflict with another human organization, another nation, it devolved into violence and destruction. We failed to *avoid* war. We failed to prevent it."

I rubbed her shoulder. "As the saying goes, you were only human. Preventing a war is a lot harder than it looks." I was starting to understand. It was tragic, but I think I was starting to understand. "So ... so you went to Eden to ... to validate your—"

"We went to Eden with our own set of prejudices." She shook her head. "Maybe I should have ... Drake had lived on Circe for centuries. He worked right there at the Institute."

"The Antigone—?"

"Yes. Maybe I should've used someone else. I thought it would be enough that he was a man, but ... but Drake agreed with me on *everything*. We were, we were simpatico, tuned into each other. Maybe I should have gotten someone from Draco, from Earth, maybe, or someone like you. Someone who had a different perspective, a different agenda. A different bias."

"Maybe. I don't know."

"When Steel wanted to save the children— Listen to me. 'Save the children.'" She laughed, "We wanted to save them from dying. The Edenites wanted to save them from not dying." Memories returned to her, touched her, softened her. "John just wanted Steel to be happy. His 'wife.' " It was painful to hear her say the word 'wife.' She said it like it had been said to me so many times back when I was married. Like the very idea of having a wife was contemptible, pathetic. " 'Estelle,'" she said, in the same tone. "It was almost comical. Her name was like some mystical song to him, yet he put her through childbirth."

I tried to swallow whatever bile was rising up in me. After all, it had been a long time since I'd been married. But I couldn't keep silent. The anger slipped out, "You might want to curb your judgment. Unless you've actually been in that situation."

"Situation?"

"Married. To someone you love. Who loves you. It's not really something you can look at from the outside and understand what's going on. Isn't that why you went to Eden in the first place? To try to understand that stuff? It sounds like you pre-judged a lot more than who causes wars."

She looked at me, then looked at the deck. "I don't know. Maybe so. We tried, Mo, we really did. I tried, but I was a product of my culture, too." Something made her sad, ashamed. "In the end, he just wanted her to get what she wanted." She shuddered at a memory, "But none of us, none of us gave even a thought to what John might have wanted." I could tell she was recalling conversations, confrontations that had taken place years ago. "It wasn't, it wasn't just that we knew the children would die if they stayed there with him. It was," she looked at her lap and shook her head again, "it was that he was male. A man. We simply assumed his desires would spring from ... I don't know ... from baser instincts, more primitive, more, more violent, possessive instincts. We just dismissed them. They didn't enter into the discussion at all. If he brought them up I don't think we even noticed." She looked at me: alone, lonely, maybe, or maybe bereft. "We just rode over him. We rode over him. I wouldn't do that to you. I wouldn't. I don't think I would." Then with renewed passion, "It was because it was a male dominated society. We thought that Eden's whole ethos and mores were somehow more primitive than ours because it was a male dominated—"

"How can you keep saying that?" I asked. "What makes you think that Eden's society was male dominated?"

"Well, it's obvious—"

"I saw how it worked. I was there. Men and women went to Eden to build a civilization. They built it and shaped it for the benefit of their children. Men *and* women. Their decisions and attitudes and everything they did shaped their society for the benefit of children, not the benefit of men."

"Perhaps, but men still benefited."

"You talk like men built their culture all by themselves. What did the women do for the last thousand years, just sit around wishing things were different?"

"Mo, men have ways of dominating—"

"You think women are the only people men try to dominate? We try to dominate each other as well. You could write a history of humanity as a series of events where men stood up to other men who were trying to dominate them." I remembered the newbies on Valhalla, fighting alongside them. "Stood up to them and fought them for what they thought was right. Risked injury, risked, risked death, risked *everything*. Are you trying to tell me that women don't have the courage to do that? What, men are aggressive and women are cowards? Is that your position?"

"You don't understand—"

"I understand. I just don't agree with you. It isn't about being dominated. It isn't about being intimidated. My— my— the man I'm named after kicked the most powerful empire on Earth out of his country. Without firing a shot. It isn't about being big or small, strong or weak, loud or soft. People shape their world by the things they do," surprising tears came to my eyes for the things I had done, "and the things they fail to do."

"Mo, men have held the reins of power throughout most of history. They're responsible for almost all of—"

"You remind me of the old days. The old days. Back then everybody looked for a group of people they didn't belong to and then blamed everything on them. Conservatives, anarchists, pacifists, Hindus, patriots, conservationists, women, men—anybody you *weren't* was at fault, was the problem, was what was wrong with the world. It's awfully easy to look at something you don't like and decide it was made by somebody else."

Archie thought about this for a long time before she said, "So ... so you're saying that, that women had as much voice in creating the civilization on Eden as men?"

"I saw their voice everywhere. In their families, in their businesses, in how wealth is distributed, how power is used—"

"Okay. Okay, I think I see what you're saying, but," she looked at me and I could see her scientific curiosity was engaged, "do you think—I mean, I mean, wouldn't that mean that women also had an equal voice in creating the original civilizations on Earth?"

"I don't know," I threw up my hands, "I know the feminists didn't think so, but ... but what's the alternative, Arch? That for thousands of years women just cowered in the corner afraid that men might be mean to them if they spoke their minds? Are women as courageous as men? As brave? As willing to risk violent reprisal, injury, death to stand up for what they believe? For what they think is just and right? Men did that over and over again. They threw off their oppressors or they died trying. Are you saying that women were too timid or, or too weak to do that? To even try? My wife was one of the most courageous human beings I've ever known. My—my mo—my mo—god DAMN it!" Every time I ran into the concept of my maternal parent I had no word. The word I had wasn't the word I wanted, wasn't the word I needed. I shook my head and went on, "If you're courageous enough to be willing to risk everything you have, everything you are, you can't be dominated by anyone, not for long. Certainly not for thousands and thousands of years."

"But, but—" I could see her chewing on the problem, "but why—? Why would women help create a culture where men had all the power?"

I shook my head. "Well, I guess the answer to that question depends on how you define 'power.' Do you think women don't have any power on Eden? Was Louise 'dominated' by John? What about Mrs. Fogarty's daughter and her husband? You know, the couple that ran the boarding house? You think he dominated her? It seemed to me like he just kept his head down and tried to stay out of the line of fire."

Arch thought about that for a while. Then she said, "So you're saying that, that men had some kinds of power and women had other kinds of power and it all sort of balanced out?"

"I don't know. Maybe it's not about power. Maybe the reason women never threw off their oppressors is because they didn't think they were being oppressed. Maybe a woman who was married to a man who spent his whole life down a coal mine trying to support his family didn't think the man was a chauvinist pig, even though he didn't want her to have to work down there with him. Maybe everybody was just doing the best they could. I can't, I can't tell you what ancient Earth was like—I'm not that old—but that's the way it looked to me on Eden. It seemed to me that women had lots of power and men had lots of power and there was an ongoing conversation about how that power would be used. But it was always, *always* ultimately decided by what was perceived to be best for their children. Always."

Archie considered this for a long time before she said, "I'll have to think about this. It's an interesting perspective. I'll ... I'll have to think about it."

I laughed and shook my head, "Actually, it was children that I originally wanted to talk to you about. I mean, before we got, you know, side-tracked."

"Children?"

"Yeah. Our captain's children."

"What ... what about them?"

I considered my words carefully. I wanted to understand what had happened, why it had happened, and at that moment I was feeling closer to Archie than I ever had. Her ability to perceive her own prejudice, her own bias, was very reassuring to me. We'd been through a lot together—she'd nursed me back to health at Neuschwanstein, I'd helped get her down the escarpment on Eden—but I don't think I'd actually trusted her until that moment. Her relationship with Steel was obviously very complex. It was hard to say who was calling the shots and when. And what I wanted to discuss was delicate, had always been delicate back to the beginnings of the craft of human conversation. I finally said, "The thing I can't understand is how. How could Steel get pregnant? Where did she get the eggs? Unless I'm completely off the mark she has to be several centuries past menopause. And unless rich people are completely different from everybody else, she had her eggs harvested before she hit puberty anyway."

Archie didn't say anything for a while. When she did speak she was very careful about what she said. "Steel is very ... um ... wealthy ... I don't think I want to— That is, I think I'd prefer you get this information from her. We ... we had some profound, um, profound disagreements on ... on how to best, uh, proceed." She smiled at me, "I'm sorry. This probably isn't helping very much, is it?"

"Not really," I smiled back, "except for the part about her being wealthy, which I think I already knew." I looked at my hands and wondered. What would I have done had I been Steel? What would I have done had I been an incredibly wealthy, powerful, female human being faced with the opportunity, the challenge, of traveling to a place like Eden? To travel back in time to a previous epoch, as alien to us as anything I could imagine. What would I have done? I couldn't get Archie to say anything more about it.

CHAPTER 29

On black velvet: five jewels sparkled beside an immense jade dome. Plato Park, its geometric components hewn and polished, tumbled metallic in low orbit above the aquamarine hemisphere of New Moorea. The tiny moonlets, works of art in themselves and far too small to produce significant gravity, would not be visited directly by the Lightdancer or any starship. A small fleet of spherical shuttles, gaudy bubbles in primary colors powered only by Musadhi graviton impellers, communicated between the moons and any visitors. They also served to carry laborers, material and supplies up from and down to the surface of the planet.

One was carrying us toward an unfinished, nickel-iron icosahedron. Through the panoramic view port of our shuttle we could see it rotating slowly, miniature in the distance, beyond its polished companions. Triangles faceted one third of the moon, the remainder was still pitted and cratered. Yuri's friend Eddie had agreed to meet us in his workshop on this final piece of his homage to Platonic idealism.

He would not meet all of us. As always, when the Lightdancer was in space, one of us—in this case a very special one of us—stayed behind, floating in the habitation module as the ship fell around New Moorea. The image of her tousled hair drifting around her face as she bade us goodbye was engraved on my memory.

We gazed into infinite blackness as geometry rolled toward us. What was diminutive for moons was colossal for sculpture: jewels grew to toys, to houses, to mountains: a tetrahedral pyramid with edges four kilometers long swelled toward us, loomed over us, fell past us, lit the awe in our faces with silver light glinting off endless planes, endless plains. We fell into the garden.

She should see this, I thought. She might not get another chance. She should get a chance to see everything. No one gets to see everything, but she should get a chance, she should get a chance—

The next moon, cubical, was even larger, but scale was beyond comprehension, distance ungraspable. Each square face was vaster than a small county: perfect, featureless, mirroring the bottomless cosmos or the watery surface of New Moorea or the blinding fire of its star as the mirrors turned. The absurd afterthought of the microscopic bubble in which we traveled drifted past, affecting nothing.

"I wish Alice would have come." Steel was worrying, as I was, as I suppose we all were. Her features were lit from below by control panel displays. Ham was strapped in beside her, hairy arms wafting in microgravity. That had been a problem. Ever since we'd heard that Krupp was back online Steel kept Ham with her always, but he could only be in one place at a time.

The conversation before we'd left the Lightdancer had been short and confrontational. Alice was getting tired of all the fuss over her and she was going to do what she was going to do, Steel's concerns notwithstanding. Someone had to stay aboard the ship; Alice elected herself for the job. Well, at least Ham would stay with her. NO! She didn't need Ham to stay with her. She would be FINE. She just wanted to be alone for a little while. OKAY?

That sort of thing.

So Alice was alone, unprotected, floating around on a starship falling through space and somewhere in that same space was a hypertrophied body-builder with anger management problems and I couldn't do a damned thing about any of it.

"Alice will be all right," Arch offered, but it landed on barren ground. Where Steel had once seemed merely unattainable, she was now unavailable. Under siege from Krupp or from her own emotions, we couldn't tell. Her communication with us had become terse and barely functional. I knew she was grieving. I don't know what the rest of the crew thought.

Take the great pyramid at Giza and make it twice the height of Everest. Mate it to its twin—base to base. Polish each face mirror-smooth with just the faintest hint of the swirls of interior geology marring the surfaces. The third monolith, an octahedron, tumbled toward us gigantically, overwhelmingly. We slid past an apex unnoticed.

"Your friend must be quite a guy," I said to Yuri, staring up or out or down at mind-altering mathematics.

"Eddie's a maniac. I like him," Yuri replied. "This stuff is pretty wacked, even for him. I think he's trying to get over a girlfriend or something. I haven't really talked to him in a while. You know, talked."

"Well, he's kept himself busy."

"Yeah."

The fourth sculpture, faces pentagonal, rolled toward us like a fantastic gaming piece, a cosmic twelve-sided die. Blank, unreadable, it told us neither our future nor our past. It was ordered perfection in the chaos of night, serene, knowing, but not speaking. Like so many gods before it, it left us to our own devices, hoping for the best.

As we silently swam through the ether toward the final movement in this celestial opus, the spiritual symmetry of our surroundings caressed us, entered us, coaxed us toward tranquility, balance. But we would not succumb. We couldn't. We were on a quest, all of us, together. Wounded, perhaps, broken in ways, but still bound to a course we would not turn from. Balance was our enemy, dissonance our ally. We needed to keep toppling forward, always forward toward our goal. I looked around at all of us and wondered what I had been like before Steel found me. Could I even remember?

It all came back to Alice. Worries gnawed at me. Unknowns multiplied exponentially as our distance from her grew. Even so, I could understand her resistance to our concern. What a hassle! What a hassle to be that important to people, so important that they constrained your choices in the name of keeping you safe. Keeping her safe, her eyes and her smile and her hands that never quite knew where to go. Keeping her safe.

"How's that arm working?" Yuri asked Arch.

Archie flexed and twisted the smooth machinery that Yuri had manufactured for her on the ship—certainly not as good as a cloned arm, but better than nothing. "It's amazingly graceful," she said. "Elegant. A little heavy, though. I'm having trouble getting used to my new center of gravity. Throws me off balance sometimes."

"Sorry. It was the best I could do—"

"Oh, I'm not complaining. It's kind of wonderful. I just have to get used to it, that's all." She examined it as though it were magical, unreal. No one had seen a prosthetic in centuries. Was it significant to her that a man had made it for her? A male? No, that was unfair to her. She had seen; she had understood. She hadn't been on the net on Eden, hadn't been able to meld with John Cheatham. He had been alien to her. She had felt threatened, afraid, surrounded by strange, unpredictable beings that were different from her. Was that bigotry? Or just xenophobia? Anyway, she had seen.

As the final moon rotated nearer to us, previously unseen details brought the gigantic scale of the project into focus. Tiny scaffolding bordered the carved surfaces, scaffolding built for fleas, for gnats, for microbes. Only two of the immense triangular facets seemed to be finished: polished to an exquisite luster. Three more were in various stages of reduction. Dust and detritus sparkled in the space above the work areas. Insignificant flashes signaled where rock was being cut with coherent light. As the moon continued to turn machined precision was replaced by random desolation, a surface pulverized for thousands of thousands of thousands of years.

In a larger crater a Quonset hut covered in regolith was our destination. From altitude it looked little more than a dust worm on the floor of the impression, but grew as we descended to a hangar capable of housing more than one of the little balls in which we flew.

Marcus said, "I hope he has everything ready. We still need to refuel and resupply consumables before we head out." He didn't say it but we all knew he meant 'head out to Brainard's Planet.' This was our last stop. There was nothing else we could do to delay the trip to our final destination. "Did he tell you where we would be picking up the lasers?" he asked Yuri.

"Yeah. I mean, no he didn't, but I'm sure he'll have them all ... you know, he'll have them. Eddie's all right. It'll be fine." Yuri seemed distracted still, outside of himself somehow, but he didn't seem worried about Eddie coming through. "It'll be fine."

Marcus regarded him with what seemed to be concern, then turned his gaze forward as huge pressure doors opened and we entered the squat structure. After they closed behind us we could hear air filling the compartment before a second set of doors opened and we moved forward into the interior. Our shuttle didn't land so much as it was grappled to the surface. We heard and felt machinery attach to us.

Yuri said, "Hmm. I just thought of something."

"What?" Tamika asked.

His expression attained some of his old quizzical amusement. It was good to see. He said, "I just realized: we're taking ray guns to a planet full of hostile aliens. Hah," he kind of laughed, "Where's Buster Crabbe when you need him, huh?"

We all stared at him blankly.

He looked around at us, "C'mon!" He looked for recognition, but we had none. "Buck Rogers! Flash Gordon! You gotta know who—" But we didn't. He shook his head in despair, "I'm surrounded by philistines."

Maybe he was. We had no idea what he was talking about: some ancient movie? Who knows. He abandoned us as lost causes and hopped online. "Eddie? We're here. Are you around? Eddie?" He waited. And waited.

"Well?" Marcus asked.

"Eddie's okay. It'll be all right." He hopped online again. "Hey, Eddie, pick up. We're here." He listened for a while. "Oh, okay." Then to us, "It's okay. He just forgot we were coming. He's been working. He's on his way."

Marcus rolled his eyes. "Well, what are we supposed to do while we wait?" he asked.

"I dunno. I suppose we could unstrap."

So we did. And the compartment was immediately filled with bouncing bodies. The smallest shove by foot or hand or elbow against anything at all sent us floating into the air to turn and twist and fall ever so slowly back down.

"Ham! Ham, it's all right. It's all right." Steel stroked his head, gazed into his eyes. His panic subsided. "It's all right."

"It'll be all right," Yuri repeated, "Eddie'll be here in a minute."

A hatch opened in the floor of the hangar and a very strange being glided out. Gangly to the point of being spider-like, his hair matted in dreadlocks a meter long that floated out in a starburst around his angular face, a full body tattoo had rendered his skin the color of ripe cherries.

"Eddie!" Yuri shouted and went through the hatch that Jemal had opened. As he hit the floor of the hangar he took a little excited hop that sent him soaring into the air. "Whoa!" he said as he turned completely over before starting to settle back to the decking, "How do you move in this place?"

"Takes practice," Eddie replied with a broad, toothy smile as the rest of us carefully made our way out. As he got closer we could see two little skeletal cages on each of his shoulders, actual bone that had been genetically modified to pierce his skin, like teeth, and form small display cases for scale models of his artwork: tetrahedron and cube floating on the left shoulder, octahedron and dodecahedron on the right.

Yuri noticed this as he came back to earth and grabbed Eddie by the arms. "Hey, nice jewelry! Where you gonna put the fifth one, on your head?" He laughed.

"No, no," Eddie replied, "When the fifth one's finished, I'm leaving. Somebody else can do the advertising. I've been up here for almost two centuries." His voice was broken, patchy, a sustained growl.

"Two?" Yuri asked, "I thought it was only one."

"Where have *you* been?" Eddie asked.

"Oh, you know, here and there." They laughed and hugged each other. "It's great to see you, man."

"Great to see you, too. Come on inside. I'll show you around. Who are your friends? I wasn't expecting so many people."

Yuri introduced us as we skid-floated toward the hatch in the floor. We had barely enough weight to gain any traction. When we'd exchanged names Yuri said, "I can't believe you're actually going to pull this off. How much was the original bet?"

"What, with Soraia?" Yuri nodded. Eddie replied, "Ten DCUs. I'm gonna make her pay up, too."

Yuri cast an assessing eye toward Eddie. "How is Soraia, anyway?"

Eddie's visage darkened a little, not much. "She's all right. I guess she got into astrophysics or something. Went back to school somewhere down in the home worlds. Last I heard she was out beyond Monoceros, studying the Rosette Nebula, I think."

We entered the hatch and started down a descending passageway lased out of the metal interior of the moon. We floated, fell, occasionally putting a hand or foot to wall, ceiling or floor, pushing ourselves along.

"Ten DCUs, huh?" Yuri asked, "How much is this place costing to make?"

"Oh, I don't know. I think it's up around four or five trillion now. You'd be surprised at the different groups that got interested in the project, though. Fundraising's been pretty good. Most of it's being paid for by mining proceeds."

"Oh, right," Yuri answered. "Shaving the surface off these rocks must bring in a nice chunk of change."

"Incredibly high-grade ores, yeah. But it's not just the surface."

"Oh?"

"We hollowed out this whole moon. I'll show you." We'd arrived at the doors of a Musadhi lift. Eddie ushered us inside. "You might want to turn upside down." He did so, pointing his feet at the nominal ceiling. "The lift descends a lot faster than you'd fall here."

As we followed suit Marcus said, "Where are the lasers?"

"Lasers?" Eddie replied. "We got 'em all over the place. Why?"

"Well ..." Marcus looked to Yuri.

Yuri said, "You said we could have some, remember?"

The lift started to descend and we settled to the ceiling. A faint sensation of actual weight became apparent, but it was upside-down weight; our heads were pointed at the center of the moon, yet our weight was on our feet.

"Oh, yeah," Eddie responded, "we ought to have some that will fit your purposes. What are you using them for again?"

This time Steel and Marcus both glared at Yuri. But Yuri was on it: "Come on, Eddie, I told you this. It's this crazy project we're doing. I can't talk about it. It's all proprietary, you know, syndicate stuff. Remember?"

"Right, right," Eddie grabbed a handrail and turned himself over as the lift began to slow. We did the same but not nearly as gracefully. "Sorry, I've been in a million meetings this morning, besides actually trying to get some sculpting done. I'll tell you; this is more like running a corp than making art." He smiled. "I knew I was taking you down to the shop for some reason, I just couldn't remember what it was."

The lift doors opened and we walked out onto a polished metal floor about fifty meters wide. A ceiling of the same material angled away from us, but there were no walls. Eddie led us over to the edge of the floor and we stared into the abyss at the exclamation point marking the end of his geometric thesis. We were standing at the acute junction of three huge structural beams and the interior of the icosohedron. The ceiling faceted gargantuanly away from us in polished triangles five kilometers on a side. Over the edge of the beam and down we saw ... what? A nest, a maze, an Escher etching rendered Brobdingnagian. The beam we were on defined one edge of a dodecahedron that had no sides, a cage of empty pentagons that had been fitted or carved to touch the inside of the icosohedral moon at each apex. And inside that the triangles of an octahedral cage, and inside that a cube and then a tetrahedron and inside them all a shimmering, undulating, transparent crystal sphere a kilometer across that bulged and trembled, wobbled and rippled.

"That's our water supply." Eddie pointed to the sphere far below. "Come on, the shop's this way," and he glided off, skimming the surface of the beam.

There was a tow cable running down the edge of it, nothing more than a metal rope a half-meter off the deck with little hand holds to pull you along. As we made our way through Eddie's masterpiece, floating along from one member to the next, descending into the center of his colossal mathematical filigree, his overpowering expression of symmetry, balance and peace, something odd struck me. Odd not only in what it was but in how it occurred to me. It struck me that not everyone was going with us to face the dangers of Brainard's Planet. Almost everyone wasn't. They were involved in something else, something trivial or profound, stultifying or ecstatic, boringly routine or startlingly unique. Whatever it was, it wasn't fatal or even potentially fatal. They were going on with their lives, which would go on. They were in no danger, none at all. They might be injured or get sick, but they would be fixed, healed, repaired, put back together. They were okay, would be okay, always and forever. How happy, I thought. How happy to be okay, just to be okay. We could all join Eddie and help him finish his sculpture, or go down to New Moorea and find jobs somewhere or run away and join the circus or do something really important but safe, all of us safe.

But Alice wasn't safe. She was under sentence of death and we were going to place ourselves in danger to save her. We wanted Alice to be okay, needed her to be okay.

Had I been okay on Vesper? Shacked up with Sheila, drinking on credit at 'Burbs' place? I had been safe. I had been in no danger, but was I okay? How do we know if we're okay? Was Matessa okay as she was taken away from the people she loved by the uncaring suits at Planetary Tectonics to be brutalized and used for six decades and then released back into the gentle, welcoming arms of Kindu? Was she okay? And what of the poor man on the dock who was so upset at seeing her go?

And what of Alice? What of her genesis? What if what I thought and what Archie had implied was correct? That Steel had, through her wealth and connections, implanted stocked, functioning ovaries in her body, deliberately placing herself in a position to be, to be fertilized, impregnated, to be filled with life and swell with life and bring life into the world. Did that make any difference? What if her motives were noble and enlightened? What if they were self-serving and cynical? Did it make any difference? Would I prefer to have never met Alice? Would I prefer it if Alice had never been brought into the world? Would I be okay now if Steel had never found me? I looked over at her as we floated along, her body so relaxed and fluid, her face so taut with worry or recrimination or anguish.

And the worry and anguish were real. What if something happened on the Lightdancer with Alice there all alone? What if something happened? What if a meteoroid struck or the pressure hull failed or the heating system or the cooling system or the carbon dioxide scrubbers or what if the food on board was tainted or the water recycling system broke down and she was poisoned or sickened and we couldn't get back to her in time? If she ... if she *died* ... if she died, that would be it. She would be gone forever and we couldn't bring her back. We couldn't ever, ever bring her back no matter how much we loved her or how hard we tried. Lost to us. Like John Cheatham, like Louise, like Drake. Like my wife. Lost. Forever.

The friendly banter between Yuri and Eddie seemed more surreal to me than our angular surroundings. Yuri was saying, "Do you realize that not one of these people knows who Buster Crabbe is?"

"You're kidding me. Buster Crabbe? He was one of the first serial stars."

"You don't have to tell me. The only actor of his time to play all three top comic book heroes—"

"You can see his influence throughout the whole century, on Johnny Weissmuller, Steve Reeves, Christopher Reeve, even Mark Hamill and Harrison Ford ..."

And yet, why shouldn't Yuri get to chat with his friend about this and that and nothing much? Why not one last pleasant, idle conversation before we plunged into the toxic, lethal soup of Brainard's Planet?

"They don't watch movies. They don't watch television shows, none of the ancient art forms."

"That's the problem with our culture today. No foundation, no sense of history. I mean the twentieth century was so pivotal. It's the earliest time we have that's actually recorded. We can actually see and hear people who aren't on the net, were never on the net, who had no conception of it, no conception of consciousness or astronomy or mathematics or ethics or even their own perspective, never mind anyone else's."

"That's what I keep saying ..."

It occurred to me that I probably *should* know more about these people. Buster Crabbe, Dotie Foster, Annette—who was it? Yuri's dream woman. If I was ever going to get serious about acting, if I was ever going to catch up with Shaughnessy again, rejoin the troupe, maybe get into reality acting ...

What was I thinking? Would any of that matter? If we lost people on Brainard's Planet or if what we found there couldn't save Alice, would any of the rest of it matter?

We'd made it down to the deepest part of the moon, deposited at the center of one of the beams defining the tetrahedron. We were close enough to the water sphere to hear the slow motion waves tumble and merge. A huge black shape flashed past me to arch up into the air above me, tapered, the white belly ribbed, flukes trailing water.

"Is that—is that a WHALE?" I asked as I watched it slowly tumble end over end, arching through the air, diminishing as it rose.

"Oh, yeah, sorry," Eddie replied. "I shoulda warned you. We have three pods of humpbacks here." It continued to rise and tumble, throwing off slowly wobbling drops of water as it arched over and started to descend. "Of course, they can jump a lot higher under this gravity. They have a lot of fun."

"But, I thought, I mean," I watched it slowly drift downward, down toward the surface of the roiling sphere, "I thought this was fresh water," and enter it, sending out concentric waves that rose and peaked and released sheets and ropes and undulating globes of water that rose and spread and hit the side of the beam we were on and thinned and divided into smaller sheets, thinner ropes, smaller globes.

"Oh, no. Think of it as our ocean. We have a whole hydrologic system here. A climate, if you want to call it that. Look up there." We did. Looking up, you could see that each beam in the nest of shapes had a light trough running down the center of its lower surface. "That's sunlight fed in from ports on the outside. It's the only way you could light a space fifteen kilometers across. The sunlight evaporates the water, gives us weather. It rains in here. Gets cloudy, foggy sometimes. You happened to catch us on a clear day. But when it rains we collect it, use it, clean it, then flush it back into the ocean."

"What do they eat?" Tamika asked.

"What they usually eat. We have a whole marine ecosystem in the sphere. Waste and remains rain down to the center where we collect them to fertilize our hydroponics farms."

Yuri clapped him on the shoulder. "You're insane, Eddie. You've always been insane."

"Yeah, a couple of my artisans want me to put floating gardens at different levels. I mean, they wouldn't actually be floating—we'd have to put little Musadhi filters in each one—but in this gravity it wouldn't take much."

"You mean little islands in the air?" Steel asked. I was almost startled that she would offer that much conversation on any topic other than Alice or the mission.

"Yeah. It might be fun. Dive from an upper beam to a little floating jungle, then soar over to another one. Finally take a long dive into the ocean. Might be fun."

'Fun.' How alien that concept had become to us. I could see it on the rest of the crew's faces, too: a longing for simpler times, easier decisions. All except Steel.

"Anyway, the shop's over here."

Eddie led us to a spot indistinguishable from any other. An elliptical piece of the deck opened and let us descend inside. As we did I asked Steel, "How's Alice doing?"

"I don't know," she replied. "She's not picking up." She didn't make eye contact with me. I don't know what she was looking at, but it wasn't anything visible to me. Surrounded by people who were risking everything to help her, she was utterly alone.

"Try not to worry. We'll be back there soon."

She didn't respond.

"So, lasers," Eddie was saying. "We got lasers. We got lots of lasers. What were you looking for?" Equipment of all kinds was organized on long tables and shelves. If there were any lasers there you could have fooled me.

"Well," Yuri replied, "something light, portable, handheld. Something we can aim."

"Sure," Eddie said. "We call those 'ray guns.' " Yuri looked around at us wanly. Then he got into an extended discussion with Eddie about all kinds of technical aspects— power requirements, weight, range, burn time. In the end he gave us seven small hand-held pistols with backpack power packs and two larger devices that could be set up on tripods and used at a distance of up to half a klick. We crated them up and started hauling them back up to the surface.

All the way up Eddie and Yuri continued yakking about various stuff. There was an almost enforced casualness about it, like they were both agreeing to ignore the fact that we all seemed kind of subtly terrified. When we got back to the top and were about to enter the Musadhi lift, I turned around to take a last look at the transcendent marvel Eddie had carved out of wandering rock and metal. The rest of the crew did the same. I wondered if they were thinking what I was, that none of us might see this place again. This place or any other place.

We got back up to the hangar and stowed the lasers in the shuttle. Yuri turned back to Eddie and said, "Well, thanks a lot. This really helps. I don't know what we would have—well, anyway, thanks."

Eddie looked Yuri in the eye, concerned, puzzled. "What the hell are you guys up to?" he asked. "I've got to say, you are giving off some of the strangest energy I've felt in centuries. Is everything okay?"

"Oh, yeah," Yuri shrugged, looked around at Steel, Marcus, Tamika, "We're okay. We're just, you know, under a lot of pressure, you know, schedules, deadlines—"

Steel came forward and said, "You really have helped us a great deal. You've taken part in something very important. What we're trying to accomplish may ... may change the world. I've, I've said too much, but ... but, thank you. Thank you very much." She took his hand.

Eddie looked at Steel and the rest of us like he was trying to define us somehow, or engage us or save us or maybe just console us. "Yeah, sure," he said. "Try not to hurt yourselves with these things."

"No problem," said Yuri, "I'll call up the manuals you gave me. We have time to learn how they work before we have to use them."

"Okay, well, keep in touch, huh? We should try to see each other more often. Two hundred years is too long."

"Yeah," Yuri answered. "Yeah." He gave Eddie a hug, "Well, 'bye."

" 'Bye. Keep in touch."

"Yeah."

We filed into the little ball and closed the hatch.

CHAPTER 30

"**P**ick up, Alice. Please." Steel's voice rose above the whirrs and hums of the shuttle. The soft glow of the control panel etched lines into her face as the Lightdancer loomed large in front of us. We were nearing the personnel airlock that led directly into the habitation module—where most normal people enter their starships. Alice had been silent since we'd left.

"*Please,* Alice. Pick up. Answer me." Steel allowed herself no familiarity or endearments with Alice in front of the crew. Once again she showed she could be one person in one setting and quite another somewhere else, and again I wondered who she really was. Steel? Estelle? The person who married John Cheatham or the one who lived in a castle? Or the one who'd picked me up on Vesper? Were they even distantly related?

"I'm sure she's all right," Marcus said. "Everyone needs a little down time now and then." For all the effect it had on Steel he needn't have bothered.

The shuttle rotated and mated with the Lightdancer. Pressures were equalized and hatches opened. We picked up the crates, our arsenal of lasers, and pushed off. As we pulled our cargo into the lower passageway of the ship, a very welcome visage floated toward us.

"Alice!" Steel exclaimed. "Where have you been? I've been bulleting you."

"Yeah, I know," Alice replied. "I've been online, scoping New Moorea. Did you know there's nothing but little islands down there? Anyway, there's a re-boot party happening in Paopao, well just outside of it. On the beach. I figured since I missed the one in Kindu I'd stop in. So anyway, that's where I'm going." She floated past us into the shuttle. " 'Bye."

"Alice—" Steel started.

"You've gotta go down to the surface to get supplies anyway, right? Well, that's where I'll be. See ya." And she closed the hatch.

Steel just stared, immobilized, as the hatch on the Lightdancer closed, too, and we heard the shuttle detach. Alice was on her way to the surface. Marcus said, "Captain, we need to get these lasers stowed before we can get under way."

Steel shifted her gaze to him, distracted, trying to focus on what he had just said. "Yes. Yes, good. Take us down to the surface as soon as you can. Do you know where ..." She looked back at the hatch where Alice had disappeared. "Do you know ..."

Tamika said, "Um, the refit facilities are on the main island of New Papeete. I believe Paopao is on one of the smaller islands close by. Some kind of underwater mining concern is just off the coast, I think, past the reefs. No corporate stuff, just a small operation."

Steel looked at Tamika, but there was no recognition there. "Yes ... yes. Take us down as soon as you can." Then with unexpected fire, "I'm tired of being weightless. Just get us under acceleration." She pushed off a bulkhead and flew down the passageway.

"Why shouldn't she go to a party?" Yuri asked me for the third time. "She should be able to go to a party if she wants." We could see the village of Paopao ahead of us at the top of a small bay. Our open skiff skimmed past jagged volcanic remnants soaked in jungle, bounced across shallow, aquamarine waves. Yuri and I had been dispatched by Steel to collect our errant patient while the rest of the crew was on New Papeete getting the Lightdancer stocked for our voyage to the planet of doom.

"I think," I started, "I think Alice is getting the benefit and the burden of about a thousand years of pent-up parenting." It occurred to me that Steel had even less training in how to parent than parents did back in the days when there *were* parents. When she'd told Yuri and me to fetch Alice she had seemed stunned, at a loss. She didn't know what to make of Alice's abrupt departure. It hadn't occurred to her that Alice *could* decide to do something on her own. She seemed to feel that Alice didn't like her anymore, that if she went to bring Alice back, Alice wouldn't come. She needed someone else to do it. Someone Alice would trust, would like, would cooperate with. Oddly enough, someone male.

"Parenting? What are you talking about?" Yuri asked.

Oh, right. Yuri didn't know. He really didn't know about any of it. He didn't know about the plan to prove that Draco had started the war, didn't know about the expedition to show that 'male-dominated' societies were inherently violent, didn't know about Steel's marriage or maternity or how John Cheatham had been destroyed or anything. At that moment I decided to tell him. I was tired of the crew being divided, of feeling separated, and I figured if we all were risking so much on this voyage, everybody ought to know why it was necessary. But how to tell him? How?

"Umm," I started, "uh, this is going to sound, um, that is, ah, I'm not sure how to say this ..."

"What?"

"Um, okay, I'm just going to, you know, okay. Here goes." I looked Yuri right in the eye, as though a posture of candor would somehow help get this across. I said, "Steel bore Alice." I waited for his reaction, but I could tell that, although the names were familiar, the sentence contained no intelligible information for him.

He repeated, "Steel bore Alice," like it was some kind of code he was supposed to break. "*I* bore Alice sometimes. Wait a minute, 'Steel *bore* Alice?' You sound like Johnny Weissmuller. You mean Steel *bores* Alice?"

"No, no—"

"I have to tell you, Mo, you've seemed awfully strange since you got back from Eden. Why are you so angry at Steel? I mean, what happened to you down there?"

"No, that's what I'm trying—I mean, you're probably right. I am—well, I don't know if I'm *angry* at her, but," but he was right. I was angry at her, "but that's what I'm trying to tell you."

"What?"

"Okay," I thought, "try this. Steel ... Steel carried Alice." No, I could tell that wasn't going to get the job done. "Um, she, she ... she delivered Alice." How could I say this? "She incubated Alice." That sounded weird even to me, but obviously not as weird as it sounded to Yuri. "She, she had Alice. She begat Alice."

"*What* are you talking about? I think you're starting to crack under the strain."

"No, no. Okay," I thought again, "okay, how about this? Do you know what the word 'mother' means?"

"Mother?" He examined me like he thought he might have to sedate me. "You mean like 'mother of Lao-Tse?' "

"Right!" I said, "*That's* what Steel is."

"She's a curse?"

"No—"

"What have you got against Steel? I know she can be, you know, odd, but—"

"Yuri, I don't think you have any idea just how odd Steel can be. I know this is difficult, but try to follow me here."

"I'm trying."

We could see the docks of Paopao nearing. I needed to get this across before we found Alice. I didn't want to be talking about it in front of her. She'd been through enough. "Um, you know that Alice was born on Eden."

"She was *what* on Eden?"

"You know, *born*. Born instead of hatched."

He looked at me for a moment, then he got it, "Oh, right, she would have been. Yeah. Why are we talking about this? It's kind of, you know, I mean I don't want to think about Alice sliding out of someone's body. It's kind of disgusting."

"Yeah, I'm sorry, I don't mean to—but it's not just, I mean, it wasn't just anyone's body. It was ..." the image of someone sliding out of Steel's body shocked me, stopped me, and *I* had slid out of—I mean, I had—I had been—"It was Steel's. You know, Steel's ... body." If it was shocking to me, it was inconceivable to Yuri. Incredulity spread across his features, rendering them slack, paralyzed. He didn't even try to speak. He just stared. "I'm not making this up. Steel told me, herself."

"Why would she say something like that?"

"It's true, Yuri. I know it's true. Steel was married. To Alice's ... other parent. To her, to her father."

"No, no, you're wrong. She would have told me."

"Why? Why would she have told you? Does she tell anyone anything she doesn't have to? Has she ever told any of us anything beyond what she thought we needed to know?"

That brought him up short. He stared off at eroded volcanic spires as he said, "But wait a minute wait a minute it doesn't make sense. You're telling me that Alice is the result, the the the product of sex, of two people, a man and a woman having sex."

"Right."

"But Steel can't do that. Nobody can. You could have sex with her as much as you wanted. It wouldn't result in, in a, a—"

"I know. That's right. I think she—I mean, she must have, before she went to Eden, I think maybe because she was going to Eden or, or maybe she went to Eden because she had it done or, I don't know, but she had to have had herself, I mean she had to undergo some kind of ... she had to have had herself ... prepped. Altered. You know, made ... made fertile."

"You're talking about her like she's some kind of breed stock."

"I know, I'm sorry. I don't know how to talk about it."

"This is absurd. You're telling me that after all the skag femmes gave us about marriage and reproduction Steel went to Eden so she could get married and reproduce? That's too fricking strange."

"I know, I know. I don't know why she did it, but I know she did."

"She was 'married'? That's what she said, 'married'?"

"Yeah, that's what they do there, on Eden, they get—she was married to, I mean, I met her ... her husband, before he died, before he killed himself."

"He ... he *killed* himself?"

"Yeah."

"Why?"

"A lot of reasons, I mean, it was complicated."

Yuri studied me for a moment then looked out over the water. "Complicated," he repeated, "Holy skag. I thought he just, you know, just ..." He killed the turbine. The boat slowed, stopped. We rocked on transparent water, suspended above white sand. "Alice must be ... I mean I can't even conceive of what she must be feeling. It's hard to imagine what it's like to have ... you know, ancestors. Fathers and stuff." Disinterested fish swam beneath us. "I couldn't figure out why Steel's been so upset. This ... this is ... What happened?"

I told him what I knew. At the end of my story I don't know if either one of us was any closer to understanding, but it felt good to have him with me again. We were both confused, but we were confused about the same things.

He finally said, "It doesn't matter. None of this matters. We still have to save Alice. That's what matters." I nodded in agreement. "But I'll tell you one thing: if Alice wants to stay at this party until she's the last one standing, she gets to." He looked at me.

"Yeah," I said, "sounds good to me."

"Okay," he said, and started up the turbine again.

I looked back at our other companion—the one Steel had sent along with us to make sure Alice stayed safe. "How're you doing, Hamster?" I asked.

He pursed his lips and lifted his chin. I guessed that meant he was okay. Beyond him the bay opened out into the strait between us and New Papeete: the island's verdant slopes blued by distance, surmounted by the kilometer-tall black needle of the Lightdancer. As I watched, a similar needle appeared high in the sky and descended on the blue sparks and blur of high-energy gravitons. "Hmm. Another starship's coming in," I said. As it got closer I could tell it was significantly larger than ours.

Yuri glanced back at it. "Yeah. Looks like an eleven-seater. Maybe even a thirteen."

We didn't think anything about it. We were clear out at the edge of the galaxy and nobody knew where we were. If anyone was going to visit New Moorea there was only one port. Yuri steered us up to the docks at Paopao.

As I hopped up on the wharf I hopped online. "Hey, Alice, where are you? Steel decided to let us out to play for awhile, too."

[Who's us?] She responded, and I was glad to hear her voice. I was afraid she wouldn't pick up for us at all.

"Just Mo and me," Yuri said. "And Ham."

There was a silence. Then: [Okay,] she replied, [I guess the three of you are frilly enough for this party.]

I looked at Yuri. " 'Frilly?' " I asked.

"Must be fresh slang. I've never heard it before."

I hopped back on, "We'll try to get frillier before we get there. Where is it?"

[Ask anybody. They'll tell you.]

"Okay, we'll see you in a bit."

[I'm not ready to go back yet.]

Yuri and I regarded each other. "We're not here to make you do anything you don't want to," he said. We had been, actually, before we'd decided to mutiny.

[Just checking up on me, huh? I wish Mom would stop worrying.]

Yuri looked at me quizzically. "*What'd* she say?" he asked me.

"Oh, uh, 'mom.' It's a word for, um, you know, maternal parent. She means Steel."

This didn't seem to help, but finally he shook his head. "Too fricking strange," he said.

The directions we got from the local at the dock were simple yet poetic: "Just walk down the beach. The party will find you before you find it," and it did before we'd gone too far. It was less organized, more spread out, than Matessa's party in Kindu. Small groups hung among coconut palms or on white sand or in the water, talking or making music or having sex.

We looked around for Alice, but she spotted us first. Ham made it difficult for us to blend in. She ran up and gave him a hug. Scratching his ears, she introduced a man who had walked up beside her: "This is Leos." He nodded to us like, I don't know, like we didn't belong there or something. "We're gonna go have some sex," she continued. "Make yourselves at home. There's food around. Sorry, Yuri, there's no surf. You'd have to swim out past the reefs."

"I'm all right," Yuri said.

"Okay, well," she took Leos' hand. "I'll be back in awhile." She waved to us and then turned to him and said, "Hey, you wanna log on while we do it?"

"Sure," he replied and they ran off together.

What could we do? We stood there on the beach looking after her. "This is good," I said, finally, and I'm pretty sure I meant it. "This is what she should be doing now."

"Yeah," Yuri responded.

"Just ... living."

"Yeah."

They disappeared behind some rocks. We regarded the rocks for a while, then the palm trees and finally the ocean before I asked Yuri, "Did you ever, in any of your lives, think you would be involved in something like this?"

Yuri kept gazing out at the gentle waves. He smiled. "No," he said, "I never dared to hope."

As I wondered at his meaning a small group of musicians to our left started an improvisation. Other people gathered around, and one or another of them would chant or sing. After a while we came to understand that these people were all in their second lives. They called each other 'twobies.' They had all spent their first lives indentured to one corp or another and were now on their maiden voyage as free souls. No wonder they treated us like outsiders. We were hundreds of years older than they were. Our lives were measured in 'lives'; theirs were still measured in years. I thought: how nice for Alice to be able to spend some time around people her own age. None of these folks were more than a century older than she was.

[Yuri, Mo. Where are you?] Steel's urgency brought us both to full attention.

Yuri replied first. "Um, we're, ah, outside of Paopao."

[Where's Alice? I need you back here now.]

"She's, uh ..." I started.

"Why? What's wrong?" Yuri cut in.

Steel logged on. Yuri and I both stumbled a little as we were suddenly viewing the universe through Steel's eyes, and Steel was looking at Krupp, all two hundred kilos of him. He was ranting, "Did you think I wouldn't find you? You think you're the only one with connections on Circe? That skag Lysistrata always knew when to cut a deal. She didn't let me down."

Steel was playing for time: "But how did you find us *here*? Nobody knew we were coming here. *We* didn't know we were coming here." As she spoke she panned her vision around the room for our benefit. Krupp wasn't alone. His tall friend Daimler was there as well, looking helpless and unhappy, and there were about a dozen SyndicEnts, each of them almost as big as Krupp.

"Holy frickin Buddha," I said.

Krupp continued, "That's what makes me so angry. You're not just crazy, you're stupid."

"Thank you," Steel responded. "It's nice talking to you, too."

"Is this helping us resolve—" Daimler started.

"THERE'S NO INTERSTELLAR TRAFFIC GOING TO EDEN," Krupp shouted. "GET IT? One neutron exhaust stream heading to Eden, *yours*. One stream heading away from Eden. YOURS. Aimed straight at New Moorea. YOU SEE? You don't think things THROUGH."

"I think things through," Steel answered.

"Let's try to stay on topic," Daimler began, "We need to—"

"She doesn't CARE!" Krupp shouted. He turned back to Steel. "Do you even KNOW how much it costs *per second* to operate a starship?"

"Okay, Captain," I said, "we're on our way."

[As fast as you can,] she replied and she logged off.

Yuri hopped online, "Um, Alice?"

[Yeah, yeah, I heard. I'll be there in a sec.] She sounded a little flustered, a little frustrated, but mostly just tired of the whole thing.

I said to Yuri, "It looked like they were in the warehouse where they were getting supplies."

"*A* warehouse, anyway," he answered.

"Well, she'll feed us the location."

"Yeah. Jesus, how long did it take us to get over here?"

"We're gonna have to do better going back."

"Yes."

I hopped on, "Alice?"

[Yeah, yeah, keep your pants on. I'm trying to get *my* pants on.]

"Okay, we just need to get going," I finished.

[I know, I know.]

I saw her hopping around the edge of the rocks adjusting clothing as she went. Then something else occurred to me: "Christ, Ham is with *us*."

"Yeah?" Yuri answered.

"Krupp is with Steel."

"Yeah."

"We need to get back there."

"Yeah. C'mon, Alice!"

"I'm coming."

We covered the distance back to the docks as fast as we could, hopped in the skiff and opened the throttle. We didn't want to bother Steel—she had her hands full—but it was awful not knowing what was going on. The minutes dragged by as we raced across the strait back to New Papeete.

As we pulled into the harbor two black needles towered over us: the Lightdancer and the much larger needle that had to be Krupp's ship. It had been almost an hour since we'd last heard from Steel. I hopped on: "Captain, we're here. Where are you?"

[On the main road from the spaceport. We're in the third warehouse down.]

"What do you want us to do?"

[Just get here.]

The spaceport was built out over the water. The warehouse she was talking about was only a couple of blocks from the docks. We started running. Then I saw Archie sprinting toward us from the Lightdancer. She either didn't see us or she was just in a hurry. She got to the door of the warehouse and disappeared inside.

I started to say, "What was she carrying?" when Steel logged on again. We had to slow down. You can't really keep your balance when you're looking at two different realities at once. Superimposed on the street in front of us, the dingy interior of the warehouse invaded our vision. Steel glanced to each side. We could see through her eyes that she was flanked by Marcus, Tamika and Jemal. Krupp seemed to have calmed down, but we could tell Steel was very tense. Surrounded by all that muscle, who wouldn't be?

Daimler was speaking: "—must understand, Estelle, that we can't let you do this. It would harm the very people you are trying to—"

Krupp cut him off: "We're not GOING to let you do this." He signaled to his drones. "If you can't see reason then I swear to Krishna—"

There was a crash to Steel's left. She turned to look at the source and we had to stop moving completely as we saw Archie break through an interior door. She staggered a little as she waved her right hand and the room erupted in screams. Steel turned back to look at Krupp and his army. They fell apart. It was too strange to be horrifying. It was like someone had taken a scalpel and just sliced through them. Where there had been a line of behemoths moving toward our friends, there was now just a pile of legs and torsos and severed arteries pumping blood. Steel logged off and we were abruptly in the street again.

We stared at each other dazedly, trying to take in what we had just seen. Yuri said, "The lasers. She had one of the lasers." He started running toward the warehouse. "Oh, Shiva. Archie—" He opened the exterior door and went inside. Alice and I ran after him. Ham lumbered along behind.

We ran down a corridor toward a broken door. Archie was yelling: "Damn it. SKAG! I lost my balance. I just meant to stop them. I didn't want to ... I didn't know this thing was so powerful."

Alice and I got to the door and walked into a charnel house. Yuri was holding his hands to his head and saying, "Oh, Shiva, oh, Shiva," over and over again. Daimler had not been standing by Krupp and the SyndicEnts. He was not harmed, but the rest of them were screaming and losing blood fast. A wavy plane of daylight streamed in where the laser had cut through the wall behind them.

Marcus recovered first. He hopped online. "Hello? Hello. We need nanodocs at warehouse number three. There's been an accident ... Yes, um, thirteen men are down. We have arterial bleeding. Yes. Yes." He hopped off and ran over to a pile of webbing and straps used to lift the crates that were stored there and started shouting orders. "We need tourniquets. Grab anything that ties and start tying off these wounds!"

The laser had sliced through them like they were paper, rising unevenly as Archie had stumbled. The nearest drone had lost both his feet. Krupp, roughly in the middle of the line, had lost both legs at the upper thigh. The farthest from Archie had been cut in two from his right hip to the left side of his waist. Yuri worked feverishly, almost manically: grabbing straps and tying them off and moving to the next and doing the same again and again and again. We all worked as fast as we could, but there were fewer of us than there were of them. By the time the nanodocs arrived we'd lost five, Krupp included. I just couldn't bring myself to work on him. I guess I was saving him for last. He would have to re-boot along with his four drones. I wondered how Steel was going to pay for it; it seemed like we were spending credits like entropy had caught up with us and it didn't matter anymore.

As we were finishing up and getting the survivors into the 'docs and the rest off to the hospital I had a chance to stop and look around. Everyone but Steel and Daimler were pretty gory. All of the crew had waded in kind of heroically, I thought, trying as hard as they could to save these people from having to 'boot. We were all in various levels of shock, but I noticed Tamika had collapsed in the corner shuddering and crying. Now that the crisis had passed and we had done what we could, she was faced with the full impact of what she had seen. We all were. Jemal was comforting her. I was too tired to even do that.

Daimler was online with traffic control: "These were *my* drones and *I'll* take care of them." Evidently traffic control didn't take kindly to the news that thirteen of its parts had been damaged so flippantly. Daimler was getting quite heated, "Kristel is a member of the Bayernische Syndicate and what she does or does not do is no concern of yours!" He listened. "Of course we'll pay for them. Who do you think you're dealing with?"

Who the heck was 'Kristel'? Was Archie working under an alias too? That's the only thing I could think of. I mean she was the one who fired the laser, but it didn't seem possible: Archie a member of a Terran syndicate?

Daimler went on, "Yes ... yes. I don't care what account ... I don't have the time or the patience to deal with this right now ... I DON'T CARE. Put it on the Valhalla account. Yes ... yes. Thank you." He turned to Steel, "Incompetent bureaucrats!"

I hadn't heard the name 'Valhalla' refer to anything but the planet in over a millennium. Now I'd heard it from Steel *and* Daimler. I didn't like it. And who the hell was Kristel?

Steel was speaking to Daimler, "I'm sorry this turned into such a ... but you saw what he did! He was going to physically restrain me. *ME!*"

"Estelle, you have to know that what you're doing is affecting all of us. I have to agree with Kr— with— with—" He glanced at the rest of us. We were standing around looking like butchers badly in need of a bath. "You're going about this with absolutely no regard for what it's costing, for what it's *going* to cost."

"What it's going to COST? You DARE talk to me about what it's—"

"All right, all right. Perhaps we shouldn't be discussing this in front of your—"

"I need to get to my ship," Steel stated. "Unless you have any more thugs you're planning to throw at me?"

"Estelle, please," Daimler hung his head, shook it. "Kristel's methods—"

"He prefers to be called 'Krupp.' "

"Yes." He glanced at us again and tried to sigh away an ancient pain. "Yes, of course. Krupp. Her methods—his, his methods are not always—"

"I see no possible purpose this conversation could have. If you want to continue it I suggest we meet again after I get back."

"After—" he sighed again. "Where are you going? At least tell me that."

Steel turned to her pilot. "Marcus, how many more loads do we have to transfer to the Lightdancer?"

"Two, maybe three, Captain," Marcus replied.

"Get it done," she said and started to leave.

Daimler put his hand on Steel's arm and spoke quietly, desperately, "We KNOW you're interested in longevity. We KNOW you want to extend the time between 'boots. We—"

"Let go of my arm," Steel said. He did. She turned and strode out of the room.

Daimler stood there for a moment, angry maybe, or maybe just lost. Then he saw us all staring at him and the anger won out. He spat at us, "I believe you've been given an order!" and followed her out.

CHAPTER 31

E ven Marcus couldn't think of anything to say for a moment. We stood there on blood-soaked concrete, arms crimson, faces and chests bespattered.

"Krupp is a woman?" Archie asked.

"He's my aunt," Alice replied.

"I mean he *was* a ... He's a trans—" Then Alice's statement registered with her, as it did with me. "What did you say?"

"He's Mom's identical twin. Well, he's not so identical anymore, I guess."

This news, as alien to reason as it was, seemed inconsequential after what we'd just been through. Even though no one had been in any real danger, we'd still reacted physically to the sight of so much agony and carnage. Our adrenaline had spiked, we'd gone into overdrive. It *was* a real emergency. It wasn't just the money. They were wounded, in horrible pain. Our memories were filled with the echoes of screams. At that moment we had no emotional energy left to process Alice's simple announcement. Then I looked at the faces of the crew and realized that Archie and I were the only ones who'd even understood what she had said.

I could tell when Marcus decided that, whatever Alice had said, it wasn't his problem. He was the exec. His job was to fly the Lightdancer and lead its crew and he had an order to follow. In the midst of the spilled fluids of human beings, this gave him comfort, purpose, a sense of direction. He watched the last of the nanodocs leave with its wounded cargo as he said, "Let's get these supplies on board. Tamika, are you all right?" Jemal helped her stand up. She nodded and wiped her nose on the back of her arm, which just smeared the blood around. "Belay that last," Marcus amended. "We need to get cleaned up." He saw the long gash in the wall behind him. "And we'll need to repair *that*. Yuri?" He looked around. "Where's Yuri?"

He wasn't in the room with us. We called out to him but there was no response. Marcus hung his head and mumbled, "Goddamn it." He ratcheted himself back up and said, "Let's get back to the ship. Shower, change and be back here in an hour."

I was walking down the passageway to my cabin, clean, renewed and looking forward to putting on a fresh coverall, when Archie came up to me. Her hair was wet and she was wearing a robe but she did not look renewed. Her eyes were red-rimmed seas of angst and fear. I couldn't tell if she was more afraid of the future or the past, but it was overwhelming her. Even for a surgeon, cutting people down like they were corn had to have been a shock for her.

"Mo, I'm—I'm ..." She folded herself into me, her arms, one flesh, one metal, across her breasts, her head leaning into my chest. "I'm—I'm—I'm—"

I put my arms around her. "Archie, what is it? Slow down, breathe. All those guys are going to be okay. They'll be fine. What's wrong?"

"No, no. I'm—I'm worried about Yuri. He hasn't come back. He's not picking up for anyone. We don't know where he is. Nobody knows where he is."

"Well," I thought, "where could he have gone? It's a small island. We'll find him—"

"That—that's not it. It's ... it's something he said to me while we were working on the ... on the victims. He said, he said—"

"What, Arch? What did he say?"

She shuddered. "He said, he said he never meant for them to be used on people."

I knew what she meant. The lasers. Yuri had seemed pretty distressed. "Oh, okay. Okay, well I'm sure he didn't—"

"That's not all. It was what I said." She looked up at me, "I said I lost my balance." This seemed like it was a much bigger admission to her than it was to me.

I thought back. "Yeah, okay, I remember you saying that. What—?"

"Don't you remember? On the shuttle. I told him his arm threw me off balance." She held up the prosthetic he had made her. "But it wasn't his arm. It was Steel logging on right when I was breaking through the door that made me stumble. I'm afraid— I'm afraid—"

"It's okay, Arch. It'll be okay."

"No, I'm afraid he'll blame himself, or— or— or blame me. I'm afraid—" I hugged her. "We have to find him, Mo. You know he's been upset lately. He's— he's— he's been ... We can't do this without him. We have to— we have to— He knows how everything works— I mean, I mean I don't want him to— to—"

"Okay, Arch. Let me talk to Marcus." I hopped online. "Hey, Marcus?"

[Yes.]

"Um, can you get the rest of the stuff loaded without me?"

[Why?]

"Well, Archie tells me Yuri's still missing, that he's not picking up for anyone."
There was a silence. [Do you think you know where he is?]

"Well, if he's anything like me, yeah, I think I might have a pretty good idea."

There was another silence as Marcus considered my proposal. Then, [All right. Let us know if you need any help. Steel wants to lift at dawn.]

When I got out of the Lightdancer, the sun had already set, but it *was* a small island and a small town. I didn't have any trouble finding the section I was looking for. It was lit up under the tropical night. The joints got cheaper, but no quieter, as you got farther from the waterfront. Every once in a while someone would remember a man fitting Yuri's description. I kept working my way uphill.

I finally found the street I'd probably been looking for all along. A handwritten sign said, "Paradise Alley." It took me back to Spam-town and 'Burbs place, Vesper and Sheila. I wandered up the street going from joint to joint.

I found him in the last dive in the alley. It was late, but this was a mining town; the place was still hopping. A band pulsed on a small stage in the corner. People danced, or just weaved back and forth. Lights, blue and red, spun and flashed on sweating bodies. I saw Yuri sitting at the far end of the bar, right next to where the wait staff picked up their orders. He seemed to have washed himself up a little, but under the colored lights it was hard to tell. I called to him and he lifted his head and looked at me through heavy-lidded eyes. He looked pretty stoked.

"MO!" he said, "Hey, man! Have a seat! Have a drink!" His speech was slurred. He turned to the bartender, "Hey, Jac, this is my friend, Mo." He patted me on the back. "He's named after Mahatma Gandhi, did you know that? Mahatma FREAKIN' Gandhi!"

Jac said, "Is that right?"

I nodded to him and said to Yuri, "Listen, Steel wants to get going—"

Yuri wrapped his arm around my neck, "Yeah, yeah, yeah, wants to get going. Wants to get going. Hey, Jac, do you know who Mahatma Gandhi is?"

"Can't say that I do."

"No. No." Yuri shook his head loosely. "You don't. That wasn't his name. His name was Mo, like my friend here. Mo-o-o Gandhi. Mogandhi, Mohandhi, Mohandhigandhi, but they called him Mahatma, you know? Out of respect."

"Okay, Yuri." I tried to get him off of his stool, but it was like trying to pick up mercury with a pair of tweezers. "That's enough history. We need to—"

"Yeah, yeah," he slipped away from me again. "Hey, Jac, what was I saying just now?"

"What? When?" Jac asked, pulling a draught for a pretty waitress who had appeared from somewhere.

"Just now," Yuri repeated, "You know, what was I saying?"

"Something about your officer." Jac handed the brew to the woman and turned to get a bottle from behind him, turned back and started filling more glasses.

"That's right," Yuri agreed. "My commanding officer. What'd I say? Mo should hear this."

Jac finished two more drinks and placed them on a tray. He sighed with the tolerance of a good bartender as he thought back, "You said, 'Never fall in love with your commanding officer.' " He turned back to get another bottle.

Yuri pointed a finger at him and winked. Then he turned to me. "Jac knows what he's talking about. He's a wise man. Never fall in love with your commanding officer."

"All right, Yuri, I'll keep that in mind." I tried to get him standing again. And failed.

"No, no, no," he wagged a finger at me. "Never. Never ever ever fall in love with your commanding officer."

"Who do you mean, Steel?" I asked. "Don't worry, I'm not in love with her."

"Who? Steel?" He waved away the absurd notion. "No, no, no. Steel's not an officer, she's a socialist." He laughed and shook his head, "A social ... social ... lite. A socialite. SociaLITE. Social light. Light of the party. Life of the party. No, no, no. Never fall in *love*," he stressed the word, "with your commanding officer. Bad idea. Baad, bad idea."

"Okay, Yuri. I won't. Now let's—"

"Hey, Jac," he turned away again, "you ever been on Alcyone four? Alcyone eye-vee?"

"I dunno," Jac laughed, "maybe." I don't know if he was laughing at Yuri or at my attempts to get Yuri to leave.

"No, no, man, Alcyone four, where they had the camps. The camps. Prisoner-of-war camps."

Jac shook his head, "I don't know."

Yuri leaned into me as Jac turned away again, "You know they turned men into women there."

"Okay, Yuri—" I started.

"No, no. They did. Turned 'em. Knocked 'em up. Made 'em have babies. Show 'em what it was like. What it felt like. I was there. I saw it."

"You were on Alcyone IV?" I asked. I remembered the holos at the Antigone Institute. Forced sex change wasn't all that had happened there, or even the worst that had happened. "During the war?"

"I was in the army, man! The D. E. F! I was a conscientious objector and they made me a medic. Can you believe that skag? A freakin' MEDIC!" He spread his arms out and laughed at the ceiling. Fans cut lazy circles through the misty air. Dancers pulsed and flowed.

"You were in the Draco Expeditionary Force? Jesus," I said, "how old were you?" I didn't even think of the etiquette, it just came out.

"I was a freakin' newbie, man! Eighteen, nineteen. Generals like 'em young and spry. You know the root word of infantry, don't you?" I didn't, but he was on to something else. "Alcyone IV. We were there to bust 'em out. Let 'em loose. Set 'em free."

"Okay, Yuri. We really gotta—"

"You been to Alcyone IV?"

"No, I—"

"They got jungles there. In the tropics. Lotsa jungles. That's where they put the camps. In the jungles. Freakin' jungles. Fulla ... stuff."

"Yeah—"

"I was a medic. A little Ranger outfit. There was only eight of us. Six rangers, our pretty, pretty lieutenant, and me. I was a medic."

"Okay—"

"Lieutenant Cooper. Cooper. Cooper, Cooper, Cooper." He smiled. "They didn't like her. Didn't like 'em. Women. In the army."

"Who didn't like her? The rangers?"

"NO," he yelled, "the YIN, man, the FREAKIN' Yin!" He waved his arm, maybe for emphasis, maybe because his arm was no longer answering to his higher brain functions. "Didn't like 'em. Thought they were traitors. Thought they shoulda been Yinified, Yinboozled, Yinimated. Yiminated, Yiniminate—Yini—Yininimate ..." He threw his head back and yelled at the universe, "FREAKIN' SKAG!"

"C'mon, Yuri," I glanced at Jac who was looking at Yuri like he might have to call the bouncer. "Sorry," I said, "How much does he owe you?"

"He's paid up. Just get him home, all right?"

"Yeah, good idea. C'mon—"

"FA'izeh's Firecats," Yuri mumbled. He seemed to have calmed down again. "You ever hear of FA'izeh's Firecats?"

I managed to get one of his arms over my shoulder and lift him off the stool. He was so far gone I was afraid what he might let slip. "We need to get back to the ship, Yuri. We gotta get going."

"Places to go, people to see ..." He was a little more stable than a plate of overcooked pasta, but not much. I tried to keep his feet under him as I walked him toward the door.

"Johnson's johnson," he said with a chuckle. "Johnson's johnson. You ever hear of FA'izeh's Firecats?"

"You asked me that one already." A pretty miner opened the door for me and we fell out into the night.

"They were tough. They knew their skag, man. They gave us a lot of trouble. Revolutionary Guard unit. Elite all the way—" He stumbled off the curb and almost pulled me into a light pole.

"Okay, Yuri, try to—"

"Course, they didn't know about *me*. I was a medic. I didn't go on any raids. I was a medic."

"Yeah, you told me." I continued to steer him down the alley.

"I think I'm gonna—" An unbroken stream of clear, slightly used beer and whiskey launched out of his mouth in a high, rainbow arc and splashed a few feet in front of him. I saw a trash can and maneuvered him over to it. He folded over the lip and continued to empty himself. When he was finished he collapsed on the sidewalk. He wasn't finished talking, however. I figured it would be easier if I just let him run down, so I sat beside him and let him talk.

"They didn't know about me. I was off takin' a leak. We were way out in the bush somewhere. The guys were asleep. Johnson was on watch. He had this big ol' johnson—that's why we called him Johnson. His name was Andy. But he had this big ol' johnson. They chipped him. Snuck up on him and chipped him. You could do that back then. Things were slower. Memory uploads took five, six seconds. They had to chip him or the guys would've woke up. Wokened up. Awakened. The guys would've awakened so they chipped him and cut off his johnson. They didn't need to do that; they just did it. They had a use for it. They had a plan. They had a plan to use Johnson's johnson."

"Yuri, maybe we better—"

"No, no, this is a funny story. They had a plan. It was a good joke." He fought off my attempts to get him standing again. "Just a second, just a second. Just— just wait a second. It's a good story—"

"Okay, Yuri. Tell me the story."

"They had a plan, see? They chipped him so the guys wouldn't sense he was in trouble, right? The guys or the lieutenant. Over the net the guys could tell if he was in trouble so FA'izeh's Firecats chipped Johnson and snuck on into camp with Johnson's johnson. Get it? FA'izeh's Firecats? Johnson's johnson? There's an alliterative theme thorough going— going through ... Anyway, I was coming back from takin' a leak when I heard 'em."

"Yeah?"

"They'd chipped two more of the guys. I saw 'em lyin' there with the backs of their heads gone. They had the other three tied up on the ground and the lieutenant tied to a tree. I was just a scared skag. I didn't have any weapons; I was a medic. I was just a scared little skag, hidin' in the freakin' bushes."

"I probably would have done the same."

"Just a scared little freakin' skag hidin' in the freakin' bushes."

I put my arm around his shoulders and pulled him into me, "Yuri—" He was sweating now, and trembling.

"They'd stripped the lieutenant. She had really pretty breasts. They made the guys watch while they cut 'em off. Then they sewed Johnson's johnson onto her. You know, between her ... so she'd look like— See? That was the joke. If you were fighting the Yin you had to be evil. If you were evil you couldn't be a woman. If you weren't a woman you had to be a man. It was kind of a syllogism."

"Oh, Shiva ... "

He started swaying back and forth. "How do I save myself, Mo? How do I save myself?"

"Yuri, you were unarmed. You said—"

"No, no, no, you haven't heard the joke yet, man!" He grabbed my shoulders and shook me, "They didn't KNOW about me! I was the freakin' medic!"

"I know—"

"No, no, no. After they sewed Johnson's johnson onto the lieutenant they chipped her and the last three guys, see? That was it! That was everybody. They knew we were the only unit in the area; we'd been harassing each other for months. After they chipped everybody they were safe, safe and sound all around. There was nobody left. Nobody left. They had a little victory celebration, a little party. They all got hammered and passed out."

"Okay—"

Yuri was crying now, "I was in love with her, Mo. I was in love with the lieutenant. My Cooper. My Cooper. My heart squeezed in my chest every time I looked at her. When they hurt her ... I wasn't a philosopher back then. I didn't even know what a syllogism *was*. I didn't get the joke! It just made me angry. I got so angry." He punched the wall, left blood and skin on the wood. "After they all passed out I crawled over to my kit. I didn't know how to use any of the weapons; I couldn't even take the safeties off. I was just a scared little skag, but I was so angry. I could feel the blood in my veins like my body was going to explode. My heart ... my heart ... I got to my kit and got out my little surgical laser. I could pop out a chip in a nanosecond. They blew the backs off the guys' heads, off the lieutenant's head. They messed up her hair. Her hair ... I didn't need to do that. I knew right where to aim. A nanosecond was all it took to pop out a chip. Just lengthen it to a millisecond and you burn right through the brain stem. No heartbeat, no blood to the brain. It just made a little pop. A little POP! One dead woman. POP! Two dead women. POP, POP, POP! Three more dead— dead—"

Yuri looked up into my face. His eyes were pools of torment, of agony unendurable, inescapable. "I *killed* five women, Mo! I murdered them. I didn't need to. They were passed out. I could have run away but ... but ... I was so *angry*! I shouldn't have gotten so angry."

He fell into me, his head buried in my lap, his body racked with sobs. All I could do was pat him on the back and say, "There, there. There, there."

I remembered the rage. It was all over the net at that time, the rage of the Yin against all that was male. Rage far too powerful for any military professionalism to contain. It wasn't bad at first, but as the war wore on, you could feel from the news reports how soldiers on both sides were becoming inured to the violence, the suffering. Mangled bodies that had been too horrific to even imagine before the war began had become all too familiar, just part of a day's work. As each new unspeakable act led to another and another, the unthinkable became thinkable, then routine, then even desirable. Thirst for justice devolved into a lust for vengeance and finally just a habit of hurting people. I held Yuri and rocked him for a long, long time.

He quieted after a while. I said, "Okay, Yuri, let's get back to the ship, huh? We still have to save Alice, don't we?" But he was passed out, his features childlike, at peace. I hopped online, "Marcus?"

[Yes?]

"I've got him."

[Good.]

"But he's, um, he's passed out. I don't think I can carry him back to the ship."

[All right. I'll send someone to help you. Where are you?]

"We're sitting in the street. It's called 'Paradise Alley.' I'll stay logged on. Just home on me. You'll find it."

[Very good. Jemal should be there in a few minutes.]

I didn't have to wait long. Jemal and I hoisted Yuri up and started dragging him back to the spaceport. I asked him, "How is everyone? Did you get everything loaded?"

He answered, "Yeah. Yeah, it's all ready to go."

He sounded a little tentative, so I pressed him further, "Is everything okay?"

"Yeah," he said, "I guess. Tamika's pretty, you know, she's still pretty messed up, I guess."

"Yeah, that was rough at the warehouse."

"It was. I don't know if she's gonna, you know, she kept crying on and off all night. I don't know if she's gonna be able to ... I think she might be thinking about, you know, thinking about ..."

"What? Leaving? The crew?"

"Yeah, maybe. She's just pretty messed up."

When we got back to the Lightdancer, the sky was getting light in the east. Everyone was waiting for us outside the ship—everyone but Steel. She was evidently on board still discussing things with Daimler. Yuri roused enough to sway on his own feet, but not enough to realize how happy everyone was to see him.

Even Marcus was happy when he said, "Clean him up. Get him to bed. We lift in forty-five minutes."

I sort of steered Yuri up the gangway and we all started to file in. From behind us Jemal said, "Um, Marcus?"

Marcus turned back. Jemal was still on the ground. "Yes?"

"Um, I was thinking, uh ..."

Marcus looked him up and down. He said, "It's time to get on board, Jemal. Let's go."

"Yeah, I mean, yeah, I was thinking that I might, um, um ..."

"Whatever it is, we can discuss it on the ship." We waited. So did Jemal.

He finally said, "I don't think I can."

"What?" asked Marcus.

"I don't— I don't think I can. Get on. I don't think I—"

Marcus said, "Jemal, we need every one of us. Seven for the engine and a Captain. That's what we have. That's what we need. Now let's get aboard."

"I think I'm gonna— I think I'm gonna stay here. Sir."

"Jemal—" Marcus closed his eyes, sighed, and hopped online, "Captain, we have a problem. I'm sorry to interrupt you but I think you need to come down here."

We all just stood there while we waited for Steel. She arrived at the hatch and said, "What is it?" She looked like she'd been up all night.

Marcus looked to Jemal. Jemal, naked and alone, looked up at our Captain.

"What is it?" Steel repeated.

"I'm sorry, Captain," he finally said. "I'm sorry."

"What?" she asked.

"I— I don't think I can do it. I don't think I can do it. I'm sorry."

"I don't understand. Do what?"

"I don't think I can— I mean— I think I'm gonna stay here. On New Moorea. You know, maybe get a job, or ... or something. I'm sorry."

I didn't know what Steel was going to do. She stood there, expressionless, motionless, on the edge of eternity.

"I'm sorry, Captain. I just— I just—"

Steel walked down the gangway to him. She embraced him and said, "Thank you, Jemal, for everything. You won't tell anyone about us, will you?"

"No, Captain, no! I won't— I just— I just can't—"

She hugged him again. "I know. I'm amazed any of us can." She looked him in the eyes. "Goodbye, Jemal."

"I'm sorry, Captain."

"It's all right." She turned and walked up the gangway. As she passed Marcus, she said, "Let's button her up."

Marcus turned and said, "But, Captain, Daimler is still on board—" But she had already disappeared inside.

We all said goodbye to Jemal, hugged him, grasped his hand. He was us. He was the 'us' that was going to survive. Then we turned and did the bravest thing any of us ever had. We stepped aboard the Lightdancer.

PART VII
BRAINARD'S PLANET

CHAPTER 32

[Marcus, take us up. I want us off of New Moorea *now*.] Steel was somewhere deeper in the ship, maybe the common room.

"I'll have to get clearance from—" Marcus started.

[Then GET IT.]

Marcus immediately became very efficient. "Tamika, you come with me to control. Archie, Mo, take care of Yuri—"

[And send Ham to me.]

"Where are you, Captain?"

[In my quarters.]

"Alice, would you take care of Ham?" Marcus asked.

"Sure," Alice replied, "C'mon, Ham. Let's go see Mom," and off they went.

Marcus and Tamika looked at her strangely. "*What* are you calling her?" Marcus asked, but Alice was already on her way.

"It's a word for maternal parent," Yuri slurred as Arch and I each hoisted an arm on our shoulders. "Our Captain was married."

Marcus looked sharply at Yuri, then Archie, then me. "Take care of him. Get him to bed." Then he turned to Tamika and said, "Let's go."

Whatever clearance he needed to get, it didn't take him long. Arch and I were still showering Yuri when we felt the little thump of gravity shift that was the impellers taking us into space. As we were maneuvering him down the passageway to his cabin, we heard the hatch to Steel's quarters open and Daimler's voice:

"Have you lost your mind? Where are you taking— You can't just— This is *kidnapping*!"

Steel's voice fired back, "What do you call forcible restraint? That's what you were going to do to me."

Daimler appeared around the curve of the passageway, headed for the personnel airlock, I guess. Steel was right behind him. "Estelle, I demand you set this ship—"

"My name is *Steel*!"

"All right, all right, whatever you want to call yourselves. Just put this ship— You can't— you can't just— I'll bullet traffic control—"

"No you won't."

Daimler turned back, looked at her, stymied. Then a new level of anger informed his voice. "Then tell me where we're going. If I'm trapped—"

"Brainard's Planet."

"What?"

"We're going to Brainard's Planet."

Alice and Ham came up behind Steel. Ham, sensing the tension I guess, interposed himself between the Captain and Daimler. Daimler regarded Ham, turned and looked at Arch and me holding up Yuri. He said, "You should know you don't need that ridiculous monkey to protect yourself from me. If you're going to forcibly abduct me I deserve to know where—"

"We're *going* to Brainard's Planet," Steel repeated.

She must have bulleted Marcus and Tamika; they came around the corridor from the other direction, effectively surrounding Daimler. Not that we were threatening him, but he couldn't really go anywhere. He looked around at all of us incredulously. He said, "Kristel was right. You are insane. What do you think you can— Is this about the little pets you picked up on Eden?"

Steel seethed. "Little *pets*?"

"Look, I'm sorry Jacob was destroyed. It was tragic. But you shouldn't have been on Eden in the first place. Those people aren't even human anymore. The boy's destruction proved that."

Alice was standing right there.

Steel spoke with controlled rage: "Alice is my *daughter*."

Daimler looked at her with real bemusement, "Your dotter? What the hell is that supposed to mean?"

I don't think Steel really realized whom she was speaking in front of, she just wanted to pound the information into Daimler. "She is my child. My offspring. My descendant. I was married on Eden, just like you were married. I became pregnant. I bore two children, Jacob and Alice."

Any circuit breakers that hadn't already tripped in Daimler's head now opened. He stood there, his mouth agape, eyes blinking. "What kind of sick, perverted—"

Steel raged. "*Perverted*? You call *me perverted*?" She turned to me. "Mo, you should understand this. When this man's wife," she stabbed a finger at Daimler, "was lost in the War of Liberation he decided to *clone* her."

Daimler lowered his eyes. "Estelle, please."

She spat back at him, "But that isn't the good part, is it, my love?" Daimler put a hand to his forehead, hiding his face. Steel's voice cut like a scalpel: "No, the good part is that his wife turned out to be genetically predisposed to bifurcating zygotes."

I thought for a second. "Identical—" I started.

"That's right. Identical twins. And when the little zygote bifurcated, *this* man," the finger stabbed again, "*this* man decided to keep *both* embryos to see which one turned out to be more like the original. After having us carefully reared and groomed for two decades, two *decades* for the job of replacing his wife, he chose *me.*"

Daimler tried to regain his dignity. "All right, Estelle. I think we've heard enough—"

Steel barked a humorless, hollow laugh. "Have we? Have we heard enough? Don't you want to tell them how much you *loved* your wife? How you couldn't face living the rest of eternity without her? Don't you want to tell them the sick punch line to this whole sordid little tale?"

"Estelle—"

"Don't you want to tell them that your wife was killed by weapons *you* sold to the Yin?"

This last was like a physical blow to him. He sagged, his voice broken. "All right," he said, "all right, Estelle, can we please ... can we please just— Do we have to do this in front of these people?"

Steel glanced around at us. She seemed to realize what she had just exposited to us. We weren't supposed to see this stuff. This was private, private in a way most people didn't even worry about anymore. But Steel and Daimler were members of one of the syndicates—the last aristocracy, a plutocracy of unimaginable wealth and fanatically guarded secrets. Archie had told me that none of them were on the net. They lived in their own universe of power and riches and if you weren't one of them you didn't get to know them or anything about them. Steel tried to recover herself, or cover herself, but she was still angry. She looked at the bulkhead, the deck, anywhere but at us. Finally she said, "Crew, dismissed. Marcus, configure the ship for interstellar jump."

Marcus answered, "But, Captain, we still need to refuel—"

"Well do THAT, then," she snapped, and turned to go back to her quarters.

Daimler entreated, "Estelle—" and followed her down the passageway.

We were left to contemplate our future. Jemal was gone. Daimler would take Jemal's place on the navnet when we boosted for Brainard's Planet. He would take Jemal's place in the engine when we freewheeled. We would be melding with him, sharing our minds, our perspectives, with him.

"Get Yuri to bed," Marcus ordered. "Tamika, I'll take first watch. Relieve me in four hours. The rest of you try to get some sleep. We've had a long night."

We had to spend the next several days refitting the ship while our Captain and this newcomer argued in her quarters and the Lightdancer drove in toward New Moorea's star and the antimatter station there. These were days of mounting tension about our new crewmate. The dynamic on the Lightdancer had changed once again, but now the six of us pulled closer together while the two rich people fought it out in chambers closed to us. We talked as we worked, our conversations moving from explanation to defensiveness to simple wonder at the whole story. Archie's perspective on it was so different from Alice's, from mine. For Arch it was a tale of changing the world, improving it, addressing injustices, making things right. For me it was more a story of human frailty and flaws, a twisting journey of people doing the right things for the wrong reasons and the wrong things for the right reasons. To Alice it was simply her life. Marcus, Tamika and Yuri had to take it in as best they could.

On the third day Yuri and I were working on the auxiliary machinery that supported the engine when he dropped the wrench he was using. "Holy skag, my hand still hurts. What the freaking hell did I do to it?"

I looked at it. It was swelling and turning some nice shades. "You had a disagreement with a wall."

Yuri looked at me. "About what?"

"I think you objected to its location."

He shook his hand. "Stupid wall." He returned to tightening the fastener we'd been working on. "I must have been having a good time."

"It was quite a party."

On the day before we changed out the antimatter core, Steel called a meeting in the common room. It was the first time all eight of us had been together since the fight in the passageway. As we filed in Steel and Daimler were already there, seated at the table where so many good meals and inspired, ecstatic conversations had been held. All that seemed very long ago. We joined them quietly, waiting for our Captain to speak.

It was a new Captain who faced us. She was guarded, formal. The easy warmth with which she had interacted with us when I first met the crew had become too expensive for her. We knew too much about her now. She wasn't comfortable with being visible, comprehensible. Her mask of exquisite beauty and mythic wealth had been replaced by the naked face of a desperate human being, haunted by her past, her mistakes, her arrogance and impudence and more than anything her fear that she wouldn't be able to pull this off. Haunted as much as any of the rest of us were. I wonder if she sensed or understood that we felt closer to her because of her exposure. Maybe that's what she didn't like.

"As you know," she started, "we have a new member of the crew. Although I have known him for a long time, you have not. He has joined us ... not under the best of circumstances, but then neither did Mohandas, and he has worked out fine." That made me feel better. I guess. "We're going to have to work together, so I wanted you to have a chance to meet him, get to know him." She waited, or just stopped speaking. Then, "Do you have any questions for us?"

We sat there, wondering what to ask and who would ask it. As the silence lengthened, we felt pressured to ask *something*, anything, just to show them we were interested. And we were certainly interested. But of all the impulsive decisions Steel had made on this voyage, letting Jemal go and pressing Daimler into service seemed the most ill conceived.

Marcus finally rescued us. He asked Steel, "Have you briefed this man fully about our mission?"

It was Daimler who answered. "Estelle has—" he started, then "Stee—" He cleared his throat. "I'm sorry, I'm just not—" He tented his fingers, gathered himself and started again, "Your Captain has told me about your technological breakthroughs in dealing with Brainard's plague." He glanced at Steel, but she was focused on the same thing she had been since she started this expedition. He continued, "They are remarkable and have certainly altered my views on this project. She has ... has spoken to me on the advisability of harvesting the eco-system on Brainard's Planet." He glanced at Steel once again, then went on, "If there are ... profits to be made, then the Bayernische syndicate wants to be in the, in the vanguard of this new area of research and resource utilization." The guy was a freaking brochure.

Yuri asked, "But do you know why we're doing this?"

Daimler seemed to gather his forces as he considered the question. "Your motives are really of no concern to me." Yuri started to respond, but Daimler plowed ahead, "But I must say the quixotic nature of this whole endeavor is quite distasteful." Again Yuri tried to interrupt, but Daimler kept talking: "And I have a very real fear that you people have no idea what you are planning to unleash on the world. If what Estelle tells me is true, there are revolutionary medical advances to be made. These advances will surely bring turbulent, if not disastrous social and economic disruptions to human civilization. You understand, I hope," he pinned each one of us with his gaze, "that extending the period between longevity treatments by as little as a factor of three would cause our economic system—a system that has been carefully crafted and perfected over centuries—to cease to function. It will collapse and there will be the most dire dislocation in every level of society."

"People won't have to go into the trades anymore," I said, not without a certain amount of animosity. "You want to talk about dislocation; let's talk about that. Let's talk about turning people into machines. Let's talk about owning human beings."

Daimler stared back at me. "Our system of indentured service enables all people, *all* people to have medical. It enables *all* people to re-boot. It's the only way we can afford it. It's not perfect, but it works."

"How old are you?" I asked, not really caring how rude I was being.

Daimler puffed up like an adder and barked, "Who do you think you're speaking to?" He turned to Steel, "I don't have to subject myself to this—"

"Answer his question," Steel replied.

I beat him to it: "Are you old enough to have been around when the first projects were started? Hmm? You know, the ones around Alpha Centauri, Procyon, Barnard's star?"

"I *funded* some of those projects! Not that it's any concern of—"

"You funded the Valhalla project?"

"My syndicate did, yes." Then he stopped and looked at me. My expression probably wasn't very friendly. "Why?" he asked, in a very different tone.

"No reason," I answered. Then I went on, "I think humanity will probably survive any dislocation we create."

Daimler stabbed a finger at me, reminiscent of the finger Steel had stabbed at him a few days ago. "Just the sort of shallow, flippant, fuzzy-minded thinking I would expect from one of you people. I think you need to remember that you are an employee of one of the oldest syndicates on Earth—"

Yuri finally succeeded in interrupting him: "I think *you* need to remember that we're not drones of yours. We're not SyndicEnts that you can turn on and off at will." He leaned forward. "And where we're going, a person can actually die."

Daimler stopped. This was out of his experience. It was out of all of our experiences, really. The word 'die' in relation to human beings still sounded alien, bizarre. "What do you mean by that?" Daimler demanded.

Yuri leaned back in his chair again. "I don't know," he answered blandly, "I guess I'm just saying it pays to be polite."

"What he's saying," Marcus' calm, steady voice displaced the belligerence in the room, "is that Brainard's Planet is a very dangerous place. If we are to do our work there and survive the experience, we need to function as a team. We have to be able to count on each other. Are we going to be able to count on you?"

I don't think Daimler was used to this kind of exchange. He looked off-balance, out of his element, fighting to keep his feet on ground that kept falling away from him. Then a clear, sweet soprano lifted the music of the conversation to another realm: "Daimler, these are my friends. They're doing all these things, taking all these horrible risks, for me."

We all turned to Alice. What she was saying was so simple and so excruciatingly true that I could barely stand to look at her. The purity of her beauty was so overpowering as to be physically painful.

Daimler didn't seem quite so affected by it as we were, but he didn't regain his balance, either. If anything he was more uncomfortable than before. He looked at his hands: "Alice, I hope you know how fond I am of you. Of Jacob, too. Having the two of you around was very ... refreshing, very surprising. When Jacob was lost it affected us all. Then when you and Estelle disappeared for so long—more than three decades—we were horribly concerned, worried ..." He paused. We waited.

"But?" Archie said.

I could tell Daimler didn't like to be interrupted; more than that, he wasn't used to it. He didn't exactly glare, but he wasn't happy, either. "There are larger issues to be considered," he said.

Arch came right back, "Let me assure you that we've considered those issues and made our decisions."

Marcus asked Steel, "What sort of risk does this man present to security?"

Steel stared straight ahead. "I'll deal with that," she said.

Marcus said, "And you vouch for him? To be a part of our operation? A part of the crew?"

Steel turned and looked long and hard at Daimler. "We are going to Brainard's Planet and we are going to find a cure for Alice's condition. That's what's going to happen." Daimler met her eyes, not defiant but not really compliant, either. After a moment of this she said, "If there are no more questions, you're all dismissed."

A little while later, as Yuri and I were eating lunch, I said, "I thought that went well."

"We are so freakin' screwed," he answered.

CHAPTER 33

[1\TC>F.S.LightDancerRequestingTrafficUpdate<1/TC]

Marcus' digital voice was calm, smooth in our minds. We were in the control room, each of us in our assigned seat. Daimler occupied Jemal's station.

[TC\LD1>YoureClearForPre-filedJumpNew MooreaM5Globular<TC/LD1]

The antimatter core had been replaced. We had swung around New Moorea's star to slingshot us out of the disc of the Milky Way. This had come as a surprise to me. Earth and the sun lie in a minor thickening of gas, dust and star formation called the Orion spur, which lies between two major arms: the Sagittarius, closer to the center of the galaxy, and the Perseus arm, which lies farther out. Brainard's Planet is in the relatively dust-free area between the Orion spur and the Perseus arm. Since New Moorea was in the far outer, or Cygnus arm, I assumed that we would be heading back toward the center of the galaxy. But our destination wasn't exactly on the Grand Tour of human occupied space. We needed to come in by the back door.

[TC\LD1>Advise:PostPanDimensionalTranslationF .S.LightDancerWillBeOffNavNet:Respond<TC/LD1]

[1\TC>Understood<1/TC]

So we were heading over twenty thousand light years north of the galactic plane, into the galactic halo, to the outskirts of the M5 globular cluster, ostensibly to research this ancient relic of the earliest ages of the universe. But what we were really doing was leaving the NavNet. Once there we would immediately turn around and head back into the Milky Way. We would be able to see it as a galaxy, would be able to see all of human occupied space at once, see the spiral arms, the dimmer areas between them. The twelve hundred light years between Earth and Brainard's Planet would seem insignificant—merely the distance between the crest and trough of one starry wave in the galactic ocean.

[*\1 >CONFIGURESHIPFORJUMP<*/1]

Even Steel's digital voice was hard. The sadness was gone, as was the compassion. All that was left was her unbreakable resolve to wrest a desired result from an uncaring universe.

[1*>CONFIGURESHIPFORJUMPAYE<1/*]

Marcus responded. We heard the torch extend.

[*\1 2 3 4 5 6 7>FINALNAV<*/1 2 3 4 5 6 7]

The crew's unitary mind, flavored now with Daimler's arrogance and missing Jemal's gentle quiet, dipped into the net for the last time on this voyage, perhaps the last time ever. The zeros lined up.

[*\1 2 3 4 5 6 7>ENABLE<*/1 2 3 4 5 6 7]

We were on our way.

The jump was a tough one, and it wouldn't get any easier. Steel's system had to bulk us up to withstand the robust gravity of Brainard's Planet, almost twice that of Earth. This not only meant more muscle mass, but greater bone density as well, sturdier ligaments and tendons, a stronger heart to pump blood through tougher veins and arteries that would have to withstand greater pressures. Very few human-occupied planets had gravity greater than Earth, and none significantly greater. This was why. We ached and creaked the whole way. The graviton filters helped us adapt, too. When we first lit the torch we filtered the thrust down to a standard gee. Over time we decreased the filtration until we were dealing with what we would face once we got to our destination.

The oddest thing about this was trying to catch something if you knocked it over or dropped it. As the gravity increased, so did every object's acceleration as it fell. By the time we got up to two gees, it was really annoying. If you dropped something on the floor—and we did that a lot because our timing hadn't adapted yet—it would fall like you had thrown it at the deck and then make a ridiculously loud sound when it hit. If it bounced, it would bounce twice too fast: WHAPwhapwhapwhapwhap! Like it was demanding your attention. It made us all edgy, even though everybody but Daimler and me had been through this once before. I would regularly hear something crash to the deck and then somebody say something like, "All right, all right! I'm sorry I dropped you! Leave me alone!"

It didn't help that we knew we would be off the NavNet when we got to M5. We would have to find our way back to Brainard's Planet the way people had done it in ancient times, back when I was a lot younger. We had records of where everything was when we left New Moorea. We knew precisely how fast and which direction everything was moving and how much time would elapse before we jumped for Brainard's Planet, but still, twenty-thousand light years is a long, long way and everything is moving and interacting all the time. *And* once we got to M5 we wouldn't have any visual input that was useful. The light we would be seeing from the Milky Way would be over twenty thousand years old. I brushed up my old astrogation skills, but back in those days we were making jumps of five, ten, *maybe* twenty-five light years at the very most.

It became obvious that Daimler didn't want to get to know us. He would only stand watches with Steel. This screwed up the watch schedule and meant that there were only two people on those watches. You can fly a starship with just two, but it's taxing and there wasn't any reason to, except that Daimler didn't want to meld with us. It impacted us in another way, as well. We ended up pulling eight-hour watches. With Steel and Daimler on the first watch it meant that Marcus, Yuri and Alice always had the second and Tamika, Arch and I always had the third. It was okay, but we never got mixed together, never spent any time with each other, and when you're looking at freewheeling, you want to have as much rapport as possible.

Fortunately, we were trying to hit a spot about four light-months from the outermost stars of the cluster. I'm glad it wasn't any closer. We ended up less than one light-month from the nearest star with a couple of comets even nearer. It would have ended things really fast if we'd come out in the middle of the star's Oort cloud. Seven of us would have uploaded onto the net to await new bodies to be grown for us and Alice wouldn't have and that would have been that.

Marcus demanded a meeting with Steel and Daimler before we jumped for Brainard's Planet. We had come to a halt relative to the cluster and were already accelerating back toward the galaxy on the impellers so we had gravity to push us into our chairs. Too much gravity, but we were getting used to it. Steel had extended the habitation module. Through the port windows in the common room we could see M5, an explosion of stars that filled a third of the sky. Looming over us was our home, much dimmer, much farther away, its cloudy arms sweeping the night: the island universe we would try to return to.

"We have to do better than this," Marcus said. "Missing our target by more than three light *months*? We can't afford to do that in the galactic disc. We *have* to be synched up when we freewheel. We have to."

Daimler started, "There are very good reasons why—"

"I'm speaking to my Captain," Marcus interrupted, not shouting, but then Marcus never needed to shout to get his point across. "If this discussion requires your input—"

Before Daimler could respond Steel answered, "Of course you're right, Marcus. I allowed this ... unorthodox practice because I knew we had plenty of room to work with out here. If we had been able to execute an accurate jump, then I was prepared to let it continue. Obviously we weren't." She thought for a moment, glanced at Daimler. "We will stand regular watches from here on out."

"Estelle—"

Marcus stood up and slammed his fist down on the table. "You are not a passenger on this vessel; you are a member of the crew. You will address our captain as such."

Daimler looked like he'd been kicked in the stomach, but he recovered quickly. "You pathetic little—"

"As executive officer, it is my duty to maintain discipline among the crew. As a watch stander, as a part of the engine you *are* a member of this crew. This vessel does not belong to you—"

"In that, my friend, you are profoundly wrong." Daimler rose from his chair and stared hard at Marcus, "This vessel does belong to me. The food you eat, the water you drink, the air you breathe belongs to me."

Marcus stared back at him, glanced at Steel, then back to Daimler, "Are you relieving our Captain of command? Are you ready to go on the net and make record of such relief? We are a starship in space. Interstellar law is quite explicit—"

"Interstellar law is explicit about kidnapping, too—"

"Do you wish to report a crime?"

Steel raised her hand. "Daimler, please sit down." Nobody moved. "Please ..." Steel repeated, "Sit down." They both remained standing so Steel stood up, too. She put a hand on Daimler's shoulder. "It is essential to me that one particular crewmember's body is not exposed to anything that would cause it to cease to function."

Daimler broke his eye contact with Marcus to look at her. "I understand why you would feel that way, but—"

"The only thing that matters right now," Steel interrupted, "is that I *do* feel that way." For a moment no one moved. Then Steel said, "We will stand regular watches. Marcus, generate a watch list."

So we finally got to know Daimler, after a fashion anyway: kind of like we knew Steel. You occasionally pick up stray thoughts or feelings when you're synched in to navigate, but I think Daimler was as practiced as Steel was at compartmentalizing himself, disguising himself, hiding.

We weren't on the NavNet, so we weren't nearly as jazzed coming off watch, and we weighed too much and had a lot of work to do to prepare for Brainard's Planet: learning how to use our new equipment, the lasers most of all. All of this impacted the time we had to hang in the common room and talk, but we got closer. Some, anyway. On one watch I caught a glimpse of Daimler's wife, and he must have caught a glimpse of mine. He, Arch and I were coming off watch when he said to me, "So you were married, hmm?"

I knew why he was asking, so I said, "Yeah." I couldn't help adding, "I lost her on Valhalla."

He raised his eyebrows, "During the uprising?"

I think my facial expression gave him all the information he needed. His response was a mixture of surprise and fear. I enjoyed his discomfiture, but ... I don't know, Arch was right there and I ... I mean, why do we reassure people in situations like that? I should have let him sweat. "It was a long time ago."

He didn't seem all that reassured. "I see. I'm— sorry."

"Yeah?" 'Sorry' seemed inadequate.

"That was a very tough decision to make. To pull out of Valhalla."

"Forgive me, but I think it was probably a lot tougher on us than it was on you."

"Of course." He sighed. "Of course. We knew it would be— would be— But we really felt we had no choice. It was either that or abandon some other project. Valhalla was where it started. We couldn't afford to let it spread—"

"I guess they were upset about watching their friends die." The word 'die' seemed to reverberate around the passageway. It upset me to realize how much it had crept back into my vocabulary. It certainly upset Daimler:

"Well— well, everyone was compensated—"

I turned on him, "Yes, after the suit was settled all of us got some cash. Now, what was it I replaced my wife with? Oh, right, I remember. Investments."

Daimler looked at the floor. "You must have loved her very much. I certainly loved mine."

Despite this confession I didn't really feel like being pals with him, but Archie asked, "Where did she— I mean where did you— lose her?"

We turned into the common room and had a seat. "It was right before the end of the war," he said. "The blockade of Circe had been going on for ten years. We all figured that the Pleiades would capitulate in a matter of weeks. Months at most. Still, I asked her not to go."

"Go where?" Archie asked. I guess I was mildly curious, too, but mostly I just hated him.

"Shangri-La."

"Oh," Archie said. 'Oh' was right. The Yin had nuked Shangri-La. They just didn't have the resources to build a space navy big enough to break the blockade around Circe, and the blockade was having a devastating effect. Women were starving to death and unable to re-boot. So the Yin decided they would show Draco that they could still attack wherever they wanted to. Shangri-La is way down in the home worlds, around Xi Boötis, only twenty-two light years from Earth. They were hoping for a huge propaganda victory that would cause Draco to withdraw. It didn't work. Two days later the D. E. F. wiped Boleyn off the face of Circe and three weeks after that the Treaty of Alcyone was signed. The Yin agreed to come back on the net. Draco agreed to allow the Pleiades to remain politically independent. The whole thing had basically been for nothing.

"And you sold the nukes to the Yin?" I asked. Like I said, I hated him.

"Well, not exactly—"

"What do you mean? You either did or you didn't." I just wanted to make this skag squirm in his own guilt. I'm not sure why he felt he needed to defend himself to me— maybe it was because he had seen my memory of Valhalla— but he did:

"They developed the nukes on their own, but we sold them most of their defense architecture. I suppose if we hadn't, the war would have been quite different. It might not have taken place at all."

"I hope you made a profit." I wanted to destroy him. I wanted to shred him. I wanted to dump him into a star the way we had dumped Drake. And then jump in after him, maybe. I don't know.

"At the time," he intoned, "we thought we were being socially progressive."

"By selling arms to people?"

He turned to me. "What would you have done? The Pleiades were a small group of women wanting to try something new and different. Wanting to experiment. They were facing the overwhelming might of Draco. They came to us for help. We thought that if we gave them the means to defend themselves—"

"Sold them the means—"

"All right, *sold* them the means. Businesses exist to make money. The point is, we were hoping that this would calm things down." He sighed. "What it did was embolden the more radical faction of the Yin to pass the Independent Network Act and start their gender purification program."

"You had to have seen that coming! They'd been talking about it for decades—"

"I suppose we should have, but we didn't."

There didn't seem to be anything else to say. We sat there for a moment, then Arch got up and started making some food. Finally, to break the silence or maybe just to keep messing with him any way I could, I said, "So what's the deal with all the names?"

He left his wife on Shangri-La and brought his gaze back to me. "Names?" he asked.

"Yeah," I responded. "Steel, Estelle. What's the big deal?"

"Oh," he said, and he looked like the past might eat him alive right then. He stared at the wall, while he decided whether it was worth explaining to me. Finally, "It's their little joke they like to play on me."

"Joke?"

He smiled grimly. "It's something they discovered when they were playing together one day. Kristel: Krupp. Estelle: Steel."

"I don't get it."

He sighed. "The Krupp Steel Works were notorious back in the twentieth century for employing slave labor to manufacture armaments for the Nazi regime on ancient Earth. My name—the Daimler name—was also associated with that regime. They never seem to tire of reminding me of that."

That was it? Steel called herself that just to annoy Daimler? "She seems to take her name pretty seriously."

He looked hollow, lost. "I suppose it gives them a sense of their power over me." He rubbed his eyes, then looked up at Archie. "That smells good, but I don't think I could eat anything right now. I think I'll get some sleep." He pushed his chair back, fought double gravity to stand up and trudged out of the room.

When he had disappeared down the passageway I turned to Archie. "Holy skag," I said.

"Yeah," she replied. "He must have cloned them right after the war. Can you imagine? Their relationship has been going on for more than a millennium."

I shook my head. "It couldn't have always been like *this*, could it?"

"Like what?"

"You know: fighting, mocking, belittling ..."

Arch stared after him. "I don't know ... I don't know." She held up a pan of pasta. "You want some of this?"

"Yeah, looks good," I answered.

We ate in silence. When we were finished Arch said, "How about we go have some two-gee sex? It'll be good for our core muscles."

"Yeah, okay," I answered. We put away our dishes and headed to her quarters.

I sat up in darkness—gasping, sweating. I couldn't call out. I couldn't ... I couldn't remember the word. Sheets rustled. A gentle hand brushed my shoulder, slid down my arm.

"What is it, Mo?" Archie's voice was like dry leaves blowing. She sat up beside me, cleared her throat. "What's wrong?" She smelled of sleep.

I wanted to answer, but I couldn't. My chest wouldn't work that way. I couldn't catch my breath. "I— I—"

"Did you have another nightmare?"

I stared at the darkness. I managed to nod. Arch slid her hand down to mine, rested her chin in the crook of my neck, kissed my jaw.

"It's okay," she murmured. "You're okay."

"Yeah," I managed to get out. "I'm ..." My breathing was starting to slow but I could feel my heart pounding.

She rubbed my chest, draped her other arm over my shoulder. The liquid softness of her breasts warmed my back. "What did you dream? Was it the same one?"

"They're—" I breathed, "never quite— I mean they're always ... similar. It's ... kind of ..."

"What was it?" She held me. "Tell me."

I blinked, looked around, came back to the world. "It was— they're always about my— about my— you know, my— That's just it. I can't think of the word. I can't think of the— I can't think of the word."

"The one for your maternal parent? What you called her?"

"Yeah. Yeah, she's—" I rubbed my forehead, my eyes. "She's in danger. The house is burning, or, or someone is chasing her ... something, something is chasing her or the house is burning or they're going to do something to her or ... or something is chasing her and I can see it ... chasing her through the burning house. It's a ... something, some kind of ... I can see her silhouetted against the flames. She's on the balcony and the roof timbers are falling and it's getting closer to her ... I'm hiding ... I'm hiding in a good place ... a good place. I want her to ... I want to call out to her, to ... to show her my hiding place, to tell her to run, but I can't ... I can't think of the word ... I can't call out to her because I can't think of the word!" I was twisting the sheets in my fists.

"Shh-sh-sh-shh," Archie rubbed my shoulders and down my arms. "It was just a dream. Just a dream." She put her cheek on my shoulder and wrapped her arms around my waist. "It was very profound, very ... moving to watch the children with their parents on Eden. It wasn't always nice, but it was always ... intense. The feelings, the emotions were very intense, very ... saturated. I saw a woman actually hit her daughter once. It was ... I don't know ... disturbing."

I was breathing more easily. Archie's voice was soothing, like my— like my— like *her* voice was. My mo— whatever I called her. "I can't understand why I can't remember what I called her. I remember what I called my father, all the things: Dad, Daddy, but my ... my ... I can't remember *anything* I called my ..."

"I don't know," soothed Archie.

"I wouldn't have erased it. Never. Never. I never would have erased it. I mean ... I mean I'd forgotten the word 'sister,' but when I heard it again I recognized it. I was ... devastated that I'd forgotten it, but it had been so long ... so long ago. But

I recognized it when I heard it. I remembered then. I remembered. *Why* can't I remember ... remember the word for ..."

"Steel was never a very good mother. On Eden. I mean, I don't think she was. I don't know. I can only compare her to my caretakers where I was hatched, but ... I don't think, I don't think she has the right, the right emotional makeup or the right background or something. Some of the women there took to it very naturally. Others ... It was surprising to me."

"What?"

"Just the range of capability. It was very difficult not to intervene. The parents would ... would lie to their children sometimes to get them to behave or to ... to establish dominance over them. We could see it when damage was being done, when emotional injuries were being inflicted. But we weren't there long enough to see what the long-term effects would be. I wish we could have ... I wish ..."

"You wish Steel hadn't tagged along and screwed everything up?"

Archie sighed, "Yeah, I guess."

"I wish I could remember what I called my ... I don't understand it. I don't understand why I can't ..."

"Hmm." Archie's tone brought my eyes to her.

"What?" I asked.

She looked thoughtful. "I don't know. I might ..." She kissed my jaw again. "I might check some things. I wonder if my security clearance still works."

"What do you mean?"

Her brow furrowed. "Let me check some things. I'll see what I can find out."

I didn't know what she was talking about, but I said, "Okay."

"Do you think you can go back to sleep now?"

I nodded.

"Good," she said, and lay back down. "This gravity wipes me out."

CHAPTER 34

We came in tight and hot, our neutron plume preceding us, blowing a hole in the corona of the star that gave life to Brainard's Planet. The two research satellites orbiting there—Draco's and The Pleiades'—were focused down, not out, constantly scanning the world's surface for any hints that might unlock the mysteries of the biosphere. Still, just in case they were glancing our way, we slid close past the stellar surface and into a trajectory that would keep us between the sun and the planet so the fire of our exhaust would be swallowed up in the fire of the star. High-energy gravitons would give us away immediately so we throttled the torch itself back to just two gees, eliminating the need to use the Musahdi filter or the graviton impellers at all. We rode the neutron stream, decelerating all the way through the system, past the three inner planets and into low orbit.

Draco and The Pleiades could have made it a lot harder on us, but bureaucratic intransigence had trumped common sense. They could have divided up the chores of studying Brainard's Planet and put their respective probes in completely different orbits, but, of course, they both wanted to study the same things. The major colonies were in a particular area that was in daylight at a particular time, so both nations had put their probes in the same polar orbit, the one following the other by a few hundred klicks. This made it easy for us: we simply inserted a half-orbit behind them, always keeping the bulk of the world between us and prying eyes.

But to move around on the surface, we needed a disguise. This was why Steel had made a reality of Brainard's Planet the last time they were here. Some of the slugs' colonies had moved since then so our first task was to re-record the entire planet. This took more than a week in orbit, but as soon as we were finished Yuri hacked into the two research satellites and started feeding our version of reality into them. Someday some dusty exobiologist might notice the substitution, but we would be long gone by then.

We each visited Archie in the medical bay, Drake's penultimate resting place. A lot of changes had been made. Yuri had managed to design a lot of new equipment that we hoped would let us analyze samples of the Brainardite slime, the 'plants' and perhaps even samples of tissue taken from the slugs. But that wasn't why Archie had sent for us. When your body is in real trouble you don't have time to think about getting on the net and uploading, it's done automatically. Since we weren't on the net, if even one of us did a comprehensive memory dump onto Steel's system, it would overload, causing it to crash. So she needed to disable our upload reflex. This made sense, but was one more reminder that we would be on our own on Brainard's Planet.

At the end of the final work shift, before our descent to the surface, Steel gave us a somewhat stilted motivational speech in the control room; then she and Daimler bid us goodnight and retreated to her quarters. It made me sad, and angry. If there was ever a night when we all should have been together that was it, but she couldn't afford it. We were the only human beings within light years, cut off from the net, unable to communicate with anyone but ourselves. Beyond the thin skin of our starship there were literally quadrillions of kilometers of cold vacuum before you got to the first human-occupied planet. But as alone and lonely as we were, it wasn't lonely enough for her. It seemed that John Cheatham's death had taken something from her so profound that she couldn't overcome it. She had been betrayed by mortality and she wasn't going to trust anything anymore, not even her crew. In some ways, not even Alice. It wasn't that nothing but the quest mattered to her anymore; it was more that nothing else even existed. We were no longer people to her so much as we were imponderables— parameters of the problem that couldn't be quantified or extrapolated. Maybe she was just terrified of losing us the way she had lost Drake, the way she'd lost her son, her husband. I don't know. Whatever it was, she left us to ourselves.

Nothing remained to be done. Everything was ready. We were left to float through the Lightdancer's quiet, darkened passageways looking for solace, for absolution maybe, or for company, or for peace.

One by one we drifted into the common room. It was lit as by a giant aquarium; the calm blue light of the sun-drenched world turning beneath us flowed in through the crystalline ports. We seemed to have a shared need to look at our adversary, our goal, the source of our fear and hope. We didn't say much, just gazed out at the planet of doom. It wasn't a recorded reality we were looking at; it was really there. The southern ocean, bright as beaten steel, washed the ragged coastline of the north. Gentle wisps of lacy, lazy cirrus caressed the land. All was soft, quiet and still.

If you looked closely, you could see a colony now and then as a tiny brown smudge. They were down there, the slugs, roaming about as they had for the last five hundred years and who knows how much longer. For all of our study, our ignorance of the Brainardites was almost pristine, as was our ignorance of the universe, even our ignorance of ourselves. Here were the very same slugs that Brainard had discovered and tried to contact. All of the life forms down there were the same individuals that Brainard's expedition had seen. Nothing died there— not plants nor animals nor their friends or relations. Life moving, interacting, but never expiring. And yet it took every bit of technological wizardry that Yuri could come up with to keep it from being lethal to us.

How had it happened? How could an ecosystem achieve such an incredibly delicate balance that *nothing* died? Was this simply another possible scenario in an infinitely diverse creation? Could it have happened this way on Earth? Did we just miss out on the evolutionary jackpot and so have to suffer the slings and arrows of outrageous fortune? Or did the Brainardites happen to pray to the right god, or somehow just avoid falling from grace?

We were going to try to find out. We'd cobbled together our gadgets and tools and we would descend into the terror. We would bathe in the pool of immortality and death and try to bring away the forbidden fruit. At one time or another each of our eyes wandered to Alice's sweet face. She glowed in the blue light of reflected ocean, very pensive, very solemn. I wanted her to smile, to laugh. I wanted to solve the problem.

And then she did laugh. "Hey, Yuri! It's our last night in microgravity. Let's go screw our brains out!"

Yuri laughed back at her. "You're on!"

She kicked off the wall and swam over to him. They hooked arms and legs and became a tangle. "You want to log on while we do it?"

He laughed again. "Why not?" They sailed out the hatch and down the passageway.

Tamika looked at Marcus. "That's not a bad idea."

Marcus smiled at her, then turned to us and said, "Have a good night." They followed Alice and Yuri.

Then Arch looked at me. When something makes sense it just makes sense, but I'd noticed something and I needed to speak: "You know, Alice has been doing that a lot."

"What?" Arch asked.

"Logging on with her partner while she has sex."

Arch looked after her. "Hmm. I guess she's ... I don't know, lonely?"

"Maybe." I thought about Alice and me, when we had logged on together. "Maybe."

I took one last look out the port at the place that had come to define my life. "Come on," Archie said. "It'll still be there tomorrow."

"Yeah," I answered.

As we swam out of the hatch, the Lightdancer passed into the shadow of the world.

The brakes had kicked in and the gees were building to maximum. We were on the final rotation. Brainard's Planet was no longer a planet to me. The horizon was flattening, the black sky was turning indigo and then blue and then I was weightless as the hook released and I plummeted toward the only alien biosphere humanity had ever found. As air resistance increased, I reached terminal velocity and I was floating rather than falling, buffeted on a mattress of air. Looking around I could see my six companions, stomachs down, arms out, knees bent to the gale. We had almost eighty kilometers to fall before the parasails would open. Death spread out like a map below us.

Even falling through the sky toward the place that had killed so many of us, I felt improbably safe inside the e-suit Yuri had designed. It was really solid, tough. Impressive. I felt like I could swim through a nuclear reactor or take a nap in raw sewage and be just fine. And we had learned a lot. Just knowing that the plague was caused by the slime the Brainardites secreted gave us tools Brainard hadn't had, or even Steel, the last time she'd been here. Unlike Brainard's expedition or Steel's first trip here, we were aiming for the desert north of the tropical belt of life that clung to the edge of the southern ocean. If we had a mishap on landing we would be away from any life forms. It might give us a little more time to deal with damage or trauma.

Our home had preceded us. For the past several days we had been dropping packets to the landing site, two of which had inflated and would serve as our habitat and laboratory. All of them had Yuri's surefire anti-plague system built in, but hopefully they were far enough away from the inhabited zone that it wouldn't matter. After we hauled all the supplies into the habitat we would be able to stay on the surface for a couple of months—little enough time to discover a way to save Alice.

I bulleted Yuri, "It looks beautiful from up here!"

[It's pretty beautiful down there, too. Otherworldly seems inadequate somehow. Wait till you walk through the tube fields. It's like nothing you've ever experienced.]

"I can't wait. I think."

Yuri laughed. [Yeah, we'll need to be careful.]

[You see the small colony to the southeast?] Steel's voice was focused. The six of us acknowledged. [That's our primary target. We'll try to get samples there.] As we continued to fall, smaller things began to resolve. I could see a main trail leading to and away from the village or hive or whatever you wanted to call it. I couldn't see any individual Brainardites yet, but the mauve/pink of the surrounding tube fields was becoming more intense.

A thin cloud deck was moving in from the west. It thickened to near-opacity as we fell toward it and now I could tell how fast I was falling. It rushed toward me and slammed into me insubstantially, like faeries or fading hope, and I was through it and could really start to look around.

Tamika said, [I can see the hab and lab.]

I could see them, too: two tiny white spots. They were about five klicks from the nearest tube fields, resting on a rocky plain just south of a fair-sized canyon.

Alice called out: [There they are!]

I looked where she was pointing, south toward the trail, and I saw them: beige, double-ended teardrops with crab-shaped carapaces swaying on their backs as they ponderously moved along.

Yuri: [Must be market day.]

Archie: [Yeah, everybody's out and about.]

Marcus interrupted: [Let's cut the chatter. We're coming up on parasail deployment. Disperse.]

We spread out to allow our sails to open and in a few moments they did, simultaneously, just like clockwork. Smooth sailing. The rocky surface of the planet of doom gently rose up to meet our feet. We released our chutes and were down.

After ten days of floating in orbit we were back in the realm of acceleration. I could feel Brainard's Planet pulling on me: my arms, my head, the fluid in my inner ears. It wanted to crush me, to suck me down into its very core. I started walking toward the habitat, my footfalls like timpani, like thunder, like the sound of the end of the world.

It took us three days to get the supplies stowed and the lab up and running. We also trained with the lasers daily—getting used to the weight, to the range and intensity controls. We burned a lot of rocks.

On the evening of the third day Steel gathered us together in the habitat. As I sat down at our little table my arm brushed against a fork and knocked it to the floor with an absurdly loud CRASH! We all jumped. It was so annoying. I picked it up and placed it carefully back on the table.

Steel looked better now that we were finally here. Memories of past tragedies were being replaced by hope, or mania, or maybe just the comfort of knowing what needed to be done next. She was made of electricity as she took us in—Archie, Marcus, Alice, Yuri, Tamika, and myself. Daimler was on the Lightdancer with Ham. I wondered how they were getting along. I wondered what deals Steel had made with him, or he with her. The thought crossed my mind that he might steal the ship, but that was silly. Where could he go without us? We were the engine.

She almost vibrated as she started to speak, barely able to control the emotions coursing through her. This was where we would make the whole venture pay off or not. We would save Alice's life or we would fail to save it; there was no third option. She negotiated with the pressure as we negotiated with our weight. "We are here to find out as much as we can about the biological processes at work here. Not just how the plague works, but how the Brainardites work. We all ... we all know what we're ultimately looking for—" she had to stop, her throat full. For a moment she was unable to even look at us. Then, "and I'm confident we'll find it, but I want us to be systematic. I want us to be methodical. More than anything I want us to be careful, to be safe." Again she had to stop speaking. Memories filled her eyes with water. "Tomorrow I just want to go into the tube fields. Not too deep. Just go in and take some samples of the tubes, the spider-plane trees."

Archie said, "I'd like to collect a few of the smaller sluglets and zooids." She pronounced it 'zoh-oids.' It meant 'animal-like.' Most of the perambulatory life here resembled the slugs, only smaller: soft bodies with nothing you could call limbs—no endoskeletons, and no visible sensory organs. Most of them had some sort of hard shell or carapace on their backs and they just wandered around, seemingly aimlessly, never in a hurry. Nobody was in a hurry here except us.

Steel answered, "That's fine. Tomorrow, though, more than anything, I want us to test our new procedures. Marcus?"

Marcus finished checking something on Steel's system and then looked at all of us: "We'll all carry hand lasers. Archie, Alice and Yuri will collect samples and specimens. Mo will flank to the left. Captain, you will flank to the right. You two will be our lookouts. Report anything unusual, unexpected, especially anything moving quickly. Tamika and I will cover from the rear with the two long-range cannons. If anyone spots anything moving toward us at any speed that seems at all threatening, we will retreat beyond the edge of the tube fields. We've never seen anything venture out onto the desert. If something does pursue us onto the rock we will continue to retreat. Only if someone is overtaken or the laboratory or habitat is threatened will I give the order to fire. I and *only* I will give the order to use the lasers. We need to remember that the lasers are probably the most dangerous things on this planet right now, to us as much as to anything else."

We regarded each other with gravity but also with an awed bemusement. We certainly knew the danger we were facing, but no one had heard this sort of language in over a thousand years, not since the end of the war.

"I haven't detected any evidence of Brainardite biology beyond the edge of the tube fields," Archie said. "I think this will be a good place to ... It was a good idea to set up base camp out here."

Steel examined Yuri with some of her old camaraderie. "Everything's functioning very well. Great work."

Yuri smiled, but he said, "We'll see."

This caused Steel to soften her posture; her eyes dropped for a moment. "We'll leave camp first thing in the morning, spend six hours in the field, then back to camp for lab work and analysis. I suggest we all get some sleep."

We paired up and wandered to our bunks: me and Archie, Marcus and Tamika, Alice and Yuri. The six of us had kind of settled on partners. It happens sometimes, particularly under stress. Steel went to her bunk alone.

After a quiet night and a quiet breakfast we climbed through hatches in the outer wall of the habitat and into our suits. Yuri had set up the e-suits so they would always stay outside; no surface that came into contact with Brainardite life would ever be in the hab or lab. We slid into them through hatches in their backs, closed up and detached from the hab wall. Five klicks of bare rock separated us from the tube fields. We could see them; the horizon was significantly farther on Brainard's Planet than it was on Earth. It made the fields seem closer than they were.

The e-suits worked great. It was almost effortless to walk, but it took significant time to speed up, slow down or change direction. It wasn't like running around naked. We sounded like an ancient cannonade as we tromped over the rock.

We were nearing the closest tubes when Yuri's voice filled my auditory lobe: [HEY! Hey HEY! Mo! Look what I found! Look what I found!]

I turned and lumbered over to him. Everyone turned to look. "What is it?"

He bent down to the ground and picked up a small stone. It glinted in the morning light as he held it up to me. [Look!] It was a little chondritic meteorite. About the same size as the one I had found on Mars so many centuries ago; the one Krupp had ripped off of my shoulder. [What are the chances, huh? What are the chances? I mean this place has a pretty thick atmosphere. How many of these guys make it to the surface? And yet here it was, right where we were walking!]

The others gathered around to look as he placed it in my hand. I just stared at it. It really was quite similar to the one I had lost, a little smaller. [What are the chances?] Yuri continued, [I know it can't replace your first talisman, but, but how many people have a talisman from Brainard's Planet? You know? What are the chances?]

Looking into Yuri's faceplate, I saw his dancing eyes. I could feel everyone lift as if the curse had been broken. Holding up the little rock so they could see it, I said, "Thank you, Yuri. Thank you very much. This is— this is really—"

[What are the chances, huh? What are the chances?] He clapped me on the back.

[All right,] even Marcus' voice seemed buoyant, [we need to stay focused. We have a lot of work to do.]

I placed the meteorite in my sample pouch—we all had them in case we came across something we wanted, and formed back up. The tube fields were only fifty meters away.

Walking toward that softly undulating carpet reminded me of Lawson's Crossing on Eden. Once again we were approaching someone else's home unannounced. Were we welcome guests or feared invaders? Or did we just not matter to the Brainardites at all? The tubes right on the edge of the desert were small—as thick as my wrist and coming up to no more than my knees—but soon we were weaving our way through thigh-thick polyps that reached up to our chests. They responded to us: shrinking away as we approached and then curving toward us—swelling, blushing in a sensual, almost sexual manner, then reaching for us as we moved on, longing for a moment and then forgetting our passage altogether. If you touched them their surface texture would roughen, dimple, I guess, like a woman's aureole.

[Mo, heads up. You're a lookout, not a tourist.]

"Sorry, Marcus. I mean, yes, sir." I lifted my gaze to scan above the swirling salmon sea. A little farther in I could see spider-plane trees punctuate the pink carpet here and there, their web-like fronds obsidian black supporting billows of shuddering, turquoise platelets shot with gold and lavender.

"The *tubes* sure notice us," I said, to no one in particular.

[Yes, but they don't build anything and they certainly don't talk,] Archie responded.

"I was just wondering why they would but nothing else does."

[You and everyone else. This is a very strange place.]

We moved farther into the field, taking samples as we went. Yuri and Alice each collected several sluglets and 'zooids.' I never saw any. They didn't crawl very far up the tubes; you had to be looking to catch them, and my focus was mostly on the horizon looking for danger.

Archie decided that she would collect tube samples from the very edge of the field where they were smallest. [I'd rather get a complete specimen,] she said, [And I just don't want to harm anything if I can help it.] Knowing that everything here was at least hundreds if not thousands of years old put a tremendous pressure on us to not step on or even bruise anything. The place was a living museum and we were on the wrong side of the glass.

When we got back to the edge of the field at the end of the day, Arch bent down to look at a small pink, weaving individual and started a discussion with Yuri about whether she should pry the tube loose from the rock or chip off the piece of rock with the tube on it.

[When the slugs move them they just seem to detach, but I can't see how they do it. It must be chemical or, or biological. These little guys are stuck fast.]

[I'd just take the rock with it,] Yuri answered. [It looks like sandstone. Something sedimentary, anyway. Can you pry a piece loose?]

[I think so.]

At that moment an incredible basso profundo thrumming swelled over us out of the south. It grew and throbbed and waned and grew again. Everyone turned to look. It was so powerful I could feel my suit vibrate, resonating with the surging waves of sound.

No one seemed to be particularly worried, so I took it upon myself to say, "What the hell's that?"

[Evening prayers,] Alice answered.

"What?"

[You'll see it when we go into the colony. It's what made Brainard think they had a religion. It's very powerful to see. Up close.]

"I'll bet. It must be really loud."

[No, it's just such a low frequency. It travels a long way. Look at the tubes.]

I did. You could see them vibrating subtly like thousands of amplifiers.

Archie worked at the rock for at least half an hour, accompanied by that ominous, pulsing drone, before she finally said, [There! Got it loose.] She stood up with her prize. Surrounded by all of us, it didn't know which way to reach. It was strangely romantic. It swelled and throbbed and stretched for us, one after the other—turning, twisting, blushing a deep rose, almost violet.

"It sure seems like it's trying to get our attention," I said.

[I know,] said Archie. [Why the display? What's the purpose of the color? Nothing has any eyes here.]

[Maybe just a byproduct of some biological process? You know, just a ... just a coincidental byproduct of something ... or something?]

[Look out, Marcus. You're starting to sound like me.] Arch carefully put the tube in a collection case. [I think we can head back for today. I have lots of stuff to study.]

[All right, let's go,] said Steel. The bass throbbing ceased then as abruptly as it had started, leaving only the soft wafting sound of the tubes rubbing together as they slowly danced. It wasn't until then that I realized we'd let our guard down. We were on the edge of the field and all of us had focused on the little tube. It was so hard to think we were in danger here—everything soft, gently swaying, calm.

Marcus noticed me lift up to scan the horizon again. He said, [Captain, we need to maintain watch.]

[Oh, yes. Of course. Mo?]

[I'm on it.] We made our way back to the lab.

Yuri, Alice and Archie placed their specimens in trays arrayed along the outside of one of the lab walls. And me, too, I placed my new talisman in a tray of its own. We'd need to make sure it was completely sterile before I could bring it into the lab; the tiniest trace of slime would be fatal to all of us. Then we tromped around to the other side of the big, inflated igloo and backed up to the hatches there, attached ourselves, opened up the mated hatches in the backs of our suits and slipped inside.

Archie assigned us all tasks and we got busy. We did the grunt work—sorting, weighing, taking holograms, making sure everything was recorded, while Arch did the real science. Yuri had come up with a great design for the lab. All of the specimens stayed outside while we worked with them inside. Even the manipulators that stuck through the lab wall generated his anti-plague field.

Archie would occasionally emit small vocal sounds as she worked, but nothing that was intelligible to us. Then, after a couple of hours of this she said, "This is good. This is big."

We looked toward her. Steel asked, "What have you found?"

"This is incredible. This is really incredible. This is big."

"What?"

She turned and looked at us, calm, balancing. "They're multi-cellular. Made of cells. Everything we collected today is made up of little protein bubbles filled with salt water, just like us. The proteins are different than the ones we use but that's no surprise."

"So," Steel started again, "does that mean—"

"It means that all of the life that we know of in the entire universe is cellular." Archie was trying to stay calm, but her eyes burned with the fire of discovery. "We all assumed it would be, life here, on Brainard's Planet, but we didn't *know* until now. This is huge. It's incredible. My hands are shaking. Come here and look at this." She led us over to the display she had been using and called up an image. "This is the—I don't know, I guess you'd call it the epidermis—of that small tube." We could see rows and rows of little blobs on the magnified image. They sure looked like cells to me.

I said, "But wasn't that scum they found on, what planet was it, um, Paradise, I think. Wasn't that made of cells?"

Archie replied, "Yes, the quasi-algae on Paradise. But that was single-celled life. These are complex, multi-cellular organisms. We've never found anything like this anywhere but Earth. Who knows how many more ecosystems we'll discover, but, but for the first one we meet to be built like *we* are ... this is, this is huge. This is huge."

Steel asked, "But what does this mean for Alice—"

Archie turned on her, "Now, Captain, you're going to have to be patient. I'm trying to write an entire freaking biology text from the ground up. It's going to take a little time."

"We don't have time—"

"Then we shouldn't be wasting it on conversations like this one. I'm working as fast as I can."

"I just don't want us to get side-tracked. I don't want us going down blind alleys. We're here for a particular—"

"I *know* why we're here!" And just like that the tension level went through the roof. Archie stopped and took a breath. "Look, Captain, look. You see those things?" She pointed to dark spots in the middle of the cells. "Those are nuclei. Do you understand what that means? It means that on two tiny, nickel-iron specks orbiting stars that are twelve hundred light years apart, life has formed the same kinds of structures. Bubbles within bubbles. You see those squiggles?" She increased the magnification. "Those are chromosomes. Chromosomes made of deoxyribonucleic acid. DNA."

"I know what DNA is. What are you telling me?"

"I'm telling you that we haven't found any deal breakers yet. I'm telling you that this can't be coincidence."

"What can't?"

"These structures. The odds against two completely separate biospheres evolving the same kinds of structures simply by chance are more than astronomical. It means that this is how it works. Put the right chemicals together and combine them with an energy source and this is what you get. These kinds of structures."

"That's all well and good but—"

"I'm telling you that our chances of finding a cure for Alice just got a lot better. A LOT better. By orders of magnitude, I don't even know how many orders. This is HUGE."

"Oh, okay. Well, that's good, then—"

"Those are chromosomes, huh?" Yuri interjected.

"What?" Archie turned. "Oh, yes. Chromosomes. Yes."

"So these cells reproduce by dividing?"

"Well, I haven't seen it happen yet, but, yes, I assume they do."

"They reproduce."

"What are you driving at?"

"Well, it's just that … it's just that nothing reproduces here. Right? At least on a large scale, nothing reproduces. We're looking at the same individuals, the same *number* of individuals that Brainard saw five centuries ago."

"Oh, right. Yes. Yes, that's still … yes. We still have a lot of work to do."

"I just don't get it." Yuri took another look at the image on the screen. "I mean everything we know about terrestrial life is dynamic. It's constantly changing—

bell curve growth patterns, populations growing to fill an ecological niche, then overfilling it, then declining. There's none of that here. There's no population growth, no decline. It's static, at least for the last five centuries. Static. I don't get it."

"It's like a utopia," I said.

"What do you mean?" asked Alice.

"Oh, you know, those thinkers on Earth back in the— what was it, the eighteenth or nineteenth century I think— they thought that they could work things out to a certain point and then they'd just stay that way: perfect forever. I think they were called Utopians ... no, no, Marxists, something like that. There were other groups, too. They each had their own prescriptions for achieving a perfect world."

Alice said, "That would be nice."

"What would be nice about it?" Yuri asked. "Stasis is death. Change is the most sublime aspect of the universe. And, anyway, even if it were desirable, or possible, to make things perfect, you're talking about a manufactured condition. An artifact. What we have here is a natural system. I don't see how it works, how it *could* work."

"I just meant it would be nice if there weren't any problems," Alice replied. Steel put a hand on her shoulder. Alice didn't quite shrug it off.

Yuri answered, "I suppose. Maybe. But if there weren't any problems, what would we *do*? Just wander around?"

"Well, for one thing I wouldn't be dying," Alice answered.

Yuri looked stricken. "Oh, Alice, I'm ... I didn't mean to say— Of course, some problems are ... I wasn't saying ... I meant—"

"It's okay." She looked at him with real kindness, affection. "I'm okay."

"That's what the Brainardites seem to do," I said. "Wander around."

Yuri checked in with Alice for a second, then responded, "Yeah, yeah, but still what are we saying? I mean all of the architecture is present in these cells for mitosis, right? Which suggests that that is how they reproduce."

"Well, they have chromosomes. That's correct. I haven't identified all of the internal structures," Archie answered.

"It suggests that they *do* reproduce."

"I would say so, yes."

"Why?"

"What do you mean?"

"Why would they? Reproduce?"

Archie thought for a minute. Then, "I'm not sure what you're— I mean, I don't know if there's a *reason*, per se. It's just how it works. This chemistry self-replicates. That's what it does."

"But to what effect? In this ecological system. What does cellular reproduction *do*?"

"Umm, it would replace worn out cells—"

"So we're saying that, at least at a cellular level, there is death here."

"I guess so. I don't know. I haven't seen any cells die. I haven't seen any reproduce."

"Right, right, but the architecture is there."

"It is."

"So, if they *do* reproduce, they reproduce at *exactly* the same rate as they die off."

"Whoa," Archie pushed her hair back and looked at the ceiling, "*that* seems far-fetched."

"That's what I was thinking," Yuri answered.

"This whole place is mind-boggling," said Marcus.

"So, Draco and The Pleiades have been observing this planet for five centuries," I said.

"Right."

"I assume they've done some kind of census."

Archie said, "Every decade. I have the figures. Same numbers every time. They don't have the resolution to get the smallest organisms, but for all the larger ones the populations are absolutely stable."

"Hmm." I thought. "How many, what would you call them, species? How many have they identified?"

"Well, one of the things that defines a species is the ability of its members to reproduce with each other, so—"

"Since Brainardites don't reproduce—"

"Right. But they have identified around twenty-five hundred discrete physical types."

"Twenty-five hundred."

"That's right."

"How many terrestrial species are there?"

"True terrestrials or including all the ones we've created to survive on other planets?" Yuri asked.

"Just the ones on Earth."

"Well, it used to be more, but there are still around thirty million."

"Hmm. We've got the Brainardites beat there."

"You see? This is what I mean," Steel interjected angrily. "We don't have time for this!"

"Okay, okay," Archie said. "I've found some other stuff. It might be important, too. It's certainly important to science."

"I don't care about science. I just want— I want to get Alice—"

"Yes. We all do. Look at this." Archie called up another image. "This is one of the sluglets." She focused down through the body, in and out so we could see the internal structures. "You see? It has organs. Specialized organs. Once again, we assumed life here would, but we didn't know until now."

Tamika said, "That— that looks kind of like a ... Is that a digestive system?"

"It's what it looks like to me. But notice ..." She focused forward and then to the rear of the animal, if it was an animal.

"Where's the mouth?" Marcus asked.

"That's the thing. There's no mouth. No entrance, no exit. But all of the internal structure is there. It's a digestive system with no way to get any food into it or waste out of it." We all shook our heads in wonder. "There's more. Let me change the sensitivity. Okay. You see that?"

"Nerves. A nervous system." That was Alice.

"Looks like. But look, no sensory organs anywhere. No eyes, no ears, no olfactory organ. All the motor neurons—I'm calling them neurons because that's what they look like to me—all of them look fully developed. But you see these?" She pointed to tiny parallel strands on the screen. "These look like sensory neurons, but they're stunted. It's like they have some tactile sense, perhaps even a sense of taste on their skin, but it's very attenuated compared to ours, very rudimentary."

"What are these concentrations of nerves up here?" Tamika asked.

"Right," Archie answered. "What are they? Are they the beginnings of sensory organs? Maybe. Maybe Brainardites take so long to evolve that they're all still waiting for their eyes and ears."

"I don't see how they could evolve at all," said Yuri. "If they don't reproduce how could they evolve?"

"Right. You're right. I don't see how, either," Arch answered.

"So," Yuri rubbed his forehead, "are we saying that the biosphere as we see it now, these complex organisms, this whole biological complex, somehow emerged full-grown out of the head of Zeus? One day we have a proto-planetary disc swirling around a star and the next we have a fully populated planet? With intricate interactions and an absolutely stable population level?"

We all stared at the conundrum for a moment. Finally Arch said, "I don't know." She thought a little more, but could only come up with, "I don't know."

The next few weeks were like that. We'd go into the tube fields, a little deeper each day, and collect samples and specimens. Then back to the lab for cataloging and analysis. Each morning we'd take the previous day's samples and place them back where we got them. It was becoming almost a fetish. These things had been here for so long we didn't want to do anything that might upset the balance in this remarkable and baffling place.

Meanwhile, a small miracle was taking place before our eyes. Maybe it was a big miracle, I don't know. It was hard to notice at the beginning. I guess the first thing that caught my attention was how Yuri was starting to behave, like the hollow shell of fatalism that had kept him propped up for so long was filling up with something wonderful. Even in the crushing gravity of Brainard's Planet, he seemed to have a lighter step; his head seemed closer to the sky. His eyes, which had always been friendly, now projected a warm approval of the universe that seemed unbounded. And then there was what Alice was starting to do to the bunk she was sharing with him. It wasn't anything much at first. She was taking the material that our supplies had been packed in and making stuff with it. The first thing was a little kind of drape or shade that she put over the lamp in their bunk alcove. Then a few woven garlands appeared that she hung like bunting over the bed. After that she made a curtain that she could pull closed, giving them a little private cave to sleep in.

We all noticed this going on but we didn't think much about it until, at the end of a long, hard day in the lab, Arch turned to Yuri as she might have to any of us and said, "Well, I'm beat. You want to go have some sex?"

Alice moved to Yuri's side with surprising alacrity and put her arm through the crook of his elbow. She gave Archie a look that I swear could have kept the plague at bay. Arch was a little stunned. She actually retreated a step, saying, "I'm— I'm sorry. I didn't— I mean, um, what's going—?" Then she recovered a little and turned to me with a small smile on her face and said, "Hey, Mo, you wanna go have some sex?"

Moving adroitly to the rescue, I said, "Sure. Sounds good to me. Shall we?" I gestured to the hatches that led to our suits and thence to the hab.

But what brought it home to me was the time we were working late in the lab and Alice and Yuri had already called it a day. Archie asked me to get something from the habitat so I suited up and went over there. When I de-suited into the hab I could hear soft music playing, some old ballad from the thirty-fifth century maybe. I turned around and saw Yuri and Alice slowly dancing with each other in the middle of the room. They were wrapped around each other and just gently swaying, their eyes closed. I decided that Archie could do without the item she had requested and slipped back into my suit.

In an odd way, none of us were surprised. If Alice had chosen someone, we couldn't think of anyone we would want for her more than Yuri. On the other hand, we were confronted by pure monogamy. In our culture it was just strange. We recognized it, but we weren't quite sure what to do with it. We treated it a little reverently. We didn't talk about it, just gave each other a quick glance now and then to confirm that we were all witnessing the same thing. But it was unmistakable, inevitable in a way. After all, Alice had spent the first half of her life in a place where this was how it worked.

How can you want to save someone's life 'even more'? But we did; we all wanted to save Alice even more than we had before. We worked harder and longer, but the Brainardites got no less baffling. Archie kept looking for cell division actually occurring in Brainardite life, but she never caught it. We didn't know if it was happening when we weren't looking or if it just wasn't happening.

Then one day the slime arrived at the lab. We hadn't encountered much of it; we hadn't been close enough to the slugs yet. So it surprised us. On the way back one evening we saw a little trail of it reaching from the tube fields all the way to the base of the lab. It went up to the wall where the specimen trays were. Yuri's field obviously worked; the slime got right up to the inflated wall of the lab but was repelled by it. It didn't actually touch it. The same with our suits: if we accidentally stepped in it the slime beaded up and slid off, leaving no trace. But Archie was excited. She didn't think she was going to have any slime to look at until we went into the colony, or at least onto the slug trail leading to the colony. She produced a little special scoop that Yuri had designed, powered it up, and scraped some of the most dangerous stuff in the universe off of the rock. She placed it in a special tray designed to hold it. We looked at it for a moment.

[It's like it followed us out here,] said Marcus.

[It's not sentient. It can't make decisions,] answered Archie.

[Then why is it here?] Tamika asked.

[I don't know. Maybe there's some pheromonal signal that it's following, some chemical signature ...] She looked back toward the belt of life to the south of us. [Let's go inside and take a look at it.]

Steel said, [Yuri, what are you doing?]

We all looked around for him. He'd wandered off north of the lab, toward the canyon. He bent over and picked something up. [I was just looking for another meteorite.]

I laughed, "You know the odds against finding the first one? You really don't think—"

[I just thought Alice might like one.] He examined what he'd picked up.

[Did you find one?] Alice asked.

[No,] he said, [this is just a little piece of obsidian.]

Archie said, [Bring it back anyway. I'll do some radiometric dating on it. As far as we know, Brainard's Planet has been geologically inert for a long time. But if that's obsidian, it had to come from one of the extinct volcanoes here. We may be able to get a read on when everything calmed down.]

When we got inside, Yuri's rock was forgotten as we all wanted to examine the slime with the new tools we had. We were actually going to find out what this stuff was made of— the stuff that had mowed us down so mercilessly.

Observed from orbit, the slime was an enigma. There seemed to be lots of organic chemicals present, but there was other stuff that no one had been able to figure out. The absorption lines were shifted somehow; it was too heavy. Everything about it was just wrong. We were hoping that some of the mysteries could be resolved close up, but no dice. Archie looked up from her instruments and said, "It's still too heavy. It's just too, too heavy for what I'm seeing. I mean it's basically a saline solution full of different proteins, *lots* of different proteins. I've recorded over forty thousand."

"That is a lot," said Steel. "Do you think any of them might be able to—"

"Help Alice? I don't know. There's RNA in there, a bunch of stuff, but that's not all. Some of the things I was expecting to find *aren't* there. I can't figure out how it gets into our cells. There aren't any viruses or anything at all larger than the various proteins. How does it get through the cell walls? How does it get through *everything*? Brainard's environmental suits? *Every*thing. There's got to be something else there but I can't find it. It's just too heavy and I can't figure out why." She sighed and pushed her chair back. "Let's take a look at Yuri's obsidian."

"Okay, look," Steel said, "this is getting out of hand. We're looking for pharmaceuticals, not minerals. There's nothing mysterious about obsidian. We're not going to find anything useful in a piece of rock. I think we need to keep pounding away at the slime. That's our best hope of—"

"Captain, do you know how to cure Alice?"

"What?"

"Neither do I. Do you know which piece of the puzzle is going to let us figure out this place? Neither do I." Archie rubbed her face. "If I spend another minute staring at that slime I'm going to ... well, I won't get anything useful accomplished, let's put it that way. I need a break. Let me just test this rock for radioisotopes. It won't take long."

Steel fumed, but let Archie walk over to the workstation that connected to the tray where Yuri's little stone resided. She did a couple of things to it, then stopped. She looked at the screen closer, then said, "Well, Yuri, it looks like obsidian. I can see how you would have thought that. But it's not obsidian." She turned to us. "It's anthracite."

We stared at her like she'd brought up one of Yuri's movie stars. "Anthracite?" Tamika said. "You mean ... you mean ... coal?"

"That's right, coal. Ladies and gentlemen," she turned back to the screen, "this is the first thing we've found here that used to be alive but isn't anymore."

CHAPTER 35

Needless to say, the discovery of coal sent everyone into an uproar. It changed our picture of the place completely. Archie tested for carbon-14 and found not a trace. That meant that Yuri's find had to be at least seventy thousand years old, almost fifty times older than I was. But if it was older than that—even much, much older—we couldn't tell; once you run out of carbon-14 you have no way to judge. This meant we needed to find some actual obsidian, or something igneous. Igneous rocks have radioisotopes in them that have much longer half-lives. If we could find where the coal came from and place it between two layers of igneous rock that we knew the ages of, we could more closely guess how old the coal was. We knew that Brainard's Planet was much older than Earth, more than twice as old. Its star was in late middle age with only another billion years or so before it swelled into a red giant and destroyed all life there.

What we needed to examine were exposed geologic strata, and the nearest ones at hand were in the canyon walls to the north of us. But the nearest wall of the canyon was a good hundred kilometers away—quite a hike in double gravity. Yuri suggested we use one of the ultra-lights to get there and Steel just about went pan-dimensional on us. First, we were here to study biology, not geology. Second, flying around on Brainard's Planet was dangerous. What if we crashed and compromised the e-suits? What if we wrecked the ultra-light beyond repair? How would we get back up to the ship? And third, we were here to study BIOLOGY!

Archie pleaded with her, "Captain, this is the first thing we've found that makes this place make any sense at all. We have to follow it up. We *have* to."

Yuri said, "We have two ultra-lights. Surely we can risk one on this."

Steel was frantic, "We don't even understand the slime yet! We don't, we don't— there are so many things right here to, to, to— We have to, we have to—

we can't just—"

"Captain, I don't know what else to do with the slime," Arch said. "It's too heavy and I can't figure out why. I've analyzed it every way I know how. I can give you a complete list of the organics present in it but I can't tell you how it does what it does."

"Then let's go into the colony. Get some slime directly from the slugs. Maybe this sample is polluted, or— or—"

Steel's mention of the colony had a chilling effect on everyone. Contemplating actual contact with the slugs scared the skag out of me. I could see it in everyone else's faces, too. I don't think we were scared for ourselves so much as we didn't want to lose anyone else. Human perspectives are so precious, so utterly irreplaceable.

"Why can't we do both?" Alice asked. "Send a couple of people to the canyon and the rest of us go to the colony?"

Alice's solution added another layer of tension. We had a procedure in place. It hadn't really been tested yet—nothing had even looked like it was thinking about assaulting us—but it was the only procedure we had. Could we afford to mess with it? I had no idea. None of us did. We didn't even know if it would work as it was. I hadn't realized how much comfort we took in staying together until I saw us contemplate splitting up.

Steel's glare was impenetrable. She wanted to be able to solve this with sheer strength, force of will. But a decision had to be made and none of us knew what the right decision was.

"We've been here for four weeks," Yuri said. "We have enough consumables to last us for another month."

Steel paced like a caged tiger, but there was no escape. Finally she said, "Daimler, have you been following this?"

[Yes.]

Great. Our eye in the sky. The man who cloned his wife. And killed mine.

"What do you think we should do?" Steel asked. I couldn't wait to hear what he said, then ignore it. There was a long pause, then:

[What do you want to accomplish here, Estelle?]

"You know what I want to accomplish," She snapped. "I want to find a— I want to have a—"

[What do you want to accomplish?]

Steel thought for a moment. "I want to have a cure in hand before we leave this place. I don't want to have to come back here again!"

[And what if you run out of consumables before that happens?]

Steel didn't like this question, but she had no answer for it. Yuri said, "We do have the capability to transport Brainardite organic materials now. We could continue our research someplace else."

Steel practically yelled at him, "Where? Who would take it? How could we get it through customs?"

"We couldn't. You're right." Yuri looked at the floor, thinking. "It's just that coal changes everything. We're no longer dealing with a static system. It's dynamic. I think we need to know how dynamic it is. What kind of time frame are we dealing with? How long has the present population been here? How did things move from dynamism to stasis? Are they really static now or are we just looking at very long lives? I think these are things that are going to affect any cure we try to come up with. I want to know what we're doing to Alice before we do it."

That last sentence resonated with all of us, even Steel. What did we need to know before we could actually try something on Alice? We had all assumed that we would find something that we understood, test it by running mathematical models, simulations, then take whatever we found back to Circe to have Alice worked on there. But how well did we need to understand it? How much information did we need to have? And what information? Which information? We were dealing with an entire biosphere, an entire planet. I understood more deeply than ever Steel's constant drive for speed. How long would it take to really find something that would work? And then there was the question we couldn't even ask ourselves: what if we couldn't find anything that worked?

[Answer the questions you can answer. The more answers you have the more efficient you'll be.]

"But what if we—"

[Estelle, you presented this to me as a legitimate corporate enterprise. If what we are doing here is to research the best way to exploit this biosphere, then we need to follow where the research leads us.]

"Captain, we have to understand this place better to even know the right questions to ask." Archie's voice was even, restrained, but we could all feel the seconds tick past, each one a lost opportunity. The merciless universe was unfolding as it would while our Captain grappled with it, looking for a way to bend it to her will.

Finally she said as if it was torn out of her, "Tamika, Yuri, you fly to the canyon tomorrow."

Alice started. "Yuri?"

Steel looked at Alice coldly. "You two have been spending too much time together anyway," I couldn't tell if she was angry or just tired. "This will give you a chance to ... to ..."

Alice moved to Yuri's side, took his hand in hers. Yuri smiled down at her, "Tamika and I will be okay. We'll be fine. We're just dealing with rocks. You're the ones going into slug central. If you promise to be careful, so will I."

Alice smiled back, but she wrapped her arms around him and leaned her head on his shoulder.

The next morning Yuri and Tamika broke out one of the ultra-lights and headed north while the rest of us headed south. Instead of three people collecting specimens, there would be only two—Archie and Alice. Steel and I would still act as lookouts and Marcus would cover us from the rear. Would one laser cannon be enough to save us if the slugs did something unexpected? Would two be enough? We kept walking.

Through tube fields and groves of spider-plane trees over gently rolling country, we eventually came to the sculptures. Brainard had called them that because he had seen the slugs sculpt them. They were always to be found anywhere near a colony. Great, weaving dykes of iron or stone, like flags or wings or ship's rudders, sinuous barriers that wove and joined and separated again. Anywhere from ten to twenty meters tall and hundreds of meters long, they sometimes helped to define where the trails went, but other than that no one knew what they were for.

'Sculpt' might be too strong a term, but Brainard had been hoping to find intelligence. He'd been hoping to have the first conversation between a human being and something else. What the slugs did was repeatedly rub up against these weaving dykes and erode them with the mild acid they secreted, the same acid that had compromised Drake's suit. But the end result was so beautiful it was hard to believe the slugs didn't want them to look that way. The proportion and flow and, I'd have to call it composition was exquisite.

It had been clouding up as we moved farther into the inhabited zone, and now we heard the gentle rumble of distant thunder followed by the percussive patter of raindrops on our helmets. We passed between a patch of weaving tubes and a trio of spider-plane trees onto the edge of the slug trail that led to the colony nearby. No slugs could be seen on the short stretch of trail that was visible. We turned left, heading for town.

[We've found a little seam on the south wall,] Yuri's voice intruded into our very different reality. [It's thin, but we can see it. We're going to land on the rim and climb down to take a look.] I saw Alice jerk upright when we heard his voice. She couldn't save him by worrying about him, but that didn't matter. Worry was all she could do.

[Very good,] Marcus said. [Keep us apprised of your progress.]

[Will do.]

Moving along the trail, we shifted to a three-pointed star. Slugs could show up from either direction so Steel and I covered our front and Marcus our rear. Alice and Arch kept watch, too, but none of us really knew what we were doing. We just tried to stay alert. For a quarter of an hour we traveled that way, the rain strengthening to a downpour. It poured off of our visors and made the rock slick. A fair-sized freshet was forming down the middle of the trail.

Marcus calmly announced: [Slugs behind us. About one hundred meters.] My heart rate spiked as I turned to look. I slipped on the wet rock and went down hard. And FAST. I mean, BAM! It's one thing when a fork falls off a table; it's quite another when you're the fork.

[Are you all right?] Steel asked.

[Yeah, yeah, I'm fine.] I wasn't. Even with the protection of the e-suit I'd really banged my hip. I struggled to get up. Thankfully Yuri's servos did most of the work.

[Nothing to be alarmed about,] Marcus said, [just some traffic. Let's move to the side of the trail and let them pass.]

Even the reality I had done on the Lightdancer all those months ago didn't prepare me for the size of the slugs. More like whales than walruses, they were ten to fifteen meters long and half again as tall as I was where their carapaces rode on their backs. Just three in this group—gliding along about walking speed, maybe a little faster—they came upon us and passed as though we were just part of the scenery. I was so close that the overhang of their shells intermittently protected me from the rain. The color displays on their sides were fairly subtle compared to the ones I had witnessed on the reality of Brainard's last sortie—just some pale blue dots and geometric figures shifting, morphing and scrolling across their wrinkled, nubbly skin. All three had similar patterns. I wondered if that meant anything. I was sure that Brainard had wondered the same thing five hundred years ago.

And then they were past and moving off down the trail. No problem. Just out for a walk. I tried to slow my heartbeat.

[Okay,] said Steel, [Let's keep going.]

We formed back up and resumed our journey.

"Couldn't we just take some slime off the trail?" I asked, reasonably, I thought.

[I don't think it would do us any good,] Arch replied. [There will be rainwater mixed in and, I mean, if we want to ensure a pure sample ...]

"Yeah." What else could I say?

[In the colony they'll be under shelter. Many of them won't be moving. It'll be easier there.]

"Right." Nobody said the job would be routine.

[Hey, everybody,] Tamika's voice.

[Yes?] Marcus responded.

[Yuri just spotted some basalts. And there seem to be several layers of volcanic ash separated by—I don't know— various kinds of sedimentary rock. It's going to take some more climbing. We may want to fly down into the canyon and land on one of the lower plateaus.]

Marcus checked in with Steel. She just seemed frozen. I understood why. The wrong decision could cost so much. After a moment Marcus said, [Very good. Let us know what you decide.]

[Will do.]

Even in the rain my first glimpse of the colony was beautiful. There's no other word to describe it—a fanciful batch of deep chocolate globes and ramps, piled up like soap suds in a bubble bath, little towers of bubbles here, overhangs and balconies there, all integrated in a marvelous celebration of randomness and harmony, glistening in the emerging sunshine.

I would have enjoyed the esthetics more if the traffic hadn't been getting worse. As we neared the colony more and more slugs were wandering here and there. None of them seemed to notice us at all, but they hadn't seemed to notice Drake either until they killed him, or grabbed him or shook hands with him or whatever they'd thought they were doing. We tried to stay out of their way as we entered the main gate—a large brown globe with a slug-sized hole cut through it.

"Alice, I want you to navigate," Steel ordered.

"Got it," Alice replied. I was glad somebody was doing that. As soon as we got inside I was lost. We had entered a system of roughly cylindrical passages. The ramps curved and climbed and descended again in no apparent pattern, crossing and branching elegantly, naturally, but more like a circulatory system than a street grid. Doors opened off into what, private homes? Cocoons? Cells? No two bubbles were the same size or shape. Some of them had metal objects on the floor, odd little knobs and twists just lying around haphazardly.

"What are those things?" I asked.

[They seem to value them,] Archie answered, [They seem to trade them, but I don't know why. No one's ever seen a slug do anything with one except bring it back to a colony and leave it in one of the rooms.] She picked one up and placed it in her pouch. [They look like iron, but I'll analyze it just in case. You never know.]

We seemed to be climbing more than descending and, after an initial left turn, generally curving around to the right. Slugs would squeeze past us without touching us then move on down the passageway. "I'm glad I'm not claustrophobic," I said.

[I am, too,] said Marcus. [Just stay alert.]

At one point the passage opened out onto a curving balcony and we could see how far we had climbed. We were looking west; the sun was starting to set over sculptures winding between tube fields and groves of spider-plane trees. We could see the trail. All traffic was incoming now. No one was leaving. We curved back inside.

[There,] Archie said. [That one.] She pointed to a cell that was occupied by a slug that was napping maybe, or meditating or pondering some unknown mystery of slugginess. [This will do. Come on, Alice.]

Marcus said, [Captain, Mo, flank the doorway. I'll take a position at that last junction.] He moved back down the passage about ten meters to where it branched, then set up the laser cannon. Steel and I took our positions as Archie and Alice went inside.

We stood there for awhile as the occasional slug wandered past, then we heard Archie say, [Skag.]

[What's wrong?] Steel asked.

[There's no slime. I forgot. They only secrete the stuff when they're moving, when something is happening that, you know, I guess upsets them or something. When they're under some kind of stress.]

[What do you want to do?] asked Alice.

[Well, it would be great if I didn't have to try to get a sample from one of these guys when it's moving. I'm not sure how I would do that.] Archie thought for a moment. [Hmm, maybe I can stress it somehow. Here, Alice, you hold the collector for a minute.]

[Okay.]

We heard a meaty thud.

[Hmm, nope, nothing.] We heard another, louder thud.

"What are you doing in there?" I asked.

[I'm slapping it.]

"You're what?"

[But I don't think I'm getting through to it. Mo? Come in here for a sec.]

"O-okay." I checked in with Steel and Marcus. They waved me in.

"What do you want me to do?"

[Just haul off and hit it as hard as you can.]

I took a look at the mountain of flesh sitting in front of me. "Um, really?"

[Yeah, you won't hurt it. I just hope it notices.]

I didn't think I wanted it to notice. I tried to remember all the crazy skag I'd done in my life, but I couldn't come up with anything that compared to this. "Are you guys covering me?" I asked.

[Oh, right. Alice, draw your laser. Um, we're gonna draw our lasers, okay, Marcus?]

[All right. You'll have to use them at your discretion. Steel and I need to stay out here, I think.]

[Yes, I agree,] said Steel. [There's quite a bit of traffic.]

[Yeah, sounds good,] Arch answered. Alice and Arch pointed their ray guns at the slug's flank. [Okay, Mo, whenever you're ready.]

That might be never, I thought, but I pulled back my fist, took a couple of breaths and said, "Okay?"

[Yeah, yeah. Go.]

I punched it.

[No, no. Harder than that.]

That wasn't what I wanted to hear, but I answered, "Right," and pulled back my fist again.

[Are you left-handed?] Arch asked.

I was pulling back my left arm. "Well, I'm kind of ambidextrous, I suppose. I eat with my right hand, but I do lot's of other stuff with my left."

[Hmm. I guess I never noticed. Okay, whenever you're ready.]

I did everything I could to prepare myself for a horrific demise, cocked my fist and then punched it as hard as I could. We waited for a few seconds, then Arch said, [No, still nothing. Tell you what,] she looked at me, [why don't you go back out into the passageway and just run right into it.]

"You want me to—"

[Yeah, just take a running start and ram it.]

Holy freakin' mother of Buddha, Krishna and freaking Zoroaster. Images of Drake's ruined body pathetically grasping for something unseen as he rotted in his pod flooded my vision. "Okay." I walked back out into the passage, pausing momentarily at the door of the chamber while a slug passed, and checked in with Steel. She looked at me like, 'What are you waiting for?' Turning back to face the napping slug, I charged myself up and started running. Like I said, it takes a little while to get going in one of Yuri's e-suits, but once I was moving I had a lot of momentum. I didn't hit it very fast, but I made a big impression. As I bounced off of it, the slug shuddered and shook. Then its skin started to get shiny.

[Yeah! That's it!] Archie yelled. She took the collector and placed it against the slug's side. [Congratulations, Mo! You're the first human being to get a slug to notice you!]

"Yay for me. Um, did it get any acid on me?"

[They secrete the acid from their ventral surface, not their sides.] Well, she could have told me that earlier. [Great, we're getting a good sample. Okay, I think that will do it. Let's get out of here.]

I happened to glance at the floor and noticed that a couple of cracks had evidently formed in the otherwise smooth surface. I bent down and managed to wiggle a little piece of the structure loose. "Hey, Arch, should I take this back with us?"

[What do you have there?] She examined the chunk. [Oh, good. Nobody's ever been able to establish what they make the colonies out of. Yes. I'll analyze it back at the lab. Now let's go before any gossip spreads about alien invasions.] I put the little piece in my pouch. It was surprisingly heavy even in this gravity, like it was made out of lead or something even denser, but it didn't look like lead. It didn't look like anything I could think of.

[Form back up,] Marcus ordered. [Mo, Steel, you lead off. I'll take the rear.] We made our way down the winding tunnel. No one tried to stop us. No one bothered us in any way, the slugs just kept going about their business, whatever that was, and after a few tension-filled moments we were back in the open air again. The system of thunderstorms had moved off to the east, a towering rampart of billowing cloud turned shockingly orange by the setting sun. Everything around us glowed fiery, rosy, in the reflected light.

[Who would have thought?] Archie said as we headed back down the trail. [Of all the different ways Brainard tried to get the slugs to notice him, nobody thought to just haul off and whack one.]

"It wouldn't be my first choice to open diplomatic relations," I responded. We kept walking, looking for the spot where we'd entered the trail that morning: the patch of tubes with the trio of spider plane trees beside it.

The sun was on the horizon when we heard Yuri's voice: [Hey, Captain?]

[Yes?]

[Um, I think we're going to bivouac here tonight. We got involved and didn't realize it was getting so late. Tamika doesn't want to try to land the ultra-light in the dark.]

There was a pause as Steel digested this news, then [Where are you?]

[We're two tiers down inside the canyon. There's a broad, flat terrace here. It'll be easy to take off in the morning, but, uh, not such a good idea at night.]

Steel stewed for a moment as two straggling slugs glided past us heading for the colony. Everyone was closing up shop for the day. Steel said, [So, you figure you have another day's work to do there, do you?]

[Um,] Yuri prevaricated, [yeah, we could probably spend another day here. There's lots of interesting stuff—]

[Goddamn it, Yuri! You did this deliberately! If you'd wanted another day out there you should have asked.]

[Point taken, Captain. But, since we're here, I mean, we have plenty of consumables. It's not going to be particularly comfortable spending the night in the suits, but it will save us a trip back and forth from the lab. Less flying, you know? Has to be safer.]

Steel gave Marcus a glare of tired exasperation. At that moment the bass throb that signaled the beginning of the slug's "evening prayers" boomed over us so loud we could feel it. We all started, then looked around at each other. Alice laughed so I did, too. This place was getting to all of us.

Steel said, [I expect to see you two back at the lab before sundown tomorrow.]

[No problem, Captain. We'll see you then.]

Marcus added, [That's an order, Yuri.]

[Absolutely. Yes, sir! We'll be there.]

[Have a good night,] said Steel, and started walking again. I could see Alice's lips moving through her visor. I think she was bulleting Yuri privately. Brainard's Planet's huge, single moon rose silver, almost full, behind the thunderheads in the east as we tromped wearily back to base.

We were all exhausted from the stress of the day so we just dropped off the specimens at the laboratory and headed for the hab. Dinner was more a matter of functional re-fueling than any sort of social gathering. Then, after the briefest of periods of digestion, we all fell into our bunks. So I was surprised to be awoken by a tap on my shoulder a little while later. I rolled over and there was Alice.

"Can I sleep with you guys tonight?" she whispered.

Archie roused, too. We checked in with each other and then I whispered back, "Sure, Alice, climb on in."

Arch and I made room between us. It was a little cramped, but not too bad. Alice snuggled in and said in a very small voice, "I miss Yuri."

Arch and I looked at each other then snuggled in closer. Arch said, "I understand. But Yuri will be all right. You'll see."

Alice's head was on my shoulder. I felt tears. She said, "I miss my dad." We couldn't do anything but hug her and stroke her hair. My heart was breaking for her. So it was almost a relief when she said, "I miss Ham. Do you think mom will re-boot him when he gets old?"

I nearly had to laugh, but I whispered, "Well, she might. She's got plenty of money. I've heard of rich people re-booting their pets sometimes."

She sighed and found a more comfortable position. "I hope she does," she said, then she fell asleep.

CHAPTER 36

The next day was a day off for most of us as Archie worked with the new sample of slime and the rest of us worried about Tamika and Yuri out at the canyon. But it sounded like there were significant developments out there. We couldn't really tell what was going on, and we didn't want to distract them from their work, but we'd occasionally pick up pieces of their conversation like, [No, that's not ... that's not ... umm, we need more resolution. Let's try, let's try grav-echo. Yeah, that's ... that's ... Shiva, this would have taken years in the old days. Holy skag. Look at that.]

Arch was getting more taciturn as she went about her labors. It was hard to tell if she was making progress or not; she just seemed focused, determined, dauntless. Lunch came and went. As she ate at her workstation, her expression became more and more inscrutable. About mid-afternoon she took a sample of her own blood and passed it through the special lock Yuri had designed for doing just that; she then used the manipulators to place it in the tray holding the slime sample. She recorded what happened but didn't say anything to us. Then she took a sample of Alice's blood and went through the same procedure. Steel tried to get her to divulge her results but she wouldn't be drawn out. She barely responded at all.

Finally she asked Steel, "Is there enough daylight left to make it to the edge of the tube field?"

Steel said, "I think so. Why?"

"I need a specimen."

"Of what?"

"Doesn't matter. Just a specimen of Brainardite life."

"All right. Let's suit up. Yuri?"

[Yeah.]

"How are you doing out there?"

[We're just wrapping up. I'd say we'll be airborne in fifteen or twenty minutes.]

"Good. We're going out to the tube field. We should be back by the time you get here."

[Okay. See you then.]

We went no farther than the very edge of the field but Marcus cautioned us to stay alert nonetheless. Arch picked up a zooid off one of the tubes. Then she found a smaller tube mounted on a loose rock. She placed them both in her pouch and we headed back. We arrived just as Tamika and Yuri were landing. They were as boisterous as Archie was subdued.

Yuri said, [You should see the stuff we've found. It's incredible!]

He reached into his sample pouch to show us, but Arch responded, [Just put the samples in trays. I'll get to them. Mo?] She handed me her specimen pouch. [I'm going to go inside. I want you to damage the zooid and the tube and then place them in the tray with the slime sample. All right?]

"Damage them? How do you mean?"

[Pinch them, poke them. Try to break the skin. Just cause some damage.]

It seemed like we were being more and more obnoxious to the Brainardites, but I acquiesced. Arch said, [Wait till I'm inside. I'll tell you when.] She went around to the other side of the lab and de-suited while the rest of us tried to avoid stepping in the trail of slime that still reached across the rock from the tube field right up to where the trays were. After a few minutes she said, [All right. Damage them and place them in the tray.]

I picked up the zooid first. I pinched it, then pinched it harder and harder until it started to squirm pitifully in my hand. Finally the skin broke and a little thick fluid started to leak out of it. I placed it in the tray as it writhed and squirmed. Then I did the same with the tube. We watched as the slime covered them both. Within moments they were completely healed.

"Well ..." I said, really intending to follow it with something insightful or profound. We stood there looking at the two healthy, happy Brainardites for a moment, then went inside just as the distant drone of the evening prayers reached us over the rock.

Arch looked very dark, very pre-occupied as we entered the lab. I would have thought after a discovery of that magnitude that she would have been at least somewhat elated, but her features were focused in a scowl of concentration.

"What made you think to do that?" I asked.

Her scowl didn't waver, but she said, "Something Alice said last night."

"What?"

"About Ham." She turned to Tamika, "Let's see what you two found out there."

We headed to what had become the geology workstation, Alice happily attached to Yuri's side. "Were you able to determine the age of the coal?"

"More or less," Yuri said. "We found a layer of basalt that was on top of the coal seam."

"Yes?"

"It has to be between three and a half and five billion years old."

"*Billion?*" Arch asked, for all of us really.

"Yeah, but that's not the big news. Take a look at what else we found." He started to manipulate the samples they had placed in the trays outside. "We found these in a thin layer just above the basalt. Once again, I'd have to say that they are at least three billion years old."

There were three thin, delicate pieces in the tray. They looked like they had been crushed; like little more than foil that had been crumpled and stomped on. "We didn't really bring a lot of metallurgical equipment with us, but I was able to get a good read with the grav-echo. You can run them through the mass spectrometer if you want."

"Were you able to determine what they were?"

Yuri nodded. "That," he pointed to the first sample, "is a piece of fairly high-grade stainless steel." He looked around for our reactions. I imagine we all looked stunned. "This one," he indicated the paler sample, "is polyethylene." Once again he checked out our faces before turning back to the display screen. "And this," he pointed to a thin chunk that was brown like the piece of the colony I had brought back, "is plutonium."

"Plutonium?" Arch asked. "Plutonium isn't brown."

"Plutonium is also radioactive. But this plutonium isn't." Yuri looked at us significantly. "Three billion years ago these slugs were able to manufacture alloys, plastics, and do something to plutonium to make it absolutely stable. Everything I've done to that little rock says it's plutonium, but it's not emitting so much as a gamma ray."

Archie stared at it in wonder.

"But get this," Yuri added, "it's just a little bit heavy."

This got Archie's attention, "Heavy?"

Yuri and Tamika nodded.

Marcus said, "Wait a minute. How do you know the slugs made these? I mean, three billion years ago there was probably a completely different ecosystem here—different dominant life form, everything."

Yuri grinned, "Check this out." He called up a reality they had taken in the canyon, but it was obviously taken in grav-echo. The translucent images were all rendered in pale green. You could see the layered nature of the canyon walls and, due to the grav-echo, you could see into the rock about a hundred meters before the resolution got too coarse to be usable. Yuri focused in on various little layers of detail. We saw the small shapes come into focus. Little pieces and shards, fragments, then larger pieces, then whole shapes preserved in the stone.

"Those are fossils!" Marcus exclaimed. We could see little impressions of Brainardite shells and carapaces, most of them broken or shattered, but some mostly or completely preserved. Lots of them were smaller, but there were also many that could have ridden on any of the slugs we had met at the colony.

"But see what happens," Yuri said. He panned up the canyon wall. "Here is the layer where we found the steel and stuff. You see?" Above that layer the fossil record stopped, just vanished. Before that point in time things had died and decomposed on Brainard's Planet. From that point forward it was obvious that they hadn't. "As near as I can tell the population we're looking at now has been here for somewhere between three and three and a half billion years." Yuri sat back, nested his fingers behind his head, put his feet up on the workstation desk and said, "So. What have you guys been doing?"

No one said anything. What could we say? I was the oldest person there and I needed to live another eighty-five centuries to reach ten thousand years of age. Then I needed to live another ninety millennia to reach a hundred thousand years, then another nine hundred millennia to reach a million. And these slugs were over three *billion* years old?

"I was thinking that this might explain the lack of sensory organs," Yuri continued.

"What do you mean?" Steel asked.

"Well, think about it. If the slugs figured out a way to live without killing anything, anything at all—I mean nothing has died here in over three billion years—what would they need sensory organs for? There's no need to hunt, no predators to avoid. No problems left to solve, really. Maybe their sensory organs just atrophied."

"But, but why do they move the colonies?" Archie asked.

"Habit?" Yuri answered.

"Habit?"

He nodded, grinning like a cat. "They're redecorating. I mean, what else do they have to do?"

We sat there for a while longer looking at our thoughts before Steel said, "All right. You've had your little junket to the canyon. You've made your discoveries; you've answered your questions. How does this get us closer to a cure for Alice?"

I'm not sure why, but we all looked to Archie. She said, "So you're suggesting ... You think the slugs ... You're saying that ... that the, the immortality here is— is— is manufactured. That the slime ..." she moved to the workstation she'd been at all day, "is manufactured."

"Is that what I'm saying?" Yuri asked. Then, "Yeah, I guess that's what I'm saying. Why? What have you found?"

Arch turned to me. "Mo? Where's that little piece of the colony you brought back?"

"Workstation 3," I said.

She walked over and fired up the screen. She did various things to the little chunk and then sat back. "It's plutonium all right, non-radioactive plutonium. They build their houses out of non-radioactive— Why would they do that?"

Yuri said, "Maybe, maybe ... maybe they used nuclear power back in the day. Maybe they built a bunch of reactors and then had all this nuclear waste to deal with and they didn't know what to do with it until they found a way to make it non-radioactive and then they found that it had some really cool architectural properties that we've never looked for because plutonium is radioactive."

Arch looked at Yuri for a moment, not really taking in what he said. Then she turned back to the screen, "And it's a little heavy. Not heavy enough to be Curium or Berkelium. Just a little heavy." She tapped her fingers on the desk in front of her. Then she said, "Yuri, can you focus the grav-echo to see subatomic particles? I'm talking leptons."

Yuri looked dubious. "Um-m-m, we're kind of set up for biochemistry, not particle physics."

"Can you do it?" she repeated.

Yuri pulled out a couple of racks and crawled behind them. He was back there for a long time. He would occasionally ask for some tool or other. The rest of us went to the hab to eat dinner then brought dinner back for Yuri, who munched on it as he continued to work on into the evening. None of us were going to bed. We waited and helped when we could. It was past midnight when he said, "Okay, try that."

Arch didn't even respond, she just moved to the workstation where the little chunk of plutonium was. Yuri was at her side almost as quickly as she got there. The rest of us gathered around. Images came up on the screen as Arch focused tighter and tighter. Finally Arch said, "What the hell is that?" She turned to Yuri, "Have you ever seen a hadron like that? Or is it a meson? What the hell is it?" She focused in a little tighter. The image was starting to pixilate. "Holy skag! They're engineering with individual leptons. With neutrinos and quarks. Look at that. They've built little machines out of neutrinos and quarks." She rolled her chair over to the slime workstation. She focused down and down. "There. Look. Different configurations, but ... Holy mother of Lao-Tse! Look at that. Look at that."

We had gone as far as we could that night. We were all buzzing but we were all exhausted, too. Alice was very content to head to her bunk with Yuri again.

The rest of us just fell into bed. But as Arch and I spooned I could tell that she was not happy.

"Are you all right?" I whispered.

She snuggled into me. "I'm ... I don't know."

"What's the matter?"

She rolled over and looked at me. Her voice was barely audible. "I'm afraid ... I'm afraid ..."

"What? What are you afraid of?"

She thought for a long time before she whispered, "You know that it was always a long shot, don't you?"

"What was?"

"Coming here. Finding a ... finding something that would ... that would help Alice. It was always ... I mean, the odds were always against us."

A cruel fist was squeezing my heart. I looked into her eyes—her sad, tired eyes. "I saw you testing the slime on your blood." She nodded. "Then Alice's blood."

She nodded again. "There was no difference. The cellular degradation and destruction progressed at the same rate, in basically the same way. Then I tested it on the little zooid and tube. I was thinking, what if the Brainardites were just kind-hearted? What if they didn't want anything to die?"

"Like Alice was saying about Ham," I said. Then something else occurred to me, "Like the vegans."

"Vegans?" She looked at me quizzically, "What do you mean? There aren't any planets around Vega."

"No, no. Not people from Vega. The vegans were an ancient cult on Earth. They didn't want to eat anything, or something like that. I forget exactly. They kind of faded out when the human race started to populate the solar system."

"Hmm. I guess the Brainardites are a sort of super-vegan."

"But what were you saying about long shots? What did you find?"

She looked at my chest while she formulated her reply. Even more softly she said, "When Steel lost Jacob in Switzerland I was back at the Institute on Circe, but of course Steel was keeping me up on how they were doing— Jacob and Alice."

"Yes?"

"When Jacob was ... was ... lost that way I was the one who compared it to Brainard's plague. The symptoms were almost identical, and the speed of the progression of the disease. I'd been doing research on Brainard's Planet. You know, it's another isolated culture."

"Like Eden."

"Right. When Jacob ... when we lost him that way it seemed like the perfect reason to— to, you know, take another try at cracking the mysteries of the ecosystem here. If we could, if we could come up with a way to protect ourselves from the plague."

She paused for a long time. I said, "Yes?"

"Steel was very enthusiastic. She said she knew people, could put together a crew. Cost was no object. I was hoping ... more than that: I thought Brainard's plague was a disease that the Brainardites had developed immunity to. That it was so lethal to us because our bodies weren't prepared to fight it off. It didn't look like they had much technology besides working with metals and building their colonies. I thought we could find antibodies or, or some sort of serum that we could use or— or modify. But you see?" She looked into my eyes, "It's not a disease. It's the opposite of a disease. It's medicine." I remembered watching the little zooid and tube heal so quickly. "The slime is just trying to heal us. It's trying to turn us into healthy Brainardites, but it can't because we're made of the wrong proteins. So it just turns us into more slime. It can take us apart but it can't put us back together." She snuggled in closer to me. "I'm afraid ... I'm afraid that Drake ... that he, that we lost him for ... for nothing. That he— that he— that he ... died ... for ... for no reason."

I held her and tried to comfort her, but I wasn't thinking about Drake. Alice was just across our inflated hut, tucked into an alcove that she had transformed into a little nest for her and Yuri. "We'll ... we'll try again tomorrow," I said, but I didn't know what I meant. If Archie couldn't find a cure for Alice, I had no idea who could. What would we do? What could we do? Exhaustion relieved me of my troubles until morning.

"What's the next step?" Steel said over breakfast. "Where do we go from here?"

Arch looked into her tea, held the mug like she was holding onto her home, but said nothing.

Marcus said, "We've made some significant discoveries. Surely we can assemble a— a— a plan of action to take us to the next ... to the next ... to where we want to be. We need to decide ... I mean, where are we right now? What do we know? What do we need to find out?"

Yuri looked at Archie like he was beginning to suspect. I tried to not look at anybody. Alice looked like she wanted to give us all the day off, just forget the whole thing for a while and goof around.

When Archie finally spoke her voice carried the weight of her knowledge, of her limits: "We've learned that instead of dealing with a primitive society here what we have is a society whose technology is so advanced that they no longer have any need to be technological. They've solved all their problems." Her eyes never left the wafts of vapor rising from the surface of her tea.

Steel responded, "So ... so, what? How can we use what we've found here?"

The curls of vapor lifted to dissipate and disappear. "I don't know," was her simple reply. "I mean, I'm sure that, given time, we can ... we can reverse engineer, we can figure out how they, how they can ... I mean we don't even know how to capture neutrinos, never mind assemble them into ... into ..."

Yuri said, "Yeah. That's a neat trick. I wouldn't even know where to start. But we know it can be done now. That's ... that's a huge advantage."

"How long do you think it would take?" Steel asked. "To, to reproduce what we've found here?"

Yuri just shook his head and spread his hands.

"But that's not the problem," Arch responded. "The problem is that the Edenites didn't have access to this level of technology or anything close to it. What's preventing Alice from re-booting has nothing to do with gadgets made from individual leptons."

Alice said, "It has to be genetic," and once again I was struck by her incredible courage. Here we were discussing her impending ... impending ... I couldn't even think it, and yet she was calmly taking part in the conversation.

"That's right, Alice," responded Archie. "Genetics is what they were good at. But we haven't been able to find the genetic trigger anywhere. We haven't been able to isolate it." Arch was working to stay positive, engaged in the problem, but desolation spread out in front of her like a desert.

Alice breathed. I could hear her exhale. I felt I could almost hear her heart beating. She was alive, living each second, each moment. She seemed to relax a little, come to a resolution. She said very calmly, "Well, I want to thank all of you for, for working so hard, for coming to this dangerous place—"

Steel cut her off, "No. NO!" She looked at Alice, "We are NOT giving up." She glared at all of us. "We are NOT through here. We have an entire ecosystem to mine, to research. There's got to be something here we can use!" She slammed her hand down on the table, knocking cutlery to the floor with a crash that was still startling even now, even after all the time we had spent in this place.

Alice's voice was very small, "Mom, I don't want to. I don't want to put you all in any more—"

"Alice. Alice, look at me." Steel grasped her shoulders. "We have supplies for another month. We have time. Look at all we've discovered so far." She turned to Archie, "What about their central nervous systems? We still don't know how they're structured, how they last so long."

"I don't think it's anything intrinsic in their structure. I think the slime maintains them just like it maintains everything else," Archie replied.

"But you don't know that. We don't know how long they would live without the slime. It could be hundreds of years. Thousands." Arch looked at her tea. "Couldn't it?" And looked. "Archie! Isn't that right?"

"Yes, Captain. We don't know how long they live. But—"

"We're not through here. We still have work to do."

"Captain, what do you want me to do?"

"We need samples of their central nervous systems at least."

"You want me to extract brain tissue?"

"We need to see how it interacts with us. With human brain tissue. What if ... What if ..."

"Mom, I don't want to graft my brain onto the brain of a—"

"Alice, you don't know what you're saying. It would only be for a little while. Just until we could figure out a cure. A few decades. A century at most."

"Mom—"

"Captain, you're asking me to perform brain surgery on a sentient being without its consent."

"How do we know they're sentient? Maybe their sentience atrophied along with their eyes and ears."

"Captain—"

"They're barely aware of their environment anymore. How could they be aware of themselves?"

"There are serious ethical questions here—"

"DAIMLER?"

[I'm here.]

"Tell them!"

Tell us what?

[Estelle, you have all the authority you need here. You don't need me to tell them anything. You're the Captain.]

Steel stared at her fists clutched on the table, "I want you to tell them."

There was a pause. Then, [All right. In case you need to be reminded, you are all under contract to your Captain and therefore to the Bayernische Syndicate. The case could be made that you forfeited any legal rights you had when you chose to break very stringent Draconian *and* Pleiadean laws by landing on Brainard's Planet. While I'm sure that Estelle wouldn't want you working under coercive conditions, these things are nonetheless true. Archie, wouldn't you say that the slime could heal any wounds you cause by surgery?]

Archie thought for a moment. "I don't know. I suppose we can assume anything we want. There's only one way to find out."

[This certainly isn't the first time that ethics have accommodated the exigencies of scientific research?]

Alice's voice was barely more than a whisper, "Mom, please. I don't want to. I don't want to do this anymore. Please."

"Alice, you need to be strong now. We'll get through this, but you need to be strong."

Archie looked grim, but said, "There's a full moon tonight. We could ... we could operate after evening prayers. That's when they're calmest, most ... most sedentary."

Steel looked around the table. Yuri and Tamika looked like they were up for anything that needed to be done. Marcus was assessing, Alice was sad and Archie was ... Archie wasn't saying anything. At that point I didn't know what I was.

"Good," Steel said. "We'll leave two hours before sundown. That should give us enough time to get to the colony before dark."

Throughout the day Archie studied every bit of information that we had about the slugs. She had Yuri modify some of our imaging equipment so we could scan the slugs' interior anatomy in the field. We certainly couldn't bring one back to the lab. Then she put together her best guess of what a kit for doing brain surgery on a Brainardite might be. She worked with a dark determination, carrying the inevitability of her crime with her. Steel spent the day with Marcus and Tamika generating possible timetables and schedules, flow charts based on this or that guess of what we might find, how we might be able to exploit it. Alice and I were involved in one way or another. Archie tried to keep her busy—I think to give her a sense of control if nothing else. Of course, none of us had control. Steel was in control.

When it was time to suit up Archie stopped as she was entering her hatch. She stood there for a moment, with one leg in her suit and one in the lab, then extracted herself. Steel said, "What's wrong?"

Arch stood for a moment, thinking. "Umm, it's nothing." She thought, shook her head. "It's nothing to do with ... with the mission. Could you ... could you give me a moment alone with Mo?"

Steel looked at me, then back at Arch. I didn't have a clue what this was about. I think it showed on my face.

Arch said, "It won't take long. Just a couple of minutes."

Steel examined us again, but said, "All right. We'll be waiting outside." She turned to the rest of the crew and said, "Let's go."

When we were alone Arch still seemed reluctant to speak. "What is it?" I asked.

She looked at the floor, looked around the lab. I didn't know what she was looking for. Then, "I just wanted to tell you about ... about your mother. About what you called her."

Oh. "Um, okay. Did you find out something?"

"Yes," she still wasn't looking at me. She drew a little arc on the floor with her toe. "That's what you called her. You called her your mother."

"What? No, no, Archie, I would remember. It was—"

"That's what you called her. Or some variation: Mama, Mom, Mommy.

Something like that."

"Well, okay. I don't know why you'd think that. It sure doesn't mean anything to me. I can't believe that I would—"

"Mo, listen to me for a minute."

"Okay."

She formed her thoughts before she spoke. "There have been times in our history when one group of people decided that some other group of people needed to change the way they behaved. Sometimes it meant changing some specific behavior, sometimes ... everything. If they didn't have the time or, or the energy or just the patience to convince them to change the way they thought, sometimes they would decide to simply coerce them into changing the way they spoke. This was usually done to 'help' the target group. Colonial powers back on Earth would proscribe colonized people from ... from speaking in their native language to help them, help them ... assimilate into the culture of the colonizers, for example. The idea was if they were forced to change the way they spoke, the way they thought would change as a natural result."

"That sounds awful."

"Yes. It never worked. If you coerce a person to change their language, it just kills their spirit and makes them hate you for it."

"Okay. What does this have to do with—"

"Usually the tools for coercion were statutory or military. Not always. Some groups didn't have access to those kinds of tools. The feminists, for example, found that ... that castigation ... vilification and, and ostracism were equally potent means of coercion."

"Arch, why are you being so pedantic? What's going on?"

She stared into the past. "I wasn't alive during the war. I was hatched just after the treaty was signed. I experienced it as history."

"Oh." She didn't need to tell me that. She didn't need to reveal how old she was.

"After Draco bombed Boleyn we knew ... I mean, they knew ... they knew that the war was lost. Or, at least, that it couldn't be won. You have to understand that by that time a significant number of us hadn't had parents. We were nurtured by groups of professionals. We didn't know what it was like to be attached emotionally to just one woman or just one man. I didn't even meet a man until I was almost two decades old."

I still didn't know where she was going with this, but I kept listening.

"When, when the Yin realized that they weren't going to achieve their goal of creating a purely female society, there was a ... a faction that had come up with a plan to at least achieve something for all the suffering they'd been through. It was very controversial and I'm sure it never would have been implemented if things hadn't gotten so awful."

She looked like she was in really bad shape. I took her hand. She still didn't look at me: "They knew they couldn't eliminate the word 'mother' from the language. It was used in too many different ways. But in many ways the concept of being a mother was what had started the war in the first place."

"I suppose so."

The weight of her story prevented her from speaking for a moment. I could tell that she wished she had some other story to tell. "The Psych Ops division had discovered a weakness in the net. They found a way to send a global command that could sever all personal, emotional attachment to any particular word." She smiled ruefully, "If they'd used the word 'Draco,' they might have won the war. Can you imagine? Eliminating all emotional attachment to the name of the nation you belonged to? But they weren't thinking that way."

And then I knew the story: "They used the word 'mother.' "

She nodded, then added, "And all its variants." Her eyes found mine. "I'm sorry, Mo. I really am."

It seemed like she was afraid that this information would make me angry. But in a profound way it was very healing. It gave me a connection that I hadn't had, to the word and to my mother. Almost without thinking I said, "I think you're one of the bravest, strongest human beings I've ever met. Thank you, Archie. Thank you."

This made her smile, shyly. She looked down as she said, "Well, I just wanted you to know. You know, in case ..."

"In case what?"

She shook her head, "Nothing. I— I just wanted you to know." She gathered herself. "They're waiting for us. We'd better go."

CHAPTER 37

Can you define the moment a person leaves the path? Is it recognizable? What is the difference between wanting to heal a human being and wanting to maintain a prized possession? Had Steel ever been able to recognize other souls or had she always moved through the universe alone? When I first met her I had wanted to possess her, but that had passed as she had transformed from a sensual image into a complex psycho-spiritual force, a locus of energy creating and destroying as she moved through time and space. What did *she* want to possess? Everything? Everyone?

With all of my questions unanswered I moved up the slug trail trying to stay alert. The afternoon thunderstorms that had become an almost daily occurrence had moved off to the east, glowing fiery in the setting sun. The world was wet. It gleamed as though freshly polished.

[Slugs to your right,] Marcus' voice was even and calm, governing all our fears as he pointed out two creatures converging on the trail from behind flowing stone. [Let's just give them some space.] We halted while they entered the trail ahead of us and lumbered homeward. Traffic was getting heavy.

I wondered if everyone else was having as many doubts as I was. I loved Alice and I wanted to save her so badly that I ached. I had grown so close to everyone here, everyone except Steel. I wanted all of us to be safe, to be okay. I moved forward, hoping, fearing, determined, uncertain. Thoughts came unbidden to me. Why had Steel brought Drake down to the surface of Vesper? She had endangered the entire population of that moon, maybe the entire population of humanity, so that her employee—her friend, perhaps—wouldn't feel the discomfort of weightlessness while he was being destroyed by the plague. Why had she gone to Eden physically prepared to conceive children? Just to get back at Daimler? Or to understand why he did what he did? Or just simple curiosity? How could she make all the decisions that she had made? How could she take John Cheatham's children away from him? How was she able to do that? How could anyone do that?

As we rounded a curve in the trail the colony came into view from behind an iron dyke that looked like it was eternally unfurling, waving, flowing in a stationary statement of motion. Chocolate globes of the colony glistened in the evening light. A pearl moon rose behind fanciful towers of bubbles; silver light competed with fire.

Steel: [We need to get into the central plaza. That's where they'll gather for evening prayers.]

Archie: [Yes.]

As we got closer to the main gate we were all getting more laconic. I wished there was more chatter. I needed to keep my mind quiet. How impoverished she must be in the midst of all her wealth. Had she ever loved Daimler? Or had that been taken away from her by the nature of her genesis? How did she define love? I had seen her eyes when she learned of her husband's death. What did it mean? How could you feel that way about someone and still do what she had done?

We entered the colony.

Yuri: [This stuff is really dense. Well, it's plutonium. What would you expect? But grav-echo barely penetrates it. It looks like if we keep to the main drag we'll get to the plaza. Umm, take the left fork up there and then keep to the right ...]

Alice looked so worried. She had such a desire to connect to everyone. And Archie had worked so hard to connect to me. Why did Steel and Daimler prefer to remain alone when the world was filled with such a wealth of humanity? We keep secrets. I had kept secrets. I had wandered off the path for a secret attraction, a flirtation, a dalliance that had cost me ... I couldn't quantify what it had cost me. Yuri had his secret, a secret so horrifying to him that he could only share it when he was absent, and yet I couldn't imagine him taking children from someone he had loved, or, more importantly, from someone the children had loved.

Should we be following orders given by a person capable of such acts? We had to in order to function at all. Perhaps Marcus had been opposed to bringing Drake down to the surface of Vesper. What could he do? State his objections and then follow orders, or mutiny and destroy the whole enterprise? As long as there was a chance of saving Alice the second option was unthinkable.

Marcus: [Slugs coming up behind.] We moved to the sides of the passage to let three enormous creatures flow by. The walls reflected the swirling, strobing colors on their sides. Flashes and fireworks and bold swaths of electric hues. Risk-free communication: there were no eyes to see what they were expressing except ours, and we would never be able to tell them what we thought about it.

We followed this last group through passageways that opened into the central piazza, a feature in all Brainardite colonies. Stars were appearing in the fading sky and the colossal moon rose crystalline, touching each dark globe with quicksilver, each crab-shaped carapace, each human environmental suit. The slugs in the open space were excited, or so they seemed by the light shows on their sides. Shapes and patterns flickered and flashed across their skin in brilliant rainbows and hallucinogenic mazes. Patterns just beyond understanding, teasing our minds with repetition and variation, developing, recapitulating, echoing, reposting. The activity continued to increase until every slug was a symphony of color and pattern, vibrating and undulating in similar tempo and style.

I don't know what started the droning. They were all aligned east to west, maybe facing the setting sun, maybe the rising moon, we couldn't tell. But the flanks of every slug started to pulse simultaneously and the world was filled with sound. I could feel it in my chest, through my feet, down my arms—the chanting of a thousand monks in the ancient Himalayas bathing us in music, in fundamental oscillation that resonated with the soul of the universe.

Archie: [Yuri? Could you set up the scanner beside the nearest one? On the right there?]

Yuri: [You got it.] The slugs were so close to each other there was just barely room to work. Stepping sideways he moved the scanner into position. The droning rose and fell, soothed and excited, lowering our pulse but raising our adrenaline.

Arch: [I'm guessing their central nervous systems will be protected under their shells, probably in the central portion of their bodies.]

Yuri: [Sounds good. How about here?] He had finished the assembly.

Arch: [That looks good. Let's try sub-sonics first. We may have to go to grav-echo. I don't want to use x-rays.]

Yuri: [Okay.] He turned on the machine. Archie gazed into the viewer. She scanned back and forth. The deep droning accompanied her, swelling and fading in complex, non-repeating patterns that always surprised, but always made sense.

Arch: [There it is. That has to be it. You see?] Steel moved to look into the viewer. Then Alice.

Alice: [I suppose so.]

Steel: [Yes. That has to be it.]

Arch: [I'll set up the probe here.] She assembled a framework that held a long needle-like instrument and aimed it at the chosen spot on the slug's skin, skin that flashed and swirled with color and shape. When she was finished: [Now we wait.]

"Wait for what?" I asked.

[Wait for them to finish their ... their evening prayers.]

"What happens then?"

Marcus: [They get very still for about an hour before they head off to their various sleeping quarters.]

Arch: [If they sleep.]

Marcus: [Yes.]

For an endless time, or a time that was not too long, the droning continued. And then it stopped, leaving an acoustic vacuum where there had been richness and mystery. The slugs quieted, the patterns on their skin fading and disappearing. They became almost inert. The night was silent, just the gentlest breeze disturbing the air. Arch approached the controls of the probe. She gazed into the scanner, lowering the probe to the very surface of the slug's skin. When she got there she stopped. For a moment nothing happened, then she said, [I can't do this. I don't think we should do this.]

Alice added, [I don't want to. I think you're right, Archie. Let's ... let's just—]

Steel moved forward. [I'll take over.] Her voice was without emotion. [Marcus, deploy everyone. I want to be ready for any reaction they might exhibit.]

[Yes, Captain.] Marcus moved the six of us to positions where we could cover Steel with our lasers, our ray guns. We were just inside the plaza, our backs to the passage that led to the outside of the colony. Marcus and Tamika flanked us with the laser canons. [We're ready, Captain.]

Steel started the probe again. It sank into the slug's flesh almost unnoticeably. From where we were we couldn't tell how deep the probe was getting but, as they say, it must have hit a nerve. As fast as a frog's tongue the slug whipped out two pseudopods, striking Steel on her shoulder and thigh. Where they struck they adhered. We knew that Steel's suit was being eroded as we watched.

[Hold your fire.] Marcus' voice was steady as always as he leveled his hand laser at the slug. We saw only the faintest beam as he hit the creature where the two pseudopods emerged from its body. The limbs retracted immediately and Archie and Yuri rushed in to pick Steel up off the ground where she had fallen. [There are no alarms, Captain. Your suit integrity is good.]

As they lifted her we could see a spreading pool of light communicate from slug to slug. They were waking up, their sides swirling and flashing. Pseudopods from three or four different slugs shot out and hit our friends. Steel was knocked on her back again. Yuri went to one knee. Arch fought to keep her balance.

Marcus said, [Captain, Archie, Yuri, stay as still as you can!] They tried to. [We have to avoid hitting the suits! Aim no closer than a meter away from them. Fire.]

Tamika and Marcus began surgically hitting the slugs with the laser canons as Alice and I used our ray guns as judiciously as we could. Soon all the slugs closest to our friends had retreated, wounded, but the colony was awake and responding.

Steel yelled: [Let's get out of here! Let's go!] The three of them joined us in the passage as the colony started to move toward us. The slugs moved faster than we had ever seen them. We turned and accelerated our suits until we were running down the twisting artery, our footfalls like artillery. Every twenty meters or so Marcus and Tamika would turn back and scan the tube for our pursuers. They weren't catching up but we weren't gaining any ground, either.

We flew out of the front gate and onto the trail. Marcus' voice actually sounded urgent: [They may be able to move faster out in the open.]

Steel responded: [We need someplace ... There!] She pointed to the waving iron dyke beside the trail. The top surface of the swirling sculpture started at the ground and rose, ramp-like, until it reached a height of ten to twenty meters, but it was far too narrow for slugs to climb up. We started up the twisting path in rich moonlight, our steps changing from thunder on rock to music on iron.

As we climbed, slugs began to emerge from the gate. When we were high enough to be able to look down on their shells, we turned back to see what they were doing. It turned out to be nothing much. As more slugs appeared through the gate their urgency seemed to evaporate and they started to slowly wander around again like nothing had happened. And still no suit alarms had gone off. We had escaped. I was gasping for air and trembling with relief or exhaustion or both.

Steel turned on Archie like a viper: [I hired you as a science officer! I expect you to do your job!]

[Captain, I— I'm sorry, but—]

[I don't need your apologies. I need you to perform. I don't know what I hit but I do know that if you had been at the controls—]

[Captain, I can't just ... I— I mean I think we need to ... we have to—] Then, as if they had never been, Archie and Marcus vanished.

It was so fast. They just disappeared. No slugs were even close to us. It wasn't until much later that I put together what I had seen. It didn't make any sense to me. I mean we had descended sixty thousand meters to get down to Eden. We knew what we were doing. It just couldn't have happened. We weren't that high up, barely ten meters, a three-story building. It simply didn't make sense. On such a complex undertaking, a mission of such profound significance, how could such a small thing, a tiny, stupid thing take two of our company? Arch had simply slipped in a puddle of water on the slick metal, she got tangled in Marcus' legs and they both went over the side. It was shocking to see how furiously the gravity of Brainard's Planet slammed them into the ground.

I think Alice was the first one to realize that they were lost. Half her life had been spent where people were unprotected. She screamed their names with a heart-wrenching anguish. Someone was saying, "They can't upload. They can't upload." I think it was me.

[I'm not getting any life signs,] Yuri was already on the move. [We need to get down there.]

He was right, but how? They had fallen on the side away from the trail, landing on solid rock beside a small field of tubes. We had to walk back down the sculpture until we got low enough to jump off. We made our way to their sides as quickly as we could, but it took several minutes. Alice was crying. Yuri kept saying: [I'm not getting any life signs.] He was the first to reach them. There were still no suit alarms. Yuri's e-suits had worked, had held up even in a fall of ten meters, but it hadn't mattered. The poor human bodies inside were broken, smashed. They didn't work anymore.

We urgently tried to think of something to do, but there was nothing to do. We tried to keep our heads like Marcus would have wanted, but Marcus was lost to us. We tried to think what medical steps Archie would have taken but it was too late for medical steps and Archie was lost to us, too. We were impoverished, devastated. We had lost two human perspectives forever.

For a long time we couldn't move, that is, we moved but we didn't go anywhere. We didn't want to move Arch or Marcus for fear of hurting them. We did this knowing that nothing could hurt them anymore. Still, the thought of picking them up with their bones broken seemed unconscionably cruel. Moving from the last place we had had them was an admission of fate that we weren't yet prepared to make. We wandered, we stood, we started to say things. We expected Marcus to pull us together, cut the skag and get us moving again, but he remained as still and silent as his fallen comrade. My dear friend. My dear, dear friend, Archie. What were we going to do?

Daimler's voice was gentle, soothing as it came to us from the ether: [Estelle, it's time to go home. Gather your friends and let's get you back up to the Lightdancer.]

Steel looked at us vacantly. Her eyes were dead. Her face was dead. Finally, in a voice that was dull and empty she said, [All right. Let's ... let's all ...] She started to walk off.

"We're not leaving them here."

She turned back, [What?]

"We're not leaving Archie and Marcus here."

[What do you mean? They're ... they're gone ...]

Alice moved to my side, [Mom, we have to take them with us. We can't just leave them.]

[Why? We can't ... we can't re-boot them. They're ... they're ...]

[We have to take them with us, mom.]

"We have to."

She stared at us uncomprehending. But she said, [Okay,] and walked back to the two inert e-suits. We decided that Yuri, Steel and Tamika would carry Marcus.

Alice and I would take Arch. We rolled the suits over onto their backs. I hadn't looked into the faceplates until then. They didn't look like themselves anymore. Their faces were distorted, broken. One of Archie's eyes had, had ... I couldn't look at it as we lifted her, but I was glad I had her shoulders and not Alice.

There was a mechanical quality to it. A certain amount of weight had to be transported back to the habitat. It had to be carried by us. Yuri figured out a way to lock the elbow and shoulder joints so the suits carried most of the burden. Still we had to stop from time to time to rest. The slugs didn't follow us. They didn't bother us at all. We walked right past several of them as we rounded the bottom of the iron sculpture. We noticed them hardly any more than they noticed us.

The lifeless globe of the moon lit our way as we trudged back to base. It was past the zenith and descending before we made it to the hab. We de-suited and went inside, but we left the bodies of our friends in their suits. There was no reason to take them out. Tamika and I lay together that night. I don't know if we slept. Sometimes we cried. Sometimes we raged. We were all so close to each other in the hab the two of us couldn't really talk without bothering everyone, so we logged on with each other for some part of that endless night. She'd known Marcus for a long time. A long, long time. She was heartbroken but more than that she was angry. I was angry, too. We raged that Steel had had to push things so far and our rage was amplified by our ambivalence. Would we have done the same in her place? Would we have risked lives to save a life with so little chance of success?

My heart was glad that Alice still had Yuri to sleep with. They took great comfort in each other. Steel lay by herself.

In the morning we prepared to leave. The hab and lab would stay behind and slowly run out of power. They would probably be discovered soon, but we would be gone. Draco and The Pleiades could puzzle out the mystery as best they could. It didn't seem to matter to us. As we were loading Arch and Marcus onto the ultra-lights, Yuri touched helmets with me: "We need to talk," was all he said. Then he went on Steel's system: [Hey, Mo. Help me check out this engine. It was running a little rough on the way back from the canyon.]

"Okay."

As Steel, Tamika and Alice went to shut down the lab, Yuri and I went around to the back of the ultra-light in question. As they disappeared behind the hab we touched helmets again. "We have to figure out a way of getting this data out," he said.

"What do you mean?"

"I mean it's all on Steel's I. S."

"Yeah, I know. But, but won't they—"

"Think about it, Mo. You saw how Steel has been behaving. She knows she can't use it to save Alice, so she's through with it. Do you trust Daimler to release it? They're going to quash it. They'll either keep it for themselves or they'll just hide it. It's illegal to come here, remember?"

"But, but none of us are on the net. How can we—"

"We have to figure out a way. Three people have given their lives for this information. I don't want it profiting some damn syndicate. I want it out where everyone can use it. Who knows where this stuff might lead us? The Brainardites don't have nanotechnology; they have picotechnology, femtotechnology. Smaller than that. We don't even have a word for it. We can't let the Bayernische Syndicate keep it or lock it away where no one will ever see it."

The problem had never occurred to me, but now I was worried about it. I didn't want Arch or Marcus or even Drake to have given their lives to profit the syndicate that had killed my wife. Yuri was right. I didn't trust Daimler and I didn't trust Steel. We had to figure out a way to get around Steel's security safeguards. But if anyone could do that it was Yuri, and he was asking me.

Of course, it wasn't until we got up to the Lightdancer that our real problem hit us in the face. We were two perspectives short. Marcus had jury-rigged the engine when they were missing only one perspective and still they had undershot their target by more than three hundred light years. How were we going to get back? We were twelve hundred light years from Earth. How close was the nearest inhabited planet? How could we even get that far? It seemed impossible. The three nearest systems had been sterilized in the plague: Elysium, Paraiso and Cielo were all within fifty light years but they were lifeless rocks. Nothing was left there. Steel, Daimler and Tamika were plugged into Steel's system, poring over maps, trying to come up with a plan, but they didn't appear to be getting anywhere.

Sometimes, though, it just depends on your relationship with a particular word. It was Alice who gave us our answer. It was in the form of a demand. Above tense, quiet deliberations that wavered between angry and desperate Alice's voice rang out: "I want to go home."

At first her response seemed childish, which wasn't surprising considering her age. Steel glanced at her testily as we floated in control. "That's what we're working on, Alice, how to get back to Earth—"

"I don't want to go back to Earth. I want to go *home!*"

Steel didn't have much patience left, "Alice, this is not the time. I don't even know what you mean. Just let us—"

Yuri said, "She wants to go back to Eden."

Steel was stunned, incredulous, "What?"

"I want to go back to Nazareth. It's the only real home I've ever known. I want to be around people my own age, who are the same as me. I want—"

The viper we had seen in Steel came out again: "Alice, stop it! That's nonsense.

It's ridiculous. We've had a setback, that's all. We're going to keep looking for a cure until we find one. We will never give up!"

"Mom, you know what Archie said. There isn't time. There are too many possible combinations of genes. That's why we came here in the first place."

"We'll make time—"

"We were gone for thirty years, mom! They hadn't made any progress. Archie said—"

"Archie is just one person—"

"Archie is DEAD! Don't you GET THAT? Archie is dead, Marcus is dead, Drake is dead, Dad is dead, Jacob is dead. How many people do you have to kill before you let go of me?"

The rage I saw in Steel's eyes took me back to the bridge at Neuschwanstein. These people—Steel, Krupp, Daimler, members of the syndicates—were used to getting their way in everything. Nothing in the universe could deny them. Their power was limitless, their appetites without boundaries. Steel kicked against a bulkhead and launched herself at Alice, grabbing her by the wrists. Alice curled up in a ball and they tumbled over each other in mid-air as Steel slapped at her again and again.

"Mom, STOP IT!! WHAT ARE YOU DOING?"

Tamika grabbed Daimler as Yuri and I launched ourselves toward Steel. Between the two of us we managed to haul her off of Alice. Our momentum carried us across the control room, and I banged my head into an instrument panel. It must have cut my scalp; blood was floating through the air in streams and globules.

Steel screamed at us, "Get your hands off me! GET YOUR HANDS OFF ME!"

I said, "Sorry, Captain. Not until everybody settles down."

"I AM THE CAPTAIN OF THIS SHIP. I ORDER YOU TO RELEASE ME!"

Yuri said, "We can't do that, Captain. Please calm down. Please."

Steel's struggles sent us tumbling, and I hit my head again in the very same place. "Ouch! Goddamn it. Please, Captain. You have to calm down."

"LET GO OF ME!"

"No."

She was still breathing hard, but she stopped her struggling. It was Tamika who spoke next: "Eden is only twenty-three light years from here." I remembered! Of all the worlds close to Brainard's Planet, Eden had been spared because it had been cut off from all human traffic. We were between the Orion spur and the Perseus arm, in a relatively dust-free part of the galaxy. We had a real chance of making Eden, even traveling in rational space. Twenty-three years would pass for the rest of humanity, but we would hardly age. Tamika continued, "We can drop Alice off on Eden and then head for Ultima Thule."

I asked, "How far is Ultima Thule beyond Eden?"

"Ninety-eight light years." That was quite a jump, but still, between the galactic arms, we just might pull it off.

Steel tried to pull free of us again, but we managed to hold onto her. "I FORBID it!" she yelled.

Tamika responded evenly, "Sorry, Captain. I'm taking control of the Lightdancer. Yuri, Mo, place the Captain and Daimler under arrest. Cut off their net access."

"You need to think about what you're doing—" Daimler started.

"You can log on from here if you want," Tamika continued. "We'll all be arrested and Alice will be returned to Eden by Traffic Control. Or you can resist and we'll eject you into space. It won't kill you, but for the second before you upload it's going to be very uncomfortable. By the time Traffic Control gets here we'll be long gone. One way or another, Alice is going home."

We heard a banging resound through the ship. Tamika said, "I think Ham heard the commotion. He seems to be upset. Alice, would you go down to his compartment and take care of him?"

CHAPTER 38

It took us four weeks—ship time—to get to Eden. After Yuri and I put Steel and Daimler in her quarters I tried to bullet Archie so she could look at the cut on my head. Things like that kept happening for a while.

We would bring Steel and Daimler their meals. Daimler would talk to us, but Steel was silent. She wouldn't even look at us. Alice tried to visit but Steel wouldn't see her. She got worse and worse. She didn't seem to be sleeping or bathing.

Tamika decided that Yuri and I would accompany Alice down the escarpment to the surface. I couldn't believe we were going to make that climb again. Tamika would stay on board to watch over and tend to our two prisoners.

Before we left I tried one last time to get Steel to see Alice. We were in orbit; everything was in suspension. I floated to their hatch and knocked. Daimler greeted me and asked me in.

Steel was looking out at Eden, turning beneath us. Her hair was dirty, her arms clutched across her chest. She looked much thinner. I spoke to Daimler, "I— I was just wondering if, if Steel wanted to see her daughter before we left." She didn't turn.

Daimler pointed at her. His voice was low and urgent. "Look at her. Is there any reason to keep putting her through this?"

I wasn't sure what to say at first. "Alice just wants to say goodbye."

"You people have made your decisions. Fine. There is no possible reason to keep her in this mental anguish."

"I— I don't—" was all I could get out.

Daimler didn't answer. He simply turned to Steel and said, "Estelle, we have a visitor. Estelle?"

She turned. Her eyes were wells of rage and grief. There was nothing left of her but anger, desperation. She rasped, "Why is she doing this to me? WHY is she DOING this to me?"

"Steel, she— she just wants ... she wants a chance to have a life, some kind of a life."

She wanted to scream but her voice was a dry wasteland. "She WANTS to have a LIFE? That's what I want to give her!" She launched herself at me, fists clenched in front of her. "YOU! You were supposed to save us! You were supposed to—" She collided with me, beating me anywhere she could reach. I was surprised at how weak she had become.

"Captain, please—" Daimler and I tried to get hold of her arms.

"Estelle, it's all right. It's all right."

She kept beating and punching and wailing until Daimler got her under control. Her eyes and nose were flinging liquid into her hair as she whipped her head around. Her chest convulsed with her sobs.

"She can't take this anymore. She needs relief," Daimler said.

Suddenly she changed. Her sobs stopped. She shrugged out of Daimler's grasp and put her arms around my neck, kissing it as she whispered, "I can give you anything, anything you want." She pulled me into her, crushing her breasts into my chest. She tried to kiss me through the floating mat that was her hair.

"Captain, this is not my decision—"

Daimler pulled her off of me again. "Estelle, this won't do. Now, now—"

She curled into a ball and started sobbing again. Daimler took her in his arms, pushed off the bulkhead and carried her back to the glass wall that looked out onto the quiet cosmos. He petted her, then came back to me and whispered, "I beg you to have pity on her."

"What do you want me to do?" I whispered back. "All of this is the result of her decisions. She chose to go to Eden, to marry, to have children, to destroy her children's family. My father would have called this karma."

Daimler said, "I call it cruelty."

"What do you want me to do?" I repeated.

"Just let me take her down to medical and erase the last two or three decades of her memory. That's all I ask."

I was shocked. I couldn't reply for a moment. I thought of all the things that I could have erased but hadn't, never would. I thought of what Yuri carried around in him, too respectful of his fallen enemies to ever relieve himself of the burden of carrying their memory.

"She— she wants to forget ... everything?" I looked at her staring vacantly at the stars and hugging herself.

"She needs to," Daimler replied. "Sometimes it's better to forget."

And what have *you* forgotten? I thought. "Can't this wait until we get back?"

"Why would you want to put her through one more second of this? Are you sadistic? Do you have some warped need for vengeance?"

How about justice? But, no, I didn't want her to be in pain if she didn't have to be. But to forget her own daughter, her son, her husband ...

I bulleted Tamika. [Yes?]

"I'm— ah ... I'm taking Daimler and Steel down to medical."

[What's wrong?]

"Umm, Steel's in a lot of pain. Daimler thinks it would be best if we ... if we wiped her memory."

[She wants to zero out?]

"No, just the last two or three decades."

There was quite some time before Tamika answered: [Well, that would certainly put her in a better legal position.] I hadn't thought of that. Daimler was covering her tracks, one step at a time. On the other hand, she really was in pain. I could see that.

"She's in pretty bad shape."

[She doesn't want to see Alice?]

"I don't think that's gonna happen."

There was another pause. Then: [All right. Stay with them. Make sure he doesn't do anything that would give them access to the net.]

"Right. Will do."

So Steel was asleep, recovering from nanosurgery when the three of us hooked onto the skyhook and started our descent, the three of us plus our sad charges. We would be carrying Archie and Marcus down to the surface. Eden was the only place I knew of where we could bury them.

Alice was stoic about her mother; still it was good to get back on the rock. It's hard to think about anything but what you're doing when you're dangling over kilometers of nothing.

We made a good descent. No goofing around, no mistakes. It helped that we had just done this a few months ago. And we had good luck with the weather. Two weeks later we were standing beside the little Buddhist shrine, the friendly stream jumping and shattering in its channel.

We dug two graves and placed the bodies in the ground. None of us knew what to say, but the ritual completed itself nonetheless. They were as much at rest as we could make them.

I said, "The Buckymobile should be about ten klicks southwest of us, if it's still there."

"I remember where it is," said Alice.

I picked up my pack, "Yeah, well, let's get going."

Yuri put his hand on my chest. I looked at him. He said, "I think the two of us will be all right from here."

Oh. Yuri was staying. Of course. He'd found a way. I should have known that. Yuri had found the woman he could save, or at least help. I would be climbing back up on my own. I looked from Yuri's face to Alice's. They were a team. "Yeah. Yeah, I'm sure you'll be fine. We'll ... um ... we'll bullet you when we get to Ultima Thule—"

Yuri said, "I don't think so, Mo."

"What? Why not?"

"Ultima Thule's ninety-eight light years away."

I didn't understand at first. It didn't matter on the net how far away we were. But then I did understand. Ninety-eight years. I felt like the Lightdancer had just been driven into my chest. "Right. What's ... what's the average lifespan on Eden?" I asked.

"About seventy years for women, sixty-five for men," Alice answered. "Some people live longer, but never much past a hundred."

I didn't know when Yuri had last booted. I knew that Alice was already effectively in her twenties. This was messing me up. When was the last time people had actually said goodbye in our culture? I didn't know how to do it. "Well ... well ... have a good life. A ... a *great* life. I— I love you both." The three of us hugged, clutched was more like it, like we never wanted to let go. But pretty soon we did.

"Take care of Ham for me," Alice said.

"I will."

Then Yuri grabbed my shoulders. "And you have to get that data out. Don't forget. You have to figure out a way."

"Right. Right, I'll ... I'll think of something."

"I'm counting on you." He gave me a whack on the shoulder. Then they turned and started down the trail.

I watched them till they were out of sight, then prepared for the ascent. When I was ready, I felt inside my medicine bag for the little meteorite Yuri had found on Brainard's Planet. I rubbed it between my fingers and kissed it for luck. It was going to be a long, lonely climb.

I was fine until the third day when I got to the hut where Archie had lost her arm. I was making myself dinner when it hit me out of the blue that she'd never gotten her new one. I don't know why that hurt so badly, but I fell apart into racking sobs of inconsolable bereavement.

But when I recovered, I had an idea. I didn't know if it would work. It seemed so simple that Steel would have foreseen it, but then, she had made so many impulsive decisions. I didn't know, but I gave it a try:

"Jemal?" I wondered if he was still on Steel's system. "Jemal? Can you hear me?"

And then he answered: [MO! Mo, it's great to hear your voice, man! How is it going? How is everybody? I've been worried sick. It's been over two decades—]

"Yeah, well, a lot's happened."

[Is everyone okay?]

"Um, no. No, Arch and Marcus didn't make it."

[They're ... they're ... They didn't—]

"We lost them."

[Oh, man—]

"Yeah, but listen."

[What? What can I do?]

"Did, umm, did you manage to get back on the net?"

There was a pause. Then: [Umm, yeah, yeah I did. I— umm, I met a guy who knew a guy who knew a guy. You know.]

"That's great. Listen, I need you to upload some data for me."

[Okay.]

"There's a lot of it. I want you to send it to Lysistrata-24. At the Antigone Institute. Got it?"

I felt a lot lighter the rest of the way up.

Epilogue

By the time I made it back up to the Lightdancer, Steel had had almost a month to recover. She looked much better; still, it was very strange to be around someone I felt I knew fairly intimately when it was obvious that she didn't have any idea who I was.

Daimler offered us a deal. Tamika and I were not to speak to Steel about anything that had happened. We were to interact with her only about the present, never about the past. In return for this he agreed to put us back on the net, pay us what Steel owed us, and say goodbye on Ultima Thule. We would have no more dealings with each other. We knew that if we told anyone about our trip to Brainard's Planet we would open ourselves up to prosecution, so we all had reason to keep our mouths shut. Tamika stipulated that none of us would get on the net before we achieved relativistic velocity. We would be out of contact until we got to the vicinity of Ultima Thule.

I didn't happen to mention that Jemal had already bulleted me to let me know that Lysistrata had received everything. Must have slipped my mind.

It took us nearly four months, ship's time, to make the voyage. Four months of back-to-back twelve-hour watches, because Tamika and I were the only ones who could stand watch. It was fairly grueling. And lonely. How we didn't hit anything is anyone's guess. Maybe my meteorite helped. We certainly made it by luck alone.

As we backed down into Ultima Thule, there came a time when we were traveling slowly enough to be in contact with the outside world. We'd been gone a long time. I wasn't expecting any messages. I didn't know if anyone would even remember me, so I was surprised to see that I had quite a few. They'd all been left in the last couple of days. There was one from Jemal, but the rest were from two women: one named Cooper and the other named FA'izeh. I recognized the names, but it still didn't make any sense. I opened the first one:

Cooper: [We don't know exactly when you'll be back in contact. Our mother is dying. Please come as quickly as you can.] This filled me with improbable theories, but they didn't really help. I opened the next:

FA'izeh: [This message is for Mohandas. Our mother, Alice Cheatham, knows you and would like to see you. She is failing and we don't expect her to last much longer. Please take the next available transport to Eden. It is very important to her that she sees you before she leaves us.]

Alice was still alive? She had to be twelve decades old. And what did she mean by the next available transport to Eden? The next message was longer:

Cooper: [Mohandas, your friend Jemal is here and can pick you up at New Jerusalem Spaceport. It's a short trip from there to Nazareth, where Mom is. FA'izeh and I are with her. If you know where our grandmother is, please bring her with you. Mom seems to think that she won't remember her. I don't know why that would be. Anyway, if you know where she is, please bring her. Oh, and please bring someone named Tamika, as well. If you can. And please contact us as soon as you get this.]

Even if Alice had waited to have children until her fourth decade, they would still have to be nearly eighty years old by now; both these voices sounded young and vigorous. I bulleted Cooper: "Hello?"

[Mohandas! Is that you?]

"Yes—"

[How soon can you get here? We think Mom has been hanging on just so she can see you.]

"Um, we're two days out from Ultima Thule."

[Good. There's a commercial transport leaving for Eden three days from now. I'll get you passage. Is Tamika there, too? I'll get her passage also.]

"Uh, yeah, Tamika is here. Um, when did ... when did Eden, I mean ... when did they start flying to Eden?"

[Oh, it's a long story. Let's just say Mom and Dad had quite an impact on this place.]

"Your dad ... your dad is, I mean, is your dad named—"

[Yes. Your friend Yuri was our father. He passed away quite a few years ago. We still miss him a lot. He spoke very highly of you.]

Even though this wasn't a surprise, it slammed into me, ripped into my heart. "Oh, well ... he was a ... was a very good friend, a ... a fine, a fine man—"

[I'm sorry. I shouldn't have been so blunt. It's just that everything is in an uproar here with Mom, and FA'i and I have been trying to handle everything. Please accept my apology.]

"Oh, no. You're fine. I mean, I mean there's nothing to ... It was just kind of a—you know—shock."

[Of course. We loved him a lot. Everybody loved him.]

That was good news. I had wondered how he was going to interact with the Edenites. I guess he did all right.

I don't know why I asked this next, it sort of came out before my mouth could stop it: "Do you know ... do you know who you're named after? You and your sister, I mean."

[Do *you* know?] she asked back. [They're such odd names. Since we're twins you'd expect us to have names like Terry and Sherry or something like that.] She laughed.

"You're twins?"

[Yes, mom says twins run in our family. But we could never find out why they named us this. Mom would always say 'Ask your father' and Dad would never talk about it.]

"Oh. Yes."

[Maybe you could tell us the story. It seemed very important to him. All he would say was that it was Mom's idea to give us these names, that Mom 'saved his life.' We never knew what he meant. I'm sorry; I'm babbling. It's just that it's so exciting that we got hold of you in time.]

"Yes, yes. I can't believe I'm going to see Alice again. This is wonderful news."

We spoke a little more. I promised I'd try to get Steel to come with us, but I wasn't optimistic.

Of course Daimler absolutely refused to even let me bring it up with Steel. I have to say that I didn't argue the point too hard; she wouldn't have gotten anything out of seeing her daughter. She really had no memory at all of any of this. And as odd as it was for *me* to be around her, I thought it would just be painful for Alice to see her.

I suppose I expected us to be met at Thule spaceport by Traffic Control, but no one met us. Nobody even seemed to know who we were, or care. It had been almost a century since Jemal had uploaded our data onto the net. I guess if we were ever news, we were old news now. The only thing on the net that seemed to have anything at all to do with us was an advertisement for a new gadget. Evidently it was the first advance based on what we found on Brainard's Planet to be developed to the point where it could be marketed. They called it LEPTONIC TECHNOLOGY!!!—breathed like it was the sexiest thing in the universe. Basically, it cheaply and conveniently erased specifically every memory of any orgasm you had ever had, so that every orgasm you experienced would be like the very first one you had ever experienced.

Oh, well. Maybe they'd do something more important with it once they got the hang of it.

I shouldn't say that no one met us. A group of Hindu proselytes with shaved heads and saffron robes were playing antique cymbals and chanting to Krishna. They gave us each a flower. But they gave everybody who passed by a flower, not just us. Evidently people were not only traveling to Eden now; Edenites were traveling to other worlds.

And Kristel met Daimler and Steel. Not Krupp. She had changed her gender again and looked remarkably like her sister. Daimler had already taken care of the financial arrangements, which were surprisingly large. We had accrued over twelve decades of back pay. With that taken care of, he said goodbye to us—dismissed us more like—and went off with the two women. Steel seemed happy to see her sister. She never looked back.

Which left Tamika and me with the last orphan in this saga. He looked kind of forlorn. I scratched his ears, "C'mon, Ham. Let's go find a room for the night." The three of us walked out of the terminal.

Eden was largely the same but remarkably different in many ways. We kept running into Yuri's engineering. Cooper hadn't been exaggerating about the impact he and Alice had had. Jemal met us at the spaceport, and we climbed aboard the hypersonic monorail to Nazareth. No sonic booms, of course. Yuri would never have put up with anything so annoying in his design.

As we pulled into Nazareth Station, we could see that the desert above the slot canyon had been transformed into a huge encampment. Tents and vehicles covered acres of rock dotted with temporary water and sanitary facilities.

"What's going on?" I asked.

Jemal said, "Oh. All of this is for Alice. But don't worry. We'll get to see her. We're on the VIP list."

There was an endless line of people sitting in camp chairs and under parasols waiting to go down the stairs that I had descended a few months ago—a few months for me, but over a century to the rest of the universe. I guess our arrival had disrupted things in a pretty major way.

We were waved through to descend into the rose light of the slot canyon, surrounded by soft swirls of textured rock. We walked beside the little golden stream, winding and winding until it opened out into the amphitheater that held Nazareth. The waterfall at the upper end of the cathedral-like space still flowed. If you looked closely, you could see tiny evidences of new power systems, sewer systems, irrigation. It was the same, but decorated with tiny, high-tech jewels here and there.

Jemal led us to the Cheatham house, where I had met John and Louise. It was surrounded by offerings—hundreds of candles and flowers and portraits, some tended, others not. The front door opened and out came two beautiful young women. I could see Alice in their faces. And Steel.

"Mohandas! Tamika! How wonderful that you could make it! How wonderful to meet you! This must be Ham! My goodness, you're a big fellow! Mom told us all about you!" We were flooded with warmth and welcome. They hugged us and kissed us and bade us come inside.

The sitting room and dining room had been turned into waiting rooms, but no one was in them. The house had been cleared for us. Cooper and FA'izeh led us up the wooden stairs to the door of Alice's bedroom. It was filled with medical equipment, but the machinery had been placed so that Alice's view of the room was uncluttered. She lay in the middle of the bed, her head propped up on pillows. She was asleep, her silver hair floating around her placid, shriveled face. Her hands, resting on the coverlet, reminded me of those of Mrs. Fogarty, who had run the boarding house where we had stayed. Alice had been transformed into a tiny elf.

"I'm going to wake her," FA'izeh said. "She's been asleep for a good while, and she'd never forgive me if I didn't." She moved to Alice's side. "Mom?" Her voice was as gentle as calling birds. "Mom? Mohandas is here. And Tamika. Mom?"

Her eyes opened, blue and clear. She blinked a couple of times and said, "Hello, FA'i. Who did you say was here?" Her voice was as tiny as she was.

FA'i waved to me. I stepped forward. "Mohandas, Mom. Here he is."

She broke into a huge smile when she saw me. "I remember *you*!" she said and took my hand. Then, conspiratorially, "We had our moments, didn't we?" With a twinkle in her eye she pulled me close. "You were a naughty boy!" She touched the end of my nose with her shriveled, elfin fingertip.

Cooper and FA'izeh looked at each other like they didn't quite know what to say and I found myself blushing like a schoolboy in front of a little old lady who was fifteen hundred years younger than me.

"It's wonderful to see you again, Alice." I'd never meant something more sincerely in all the centuries I'd been alive. "It's— it's— I didn't think I'd, I mean, it's a miracle you're still alive. How ... how did you, how did you—"

She put her tiny hands on my face. "Oh, I don't want to talk about medicine now! You people never wait to see how long the net will keep you alive. You always rush off and re-boot before you start looking like me!" She laughed.

That was right. She'd been on the net this whole time. So had Yuri. Until he— "When did you ... I mean, when did Eden ... How did you, how did you convince them to—"

"Listen to this boy," she said with a smile. "All questions! You come here and give me a hug. Careful now; there's not much of me left." It was like hugging a bundle of twigs, but I didn't mind. I would have hugged her forever.

"Tamika's here, too," I said. She approached the bed.

"Hello, Tamika! How are you?"

"I'm ... I'm fine. It's, it's good to see you, Alice."

"And we have another friend from the old days." I gestured to Ham. He came up to the bed and gently nuzzled her.

"Ham! Ham, you big puppy! You look wonderful!" She looked at all of us. "It's so good to see you all again! It's so nice to get everybody together!"

We talked for a little while, but she wore out pretty quickly. I was able to ask about Yuri. I wasn't sure how to bring it up, but she was at peace with his passing. It had been over three decades for her.

"Did ... did Yuri pass before Eden opened up to the outside world?"

She smiled and patted my hand. "It was largely because of my husband that Eden did open up."

"How did, how did ... I mean they seemed so dead-set against it. The heresy thing, the ... the ... everything that happened with your father—"

"Oh, I know. It wasn't easy and it didn't happen overnight."

"But I would have thought that, that as soon as you brought up getting in touch with the outside world—"

"We didn't."

"What?"

"I'm afraid I gave the people here a bit of a conundrum." She smiled. "You see, I *was* in contact with the outside world, and yet, I was a legitimate citizen of Eden."

"You told them who you were? Where you'd been?"

"I didn't exactly tell them; I just didn't keep it a secret. When someone would ask, I'd tell the truth. Yuri and I never advocated communicating with the rest of humanity; we just did communicate with them. Well, I did directly and Yuri did through Jemal after you had that ingenious idea. Yuri was very proud of you. Very happy that you got the data out."

Too many things at once: I was trying to be humble in the face of Yuri's praise while at the same time trying to process this. Yuri *hadn't* been on the net. None of us had been. But Alice was talking like she *was* on the net. Which is what I had thought, only there wasn't any way she could be. "Wait a minute. You ... you are on the net? How did you get back on?" She'd been on Eden. There was no way.

"I'd never been out of contact with the net. Mom didn't consider me a security risk, I guess."

Oh.

"We had to walk a very fine line. But then, Yuri kept solving problems for people, designing things, making life better. You know he was a genius but he also had the advantage of a millennium of technological advances."

"Of course."

"But most importantly, people just liked him."

That made sense.

"He'd talk about all the silly things that made human civilization so wonderful—old movies, TV shows, all kinds of crazy things. It made it less scary to the people here."

"Hmm."

"And then there was the fact that he came here. To be with me."

"Yes?"

"You see? He could have stayed out there and re-booted and kept living, but he chose to come here. Just to be with me."

"I— I— I don't see—"

"He challenged their faith."

I must have looked confused. She smiled indulgently. "Don't you see? He showed them that a person could choose what to sacrifice himself for. He made them feel, well, rather cowardly for not going out into the world, offering their ideas, and taking their chances that they might decide to leave their religion and become something else."

"Huh."

"I'm afraid I pushed him. I always wanted to get everyone back together. I think I might have been a little obsessive about it." She smiled again. "He knew I wanted it. He knew I wanted the human family to be whole again. He offered them an extraordinary promise. And he kept his word."

"What?"

"He said if we reached out, if we re-integrated with the rest of humanity, he would still not re-boot. He would allow his life to end here, on Eden. And that's what he did. He did it for me." Alice brushed at the tears that were rolling down my cheek. "Don't be sad about Yuri. You know what a heavy burden he was carrying. It was time for him to lay it down, and he never would have chosen to forget."

"No, he wouldn't."

"No."

"Your ... your ... your mom ... chose to forget."

"I know," her expression darkened. "I know. We all have our own path to walk."

We sat there quietly for a moment. Then Tamika said, "I wonder what's going to happen to their culture, to the culture here. Do you think it can survive?"

Alice looked thoughtful. "That's something they're going to have to work out. As my beloved husband used to say, 'Stasis is death. Change is the most sublime aspect of the universe.'"

We spent the night in the house. When we woke in the morning Alice had declined quite a bit. I guess seeing us again and talking about everything had taken a lot out of her. But about mid-morning Cooper came into the sitting room to get me.

"Mom would like to see you again, Mohandas."

"Oh, okay." I got up off of the settee and followed her upstairs.

Her eyes were closed, but she opened them when she heard us walk in. I sat in the chair next to the bed. Cooper stood by the door. Alice said, "Cooper, dear, could you give us a little privacy?"

Cooper said, "Oh, sure. I'll be right downstairs." She went out.

Alice regarded me for a moment, like I was a problem she wasn't sure how to solve.

"What is it, Alice?" I asked.

She thought for a moment more. Then she said, "It occurred to me ... It occurred to me that I might be seeing your wife soon."

Well, that was it for me. It took about two seconds for me to fall completely apart. My chest heaved, tears ran down my face and snot dangled out of my nose. She brought my head to her bosom and stroked my hair. "Sh-h, sh-h. It's all right, Mo. It's all right." She held me as I sobbed. Then she said, "I was just wondering if there was any message you'd like me to give her, just in case I see her."

I looked up into her elfin face, her eyes tired but still bright. I was lost, found, transformed, demolished. "I— I— I— I don't ... know—"

"Is there anything at all you'd like to say?"

I thought about my wife as the tears streamed down my face. Her beautiful eyes, her beautiful mind. Her trust, her heart. "Tell her... tell her ... tell her I'm sorry. I'm— I'm sorry. I'm so, so sorry."

Alice lifted her head off the pillow. "You're sorry? What kind of a message is that? You haven't seen her in twelve centuries and you want to tell her you're sorry?"

"I— I— I—"

"Tell you what. I'll tell her you love her. How's that? I *know* that's the truth."

And I was reborn. I didn't know whether to laugh, cry, shout to the universe or remain silent. I was new. Unsullied. Pristine. I couldn't feel my hands. I couldn't feel my ears. My head floated above the ground, unconnected to anything temporal. "Yeah," I answered. "Yeah, that would probably be better."

Alice died that afternoon. Her tiny body quietly stopped. Her unique, irreplaceable perspective vanished from the world of our senses. We had given everything we could to try to save her and she had ended up saving all of us.

The memorial service was attended by thousands of Edenites. Most of them had to stand outside the church. All of Nazareth filled with people who just wanted to be near her in this final moment. As I listened to the pastor speak about her life, I couldn't help thinking about Steel, about all the decisions she had made—the awful, selfish, shortsighted, impudent, arrogant decisions. And yet, if she had made just one of those decisions differently I never would have met Alice. Alice never would have existed. I didn't know what to do with that information. I guess women are just blessed that way.

I decided to go back to my house on Scarpus. It was summer there and the hardwood forests would be beautiful. But more than that, it was a big house, and I had new responsibilities.

Before she died, Alice had asked me to help introduce her daughters to the galaxy. They weren't going to die. They had already re-booted once. They explained it to me while I was in Nazareth. Their mother was only half Edenite; that is, their grandmother was from Earth. Evidently there was enough of the genetic puzzle left in Alice's genome to prevent her from re-booting, but when Alice and Yuri had had Cooper and FA'izeh they were only one-quarter Edenite and the genetic puzzle broke down. It was helping researchers in Draco and The Pleiades figure out how it worked—how to develop a way around it and let everyone from Eden re-boot. They figured they'd have it licked in another couple of decades. I asked Cooper and FA'izeh what they thought that would do to their culture. FA'izeh had smiled:

"People were worried about it. But Dad told them, I remember his words exactly, he said, 'The only way to find out if you're immortal is to make it to the end of time and look around to see if you're still alive. Until you've done that, all you know is that you haven't died *yet*.' "

So they've sent applications to study at the MAD Labs on Circe, the newest facility at the Antigone Institute. It's where all the hottest bleeding edge stuff is going on: the Marcus/Archie/Drake Exobiology and Leptonics Laboratories. It's where they developed that orgasm stuff. Until we hear if they've been accepted, the four of us are staying here—me, Cooper, FA'izeh and Ham.

I know what my job is now. It is as simple as it is sublime. My job is to love my wife till the end of time, or as long as I can keep from falling over. I accept this task with all of its ramifications and manifestations. I will echo and resonate with her love of the universe and everything and everyone in it. I will give her love to the cosmos as she gave it to me. I will give it to the young, to the powerless, to the people who need it. As she would have said, there's plenty of work to be done.

Speaking of work, I need to find a job. If I'm going to be re-booting Ham every fifty years I'm going to have to find a way to make more money.

Thank you, Alice.

Thank you, Steel.

Thank you, my darling, darling wife.

I love you.

Forever.

Seattle, December 25th, 2009

John Patrick Lowrie was born in 1952 in Honolulu, Hawaii and raised in Boulder, Colorado. At sixteen he left home to make his way as a singer/guitarist/flautist/trombonist in a rock 'n' roll band, sleeping in parks and communes and getting to know several hippies. After surviving the draft, he graduated with highest distinction from the Indiana University School of Music and for a few years managed to make a living as a composer and guitarist in his acoustic fusion duo, The Kiethe Lowrie Duet, garnering critical acclaim and opening for people who were much more famous than he was. He then decided to become an actor because the pay was better and the work was steadier. To this day he remains the only person he knows of who has done this. He met Ellen McLain, his wife of twenty-four years, in Arnhem, Holland on a European tour of a Broadway show and started his acting career in Palermo, Italy telling jokes to an opera house full of Sicilians who didn't speak English. Success continues to dog his heels like an angry Pekinese. He and his wife now reside in Seattle where they divide their professional time between acting in live theater and voice-acting for computer games and radio dramas.

You can find John online by visiting www.johnpatricklowrie.com or www.lowrie.camelpress.com.